FRIENDS TOGETHER

HICKORY HILLS #2

SUE STEWART ADE

ISBN: 978-1-68046-816-8

Published by Satin Romance
An Imprint of Melange Books, LLC
White Bear Lake, MN 55110
www.satinromance.com

Published in the United States of America.

Cover Design by Lynsee Lauritsen

This book is dedicated to my grandson, Hayden Ade.
1995-2019
You lit up our world.

CHAPTER ONE

Some people were born lucky. Others had to make their own luck. Today Lady Luck needed some help, thought Bucky as he sneaked down the graveled alley, rocks crunching beneath his tennis shoes. He tugged on the brim of his black baseball cap, pulling it down not to keep out the sun, but to make sure no one would recognize him.

Crisp September air nipped at his face. Jacket weather. Perfect to conceal the gun tucked into the waistband of his black jeans. The SIG Sauer was just a precaution. He didn't plan to use it.

He stopped at the rear entrance to the yellow-brick building. His eyes shifted left and right, checking the alley to be sure no one was in sight. Satisfied, he slipped on his gloves and twisted the knob. The door didn't budge. He extracted a credit card from the pocket of his black nylon windbreaker and slid it between the jam and the door. *Click.* The lock released.

A block away, the clock on the courthouse steeple bonged nine times. Most of the residents of Hickory Hills would soon be gathered at the white clapboard church overlooking the town to pay their last respects to Miss Lucille May, the town librarian. He would be in and out of the law office before the funeral began.

Slithering inside, he blinked and waited for his eyes to adjust to the windowless darkness. On his right were shelves stacked with office supplies. He turned to his left. *Bingo.* Large metal file cabinets lined the other three walls.

The job would be easy. Find the file he wanted and take it. First, he needed to make sure no Unlucky Lou had come in to work on Saturday morning.

He tiptoed through the hall and into the next room. A massive mahogany desk sat in the center of the office with floor-to-ceiling shelves of leather-bound law books behind it. The plush gray carpet was a stark contrast to the wooden floors in the hallway and file room. It muffled his steps as he crossed to the opposite door and peered into the reception area.

The black leather chair behind the computer on the counter was empty. *Cha-ching.* A rush charged through him the way it did when all those beautiful red cherries lined up on a slot machine.

He retraced his steps to the windowless room, closed the door, and flicked on the switch. Fluorescent lighting flooded the area. Circling from cabinet to cabinet, he spotted the drawer he needed and tugged it open. He rifled through the folders, lifted one out, and placed it on top of the file cabinet. He flipped through the papers, perusing the contents. His eyes widened as he focused on the document and slipped it out.

The opening door behind him creaked. He whirled around, dropping the papers.

Filling the doorway stood the lawyer, Jackson Wenzel. His signature fedora covered his gray hair. "What do you think you're doing in my files?" Jackson didn't wait for an answer. He reached into the pocket of his navy blazer and pulled out his phone.

Instinct took over. Bucky grabbed the gun from beneath his jacket, aimed at Jackson, and pulled the trigger.

Crack.

The bullet drilled Jackson's neck. Blood squirted from the wound. Jackson's mouth flapped open, garbling his words as the phone slipped from his fingers and clattered onto the floor.

His hands reached up, flailing, as he tried to staunch the blood pumping from his carotid artery and squirting onto the wall. He teetered backward and, like a felled tree, thudded into the hallway, his fedora toppling off behind him.

Bucky jerked away from the spray of blood. He waited until it no longer spurted from the wound before he inched toward the body. Jackson's legs jerked. His eyes appeared milky and flat. Something gurgled in his throat.

Bucky jumped and laughed nervously. The strange sound was a death gag. Jackson's chest labored up and down. The blood continued to pump out of the hole, soaking into his shirt and blazer. He wasn't dead, but his body would bleed out in minutes.

Maybe the saying was true. After the first murder, the others were easy. Bucky had spent months planning his first kill, agonized over every detail. With Jackson he'd merely reacted. If he was caught, he wouldn't fry. Illinois no longer had a death penalty but living in a cage might be worse.

Think. Think. Think. The stakes were too high to fold. Maybe he could still fix this unfortunate complication.

Bucky slipped the gun into the pocket of his windbreaker and bent over. He gripped the lawyer's ankles and tugged. The body slid a few inches. He heaved harder and dragged Jackson across the wooden floor, leaving behind a trail of blood. When the body no longer blocked the threshold, Bucky picked up the fedora and pulled the door closed.

He gathered the bloodied papers he'd dropped and stuffed them into his jacket. Then he opened the nearest file cabinet and randomly tossed out folders, scattering them around the room.

His eyes wandered to the supplies shelved on the opposite wall. No paint brush. He spotted a box of magic markers. Magic was just what he needed, a little sleight of hand to help the cops in this podunk town piece together the clues.

One tiny detail worried him—the kid who had ridden his bike over to see Miss May last week. What was the boy's name? Jason. Yes, that was it. Bucky didn't want anything bad to happen to Jason. But if Jason had an accident, maybe it would be a blessing. The kid wouldn't have to experience the ugliness of life.

Bucky steadied his hand and pulled a red magic marker from the box. He marched over to Jackson's body, leaned down, and lowered the tip into the pool of blood, letting it soak up the sticky red liquid. Then he placed the marker in the center of Jackson's forehead.

With one swift swoosh, the red streak zigzagged across his forehead above his bushy gray eyebrows leaving a big bloody red *Z*.

CHAPTER TWO

Tomi stood outside the terminal at O'Hare searching for her American friend, Laney Elam. The thirteen-hour flight from Tokyo to Chicago had been grueling. Her bones ached. Her body sagged. She had another four hours to travel before she reached her destination—Hickory Hills, Illinois.

She combed her fingers through her hair, letting it fan across the back of her practical black suit. Her three-inch patent-leather heels were not practical, but they made her feel pretty.

Sleeping on the plane had been impossible. She was seated next to a weary mother wrestling a crying baby. Every time the woman nodded off, the six-month-old protested with a loud scream.

"I'm Tomoe Kanai." She'd said her first name slowly the way it was pronounced, "Toe-moe-ay, but my American friend call me Toe-me." She had stretched out her arms to take the baby. "I help." The mother had hesitated, but the baby crawled onto Tomi's lap.

She had little experience with babies, but she hummed a Japanese cradle song her grandmother had sung to her. "Sleep little pigeon and fold your wings..." Tomi had been afraid to sleep. If her arms relaxed, the baby might slip off her lap. She forced herself to stay awake.

The baby snuggled so close Tomi could feel the baby's heart beating and could smell her freshly-powdered skin. Tomi felt protective in a way she'd never experienced. As a mother.

When the plane landed, and the mother took the baby, Tomi's arms ached with emptiness, and her legs were as rubbery as an octopus. But as she walked through the wind tunnel and into the terminal, a renewed strength surged through her. Her dream had come true. She was in America.

That had been an hour ago. Where was Laney? The baggage claim and gates on international flights were restricted to passengers. Laney had promised to meet her outside the terminal where the taxis and buses pulled up.

Tomi glanced at the sign above her head with the pictures of a car, bus, and taxi. The heavy odor of fumes hung in the air as vehicles picked up and dropped off passengers. People walked across the road to and from the five-story parking garage. She searched the faces, looking for her friend.

Maybe she should have listened to her parents. They had not wanted her to come to America, especially after what had happened to her brother. Her friends had more freedom than she did. Her father relied on the old ways.

Her mother, who often sided with Tomi against her strict father, had remained silent. Even her aunt and uncle, who traveled yearly to New York City on business, had advised against a trip to the Midwest. "Too dangerous. Many guns."

Tomi was twenty-eight, old enough to make her own decisions. Her girlfriends' parents didn't fawn over them in the suffocating way her parents did.

But Tomi respected her parents and would not disobey them. Finally she and her parents had compromised. If they would give her permission to go to America, she would do as they wished when she returned to Japan.

Staying in America for three months and being in her best friend's wedding seemed like a fairy tale. But why wasn't her friend at the airport? The people had begun to dwindle. Buses and taxis no longer pulled in and out. Maybe she was waiting under the wrong ground transportation sign.

She reached into her pocket and took out her phone. A tiny plastic cat with a raised paw dangled from the bottom. The lucky cat charm was supposed to bring her good fortune. The bars on the cell phone screen remained unlit. If she moved, she might be able to find a signal. She tugged at the unwieldy luggage cart piled with her two large suitcases and a carry-on bag. But if she moved, she might miss Laney.

She unwrapped a stick of Japanese gum and popped it into her mouth.

The subtle peach fragrance calmed the knots in her stomach. She closed her eyes and let the fragrance infuse her body.

When she opened her eyes, a chill tingled down her spine. She felt vulnerable standing alone outside the glass doors of the terminal. She was not schooled in martial arts like her brother. Someone could easily attack her, take her suitcases or steal her purse. She didn't know anyone in America except Laney. What if something had happened to her friend? What if she had been in an accident?

Tomi chided herself. She had been watching too many American movies. No one would accost her outside of one of the world's busiest airports. She fingered the pouch hidden beneath her blouse. At least her passport was safe. Then she remembered the story of someone losing her valuables when the string was cut.

A friend had suggested a weapon, such as a hat pin for protection, but sharp objects were not allowed on planes. She gripped the handle of the luggage cart to steady her shaking hands. She checked her cell phone again. No signal. Why hadn't she heeded her parents' warning? Why had she thought she could be an independent woman and make her own decisions?

———

P.R. tapped his fingers on the steering wheel as he inched his convertible toward the parking garage at O'Hare. Maybe he wasn't late. Maybe the flight from Japan had been delayed. If he had not pressed the snooze on his alarm clock, he might have been involved in the three-car pileup. Instead he and his car were safe, but he'd stopped at the accident and helped until the paramedics arrived.

Coming to the airport was not the way he'd planned to spend his Saturday morning. But being the younger brother of three sisters meant a woman's plans often trumped his own. He'd let his sister's friend, Quinn, who also was one of his clients, talk him into picking up a woman from the airport and driving her to Hickory Hills. He liked women—a lot. He liked the way their bodies curved and all those fruity fragrances. A four-hour drive with a beautiful woman sounded pleasant. After all, that was his name, Pleasant Rupert.

Then last night Quinn had phoned and said she'd made a mistake about the date. Something about Japan being a day ahead. The flight arrived on Saturday, not on Sunday when he'd planned to go to Hickory Hills.

The problem was tonight he had a date. Most of the time he would have just rescheduled, but this wasn't just any date. He'd spent months trying to thaw out the office ice princess. Finally, she'd agreed to meet him for drinks. He wasn't about to give Miss Ashleigh Flynn a chance to back out. He wanted to find out what was beneath her slick surface.

He'd just drive the four hours to Hickory Hills and deliver the woman. What was her name? Something that started with a *T*. He'd deliver Miss T and be back in time to show Ashleigh just how pleasant he could be.

He pulled into the parking garage, took a ticket, and climbed out of the Sebring. On the way to the terminal, he spotted a small kiosk with colorful balloon bouquets. A yellow smiley-face balloon might make up for being late.

The woman he was supposed to pick up should be waiting near ground transportation. He might have trouble spotting her among all the foreign travelers. But she should be able to find him—a tall blond guy with a goatee and mustache. He wasn't wearing a tie, not on a Saturday when he didn't have to work at the law office. He'd put on a gray sports coat over his T-shirt and jeans.

When he found the transportation sign, his day brightened. There stood an attractive Japanese woman, primly dressed in a black suit and white blouse. His sister had described her as around five feet six inches, weighing about one hundred and twenty-five pounds. That had to be Miss T.

He liked voluptuous blondes with plenty of cleavage and curvy legs. Yet something about her piqued his interest. All that long black hair was striking against her flawless beige skin. Her face was wide with high cheek bones and a rather flat nose, but somehow it all seemed to fit.

He stopped in front of her and bowed as he presented the balloon. "Welcome to America."

Her eyes brightened. *"Arigatou gozaimasu."* Her hand flew to her mouth. "Oh, so sorry. English. Thank you very much."

"Quinn sent me." He bent over, took her hand, and kissed it.

Tomi felt the warmth of his lips on her hand. She gasped and jerked back. She would not be tricked into trusting this man by his good looks and the cute bouncy balloon. Her mother's words echoed in her head. "Beware of American men."

"Aren't you Miss...something that starts with a *T*? Quinn's friend."

Maybe he was trying to pronounce her Japanese name. She said it, emphasizing each syllable. "Toe-moe-ay."

He repeated it. Then he said, "I'm P.R."

If Laney sent this man, why didn't he know her name? But he said Quinn, not Laney, and what did 'pr' mean?

The man lifted her two large suitcases from the luggage cart. She shook her head and lunged for her carry-on before he took it.

He shrugged his wide shoulders and held onto the two suitcases. "Okay, you can take the smaller one. I'll carry these." He turned and walked toward the parking garage.

Clutching the balloon and the carry-on, she scurried after him. His legs were long, and in her pretty, impractical heels, she couldn't catch him. She let out a tiny squeak that sounded like a snow monkey. "Stop! Stop!"

The man paused and looked over his shoulder.

She caught up to him. Her voice shook. "Why you take bags?"

His lips curved into a smile. "Quinn asked me to pick you up. I'm P.R."

Who was Quinn? And what did 'pr' and 'pick up' mean? She pulled out her phone. Two bars lit up.

She dialed Laney's number and waited. The phone went to voice mail. She didn't leave a message. Instead she typed the letters 'pr' into her language app. A translation popped up. "Public relations. The spread of information between an organization such as a government or business and an individual. It is advertising or marketing..."

Ah. The man must be a salesman. Was he selling the balloon? She entered the words 'pick up' and read the definition, "to take passengers into a vehicle."

Maybe the man was giving her a ride. He had taken her bags, but he hadn't asked where she was going.

She scrolled to another definition of 'pick up.' Her eyes widened. "To enter into conversation or companionship with a previously unknown person. (A brief affair with a girl he *picked up* in a bar.)"

This couldn't be happening. *I'm not a pick up. Laney promised to be here.* But Laney wasn't here, only this stranger. She reached for the closest suitcase. "I take."

He wheeled it away from her. "I've got these. My car is parked in the garage. Follow me." He turned and started across the street.

Panic seized her. He was walking away with her suitcases. What should she do? She couldn't let this stranger take her bags. Yet she couldn't go to the garage and get into a car with him.

She spun toward the terminal. On the other side of the glass stood a man in a black hat and pants. A patch on his white shirt read 'police.'

Tomi kicked off her three-inch heels. Pulling her carry-on, she raced to the entrance. The automatic doors swung open. She ran up to the man who was built like a sumo wrestler.

He immediately straightened. "May I help you, Miss?"

Her mouth opened. Nothing came out. She gulped and swallowed her gum. She tried again. This time she did not squeak. She steadied her finger and pointed to the stranger crossing the street with her suitcases and shouted, "Thief!"

CHAPTER THREE

Thief! P.R. flushed, and his large ears burned as the word echoed in his head. He stood spread-eagled in the security office as a guard ran a wand over his body. P.R. tried to explain the misunderstanding, but the burly man, whose name tag read 'Officer Levy,' wasn't listening.

"Identification," Levy barked.

He glared over his shoulder at his accuser standing on the other side of room. "I'm getting my wallet." He reached into his back pocket and slid out his billfold. He handed his driver's license to Levy. P.R. was a lawyer, and many of his clients said they'd been falsely accused. Now he understood how they felt.

As the guard examined the license, the corners of his mouth twitched as if he wanted to grin. "Not many men named Pleasant Rupert. You aren't by any chance called P.R.?"

"That's me." The security guard handed P.R. his license, and he slipped it back into his wallet.

"Well, I'll be a monkey's uncle. My dad always said P.R. Montgomery was the best paperboy he ever had. Never threw a newspaper into the rose bushes or left one out in the rain. Every morning Dad would patter out to the porch and his *Tribune* would be wrapped up and waiting."

The name 'Levy' on the officer's badge clicked. The taut muscles in P.R.'s neck relaxed. "Your parents aren't Al and Alice?"

"Yep. Mom passed on last year, but Dad still lives in the same house. That neighborhood's changing, but my brother and me can't convince Dad to move."

"I know what you mean. After my father passed away and my sisters left home, we tried to get Mom to leave, but she wouldn't hear of it."

The officer chuckled. "Maybe we should get those two old fuddy-duddies together."

P.R. didn't think of his sprightly mother as a fuddy-duddy. She certainly could take care of herself, but he still lived with her in the same house in Chicago where he'd grown up and delivered newspapers.

He'd loved the job during the warm summers—getting up early, eating with Dad, and then hopping on his bike, peddling up and down the streets. But on those cold winter mornings when the wind gusted in from Lake Michigan, his cheeks stung, and his fingers froze. Sometimes he had to plow through snow drifts more than a foot high.

But he didn't quit. He saw how hard life was for his parents. His dad had been a union electrician by day and a cab driver at night. Dad insisted his wife not work outside the home. With four kids, money was tight.

College was expensive. Even with a scholarship and living at home, P.R. had taken out loans for books and additional expenses. Delivering papers had helped him start a saving account for college, but he never thought it would help him years later.

"Have a seat and let's see if we can clear this up." Levy waved to the chairs in front of his desk while he squeezed into the big chair behind it.

After the two of them sat, he asked for their stories. "Ladies first."

Officer Levy asked Miss T to spell the name of the friend she was visiting. When she spelled 'Laney' not 'Raney,' P.R. slapped his forehead with the palm of his hand. Now he understood the confusion.

Quinn's real name was Laney. She changed it to Quinn when she'd moved to Hickory Hills because she had been on the run, but maybe Miss T didn't know that.

When Levy finished questioning both of them, he reached for the desk phone. "Give me the number of this Laney or Quinn."

P.R. scrolled through his contacts and read aloud Quinn's number. Levy dialed, and P.R. was relieved when the officer started talking to Quinn. She must have convinced Levy that P.R. wasn't a thief or kidnapper because the

SUE STEWART ADE

guard signaled P.R. with a thumbs up. Then he handed the phone to Miss Trouble.

"*Moshi moshi.*"

P.R. knew the Japanese words for the telephone 'hello,' but he didn't understand the rest of the conversation.

After she hung up, she turned to him. "So sorry. Laney say I should go with you."

P.R. was still seething as he drove out of Chicago. It was almost 10 a.m., and so far, he was not having a pleasant morning. Usually when he drove from the city, he would lean his seat back, put down the top of the convertible, and relax. Today, the top remained closed, and his seat upright.

His foul mood was all because of his passenger, Miss Tomi Kanai, asleep beside him. She could have told him earlier to call her Tomi. It would have been so much easier to remember. Tomi was slumped over, her head resting against his arm. One slight shift and she might wake. That was the last thing he wanted to do, especially after the misunderstanding at O'Hare.

In hindsight, he might have handled the situation better. He hadn't remembered her name, and even though Quinn had been his client and he knew her real name was Laney, he hadn't understood the name clearly enough to put the two together.

He glanced down at Tomi and then back to the road. Definitely not his type. Yet even after the fiasco at the airport, she was alluring. The delicate fragrance he'd whiffed earlier lingered. What was that scent? Something fruity and tempting.

His cell phone rang, jolting him back to reality. Tomi jerked up. "Baby."

He frowned. "Baby?"

She looked around and shook her head. "So sorry."

He answered the call with his Bluetooth. The name that popped up on the screen was Ace, Quinn's fiancé.

"I hear you almost got arrested," Ace said. "That mustache and goatee must make you look pretty dangerous."

"Very funny. Remind me not to let Quinn talk me into anything again."

"Good luck with that."

"Ace, you're the one who needs the luck. You're about to get hitched."

"Fifteen days," Ace said. "The sooner the better."

12

P.R. shook his head. What was wrong with Ace? Until a few months ago, he'd sworn off women and marriage. Then Quinn had stepped back into his life, and he couldn't wait to walk her down the aisle.

"How much longer before you get here?" Ace asked.

"I can make it in less than an hour if I take the shortcut through the country."

"Better stay on Highway 51," Ace said. "A few days ago Ezekiel Eggers escaped from Marion Federal Penitentiary. He might be headed to Hickory Hills."

P.R. cringed. "You mean the big albino they call Zeus?"

"Yeah, that's one of the names he's called."

"I worked for Jackson the summer he defended Zeus. The man has delusions of power." P.R. remembered the media had called him Zeus because he thought he was a god. He judged his victims, deciding who was worthy to live and who needed to die.

After the guilty verdict, Zeus had threatened Jackson. P.R. hoped Zeus hadn't come back to seek revenge. During high school, and later during law school, Jackson Wenzel had given P.R. a job. Jackson had never had a son, and at fifteen P.R. had lost his dad, so they'd forged a special bond.

Now that Jackson was about to turn eighty, he wanted to retire and have P.R. take over the practice. P.R. had declined, but Jackson told him to keep the keys to the office and give it more thought.

Chicago was where the big money and powerful lawyers were, not in a small town like Hickory Hills with fewer than four thousand people. Jackson had asked P.R. to review three files concerning his clients who had been denied black lung benefits. The cases tugged at his heart, but not enough for P.R. to change his mind about the offer. He didn't want to disappoint Jackson, so to avoid him, P.R. planned to return the files when Jackson wasn't in the office.

"Hey, Ace, tell Quinn before I drop her friend off, I'm going to swing by Jackson's office."

CHAPTER FOUR

P.R. ended Ace's call and glanced over at Tomi. "Feel rested?"

"Yes. So sorry I sleep."

He stroked his goatee in frustration. She had yet to pronounce his name correctly, but she didn't have any trouble saying, "so sorry." At the airport she'd said it more than a dozen times. His gruff voice revealed his annoyance. "Stop saying you're sorry."

She scooted to the other side of the car. "Okay." Then she added, "So sorry." She must have realized she had repeated the words. She put her hand over her mouth and said, "So sorry."

He gritted his teeth. Maybe some fresh air would help his foul mood. He pressed the button, and the top of the convertible slid open, letting in the afternoon sun. Tomi craned her head back against the seat and lifted her arms. She waved her hands in the air and laughed.

The delightful tinkling sound surprised him. She didn't seem to mind the wind whipping through her hair, the way most women did. Her cheeks glowed and she looked happy. Under difference circumstance, he might have been tempted to get to know Tomi.

Instead he concentrated on the road cutting through the flat Illinois farmland. Ahead, on his left, a combine lumbered through the cornfield. As his car passed the parked grain truck, the hopper spit kernels of corn into the bed. P.R. inhaled the sweet powdery scent of the grain swirling in the air and began to relax.

"So big." Tomi's voice filled with awe.

He spoke slowly and clearly. "It's a John Deere."

"Deer?" She leaned forward, her head turning left and right. "Where?"

He groaned. Of course, she was looking for Bambi. "Do you like music?" He didn't wait for a response but turned on the radio. Pounding rap music rocked the car. He quickly changed the station. He wasn't about to explain those lyrics.

The voice of Celine Dion singing "My Heart Will Go On" filled the air. His sisters loved the movie *Titanic*. Growing up they'd had one TV in the house. Most of the time, he'd been subjected to the girls' shows, except when Dad was home and they'd watched sports together.

P.R. admitted he liked some romances, but what was romantic about *Titanic* where one person dies and leaves the other one alone? He'd experienced being left and what he'd felt was pain.

He reached to change the station.

Tomi's hand brushed against his. "I like."

"Are you sure?"

She nodded, letting the familiar music take her to a happy time. Her brother, Hiro, had always wanted to visit America. He liked to joke about his name. "Everyone will call me a hero, just the way my name is pronounced."

Hiro knew her favorite movie was *Titanic,* so for her birthday they had taken the high-speed bullet train into Tokyo to watch it again. What was the name of the actor? Something like the inventor DaVinci. Leonardo, that was it.

Afterward, she and Hiro had eaten their favorite noodles—udon, thick wheat noodles for her, and soba, thin buckwheat noodles for Hiro. They'd sat on stools at the counter, eating with chopsticks and slurping their noodles to show their appreciation for the delicious taste.

Then they wandered through the shops. "It's cute," she'd said, picking up a tiny porcelain frog.

Her brother had bought a dragon and then surprised her by purchasing the frog. He placed it into the palm of her hand. "A frog in the well does not know the great sea," he said. "This will give you the courage to leap out of the well."

Well, she'd taken the leap to America, and at the airport she'd caused so much trouble she felt as if she'd slipped into a melon field. That's what her mother always said when Tomi caused trouble. She had apologized, over and over, yet that only irritated this man more. No wonder he wasn't called by his name. He wasn't pleasant.

She'd never ridden in a car alone with a man. Her eyes slid sideways, sneaking a peek at him. His looks were so different from a Japanese man. He was tall with light hair and blue eyes. She wanted to touch his blond hair, see how it felt. She couldn't do something so intimate, could she? But wasn't that one of the reasons she had come to America, so she wouldn't have to stuff all feelings inside? Here she could be herself. If she had an urge to touch his hair, she could reach out...

P.R. turned toward her. His startlingly blue eyes unnerved her. Heat rushed to her face. He had the same blond hair and blue eyes that made Leonardo so appealing, only with all that facial hair, P.R. seemed more like a fair-headed devil.

What must he think of her? Calling him a thief, and when she had awakened, she thought she was still on the airplane, holding the baby. That tiny heart beating against her own had stirred up strange emotions. She'd never thought much about having a baby and being a mother. On the airplane she'd felt protective of the infant. Maybe that's why her parents were so protective of her. What would it feel like to fall in love with a man and want to have his child?

She had tried to talk to her mother about falling in love with a man, but her mother hadn't fallen in love. Her parents' marriage had been arranged. "You learn to love," her mother explained.

In American movies, love between a man and woman seemed to be a beautiful feeling, not a school lesson. She had not had to learn to love her brother. Hiro was two years older, and she thought maybe he could explain romantic love, but she didn't think the maid cafés he frequented sounded romantic. "Why do you like to go there?" she asked.

"The girls look cute in those French maid costumes. They greet me, 'Welcome home, master,' and listen to my troubles."

Tomi knew the rules of the café: no asking for personal information or touching.

She didn't understand why he would want to pay someone to treat him as a master. He was the number one child. Growing up, she'd envied his favored status. Now she realized being number one was also a burden.

She pushed away the grief. Her brother had wanted to come to America. She would make this trip a happy time. She would make her own choices and break free of expected behavior.

"We're here. Hickory Hills." P.R. sounded relieved.

They passed a peaceful-looking park shaded with large trees. The leaves were beginning to change from green to shades of red and yellow. On the playground were bright colorful swings and a giant, two-sided slide. In the middle of the park was a small island surrounded by a lagoon with a picturesque foot bridge. She sighed at the tranquil setting and hoped she'd be able to come to the park and walk across the arched bridge.

In the town were many shops, but no people on the sidewalks. *Very strange.* He stopped the car in front of a yellow brick building. "Stay here. I'll be back in a minute."

"I come." Her bladder was beginning to feel uncomfortable. She slid out of the car and scampered up the steps. The sign on the building read "Jackson Wenzel, Attorney-at-Law."

P.R. unlocked the door and pulled it open. He gestured with his hand for her to enter. She stepped inside. The wooden door slammed behind them. Cold chills shivered through her. She glanced around the dimly lit room for a picture of a woman or the word 'toilet.' Seeing none, she followed P.R. into the next room. He turned on the lights and placed some folders on top of the large desk.

The light from the office spilled into the hall. Maybe it led to a toilet. She hurried to the hallway and spotted two closed doors at the end. She took a fortifying breath and shuffled into the darkness.

The hairs on her arms rose. Her legs balked. She forced herself forward, one foot at a time. She reached into the pocket of her suit and rubbed the porcelain frog. Usually she could hear her brother's voice and be calmed by his words. "You must have the courage of a tigress." Now all she heard was the thudding of her heart.

She twisted the knob on the first door and stepped into the dark room. Her nose wrinkled. The horrible, rusty metallic odor must be from a Western toilet.

She eased into the room and felt along the wall for a light. Her fingers found the switch and flipped it on. Overhead lights flickered. She inched into the room. Her foot hit something. She stumbled, barely catching herself before she toppled forward.

Light flooded the room. Red paint was splattered everywhere—on the wall, on the file cabinets, on the papers and folders scattered on the floor. She looked down to see what her shoe had bumped. Staring up at her were the glassy eyes of a man covered in red.

Not paint. Blood. She was standing in a pool of blood.

She screamed, not like a tigress, but like a frightened animal.

CHAPTER FIVE

Tomi's raw scream cut through the room. P.R. dropped his note on the desk and raced down the hall. He rushed into the open doorway. His foot slipped. He grabbed the door knob and steadied himself. His stomach heaved. Blood, lots of blood. Everywhere. In the middle of the room stood Tomi, her hands covering her eyes. At her feet, soaked in blood, lay Jackson.

P.R. leaned over and stared into Jackson's gray face. His open eyes sunk into his head. Across his forehead were streaks of dried blood. P.R. reached for Jackson's arm to get a pulse. His hand was cold and stiff, the skin purple. On the side of his neck was a gaping hole where a bullet must have entered.

P.R. moaned. He was too late. His friend and mentor, Jackson Wenzel, had been dead for several hours.

P.R.'s eyes darted back to Tomi. Her face was blanched, her body shaking. He stood and stepped toward her. He kept his voice calm. "Tomi, it's me. P.R."

She lowered her hands. Wide black saucers of fear stared at him. Gently, he placed his hand on her shoulder. She recoiled.

"Tomi. We have to get out of here."

She backed away from him and the door. He stepped closer, nudged her forward. She fisted her hands and pummeled his chest.

The attack surprised him. Her blows knocked him backward. He grabbed her wrists and wrapped his hands around them.

She spit out a string of shrill Japanese. He didn't need a translator to understand she wanted him to get away from her.

Instead, he tightened his grip and pulled her toward him. "Sh-sh. It's okay. It's okay." Even as he said the words, he knew it was not okay. Jackson, the man he'd loved as a father, was lying in a pool of blood. Dead.

P.R. continued talking softly, trying to soothe her. Something he said or the sound of his voice must have registered. She quit fighting. Her body went slack.

He let go of her wrists and wrapped his arms around her, holding her against him, waiting for her to quit shaking. When she did, he eased them toward the door. "Don't look. Don't look."

She pressed her face against his chest. He used his body to shield her from the blood and Jackson lying on the floor.

As they stepped into the hall, Tomi bent over. Her hands flew to her mouth, and she gagged. He whisked her across the hall and pushed open the bathroom door. Light from an opaque window streamed in. She broke loose, rushed to the pedestal sink, and puked.

He backed out of the room. In the hall he took out his phone and called Quinn. He should have phoned the police, but all he could think about was Tomi.

Please answer. Please answer. On the third ring, Quinn picked up.

"It's P.R. I'm at Jackson's office. He's...something...something bad has happened. You need to get here. Now."

"What's wrong? Is Tomi—"

"Quinn, I can't explain. Hurry. Tomi needs you."

He hung up and opened the bathroom door. He smelled the vomit. Two legs showed beneath the first stall. He swiped the back of his arm across his damp forehead and returned to the hallway.

After Quinn arrived, he'd call Ben. His brother-in-law wasn't the typical small town sheriff. He'd worked in Chicago before he and Belle had moved to Hickory Hills and opened a B&B. Ben had investigated plenty of murders and was used to them.

P.R. closed his eyes. Images of the bloody scene flashed through his mind. He was wrong. No one would be able to get used to murder—the blood, the gray flesh, the streaked face.

P.R. gasped. The blood on Jackson's forehead came into focus. Red lines had crisscrossed from the hair line to the eyebrows in a specific pattern—the letter Z.

Zeus.

CHAPTER SIX

Bucky turned off the graveled road and parked his car in the clump of shagbark hickories. He checked the clock on the dash. Two p.m. The tall trees hid the beige Buick from the road and the house. The family might have already returned from Miss May's funeral.

He felt another wave of nausea. Hours had passed since the murder, and still he couldn't shake the sight. So much blood. He hadn't expected to kill again. He'd read about a killer's rush. The pumping of the heart, the electricity in the veins, the euphoria. He'd felt none of that. The only things pumping through his veins were fear and nausea. He lowered his head on the steering wheel and waited for the queasiness to subside.

When he'd left Jackson's office, his clothes had been splattered with blood. He couldn't just check into the local B&B and change. So he'd hightailed it to Miss May's place in the country. He'd hidden there before. No one would be around when she was getting lowered into the ground.

He drove his car into Miss May's barn and stripped off his bloody jacket, jeans, and cap. He used the water from the faucet for the animal trough and washed off. Then he fished a pair of slacks and a button-down shirt from his duffle bag in the trunk. He stuffed his stained clothes into the bag. He'd burn it all later.

He had one more stop before getting out of Dodge, but as he unbolted the barn door, a car drove up Miss May's lane. He peeked out the barn window. A man opened the back door of the house and disappeared inside. He hadn't seen the man's face, but he was pretty sure who he was.

For three tense hours, Bucky had barricaded himself behind the hay bales in the loft. Finally, Bucky heard the car speeding away. He didn't immediately leave. He waited until he was sure the man wasn't coming back before he pulled his car from the barn and drove to Ace's house.

Now, Bucky eased himself out of the car shielded by the hickory trees and crawled on his belly toward the two-story farmhouse with the wraparound porch. Behind the house was a metal machine shed. On the other side, opposite the hickory grove, stood a field of corn almost ready to be picked. The farm belonged to Jason's father, A.C. Edelston, known as Ace.

Only two people could interfere with his plan. Jason and Ace. So far, Jason hadn't been a problem. Hopefully Ace wouldn't be either.

A movement in the trees caught Bucky's eye. His hand slid to the gun tucked into his waistband. Near the house, two kids ran into the hickory grove. Their backs were to him as they stopped near a fresh mound of dirt. Bucky recognized Jason, a dark-haired boy, around seven.

Bucky didn't know the smaller, red-headed girl with a puppy prancing around her skinny legs. The girl dropped to her knees and placed a handful of yellow goldenrods on the mound of fresh dirt. Was this where Jason had buried his dog?

Bucky hadn't meant to harm the puppy. He loved dogs. He'd been watching from the barn window the day Jason, followed by his dog, had ridden his bike to Miss May's. When Jason left, he biked down the lane, the little golden retriever scampering behind. As Jason turned onto the country road, his bike slipped on the gravel and flipped him. Jason brushed off his jean jacket and got up. The puppy lay in the grass. Jason had wrapped the puppy in his jacket and carried him home. Bucky learned later the puppy had died.

He remembered the death of his childhood pet, Slippers, a collie with four white paws. One day he'd come home from school and his older brother, Joey, was lying on the top bunk, bawling. "Dog dead, Bucky. Dog dead."

Joey always called him Bucky, not because he had beaver front teeth but after Captain America's sidekick, Bucky. The killer had been called other nicknames, but he liked to think of himself as Bucky. It reminded him of his brother.

Captain, that's the name their father insisted his sons call him, said Slippers had gone mad and snapped at him. So he dragged Slippers out to the apple orchard and shot him.

Captain didn't tolerate crying. "You boys need to learn to be men." At the time, Joey was ten, and Bucky was seven.

When Slippers died, Joey couldn't stop crying. Finally, angry at not having his orders obeyed, Captain stripped off his belt. "You wanna cry. I'll give you something to cry about."

Captain raised his thick leather strap and brought it down on Joey's back. The flannel shirt didn't protect Joey from the harsh blows. Captain, his face as red as Joey's shirt, struck Joey over and over.

Bucky was no match for Captain. Still, he lunged at him. Captain whirled around and yelled, "Quit acting like your brother or you'll be next."

Bucky choked back sobs, but held onto Captain's pant leg. "Stop hurting Joey. He can't help it."

Captain didn't stop until Joey's flannel shirt was shredded and Joey's bare back was slashed open. When Joey began bleeding, Captain came to his senses and stomped away.

Watching his brother being beaten made something inside Bucky snap. After that he didn't care about anything or anybody enough to cry again. Except for Joey.

The next day the boys found Slippers' body tossed on a pile of rubbish in the orchard. "Bucky, bury. Bucky, bury."

Bucky found a shovel. He could still smell the fresh earth as he dug a grave and buried the dog. He scratched Slippers' name on a large rock and placed it on top of the mound of dirt. All that spring Joey picked fistfuls of dandelions and scattered them on Slippers' grave.

As Bucky grew older, he prided himself on not being like Captain. But today Bucky had murdered a man. He hadn't planned to cross that line again. He'd seen the light, been rehabilitated. Now he realized no matter how hard he tried, 'the apple didn't fall far from the tree.' His core was as evil as Captain's.

Bucky scooted behind a tree and kept low to the ground as he continued to watch Jason and the girl. After about five minutes, they raced out of the trees and into the house. He couldn't search the house with the kids there, and he couldn't keep the car parked in the trees. Someone coming down the lane might spot it or him.

He dashed to the car, backed it out of the clump of trees, and onto the country road. About a quarter of a mile from the house, he found the perfect place to hide—an abandoned coal mine.

A weathered wooden sign hung over the entrance of Springside Mine. Posted below the name of the mine was a warning. *NO TRESPASSING.* The hinged gate leading into the mine hung open. Bucky ignored the sign and gunned the car through the entrance.

The afternoon sun glinted on the finely crushed coal dust packed on the ground. It sparkled like chips of black diamonds. On his left stood the boarded-up mine, on the right a slag pile and a concrete-block building. The roof on the building had caved in. The window panes were shards of glass. But the concrete building was large enough to hide his car behind.

As he drove toward the back of the building, the low fuel light on the dash lit up. He cursed. If he had to make a quick getaway, he didn't want to run out of gas. Lady Luck had certainly turned her back on him. No use staying around and trudging through the cornfield to watch Ace's house. He'd come back during Jackson's funeral. Then the house would be empty.

He turned the car around and drove toward town. Five minutes later he spotted a sign on the right, 'Welcome to Hickory Hills, population, 3,967.'

The shrill screeching of a police siren sliced through the air. Whirling red-and-blue bubble lights reflected in the rearview mirror. He tightened his sweaty hands on the steering wheel.

He hadn't been driving fast, only fifty-five, the speed limit. Then he saw another sign. 'Speed limit 45.'

He pounded his fist against the steering wheel. What was he going to do? He didn't have enough gas to make a run for it. But if his car was searched, the cop would find the duffle bag in the trunk and his gun on the passenger seat.

Bucky picked the gun up, but instead of hiding it under the seat, he kept it in his hand. He didn't want to kill again, especially a cop. In prison they did bad things to cop killers.

His stomach turned. He didn't have the grit for killing, yet his finger found the trigger. Behind him the siren screeched louder. The cruiser sped closer.

He eased his foot off the gas, steered to the side of the road, and stopped. The squad car caught up to him. His body tensed. He braced himself.

The black-and-white screeched by.

Bucky collapsed against the seat, taking long, steadying breaths. Then he bolted up. What if the cop was speeding to the lawyer's office? What if Jackson's body had been found?

Returning to the lawyer's office wasn't smart, but Bucky couldn't convince himself to stay away. He pulled the car back onto the road and drove into town. Near the courthouse, a policeman directed traffic away from the lawyer's office.

Bucky followed the line of vehicles inching forward gawking at the yellow-brick building surrounded by emergency vehicles and police cars.

The manhunt would begin. He imagined being handcuffed and dragged to jail. Then rational thoughts kicked in. So what if the body had been discovered earlier than he expected? That didn't mean the cops would be able to find him. His heart pumped faster. Electricity shot through his veins. Now he felt that killer rush.

CHAPTER SEVEN

The next day, Quinn poured tea into Tomi's cup and then sat across from her at the round oak table in the loft. "Feeling better?"

Tomi fanned her hand across the steaming tea. Even though she'd slept past noon, dark half circles hung under her eyes, and her hand shook when she picked up her cup. "A little."

"I've missed you so much." Quinn's voice filled with sadness. "We used to dream about being friends together in America, but…but never like this. Jackson murdered and you finding the body."

"My parents no want me come to America. Dangerous."

"Hickory Hills is usually safe. That's why I brought Taylor here after Chrissy died." Now wasn't the best time to tell Tomi that Quinn had witnessed her best friend being murdered by her husband, Winston. To keep him from getting custody, Quinn had kidnapped Chrissy's daughter and brought her to Hickory Hills. Another day she would explain all that.

Today Quinn explained about their names. "I needed to change our names, and I wanted us to live as mother and daughter so I'm Quincy Matthews, not Laney Elam."

"No one call you Laney?"

Quinn shook her head. "I'm Quinn, and I have temporary custody of Phoebe, who is now called Taylor."

"Where is…Taylor?" Tomi asked.

"She went to church with Ace and his son, Jason."

Tomi sipped the tea and looked around at the kitchen and great room. "So big."

"In Japan, yes. In America, no." One of the adjustments Quinn had to make during the four years she and Tomi lived together in Tokyo was the compact living quarters.

"Is this...usual American home?"

Quinn laughed. "Originally, this was a barn. The top part, the hay loft, is our two-bedroom apartment. Under this table is a small trap door with a ladder that leads to the lower part of the barn where I park the car."

"Hay...loft?"

"Kind of an upstairs used to store hay or straw."

Tomi frowned and typed the words into the app on her phone.

So many things, like the loft, were difficult to explain to Tomi. The gray barn had been part of Ace's farm and was given to Quinn's grandparents, the Elams, who had made it into their home. Grampa Elam passed away first. Last year, after Grandma Elam died, Quinn inherited the barn and a few surrounding acres.

She could still picture Grampa next to the pot-bellied wood stove, stretched out in his recliner, reading a Zane Grey western. Grandma, wearing her print apron, was usually in the kitchen baking, something delicious, like Quinn's favorite oatmeal cookies.

In the summers, Quinn had stayed with her grandparents. One summer she had brought Chrissy here. Quinn turned and gazed out the wide expanse of windows that overlooked the lake behind the loft. There, near the bank, stood the special hardwood tree. That's where she and Chrissy had pricked their fingers and made a blood pact to be friends forever. Thinking about Chrissy still made Quinn's heart ache, and always would.

Her grandparents and this loft had been the constants in her life. The interior was as old and as weathered as the barn wood exposed on the far side of the great room, but she would miss this place.

In two weeks, on September 18, she would marry Ace, and then she and Taylor would move in with him and Jason. She was looking forward to being married and the four of them forming a family. The loft, however, would always have a special place in her heart.

Footsteps clattered up the outside stairs and the front door swung open. "Mom! Mom!"

Quinn's heart fluttered with joy. She still wasn't used to hearing Taylor call her mom.

Jason and Taylor charged into the room, followed by her puppy, a golden retriever. "Is she up? Is she—" Taylor's skinny legs skidded to a stop. Her bright blue eyes widened when she saw Tomi sitting at the table. Taylor pushed her glasses up on her nose and bowed. "*Ohayou.*" Then she giggled and didn't add the formal greeting. "It sounds like *Ohio.*"

Jason elbowed Taylor. "It's afternoon. You're supposed to say *konnichiwa.*"

Tomi didn't seem to mind that Taylor had said 'good morning.' Tomi's tired face lit up, and her brown eyes sparkled at Taylor.

Jason, who had dark hair and serious eyes like Ace's, was still mourning the death of his puppy. Until this year, Jason had lived with his mother in Chicago and wasn't allowed to have a dog. The vet suspected Babe had eaten something poisonous, so Jason blamed himself. Babe's death had been overshadowed when, the following day, Miss May's nephew found her at home, dead.

Miss May was eighty-five and had recently retired as the town's librarian. At her party, she boasted, "Never been sick a day in my life. Reading. That's the key to a long life."

Despite her age, the suddenness of her death was somewhat of a shock. Miss May had been a good friend to Grandma Elam and to Quinn. Ace farmed Miss May's land and had been one of the pallbearers. Quinn was grateful P.R. had picked up Tomi from O'Hare so Quinn could attend the funeral, but for Tomi it hadn't worked out so well.

"Do you like the sign?" Taylor pointed to the red, white, and blue banner above the kitchen window. "Jason and I made it for you."

Tomi admired the banner. "So nice."

Taylor smiled, showing her two top teeth growing in. The light from the bay windows glistened on her coppery red hair.

"Your hair...so red and curly."

Taylor giggled and ran her hand through her shoulder-length curls. Its auburn red was the same color as her biological father's, but Taylor had so many changes to cope with in her life at Hickory Hills that Quinn had put off telling the child about her parentage.

To change the subject, Quinn lifted the teapot from the table. "Look what Tomi brought us." The white china teapot was decorated with fan-like blue flowers.

Taylor clapped her hands. "Now we can have a tea party."

"I have present for you." Tomi rose and went into the bedroom. She returned with two wrapped packages. She handed one to Taylor and one to Jason. Taylor ripped off the paper and held up a beautiful pink silk kimono decorated with cranes. "Can I try it on?"

"You might need Tomi to help you."

Jason's turned-down mouth said he definitely hoped his present wasn't a kimono, but when he unwrapped it, he discovered Japanese coins to add to his collection. He kept his head down and mumbled, "Thanks."

Taylor tugged on Tomi's hand and led her toward the bedroom. Quinn turned to Jason, but he'd already fled out the door. Quinn had hoped to talk to him alone and let him know it was normal to feel sad about Babe's death. Ace had tried to soften the loss by letting Jason keep Miss May's dog, Bullet.

But you couldn't get over the loss of one dog by replacing it with another. Just like Taylor couldn't get over the loss of Chrissy, the mother Taylor had loved the first four years of her life, by living with Quinn.

Taylor returned, wearing the kimono. Around her waist was a wide obi, and on her feet were thong-like sandals. As she shuffled around the room, her puppy tried to jump on her. "No, Gogo." Taylor pointed her finger at the dog. "Sit."

The puppy skidded to a stop and sat.

"Good dog." Taylor patted its head. "Shake hands with Tomi." The golden retriever lifted one paw.

Tomi knelt and shook hands.

"She was the fifth in the litter so I named her 'Go,' the Japanese number for five." Taylor's blue eyes twinkled with pride. "I doubled it because she's always on the go."

Tomi ran her hand through Gogo's golden fur. "So soft."

Taylor turned to Quinn. "Can I play outside now?"

Quinn nodded. "Maybe you can cheer Jason up. He's still sad about losing Babe."

"I told him when we lived together, I'd let Gogo sleep with him." Taylor slipped off her kimono and handed it to Quinn. Then she skipped over to the front door, and she and Gogo padded down the outdoor stairs.

Quinn didn't want Tomi to dwell on yesterday, so she brought up the wedding. "Do you want to see your dress?"

Tomi nodded.

Quinn went to her bedroom and returned with a jade green, floor-length gown draped over her arm. "This is for you."

The dress with tiny pearls along the neckline had a fitted waist and full skirt. Tomi fingered the pearls. "So beautiful."

"I made it, but it will need to be altered." Quinn handed Tomi the dress. "Try it on, and come back in here so I can pin up the hem."

Tomi carried the dress into the bedroom. When she returned wearing the gown, Quinn's breath caught. "Oh, Tomi, you look beautiful. The color is perfect with your dark hair and eyes."

Tomi blushed and bowed politely.

"Turn around so I can see the full effect."

Tomi slowly twirled.

"It needs to be taken in at the waist." Quinn retrieved a pin cushion from the bedroom and began tucking and pinning. When she finished, the full skirt made Tomi's tiny waist look even smaller.

Quinn pulled a footstool from near the couch to the center of the room. "Stand on this so I can hem the dress evenly."

As Tomi stood on the stool, Quinn sat on the floor, circling the skirt and pinning up the hem. A knock sounded on the door. Quinn rose and pulled the door open.

P.R. stepped in. "I came over to check—" The sight of Tomi standing on a footstool wearing an elegant green gown made P.R. stop.

Tomi turned toward the door. Her weight shifted and the stool tipped. In two long strides, P.R. sprinted across the room and grabbed Tomi. As he righted the stool, he kept his hands around her waist and steadied her. They were close, almost eye to eye. He was mesmerized by the sight of her and her fragrant scent.

Too soon, Quinn broke the spell. "I've finished pinning the hem. You can get down, Tomi."

P.R. swooped her off the stool. She was as light as a china doll. He set her on the floor, but kept his hands on her waist and leaned in to get another whiff of her fragrance. "I came by to check on you, and to tell you how sorry I am about yesterday."

Tomi's dark eyebrows drew together. "Sorry?"

"Your visit to America shouldn't have started that way, so I'm sorry."

"You sorry?" she repeated and wiggled out of his arms.

"Yes, so sorry."

She put one hand on her hip. "No say *so sorry.*"

"But—" He held out his hands, palms up, because he didn't know what else to say.

She tilted her head and looked up at him. Her words sounded stern and her mouth was pressed closed, but a twinkle glinted in her eyes. Was she teasing him about yesterday when he'd been frustrated over the number of times she'd apologized?

The corners of her lips quivered. Her eyebrows arched in an exaggerated expression.

She *was* teasing him. He burst out laughing. Tomi laughed, too. He stood there, reveling in their unexpected connection.

From across the room, Quinn asked, "What are you two laughing about?"

Tomi looked over her shoulder at Quinn. "Ancient Japanese secret."

P.R. and Tomi burst out laughing again. He couldn't take his eyes off her. Long black hair flowed over her shoulders, and the green dress emphasized her small rounded breasts and tiny waist. Even with dark circles under her eyes, she was breathtaking. But what captivated him more than her beauty was her joy and laughter.

"P.R., Tomi asked me about Jackson," Quinn said. "I didn't know him well, but you worked for him. Maybe you can tell her more about him and ease her mind."

P.R.'s smile faded. "Jackson was a good man. He didn't deserve to die like that."

"What about spirit?" Tomi asked.

"His spirit?" Tomi didn't answer, so he turned to Quinn. "Does Tomi mean his soul?"

"Not exactly," Quinn said. "Jackson's life ended in a violent death, and she was the one who found him." Quinn paused as if choosing her words carefully. "She's afraid his spirit might invade her body and seek revenge."

P.R. raised his brows. "Why would she think that? Jackson wasn't a vengeful person."

"She believes after a violent death, the spirit can take over another person's body."

He chuckled. "That's ridiculous."

"Why you laugh?" Tomi asked.

He turned to her. "Because Jackson is not going to seize your body."

"How you know?" Tomi crossed her arms. "Did his..." She walked to the table, picked up her phone, and searched for the right word. "Did his ghost tell you?"

"Ghost?" P.R. examined her eyes for that glint of humor. He didn't see any. Her brown eyes looked serious. But surely she didn't think Jackson's ghost was lurking nearby ready to snatch her body. He cupped his hands around his mouth and circled the room, calling, "Any ghosts here? If so, show yourself." He laughed at his own joke.

Then he gestured with his hands around the room. "See. No ghosts. You're safe."

"Why you think funny?"

"Because the idea is crazy."

"I not in crazy land." Tears welled up in her eyes.

He stepped forward. "Tomi, I—"

Before he could reach her, she hitched up her skirt and scurried out of the room. The bedroom door slammed shut.

Quinn glared at him. "Now look what you've done."

"Me? You don't seriously believe spirits can take over a person's body or that ghosts are skulking about, do you?"

"Don't you remember my experience at the Old Slave House?"

He stroked his goatee. Last summer, Quinn had led tours of the Crenshaw Mansion. The locals called it the Old Slave House because during the 1800s, the slaves who worked in the nearby salt mines were chained in cells on the third floor. "I remember you said something about the mother voices had warned you."

"Yes, and you must not have thought I was crazy because you were my lawyer and helped me gain temporary custody of Taylor."

P.R. had never experienced anything supernatural, but enough people had seen or heard unsettling things at the Old Slave House that he couldn't quite dismiss it as crazy. "Well, that's different. What I don't believe is Jackson's spirit trying to invade Tomi's body."

"It's not what you or I believe, P.R. It's what Tomi believes. You should respect her beliefs. Instead you made fun of them."

"But ghosts aren't real."

"To her they are. It's an old Japanese belief, but still widely known. Tomi grew up with her grandparents and their way of thinking."

He'd been trying to make Tomi feel better, but he'd made her feel worse. P.R. moved toward the hall. "I'll talk to her."

"No." Quinn put her hand on his arm. "She's tired."

"I only want to apologize."

"Give her time, P.R. Maybe if she gets to know you, and you act a little more considerate, she won't think you're the devil."

CHAPTER EIGHT

Monday morning, P.R. stepped into the elevator of the office building near Water Tower Plaza in Chicago and pushed the button for the tenth floor. He dreaded going to work and facing Ashleigh. After finding Jackson's body and talking to the police, he'd forgotten to cancel their date. He'd phoned on Sunday, left several voice messages, and texted, but she hadn't responded.

He walked into the office and went straight to see her. Maybe if he explained in person, he'd be able to repair the damage. He knocked on her closed door.

"Come in."

He straightened his tie and opened the door. Ashleigh sat behind her desk piled with stacks of briefs. She didn't look up from the papers in her hands. With each step forward, the temperature in the room seemed to drop.

He didn't have to guess at Ashleigh's mood. She wore mood changing polish on her long fingernails. The color today was purple.

P.R. cleared his throat. "I'm sorry about Saturday night." Her head stayed down. He waited for her to reply. When she didn't, he began to explain, "After finding Jackson..."

She cut him off with a flip of her wrist. "No big deal."

To him it was a big deal. He shifted back and forth. Maybe if they made eye contact, she would see he was sincere and would give him a second chance. Finally he said, "I'd like to try again...sometime."

Still no reply.

At least she hadn't flat out refused. He hurried on. "Next weekend is Jackson's funeral and the following weekend I have to usher at a wedding, but maybe after that?"

Her head rose. She smiled, not the icy cold smile he expected, but one that offered hope. "I like weddings."

P.R. practically floated back to his office. What was it about weddings that made women get all mushy? P.R. didn't want to be a bachelor forever. Eventually he hoped to marry, but so far, he hadn't found a woman who interested him enough to want to spend a lifetime with her. He didn't mind escorting Ashleigh to the wedding and walking her down the aisle, as long as it wasn't all the way to the altar.

———

On Friday P.R. had court, so he didn't drive to Hickory Hills for Jackson's visitation. He went early Saturday morning to the funeral to talk to Jackson's daughter. When he walked in, Michelle stood in the front of the church beside her father's closed casket. Even though she was an attractive woman in her fifties, she usually looked much younger. Today, however, her face was lined with grief, her big eyes red and puffy.

"I'm so sorry about your father." P.R. reached over and hugged her. "Jackson was a great man. One I admired very much."

"He thought the same about you." Michelle removed a tissue from her purse and dabbed her eyes. "I was the daughter he loved. You were the son he wanted."

A lump formed in P.R.'s throat.

"Daddy told me he asked you to take over his practice. I hope you accept."

P.R. couldn't meet her eyes. He didn't want to give her more bad news today.

"I brought this." Michelle pulled a piece of paper from her purse. The note had scribbly pencil images of a rocking chair, fishing pole, and pipe. "It's pretty easy to figure out he was looking forward to retirement."

P.R. pictured Jackson hunched over his desk, doodling. Most of Jackson's doodles were more cryptic.

"When I was a child, I asked Daddy if his doodling meant anything. He gave me his stern look and waggled his eyebrows." Michelle tried to imitate her father. "Of course they mean something. Everything in life means something."

P.R. responded with a hollow laugh.

"I was persistent and kept pestering him. Finally, Dad told me his doodles were a kind of shorthand. 'When you're older and go into law with me, I'll explain them to you.' But I didn't go into law, and he never explained them."

P.R. put his hand on Michelle's shoulder to console her. "I *did* go into law, and he never explained them to me either."

"I saved a seat for you with the family, if you'd like to sit with us."

The lump in his throat thickened. All he could do was nod. He sat in the front row beside Michelle and her husband, who kept a comforting arm around his wife.

As soft organ music played in the background, P.R.'s eyes rested on the closed casket with a spray of red roses and a ribbon with the word 'Father.'

P.R. remembered the fatherly way Jackson used to slap him on the back and call him son. Still, whenever P.R. attended a funeral and smelled roses, no matter whose funeral it was, he was plunged back to that eventful day when he was fifteen.

With all his usual teenage bravado, he'd swaggered into the house. But the instant the screen door smacked behind him, everything changed. His mother wasn't waiting in the kitchen. She sat on the couch in the living room, surrounded by his sisters.

She looked up at him, her eyes swollen. She wiped them with a tissue and patted the rose-chintz cushion beside her. He trudged across the worn carpeting. Already the pall of death hung in the room. Maybe Uncle Bob who had cancer or Grandma Dot in her eighties...

"Your-your father...God bless his soul."

P.R. couldn't grasp it. That morning before P.R. delivered papers, his father sat across the table eating a bowl of oatmeal. He was fifty-three, held two jobs, and never missed a day's work. He couldn't be dead.

P.R. didn't ask *how*, but his older sister Summer answered the question. "A massive stroke. He was working on the elevator in the Sears Tower."

"At-at least he wasn't driving the cab." His mother seemed to take comfort in that.

P.R. didn't feel any comfort about where his dad had died. In fact, he didn't feel anything. At the funeral his mother and sisters had gone through boxes of tissues. He hadn't shed a tear. His family thought he was being stoic, stepping into the role of 'man of the house.' They didn't know that if he allowed himself to shed a single tear, he might never be able to stop.

Not because he and his father were close—but because they weren't. His father was a hard worker who'd always provided for his family, but he never seemed to derive much pleasure from life—or his children. They didn't share father-son activities like playing pitch and catch or going on camping trips.

P.R.'s favorite childhood memory was the day he was eight years old and his father had taken him to a Cubs game at Wrigley Field. They'd squeezed into bleacher seats and eaten hot dogs, smothered in mustard and relish. They'd cheered for the Cubs, who won ten to eight against the Cardinals.

After that day, P.R. expected his father to spend more time with him, but nothing changed. His father still didn't come to his Little League games, but continued to ride P.R. about how he didn't measure up. He didn't fold the newspapers right or cut the grass short enough or take the trash out on time.

At fifteen, P.R. had given up trying to please his father. At breakfast, the morning his father died, they'd argued. Between spoonsful of oatmeal, his dad had expressed his disappointment in P.R.

"I work twelve hours a day to pay for that fancy school of yours." His father pointed his spoon at him. "And the best you can do is a *C* in geometry."

P.R. slumped in his seat and tried to defend himself. "Those theorems are hard. I'll never use them."

"No son of mine brings home a *C* on his report card."

P.R. resented the way his father came down harder on him than his sisters. "When the girls were in school, you didn't care about *C*'s on their report cards." Raven had earned average grades; Belle's had been a little better; only Summer consistently made the honor roll.

His father threw his spoon down in disgust. "Their husbands will support them." His father thought the man should be the breadwinner. Even though money was tight, he forbade his wife to work outside the home.

After his father's death, P.R. began to understand. At the time, Summer and Belle were married, and Raven lived in an apartment with a girlfriend. He was the only one left at home with his mom.

A small life insurance policy paid off the mortgage on the house, but his mother still struggled from week to week to pay the bills. She took a job at Angelo's a neighborhood Italian restaurant. P.R. dropped out of that pricey private school and enrolled in a public high school. Besides his morning paper route, he earned money by scooping snow and mowing lawns.

He buckled down and never brought home another *C*. He earned a scholarship to Northwestern and passed the bar exam on his first attempt. Some lessons, though, came too late. No matter how hard P.R. tried, he would never have what he wanted—his father's approval.

Jackson Wenzel had been the man who had taken a fatherly interest in him. The first summer after his father's death, P.R. stayed with his sister Summer in Hickory Hills. Jackson hired P.R. as a courier, but when P.R. stepped into the courtroom, he knew that's where he belonged. Jackson had recognized P.R.'s keen interest and helped him along the way.

Recently Jackson had urged P.R. to continue the fight for coal miners and their benefits. "They need someone with your drive and ethics to represent them."

When Jackson had been a young lawyer, he'd gone to Washington and pressed Congress for changes in the black lung benefits for widows and families. For Jackson the fight had been personal. His dad had quit school and begun working in the mine at twelve. By the time his dad was fifty, his lungs were riddled with coal dust, and he was so short of breath he was unable to climb the stairs to his room on the second floor.

His bed was moved downstairs. The last few months of his life, his cough rattled through the house. "I can still hear Dad hacking and see the gobs of yellow phlegm he spit up. But when he died, our family was denied black lung benefits. I've spent my life trying to make sure that doesn't happen to another family."

In principle, P.R. agreed with Jackson, but P.R. wasn't interested in sacrificing a lucrative career. The miners' cases dragged on for years before reaching a settlement, and few were successful. P.R. had finally paid off his student loans, bought a car, and was saving money for a condo in downtown Chicago.

"A more experienced lawyer might be better," P.R. said, trying to soften his refusal to Jackson.

When he rose to leave, Jackson pulled out a handful of folders. "Take these with you. Read them over. Maybe you'll change your mind."

P.R. had read over the cases and been moved, but when he'd returned the folders to Jackson's office, he'd written a short note declining the offer. He'd laid the note on the desk a few minutes before he'd discovered Jackson lying on the floor of the file room, dead. P.R. was glad Jackson hadn't read the note, not because P.R. had changed his mind, but because he didn't want to disappoint his mentor the way he had disappointed his father.

As P.R. waited for the service to begin, he straightened his tie. The top button on his starched white shirt seemed unusually confining. Across the aisle sat Quinn and Ace. P.R. had expected to see Tomi today and was surprised at the stab of disappointment that she wasn't here. When he'd ordered Jackson's flowers for the funeral, he sent her yellow roses.

He regretted the way things had ended between them. "Why does she think I'm the devil?" he'd asked Quinn.

"It has something to do with your mustache and goatee."

When P.R. was hired by the prestigious law firm of Spader, Kirk, and Lloyd, he'd grown the facial hair to make him look more mature. Other women didn't seem to mind.

The music in the church stopped. Reverend Stone stepped up to the altar. According to Belle, he wasn't a fire-and-brimstone preacher as his name implied, but a godly man. And even though he was short—his wide shoulders no higher than the lectern—to his congregation and the town he stood seven feet tall.

The church was packed with family and friends, as well as other lawyers, United Mine Workers representatives, and clients. All bowed their heads as the reverend led them in prayer.

The funeral lasted more than two hours, as person after person stepped to the podium to pay tribute to the life of Jackson Wenzel. A long queue formed behind the casket as the pallbearers carried it to the cemetery alongside the church.

Saying goodbye to his mentor and friend was more difficult than P.R. expected. But now was the time for the living, so he turned away and followed the others into the church for the funeral dinner where they would eat and tell stories about the man they'd loved.

Salads and desserts were set out on tables in the fellowship hall. P.R. shuffled through the line, filling his plate, and then moved into the kitchen for the fried chicken, mashed potatoes, and gravy.

Quinn was one of the church women serving the fried chicken. She placed two legs onto his plate. "What a great tribute to Jackson."

P.R. nodded. "I thought Tomi might come for the dinner."

"I invited her, but she wanted to rest. Truthfully, I think she's still afraid."

P.R. moved out of line and stood behind Quinn. "And you left her alone?"

"I thought it would be for a short time." She checked her watch. "It's after one, and I still have to clean up." She reached into her apron pocket and pulled out her phone. "I'll call and check on her."

Quinn put it on speaker, and P.R. listened to it ring. Then he heard a recorded message in Tomi's voice. He didn't understand the Japanese words, but her voice lightened his mood. Quinn left a message, explaining she would be at the church for a few more hours.

"Why didn't she answer?"

Quinn shrugged. "Maybe she's sleeping or maybe she went over to Ace's. I asked her to feed the dogs." A line creased her forehead. "The kids are at the Saturday afternoon reading program at the library and won't be home until after three."

"I could run by, bring her some food, and make sure she's all right."

Quinn hesitated. "Well, I have to admit Tomi liked the flowers you sent. That was very thoughtful, P.R."

"I wanted to show her I'm not really the devil."

CHAPTER NINE

Bucky flipped through the folders in the bottom drawer of the file cabinet. He slammed the drawer shut. Nothing. For the past two hours he'd searched Ace's house looking for that infernal document. Where could it be?

Today was too warm for a jacket, so he'd tucked his phone into the front pocket of his black jeans and the gun into the waistband. The long white hair and beard were hot. He swiped the back of his arm across the sweat tricking down his face.

Think. Think. Think.

It was after one o'clock. Jackson's funeral would be over. Ace's truck could pull into the drive at any minute. Bucky clenched his gloved hands and looked around the study. A large aerial photograph of the farm hung above the desk next to the file cabinet. The frame was slightly crooked. He leaned across the desk and lifted the lower corner of the picture.

Bingo. Inserted in the wall was a square safe with a combination lock in the middle. He removed the picture and propped it against the side of the desk. Interlocking his latex-gloved fingers, he pressed them backward until they popped, the way he'd seen safe crackers do in movies. Then he whirled the dial and began trying different series of numbers. Several times, the lock seemed to catch, but didn't open.

He pulled his cell phone out of his pocket and Googled A.C. Edleston.

He scrolled through the information: address, phone number, and birthday. He began with the address, trying several sequences of the rural post office box. He moved on to the ten-digit phone number. Nothing. Then he attempted the November birthday.

He twirled the lock: left, right, left. *Click.* The door on the safe popped open. *Cha-ching!* He'd just hit the jackpot.

He rifled through the safe and pulled out a life insurance policy. He whistled. Ace would be worth a pretty penny when he bought the farm. The man opened Ace's passport. In August, he'd traveled to Great Britain. Bucky didn't bother to look at Jason's passport or birth certificate, but he fingered the marriage license. Maybe he should swipe it and save Ace some aggravation.

Oh, Ace's marriage would start out hunky-dory, and then the little woman would bat her eyes at him, wanting a few more sparkly bobbles to dangle from her ears or flash on her fingers. Before Ace realized it, he would be chained with debt, and no matter how much money he made, Barbie doll would always want more.

Nah, why should Bucky take the marriage license? Ace wasn't making his life easy. He'd spent yesterday in the cornfield watching the house and waiting for Ace and Jason to go to Jackson's visitation. But Ace left alone, and the lights remained on. Last night Bucky slept in the coal mine. Coal dust had clung to his clothes, and he coughed so hard he spit up blood. No wonder coal miners ended up with black lung.

He thought he'd have plenty of time to search the house during the funeral. Only he hadn't found what he wanted.

He slid the marriage license back into the safe. According to the horoscope, Ace was a Scorpio. They possessed power and passion. Give Ace a few years of marriage and see how powerful and passionate he felt.

Bucky closed the safe and hung the picture back on the wall, tilting it slightly to the right. He'd already checked upstairs, but maybe he'd missed something.

He took the steps two at a time and paused in the doorway of Jason's bedroom. The twin bed was hastily made, the denim spread thrown halfway over the lumpy pillows. A shelf on the wall displayed Star Wars figures.

Bucky walked into the room. His fear and urgency dissipated as he was transported to his boyhood bedroom with the wobbly bunk beds he'd shared with Joey. Once upon a time, Bucky had believed in the Force. Luke Skywalker and Princess Leia, good against evil. As a kid, it had been so clear.

Bucky and Joey loved superheroes. Bucky had even drawn his own superhero comic books. Flame Boy, his side kick, Joey, and their dog battled Captain Evil. In his comics, Flame Boy always won. Captain Evil always lost. He'd learned in life that wasn't true.

For Joey's eleventh birthday, his mother had baked his favorite chocolate cake, and Bucky had been allowed to light the candles. But Captain had become irate when Joey continued to chant, "Burbday, burbday."

Captain said he didn't want other people laughing at an eleven-year-old kid who couldn't talk right. He dragged Joey from the table and up to his room where he locked him in.

Bucky begged Captain to let Joey play outside with him. "We'll stay away from the house. No one will see us."

Captain refused. But Bucky kept pleading. Finally, Captain snapped. "If you want to play with your brother so much, I'll lock you in with him."

As soon as the lock on the bedroom door clicked, Bucky panicked. The walls closed in. His vision blurred. The world turned red. He huddled in the corner of the closet, gasping for air and groping for something to help him. His fingers found the box of matches he'd stuffed in his pocket.

He struck the first match and watched it burn. The veil of red lifted. He struck another match and another.

Joey smelled the smoke and pushed back the curtain used for a closet door. "No, Bucky, no!"

Bucky didn't pay any attention. When Joey grabbed for the match, it slipped from Bucky's fingers into the open box. All the matches ignited. The fire was beautiful, swirling red, yellow, and orange.

Joey began blowing, but Bucky watched, mesmerized by the flames. The fire quickly spread and was too big for Joey to blow out. Trying to help, Bucky ran to the window and opened it. He hadn't known fresh air would fuel the fire.

The curtain across the closet burst into flames. Joey's shirt ignited. Bucky grabbed a blanket from the bed and threw it over his brother, smothering the fire, but not before Joey had been badly burned on his chest and hands. He was taken to the burn unit at the Children's Hospital in St. Louis.

Bucky hadn't been allowed to visit, but he had prayed for God to heal his brother. Jesus had healed the leper, so He could heal Joey. Every day he'd colored pictures for Joey. They were variations of the same world: a dog and two stick figures, dressed like superheroes, holding hands under a bright yellow sun.

One night when he finished his picture and was coming downstairs to put it on the kitchen table, he heard his parents arguing.

Captain's voice carried up the stairs to where Bucky hung over the rail. "It was Joey's fault. This time Bucky put out the fire. What's going to happen next time?"

"I won't let you do it," his mother said.

Bucky couldn't let Joey take the blame. When he walked into the kitchen to confess, his whole body shook. Bucky knew he'd get a beating, but he had to tell the truth. "It was me," he said. "I started the fire, not Joey."

Bucky did get a beating, but not for the fire—for lying. Captain told him to shut his trap, and his mother cried because her good little boy was trying to take the blame.

After Joey had been hospitalized for three weeks, Captain came home and announced Joey wouldn't need any more pictures. He wasn't coming home. He was dead.

Bucky wouldn't accept it. Even after the small memorial service, he continued to pray for Jesus to bring Joey back. But Joey hadn't come back.

Grief rose up in Bucky. The need for his brother was so strong he collapsed onto his knees in Jason's room. He took a deep breath and started to rise, carefully avoiding the Matchbox cars scattered around the room.

Bucky spotted a black-and-white police cruiser like Joey used to have. The cruiser had been his brother's favorite. Bucky bent over, picked up the police car, and palmed it. He moaned.

He knew when he was defeated. No use continuing to search Ace's house. The hiding places were too numerous. Bucky had found the original document at Miss May's and a duplicate in the lawyer's office. The third copy might not even be here. Ace could have stored it in a safety deposit box at a bank or somewhere else.

Woof, woof, woof. The killer whirled around and crossed to the upstairs window. Three dogs—a greyhound, a golden retriever, and a puppy—were staked near the machine shed. They continued to bark. Somebody must be coming.

He slipped the police car into the pocket of his jeans.

CHAPTER TEN

Tomi lay in bed dreaming about her brother, Hiro. Music played in the distance. She ignored it and continued to drift between sleep and consciousness. Her brother was ten and she was eight. The afternoon was hot, so to cool off they'd gone to the river near their house.

Hiro was wading in a stream, the water up to his knees. He stripped off his shirt. His chest was golden brown and hairless, but his thin arms were roped with muscles. In his hand, he clutched a long spear he'd fashioned from a tree limb and whittled to a sharp point.

She sat on the edge of the river bank, upstream from where Hiro was spear fishing. Her feet dangled in the clear water, the current sluicing through her toes. Sun shimmered on the surface, and below fish darted in and out. When a school of fish swam near, she stilled her feet and raised her hand, signaling Hiro to be ready.

He would plant his feet firmly on the muddy bottom and wait. When the fish were close, he aimed the spear a few feet ahead of his prey and threw it. Already he had speared more than half a dozen fish, enough for their family's supper.

A school of murata swirled upstream. The fish, called poor man's salmon, resembled giant minnows, and the ones with an orange-and-black stripe were spawning. When the school reached her legs, she waved to

Hiro. He planted his feet and aimed the spear. Waiting, waiting, he hurled it into the water.

"*Ichiban! Ichiban!* Number one, number one." Hiro beat his bare chest with a fist and raised the spear triumphantly over his head as he showed off the palm-sized, striped fish wiggling on the end. She hoped she got the fish at supper and would find the delicious eggs inside.

Her brother's voice faded. The music in the background grew louder. She blinked. Where was she? She turned toward a white desk and dresser. In the corner lay an empty dog bed. The fog lifted. She was in America, lying on Taylor's top bunk.

The familiar music was her cell phone. She groped for her phone on the desk. Just as she picked it up, the music stopped.

'Missed call' and 'Laney' appeared on the screen. Tomi hit redial. A busy signal. A new voicemail popped up. She listened to Laney's message that she would be back in a few hours. Tomi checked the clock. She had planned to take a short nap. That was two hours ago.

The dogs. She was supposed to feed and water the dogs. She'd call Laney, no Quinn, after she checked on the dogs.

She left on her Hawaiian-print mumu and twisted her long hair off her neck, securing it with lacquered sticks. Satisfied she didn't look like a fishmonger's wife, she dropped her phone into one of the wide pockets, slipped on her sandals, and hurried out the door, hearing it click behind her.

Through the tall trees she couldn't see Ace's house, but she found the worn footpath that Quinn had shown her. The fall afternoon was warm, and broken nut shells littering the ground crunched beneath her feet. A bushy-tailed gray squirrel scampered in front of her. It ran up the side of a tree and disappeared into the leaves.

She had never seen a squirrel outside of a cage. When she was a child, she and Hiro had gone to the squirrel garden near Tokyo and fed them sunflowers seeds. She'd worn a protective hand mitt, but Hiro fed them right out of his palm.

From above, something plopped onto the ground. She bent over and picked up a nut. The shell was too hard to crack open. She dropped it into the pocket with her phone. She would taste it later.

As she walked through the woods, clumps of dark clouds drifted in front of the sun. Shadows from the tall trees webbed on the path. The hairs on her neck rose, and a chill rippled through her. She started to turn back.

Woof, woof, woof! Through the clearing she saw Ace's two-story house and in the yard three dogs tied to a stake.

The front door of the house swung open. A man with long white hair flowing behind him ran out of the house and leaped from the porch. The sheriff had shown her a picture of a man with long white hair who had escaped from prison. Sheriff Ben said it might be the killer.

Her chest tightened. She couldn't find any air. She scrambled backward, her sandals slipping on the scattered nut shells. Thudding to the ground, she landed on her rump.

The man in Ace's yard stopped and turned in her direction. She scooted behind a tree. Had he seen her? Would he come after her? She had to get away.

Afraid to stand, she scuttled on her hands and feet. Her foot snagged on the raised tree roots. She fell into the dirt. She peeked over her shoulder. She couldn't see the man or the house. Staying low, she crawled from tree to tree. When the barn came into view, she scrambled up and sprinted toward the stairs.

She stopped on the landing and bent over, panting. Then she twisted the knob. The door didn't open. She pushed with her shoulder. The door wouldn't budge. It was locked.

She reached into her pocket for her cell phone. She pulled out a nut. Her phone was gone.

CHAPTER ELEVEN

P.R. bounded up the stairs on the side of the barn. A plastic sack dangled from his arm. He stopped on the landing and knocked on the door.

The September afternoon was warm. At the funeral dinner, he'd loosened his tie, and in the car, he'd stripped off his suit jacket and rolled up his sleeves. Overhead a gaggle of geese squawked and flapped their wings. He turned toward the lake. The geese glided across the water, landing feet first like skiers. After a hectic week in the city, the country life usually relaxed him.

This trip was different. Jackson's funeral had unsettled him, made him restless to get on with his life. He was twenty-nine years old. He had a lucrative job and owned a car. The next step in his life plan was to buy a condo in Chicago, but he needed to make sure his job was secure.

Impatient, he knocked on the door again. "Quinn sent me with some food."

The door didn't open. He leaned in and listened. Nothing. He twisted the doorknob and pushed. Locked.

He pounded harder. "Tomi, it's—" Maybe he shouldn't say his name. If she thought he was the devil, she wouldn't be pleased to find him knocking on her door, especially when she was alone. Reluctantly, he bent over and set the sack on the landing. "I'm leaving the food outside the door."

Quinn had said something about Tomi feeding the dogs. Maybe she was at Ace's house. Buoyed by the thought he might still see her, he took the steps two at a time and sprinted through the hickory grove.

Even before he cleared the trees, he heard the dogs barking. They were staked near the machine shed, their water and food bowls turned over. Taylor's puppy jumped around, begging for attention. P.R. knelt and scuffed Gogo between the ears. Then he ran his hand down the back of Ace's golden retriever, stroking the fur.

The third dog loped over and nuzzled him with his long snout. This must be Bullet, the dog Miss May had adopted through the Greyhound Project. P.R. held out his hand and let Bullet sniff it.

He played with the dogs for several minutes before he filled their water bowls from the outside spigot on the machine shed. Then he walked into the Quonset hut, checking for dog food and Tomi. Finding neither, he headed to the house and knocked on the back door. No one answered. He tried the front door. No answer there either.

As he stood on the porch, he began to worry. He didn't have Tomi's phone number and calling Quinn might alarm her. Tomi had to be here somewhere.

Maybe she was at the loft, sleeping. He'd go back and knock louder. As he walked through the tall hickory trees, he heard music playing that sounded like a phone. He patted his pants pocket. It wasn't his cell.

He followed the sound and found a phone lying on the ground near a cluster of gnarled tree roots. He picked it up. A small white plastic cat with its paw raised dangled from the bottom. Tomi's phone. He looked around. Where was she?

He swiped the screen. A grid of numbers appeared. He didn't know her password. He dropped her cell into his shirt pocket and pulled out his phone. He pressed Quinn's number.

She answered and quickly said, "P.R. I phoned Tomi, but—"

"I know. I have her cell. I found it in the woods near Ace's."

"What? Where is she?"

"I don't know. She didn't answer, and the door at the loft is locked."

"Maybe she's at Ace's feeding the dogs."

"No, I checked. The dogs didn't have food or water. Where else would she be?"

"I don't know. Go back to the loft and knock again. If she doesn't answer, there's a ceramic turtle at the bottom of the stairs with two keys inside. The silver one unlocks the loft. The gold is for the padlock on the barn door."

P.R. hung up, but he didn't rush through the woods. He kept his head down searching for clues. He didn't find any.

At the foot of the stairs, the turtle was camouflaged by a green leafy bush. He lifted the shell. Inside lay only one key, silver. He glanced at the double barn doors. The padlock usually hanging from the latch was gone.

Quinn had ridden with Ace to the funeral. Maybe Tomi had taken the car. He rushed to the front of the barn and pulled open the doors. Quinn's Ford Fusion was parked inside. He let out a breath of relief.

He stepped into the barn and waited for his eyes to adjust to the dim light. Against the far wall were bikes, fishing poles, a tarp covering a table and chairs, a lawn mower, and various tools. In front of Quinn's car, a ladder rose to the rafters.

He craned his neck and squinted at a small square cut in the floor of the loft. Quinn had talked about a trap door leading from the bottom of the barn to the loft.

He moved to the ladder and began climbing. When he neared the top, he pushed on the trap door. It gave way, unbalancing him. He grabbed for the side of the ladder and steadied his legs. He stuck his head through the small door. He was under the table in the loft. "Tomi, are you there?"

He heard a sound, but it didn't come from the loft.

"Tomi, where are you?"

"P.R., I here."

It sounded like Tomi, only her voice was below.

He ducked his head back through the door and scanned the lower part of the barn. Tomi was peeking out from under the tarp. "Why are you hiding?"

She threw off the tarp. Her print dress was streaked with dirt, and loose locks of hair dangled over her shoulder. She sprinted toward him. "Bad man...bad man."

Why was she calling him a bad man yet running toward him? Was she going to attack him again? He started to scramble down the ladder. His foot slipped. He missed a step near the middle. His arms flailed. His hands grasped for something. They found only air.

His body bumped down the ladder, his ribs cracking against the steps. He thudded onto the hood of Quinn's car, rolled off, and hit the concrete floor.

Pain shot through his head.

CHAPTER TWELVE

"P.R.! P.R!" Tomi raced across the barn and dropped to her knees.

"*Moshi! Moshi!* Are you there? Speak to me."

His eyes didn't open. He wasn't moving. All her fears vanished. She had to get help. Her cell phone was in his shirt pocket. She pulled it out and pressed Quinn's number.

She told Quinn that P.R. had fallen and asked her to come quickly. After Quinn assured her she would be there, Tomi hung up. She leaned over P.R. Was he breathing? His chest didn't seem to be moving up and down.

She continued talking, urging him to open his eyes. They stayed closed. Then she realized she was speaking Japanese. She took a steadying breath and searched for the right English words.

Lyrical sounds floated through his consciousness. He strained to understand the stream of foreign words. He wanted them to slow down and become English.

Almost as if she heard him, the words changed. "Wake up. No die."

Die. Was he dying?

He was lying on his back. His head ached. He tried to speak, but his mouth wouldn't move. He started to rise. Excruciating pain shot through his head. Maybe this was the way it felt to die. Trapped in darkness, throbbing with pain. Where was the bright light? The peace?

His throat was parched. Water. He needed water. He'd sell his soul for a cool drink of water.

Oh, no! Maybe that's what he'd done. He was in purgatory, dying of thirst and pain. His head certainly hurt like hell. Not just his head, his ribs. Each breath made him wince.

"Wake up, please."

That angelic voice made him want to slog through the pain. A hand touched his wrist. Soft fingers gently felt for a pulse. Then they slid up the side of his neck and pushed down. Did he have a pulse?

Too soon the hand and voice were gone. He moaned, wanting them to come back.

A wet rag was placed on his forehead. All thoughts of hell vanished. He opened his eyes. He focused on a woman staring down at him. Her brown eyes were filled with fear. He wanted to reach up and brush away that fear. He lifted his arm, surprised that it worked, and touched her hand. Those dark chocolate eyes melted into his.

He guided her hand with the wet cloth down his face to his lips. He sucked in, letting the water sluice through his mouth and trickle into his throat.

Tomi. He had been searching for her and here she was. Her words were comforting, her touch gentle. She thought he was the devil. But he no longer felt like he was in hell. He tried to get up. Pain shot through his ribs.

"No move." Her voice shook.

Was she still afraid of him? He didn't want to frighten her. He lay still and closed his eyes, content to just listen to her comforting words. He drifted, floating with the lyrical sounds.

"Wake up, please. Wake up."

He didn't want to wake up.

A hand slapped his cheek, stinging him awake. Startled, his eyes popped open.

Her voice changed. "Hard head."

He laughed, only it sounded like a groan. Pain stabbed his head. His hand moved to his skull. He found a small bump and winced. As much as he hurt, he'd thought it would be the size of a goose egg.

Tomi stood and walked away. He wanted her to stay.

He tried to say, 'Come back,' but it was too difficult. He closed his eyes and gave in to the pain.

Other voices swirled around him. Tomi was saying something about a bad man at Ace's house. Was she talking about him? Maybe she had seen Jackson's spirit.

He recognized Quinn's voice. "P.R., P.R."

He forced his eyes open. Quinn was kneeling beside him. "What happened?"

Above him, Tomi came into view and pointed up. "Fell."

Quinn tilted her head toward the ladder.

Footsteps stomped across the concrete. Ace knelt beside him and frowned. "Quinn, Call an ambulance."

P.R. strained to speak. "No...ambulance."

"Can you get up?" Ace asked.

P.R. struggled and with the help of Ace made it to his knees. He braced himself against the car and slowly stood. The barn began to spin. He swayed and held onto the car.

Ace threw a steadying arm around P.R.'s shoulders. He grimaced. "I'm okay."

"P.R., you've never been okay."

He groaned at Ace's attempt at humor.

"You took a nasty fall," Quinn said. "Doc Morgan needs to check you out."

P.R. didn't protest. He leaned against Ace as he guided him toward the truck. Each step sent a knife-stabbing pain through P.R.'s side. When they reached the truck, Ace opened the passenger door. P.R. slid into the seat and closed his eyes. His head was spinning. His stomach roiling. He fought the nausea.

Ace was talking to Quinn. "I'll drive P.R. to the hospital. I'm not sure what Tomi saw, but I don't want you two here alone."

"What about the kids?"

"Have Summer pick them up from the library. You drive Tomi to the police station and talk to Ben."

P.R. wanted Tomi to come with him. He opened his eyes. She was peering through the windshield. Their eyes met. He didn't use words. He let her see his need. He was asking her to stay with him; she was answering, only it wasn't the answer he wanted. She hesitated, not sure.

He blinked, letting the wall he had hidden behind for so many years crumble. She took a step toward the truck. Was she coming or going?

She opened the passenger door. He moved over and patted the seat next to him.

She slid in. "I go."

He rested his head on her shoulder. His head stopped throbbing. The pain in his side began to ease. As the truck pulled away, he relaxed. He could breathe again.

CHAPTER THIRTEEN

At the hospital, Tomi and Ace stayed in the waiting room while a nurse whisked P.R. into the emergency room. Quinn arrived a few minutes later.

"They run tests," Tomi said to Quinn.

Quinn gestured to the dirt on Tomi's dress. "Let's clean you up." Quinn turned to Ace. "Call Ben and tell him what Tomi saw."

Quinn led Tomi to the restroom where Quinn brushed the dirt from Tomi's mumu and fixed her hair. "I hope they catch Zeus."

Tomi frowned. "Zeus?"

"The man with the white hair you saw leaving Ace's."

Goosebumps pricked Tomi's arm. "Bad man."

Quinn nodded.

They returned to the waiting room. An hour later a nurse wheeled P.R. back.

"What did they find out?" Ace asked.

P.R. shrugged. "They have to read the X-rays."

The front door of the emergency room opened, and a tall woman with spiked red hair rushed in. "Summer told me you were here." She hurried over to P.R., leaned down, and hugged him.

"Holy cow!" P.R. gritted his teeth and winced. "If my ribs weren't broken before, they are now." He waved Tomi over. "I want you to meet my oldest sister, Belle. She and her husband own the Castle, the local B&B."

Tomi bowed to P.R.'s sister. Belle shook Tomi's hand, and then turned to P.R. "Be careful about tossing around the old part. I'm thirty-nine and plan to stay that way, just like Jack Benny."

P.R. groaned. "If you know who Jack Benny is, you are old." Then he raised his hand and saluted his sister. "Belle's also a drill sergeant and married to the sheriff."

"Someone has to keep you in line," Belle said.

Tomi tried to follow the conversation, but Belle wasn't wearing a military uniform, so Tomi didn't understand why P.R. saluted her. But when Belle looked at P.R., her green eyes were filled with concern, and Tomi saw the kind of love she'd felt for her brother.

"What's with the red hair, Sis?" asked P.R.

Belle fluffed out her short, spiky hair. "It's my new look for Quinn's wedding."

The doctor sailed into the room, his white lab coat flapping behind. He carried a tablet, and the name tag on his coat read Doc Morgan. He had thick-framed glasses and black hair salted with gray, but his unlined face made him appear not much older than Ace.

The doctor patted Ace on the back. "One more week and you're hitched. You have my condolences."

Tomi was confused by the greeting, but Ace gave a hearty laugh and then turned to Quinn. His smoldering look made Tomi envious. No man had ever looked at her like that—and likely never would.

Since P.R.'s family and friends were the only ones in the waiting area, the doctor pulled up a footstool and sat next to P.R.'s wheelchair. "Your ribs are only bruised, and the X-rays did not show any bleeding on the brain."

Quinn translated, and Tomi's tense body relaxed.

"Thanks, Doc. Now I can head to Chicago." P.R. put his hand on the arm of the wheelchair and struggled to get up.

"Not so fast." The doctor clamped P.R.'s shoulder. "Even though the X-rays didn't detect bleeding, you probably suffered a mild concussion."

P.R. sank back into the chair. The happy mood in the room flattened.

Tomi typed 'concussion' into her phone. A new worry settled in, especially when Doc Morgan added, "You need to stay in the hospital tonight."

P.R. protested. "I have work to do in Chicago."

"Work can wait. No driving for the next few days."

P.R. turned to Belle. "Looks like you'll have another guest at the B&B."

"Sorry, the Castle's booked this weekend," Belle said. "Raven is staying in the family's room because her husband is out of town and the twins are due next week. But you can bunk with your nephews."

Ace walked over to the wheelchair. "P.R. can stay with me. I'll make sure he behaves."

"Sounds better than the hospital or bunking with the boys." P.R. looked up at Ace. "Thanks."

The doctor turned to Ace. "He needs rest. No computer, television, or reading."

P.R. frowned. "Wake me up next week."

"No lengthy sleeping either." The doctor typed some notes into his tablet. "You don't want to slip into a coma."

P.R. threw up his hands. "What can I do?"

The doctor pushed his glasses to the top of his head. "For the next forty-eight hours, very little."

P.R. pressed his hand to his forehead. "Well, at least give me something for this headache."

"Sorry, P.R. You can take aspirin, but stronger drugs might mask your symptoms."

Tomi didn't understand everything the doctor said, but later that night after supper Quinn explained.

"I worry for his head," Tomi said, sitting across from Quinn at the table.

"P.R. just needs to rest." Quinn reached over and put her hand on Tomi's. "It's good to have you here. I've missed you."

"Me, too." Tomi knew Quinn was trying to change the subject to something pleasant, so she asked, "Do you remember day we met?"

Quinn smiled. "Yes. We were both new teachers late for our first day."

"Other new teachers were men. I no want to go in. Then you appear, running down hall."

"Do you know why I was late?"

"You missed train."

"That's what I let you think," Quinn said. "But everything in Japan was so difficult, even going out to eat. I couldn't read the menu, so I had to point to the plastic food on display. When the noodles arrived, I couldn't use the chopsticks."

"Oh, so sorry."

"I wanted to fly back to the U.S., but I didn't have money for a ticket, so I planned to teach for a few weeks and then return."

"So why you no leave?" Tomi asked.

"Because of you. It wasn't so hard when I had a friend."

Tomi nodded. "Friends together."

Quinn squeezed Tomi's hand. "Yes, friends together."

————

The next day P.R. sat between Ace and Tomi at the butcher block table in Ace's kitchen. Across from them were Quinn, Taylor, and Jason.

"This certainly beats hospital food," P.R. said, reaching for another slice of pizza. With the nausea gone, P.R.'s hearty appetite had returned. He'd devoured almost half of the thick-crust pizza topped with sausage, mushrooms, and peppers. He didn't have to ask Tomi if she liked American pizza. She had matched him piece for piece.

Across the table, Jason elbowed Taylor. She elbowed him back.

Last April, when P.R. had met Taylor, she had been a thin waif with sad-looking eyes and buzzed hair. Now she had plump rosy cheeks and hair curling around her face.

The change was more than physical. Taylor had a twinkle in her eye that hadn't been there when she first started living with Quinn. P.R. hoped the court would grant Quinn permanent custody of Taylor, but Quinn was adamant about not contacting the biological father.

P.R. glanced at the last piece of pizza. He didn't want it tossed to Gogo, lying in wait by the door. He reached for the pizza, and Tomi's hand shot out, too. Their fingers brushed. He felt a tingle that had nothing to do with his head.

"Be my guest." He removed his hand. Tomi would just say 'so sorry' and leave it for him.

"*Arigatou gozaimasu.*" Tomi scooped up the piece of pizza and bit into it.

He stifled a laugh as she devoured the whole slice. A dab of tomato sauce smeared the corner of her mouth. He signaled her by swiping the corner of his mouth. She rubbed the side of her mouth with a napkin. Then her soft brown eyes questioned his.

He was mesmerized by her eyes and by her wide mouth with full, plump lips. He wondered what it would feel like to kiss those red lips. Would they be as sweet as they looked?

Holy cow! He needed to back away from that thought. He straightened in his chair, but Tomi continued to stare at him. Not exactly at him. She seemed to focus on his ears.

He had always been self-conscious of his large earlobes, but most women seemed to find him attractive anyway.

He resisted the urge to cover his ears with his hands. Instead he asked, "Are you staring at my ears?"

Tomi's brown eyes flitted away. Her hand covered her mouth. "So sorry."

P.R. was the one who was sorry. He had embarrassed her, and now everyone at the table was staring at his ears. Taylor and Jason started snickering.

Ace cleared his throat. "What's going on, son?"

Jason maneuvered out of the situation. "I want to go fishing."

Taylor pushed up her glasses. "Me, too."

"We could take the pontoon," Quinn said.

Normally P.R. would be the first to hop on the boat, but today he was drained. "Last night the nurse woke me up every two hours. Count me out."

"Doc Morgan said not to leave you alone," Ace reminded him. "So, no fishing today."

Taylor stuck out her lip and Jason groaned. "But, Dad."

"I'll stay with P.R.," Quinn offered. "Ace, you take the kids and Tomi on the boat."

Ace's brows drew together. Even P.R. could see that Ace didn't like leaving Quinn.

"I stay," said Tomi.

"No," Quinn said. "I want you to go fishing and have fun."

"Very tired," Tomi said.

P.R. liked the comforting way Tomi had taken care of him when he'd fallen. Before anyone else could object, he said, "Yes, she can stay with me."

"Well," Quinn said and then switched to Japanese as she asked Tomi several questions.

P.R. didn't need to understand Japanese to know that Quinn was worried about leaving Tomi alone with him.

Tomi held up her cell phone. "Need help, I call."

"We'll be fine," P.R. said, waving her away. "Go, go."

Upon hearing his name, Gogo jumped up and barked.

"I'll get the poles." Jason hurried out the door. Taylor and Gogo scampered behind.

While Quinn and Tomi cleaned up the table, Ace helped P.R. into the living room and onto the couch. P.R. hadn't realized just how tired he was until he leaned back against the sofa. Within minutes, he relaxed and drifted off to sleep.

Someone touched his arm. He jerked awake. Tomi sat on the couch next to him. He checked his watch. He'd been sleeping for more than two hours.

"Tea?" she said, pointing to a cup on the table in front of him.

He couldn't remember when he'd drunk hot tea, but it sounded good. What was that Japanese word for thank you? *Arigatou.* He mangled the pronunciation, but his effort earned him a huge smile.

"Milk or sugar?" Tomi asked.

He drank his coffee black, so he shook his head. The room started to spin. He winced.

"Head hurt?"

"A little dizzy," he admitted. "Thank you for staying with me."

"Very welcome."

P.R. liked talking to women, but he wasn't sure what to say to Tomi. "I guess you noticed my ears."

"Yes, very big."

Well, she didn't have to sound pleased.

"So good," she added.

"Good?"

"Yes. Japanese saying. If man's ear lobes hold grain of rice, he be rich."

P.R. laughed. "I should be very rich."

As he sipped his tea, Tomi said, "Must be hard day."

"According to Doc Morgan I'll be fine."

"Not for head." She placed her hand over her heart. "For America."

He put his cup on the table. "America?"

She pointed to the date on his wristwatch. "9/11."

He hadn't realized today was the anniversary of the terrorist attack on the World Trade Center. He was surprised Tomi remembered.

"So sad." She blinked as if holding back tears.

He had been fourteen the day two planes flew into the World Trade Center. Until then life had been simple. His only worry, other than how to please his father, was getting his sisters out of the bathroom.

On Sept. 11, he'd been in English class, slouched in his seat in the back row. Suddenly the teacher interrupted the grammar lesson and switched on the television. The newscast showed a plane flying into the World Trade Center. He'd bolted upright. Flames shot out of the windows and licked the outside of the building. Then a smaller plane hit the second building. As he watched, the hot steel melted. The twin towers collapsed. For days the images were replayed on TV.

Even now the memory unnerved him. He picked up his cup and took a long drink. "It was a hard time."

"*Hai.*"

The lovely lilt in her voice was gone, and her soft eyes seemed far away. Why would she be sad about 9/11? He put down his tea. "What's wrong?"

She folded her hands in her lap and lowered her head. "3/11."

He thought she said *3/11.* "Do you mean 9/11?"

"No. 3/11."

This time he was sure about the date. "I don't understand. What is 3/11?"

"March 11, 2011."

He stroked his goatee, trying to figure out the significance. "Is that an important date for you?"

The memory of that day rolled over her like the black waters of the tsunami that had hit the coast of Japan. The day was not an ordinary Friday. She should have been at school, teaching. But she had taken a half day off to go with her parents to visit Uncle. Her father's older brother and family lived one hundred kilometers inland.

She had not wanted to go and begged to stay home with Grandmother, who was too feeble to make the long trip. But her parents said Hiro could stay behind.

Being a dutiful daughter, she rode the train with her parents. In her lap she carried a bowl of sticky rice balls her grandmother had made. The first earthquake struck near Tokyo at 2:46 p.m. Even though they were two hours away, their railroad car rocked back and forth so hard the rice balls tumbled from her lap and their suitcases upended. She thought the train might tip off the tracks. Later she learned the earthquake lasted six minutes. Those six minutes changed her life.

An hour after the earthquake, a tsunami hit the coast near her town. The tidal waves surged to a height of almost thirty-nine meters and crashed through the seawall. The raging water sent boats inland and flattened everything—the temple, the school, and their home.

How could she explain the devastation to P.R.? She picked up her phone and typed in the date. She handed it to him. "Please read."

P.R. looked at the screen. "I can't read Japanese."

Her hand shook as she changed the language to English.

P.R. read the words aloud, "On 11 March 2011, Japan recorded a magnitude 9 earthquake that generated a tsunami along the Pacific coastline as far as four hundred miles. Near the prefecture of Fukushima..."

He gripped the phone tighter. *Fukushima.* He recognized that name from the news clips on TV. The nuclear power plant. He made the connection. The earthquake and tsunami had happened on 3/11.

He continued reading, "Over 15,000 dead and 2,500 missing." He turned to Tomi. "Did someone you know die?"

Her sad eyes said it all. "*Hai.* Grandmother." Then she pointed to the screen and the word 'missing.'

"Someone's missing?"

She reached into her pocket and rubbed the small porcelain frog. "Brother."

He gulped down the last of his tea. He called his three sisters triple threat, yet he couldn't imagine losing one of them.

Tomi took the phone and searched again. When she found what she wanted, she handed it to him.

His eyes scanned the article. "After the tsunami, the Fukushima Daiichi Nuclear Power Plant suffered a level 7 nuclear meltdown."

Tomi pointed to the words below. "Five years after the quake, about 230,000 people who lost their homes are still living in temporary housing." She placed her finger on 'temporary housing.'

"You lost your home."

"*Hai.* My parents live in temporary housing. I moved to Tokyo to teach. That's when I met Laney...Quinn."

P.R. wrapped both his hands around hers. Tomi had lost her grandmother, her brother, and her home. What could he say that would let her know how he felt? Then he remembered her words. It wasn't much, but he hoped she would understand his heart-felt sympathy. "So sorry."

"*Arigatou gozaimasu.*"

She spoke Japanese and he spoke English, but in this moment it didn't matter. As his large hands enveloped hers, she felt safe and connected, not as a woman to a man, not as a Japanese to an American. His words and his touch had severed those boundaries.

A quiet peace she had not experienced since the tsunami flowed through her.

CHAPTER FOURTEEN

On Friday evening before the wedding rehearsal, Quinn and Tomi paused at the small cemetery beside the Hopewell Hickory Church. "This is where my dad and grandparents are buried. We're going to visit their graves. Do you want to come, Tomi?"

Tomi stared at the gray stones and thought of her grandmother and brother. Her grandmother's body had been found, but not her brother's. She had no resting place to visit for him.

A chill ran through her. She did not want to disturb the dead. "I go in church." She drew the burgundy shawl, which her grandmother had knitted, tightly around her shoulders. Wearing the soft angora wrap made Tomi feel as if her grandmother's arms were wrapped around her.

Tomi's heart raced as she opened the heavy wooden door and stepped into the church. She and her parents had traveled to Europe and visited cathedrals, even the Vatican, but this was the first time she had been in an American church.

Quinn had explained about Mary, Jesus, and God, but no golden statues adorned the church and no smells of incense wafted through the air. Over the altar hung a large wooden cross, and on the wall behind was a painted picture of a shepherd holding a small lamb in his arms.

Light from the setting sun shone through the stained glass windows, casting an ethereal glow around the small room lined with wooden benches. The tranquil peace calmed her nerves.

The door behind her opened. Taylor and Jason, followed by Quinn and Ace, nudged her down the aisle to the front row.

As they sat and waited for the practice wedding, Ace's whispers grew louder. "Quinn, that's crazy."

"No, it's practical," Quinn hissed. "I'm not moving my stuff to your house until after the wedding."

Ace was no longer whispering. "Why is that practical?"

"What if I need something at your house?"

"Then come and get it."

"Not if it's on our wedding day. The bride and groom aren't supposed to see each other."

"That's an old wives' tale," Ace said. "Besides, you don't have to move everything."

Quinn stood and put her hand on her hip. "I don't plan on moving anything."

Ace shot up. "Fine." He did not sound as if he thought it was fine. "But after the honeymoon, everything gets moved to my place. I don't want my wife having a runaway house."

Quinn frowned. "A runaway house?"

"A place for you to run away to every time we disagree."

Quinn laced her fingers through Ace's. "I'm not going to run away."

Tomi noticed Quinn didn't say she was not going to disagree. But as Quinn and Ace faced each other, their eyes filled with love, the kind Tomi yearned to feel.

Tomi remembered New Year's Eve when she and Quinn had visited the Meiji Shrine in Tokyo. Tomi gave Quinn a wooden plaque to write her wish and tie onto the prayer wall.

"What should I write?" Quinn asked.

Tomi showed Quinn her wish. 'Find love.'

"You can't find love. Love finds you."

Tomi didn't understand how love could find someone, but now the light in the church reflected on Quinn's face glowing with love.

In the back the heavy wooden door opened. Tomi turned, hoping to see P.R. After last weekend, she no longer thought of him as the devil. When she told him about losing her grandmother and brother, he had been kind.

During the week, she had worried about his head and how lonely he must be in Chicago.

But Ace's brother, Craig, and his wife, Summer, walked in. Craig was the best man and Summer the photographer. Her camera was looped around her neck, and as she hurried toward the front, she was talking on her phone.

Quinn turned toward the door, too. Tomi knew Quinn hoped her mother would come. Quinn had told Tomi about her childhood. When Quinn was seven, her father had died in a truck accident. Her mother was an alcoholic and began drinking more. She changed jobs and men often. Quinn cooked and cared for herself. When home life became too unbearable, Quinn stayed with her friend Chrissy.

Quinn had invited her mother to the wedding. Yesterday when Quinn said she wanted her mother to come, the longing in Quinn's voice sounded as if she were still that little girl yearning for her mother's love.

The church door creaked again. Tomi turned. Her heart lightened as P.R opened the door. Then a tall blonde in a tight red sheath walked in and looped her arm through P.R.'s. Tomi's smile slipped away.

Jason whispered to Taylor, "P.R. has a girlfriend."

Taylor shrugged. "Mom says he's a playboy."

So P.R. is not a lonely bachelor, thought Tomi. He likes many women. Her mother had warned her about American playboys. She must keep her guard up.

As P.R. walked down the aisle, Summer hurried over to him. "Raven called. She's in labor."

"Now?" He dropped the woman's arm and moved toward his sister. "I thought they were inducing labor on Monday."

"I guess the babies have other plans. Raven is refusing to go to the hospital until Carter arrives."

"The hospital's only a few blocks away."

"The hospital in Hickory Hills doesn't deliver babies," Summer said. "The closest one is an hour away."

P.R.'s chest tightened. No wonder Summer was upset. "When's Carter's plane getting in?"

"It landed in St. Louis about three hours ago."

P. R.'s voice rose. "It doesn't take three hours to drive here from St. Louis."

He liked his other two brothers-in-law. Craig was a commodity broker and Ben, the sheriff. Carter was a salesman and flew out on Monday morning and back home on Friday. P.R. wasn't buying what Carter was selling about being a loyal husband. He had a wedding ring on his finger, but he seemed to enjoy other women a little too much.

"Just looking, just looking," Carter once said when P.R. caught him ogling one of his dates. "A guy might as well be dead if he can't look."

The minister hurried in through the side door. "If everyone's here, let's begin."

P.R. settled Ashleigh into a middle pew and strode to the back of the church. Many of his friends had recently been hitched, so he had the usher's duties down pat. He pulled out the runner and nodded to the organist. The music signaled the wedding party to begin. Ace and Craig stood in front of the altar with the minister. Tomi, Taylor, Jason, and Quinn waited in the back.

P.R. stood off to the side and waved Tomi down the aisle. She wore a quaint shawl, knotted in front, and her long black hair cascaded over it. Her dress emphasized her waist and the full skirt flared out to just above her knees. The glow on her face gave her an innocence that touched him in a way he hadn't expected.

As she walked by, he tried to catch her eye. She didn't meet his gaze, but he got a whiff of that sweet scent he couldn't quite identify. He wanted to reach out and touch her, feel her soft skin beneath his hands. But she strolled by without a glance.

Disappointment stabbed through him. He wanted those interesting brown eyes to turn his way and light up. He chided himself. Isn't that what he'd ragged on Carter about, having one woman and looking at another?

Bringing Ashleigh to the wedding hadn't been totally his idea. It somehow made their first date more serious than he wanted. She'd ridden with him from Chicago, but he'd bought her a train ticket to return on Sunday. He planned to stay through Monday to be with Raven when she delivered.

He'd been at the hospital when his other sisters had given birth. Belle had two boys; Summer had a boy and a girl. Raven didn't want to know the sex of the twins. She'd spent the better part of the last three months in bed, trying to make sure the babies were healthy.

After they finished the rehearsal, the minister asked, "Any questions?"

Summer's phone rang. She listened and then quickly hung up. "Raven's water broke. Ben's taking her to Hickory Hills Community Hospital."

"Here?" P.R. asked. "You said they don't deliver babies."

"Well, these babies aren't waiting."

CHAPTER FIFTEEN

The next day Quinn sat at the small wooden table in the kindergarten Sunday school room. Tomi stood behind Quinn fixing her hair, which was no longer black, but close to its natural honey blonde.

"Now look like Laney," Tomi said.

Quinn ran her hand over her silk wedding gown. *Laney.* The name no longer sounded familiar. Melana Elam and that life had ended six months ago when she and Taylor fled to Hickory Hills.

Quinn had been holding Taylor's hand as they walked into this very room. The teacher had welcomed them and introduced herself as Summer. Her daughter, Kat, had taken Taylor's hand and led her over to the play kitchen. By the end of Sunday school, Kat and Taylor had become 'bestest friends.'

Summer and Quinn had become friends, too, and now that Quinn was marrying Ace, she and Summer would be sisters-in-law. So, not only would she be marrying the man she loved, but she would also be getting the family she'd always wanted. She closed her eyes and thanked God for all her blessings.

A wave of sadness washed over her. This morning her mother had phoned and said she couldn't come to the wedding. Quinn accepted she would never have the mother-daughter relationship she wanted, but the familiar ache of longing still hurt. As much as she told herself it didn't matter, she couldn't deny she still yearned for her mother's love.

The phone on her lap vibrated. She glanced at the screen. "Raven."

"Good morning," answered Quinn. "How's the new mama and babies?"

"Did you know the twins were born in Hickory Hills?"

"Raven, by now the whole town knows."

"They're the first babies born here in the last thirty years. Doc Morgan was won-der-ful," Then Raven's tone switched to mortification. "They were going to call the vet. The vet!"

"Well, Doc Morgan was pretty pumped. I was in the waiting room when he passed around his phone, showing off pictures of the babies. He said you were a trooper." Quinn didn't tell Raven how Carter had preened around the waiting room as if he had delivered the babies himself.

"Did you hear the twins' names?" Raven didn't wait for an answer. "I chose Morgan for one, and Carter chose Megan for the other."

Quinn wondered what Carter thought about his daughter being named after Doc Morgan.

As if Raven had heard her unspoken question, she said, "Well, it wasn't like I could name a girl Carter, could I? I think Carter might have been a teensy bit disappointed that I didn't have at least one boy."

Quinn switched the subject away from Carter. From the pictures, Quinn knew the twins were not identical. One girl was blonde and tiny, the other dark haired and stocky. "Which one is Morgan?" she asked.

"The one with all the dark hair like me and Doc Morgan."

At the end of the summer, Quinn had spent a lot of time with Raven, who had been confined to bed rest. Quinn was also at loose ends, with Ace and Jason in London and Taylor with Chrissy's mother. The two women had become close, each talking about their futures as mothers.

Being a parent was still scary for Quinn. She used to worry she would be aloof like her own mother. Taylor had been in Quinn's life for six months. And even though Quinn was still learning, she already knew she would never be like her mother.

Raven voiced her new-mother doubts. "What if I mess up?"

"All mothers mess up," Quinn said. "We just have to do the best we can and show our kids we love them."

With this marriage, Quinn would be entering new territory. She would be Jason's stepmother, and Ace would be Taylor's stepfather. Jason's mother, Stephanie, was in England for a year, but Taylor's father, Truman, wasn't part of Taylor's life. Truman didn't know he had a daughter, and Quinn intended to keep it that way.

Raven's voice sounded less cheerful. "I'm sorry I have to miss your wedding, but Summer promised to take lots of pictures."

A knock sounded on the door. Quinn quickly said goodbye to Raven and called across the room. "If it isn't Ace, you can come in."

"Ask me the secret word," Taylor said from the other side of the door. Taylor had decided they needed a secret code to keep people from sneaking in to see Quinn's wedding dress before the ceremony.

Tomi skirted the table and opened the door a few inches. She leaned down to Taylor. "Speak magic word."

"Cheese," Taylor whispered loudly and pushed open the door.

Taylor looked so grown up in the dark green gown that matched Tomi's. The crown of white daisies on Taylor's head was a striking contrast to Taylor's burnished red hair. Tomi wore a similar ring of white daisies in her hair.

Taylor clomped across the room, her dress short enough to show off her Western boots. Ace had wanted a traditional wedding, but balked at wearing a tuxedo. So the wedding was traditional with a little bit of country.

"Did you choose 'cheese' for the secret word so I'd be smiling big when Summer took my picture?" Quinn asked.

Taylor shook her head and threw her arms around Quinn. "No, because I love cheese…and you, Mommy."

Quinn's heart filled with happiness. Loving Taylor was so easy. Why hadn't it been that easy between Quinn and her own mother? Even if her mother had not wanted to come to Quinn's wedding, why didn't her mother want to see her granddaughter?

Taylor scooted off her lap and dropped a small white piece of paper onto the table. "Special delivery."

Quinn stared at the note. Her heart thudded. She closed her eyes and tried to blot out the folded paper, but she could not blot out the memory of her first wedding.

That had been five years ago. Chrissy was her maid of honor, and an hour before the ceremony, the best man delivered a note.

"It's from Truman," Chrissy said, handing her the piece of paper.

"Oh, how sweet, a love letter." But when Laney opened the note, her world shattered.

Truman said he didn't love her and couldn't marry her. Even now the sting of rejection cut deep.

What if Ace no longer loved her? What if he didn't want to marry her?

"Mommy, read the note," Taylor prodded.

Quinn opened her eyes. Her stomach knotted. She picked up the note. Her hands shook as she unfolded the paper. She couldn't focus on the words.

What would she say to Taylor? To Jason? Quinn wanted to be Jason's mother and watch him grow into a fine young man like Ace.

Ace was a good man. He was not Truman. She believed in Ace and his love. He wouldn't send a note. If he had a problem with her, he would charge in and confront her. She needed to trust Ace—and her heart.

Taylor shuffled back and forth. "Mommy, read Jason's note."

"Jason?" She looked down at the printed letters of a child.

"Jason said his dad gets to ask if you promise to be his wife," Taylor explained. "Jason wants to ask if you promise to be his mommy."

Touched, Quinn put her hand over her heart. "Of course, I want to be Jason's mother."

"I told him you were a real good mommy and didn't get mad at me or Gogo too much."

Quinn read the note aloud. "Do you promise to be my mother and love me, even if I forget to clean my room?"

At the bottom of the paper were the words *yes* and *no* with a box in front of each. Quinn picked up a pencil from the table and made a large black X in the box labeled *yes*. Then to reassure Jason, she added her own vow. *I do. I do. I do.*

———

Quinn stood in the back of the church watching Tomi walk down the aisle. Quinn tried to tamp down the nerves in her stomach. The pews were filled with more than one hundred friends and family. When Tomi reached the altar, Quinn nudged Taylor and Jason forward.

Jason was wearing blue jeans, a suede vest, a tie, and Western boots. Both carried cowboy hats. Inside Jason's upturned straw hat was the wedding ring. Inside Taylor's hat were soft yellow rose petals that she tossed onto the white runner.

A tuft of Jason's hair stuck up from his crown, and the garland of daisies in Taylor's hair was askew. Quinn wanted to call them back, smooth out Jason's hair and right Taylor's headpiece. But when she looked at her children, they seemed natural. Her children. Hers and Ace's. Her heart swelled.

Next to Quinn on a card table covered with a white linen cloth were a candle and a silver-framed picture of her dad and Quinn taken the summer before he died. She wore faded plaid shorts and sat on her dad's wide shoulders. Her bare legs and feet dangled onto his chest.

Quinn missed her dad, but today was harder. As a child, she had felt his love, and while sitting on his shoulders, she was never afraid she would fall. But when he died, her safety net was yanked away.

The candle flickered on the glass covering the picture, making it appear as if her dad's dark blue eyes were sparkling at her the way they always did. He couldn't walk her down the aisle and give her away, but he would always be a part of her.

The organist struck up the wedding march. P.R. nodded to her and the guests stood. Quinn gripped her bouquet of daisies, took one long steadying breath, and slowly walked down the aisle.

When she was halfway to the altar, the organist hit a discordant note. Quinn's high-heeled shoe slipped. Panicking, she searched for Ace. He was standing at the altar, looking handsome in his white shirt, suede vest, and jeans. He fixed his eyes on her and smiled. Her world righted.

No wedding or marriage was perfect. She and Ace would have to work at theirs. She would have to trust Ace and he would have to learn not to expect her to agree with everything he said. But Ace would be there to support her and Taylor, and Quinn would be there to support him and Jason.

Joy bubbled up inside her. When she reached the altar, she stopped next to Ace. His intense blue eyes locked on hers, enveloped her the way they always had. The minister, the people, the church disappeared. It was just Quinn and Ace, standing before God, vowing their love for Him and each other.

"Will you, Ace Edleston, have this woman, Melana Elam, who is now called Quincy Matthews, to live together in holy marriage? Will you love her, comfort her, honor, and keep her in sickness and in health, and forsaking all others, be faithful to her as long as you both shall live?"

Ace's loud voice boomed through the church. "I do."

"And do you, Melana Elam, now called Quincy Matthews, take Arthur Clark Edleston, known as Ace, to be your lawful wedded husband?"

Quinn's answer was softer, but her resolve just as firm. "I do."

In the center of the altar stood the empty base of a unity cross. Craig handed Ace the outline of a cross. He approached the altar and placed it on the wooden base. The cross represented the man, bold and strong. But it was empty inside, just as a man was without a woman.

Tomi handed Quinn the inner piece, an intricate, curved design that represented the woman. Quinn stepped up to the altar and placed her piece inside the cross.

Then Jason and Taylor approached the altar. First Jason inserted a post on one side of the cross, and Taylor inserted one on the other, permanently binding the cross together. Tears welled up in Quinn's eyes. Now she had a family.

The minister ended the ceremony with, "You may kiss the bride."

Quinn turned to Ace, expecting a quick kiss. He wrapped his arms around her, pulled her to him, and kissed her with such passion that she went weak in the knees. Then he swooped her up into his arms and began carrying her down the aisle.

"Ace, put me down!" She kicked her feet, trying to get free. Her satin shoe slipped off and flew into the air, twirling and somersaulting until it landed in the lap of a woman with long dark hair.

The entire church roared with laughter.

Quinn was mortified. She didn't even know the woman, but she thought the man next to her was Miss May's nephew.

The guests continued to laugh. Quinn quit fighting and threw back her head and laughed, too.

Life with Ace would never be easy, but there would be plenty of joy, and she was ready to begin the journey.

CHAPTER SIXTEEN

The wedding reception was held at the Castle, a large three-story, gray stone house with a turret in the middle and gables on each side. P.R.'s sister Belle and her husband, Ben, had bought the castle-like house when they moved to Hickory Hills and converted it into a bed and breakfast.

Belle and her sisters had planned the reception as a gift to Quinn and Ace. But as Quinn walked into the dining room, her breath caught.

The reception was decorated in a mixture of rustic and elegance. White linen cloths and burlap runners covered a dozen round tables. Mason jars were filled with water and the silverware was tied in burlap napkins. In the center of each table was a hurricane lantern with a single flickering candle. Above the tables hung crystal chandeliers with diamond-shaped prisms. Light from the chandeliers and the candles warmed the room with a soft glow.

Summer took a picture as Quinn stood between Ace and Tomi in the entrance, then pointed to a painted door near a stack of hay bales. "Stand over there."

Quinn and Ace posed for several shots in front of the wooden door. "I hope this is the last one," Quinn said.

Ace pulled his pocket watch from his vest. "We've been married more than an hour, and we're still agreeing."

Click. Summer captured the moment. She turned to Tomi. "I want a photo of you and Quinn."

Ace stepped away, and Tomi slipped next to Quinn.

"Lift your dresses and show off those cowgirl boots," Summer said.

Quinn was relieved to be wearing boots, especially after the flying shoe incident at the church. Tomi, however, had been reluctant to give up her high heels.

After several more pictures, Quinn held up her palm. "That's enough." She appreciated Summer being her photographer, but Quinn didn't want to spend the entire reception posing.

She grabbed Ace's hand and looped arms with Tomi. Together, the three of them weaved through the guests to the buffet table where washtubs had been filled with potato salad, coleslaw, and barbeque—St. Louis and Kansas City style. Quinn gasped in delight at the wreaths of cauliflower and broccoli decorated with red radishes cut like budding flowers. Beside them, tiny orange carrots arranged like sunflower petals circled dishes of ranch dressing.

Quinn felt a twinge of guilt. She was used to relying on herself. Accepting help from others didn't come easily. "I'll never be able to repay Belle and her sisters for all this work."

Ace put his hand on her shoulder and gently massaged her tense muscles. "They don't expect you to pay them back, Quinn. They're your friends. They want to do this for you."

Friends. Quinn had arrived in Hickory Hills in March, but the friendships she'd made with Summer, Belle, and Raven were lasting ones. *Forever friends.* "You're right," she said to Ace.

He grinned. "May I record that?"

Taylor and Jason joined them. Taylor looked toward the wedding cake and the tiers of plated cupcakes beside it. "Everything is so beau-ti-ful."

Quinn leaned over and kissed Taylor's rosy cheek. "Including you. Why don't you and Jason introduce Tomi to your friends?"

As they led Tomi away, guitar music drifted through the open French doors and into the dining room.

"I don't think I've ever danced with you," Quinn said to Ace, wishing she was already in his arms.

"There are lots of things we haven't done together—yet." The smoldering look in his eyes left little doubt that he was thinking about their honeymoon.

The trip would be short, three days and two nights in Shawnee National Forest. But time alone was important and precious.

He ran a finger over her lips. A ripple of anticipation shivered through her.

"Are you cold?" he asked.

She shook her head.

"Too bad. I know lots of ways to warm you up."

She smiled. "Sounds wonderful."

"So let's eat and skedaddle."

"Ace! We have to mingle with our guests, although I don't know some of them."

"I know most of them."

"*Most*? It's our wedding. We should know *all* of them?"

Ace shrugged. "Who don't you know?"

Quinn glanced around the dining room. Some of the guests were seated at tables; others were standing and chatting. Quinn nodded at the three people near the open French doors. "I think that's Miss May's nephew, but I don't know the man and woman next to him."

"The man is Stuart May. The woman next to him caught your shoe. I'll introduce you." Ace guided her across the room. They stopped near the French doors where a cool evening breeze and soft guitar chords trailed in.

Ace extended his hand to Stuart. "Glad you could make it."

Stuart shook Ace's hand. Stuart looked as if he was mid-thirties, but his brown hair had already begun to recede. Quinn had seen him at Miss May's funeral. He'd been late and hadn't stayed for the funeral dinner. But Stuart's sister hadn't even shown up. Ace said something about a squabble years ago. Maybe that's why she hadn't been listed as a beneficiary in the will.

"Guess I'll be the next one tying the knot." Stuart slipped his arm around the tall woman by his side. Her black dress and long dark hair were a stark contrast to her milky-white skin and made her resemble Morticia from the Addams Family. "This is my fiancé, Sabina Barnes, and her brother, Virgil."

Sabina and Stuart made an odd looking couple. He was medium height with a robust middle. She was tall and willowy. Stuart had a wide, friendly smile. Sabina's red lips remained closed. Maybe she was upset about the shoe incident at the wedding.

"I'm sorry about my shoe landing in your lap," Quinn said. "Ace got a little carried away."

Sabina raked her fingernails through her long hair. "Ace's shoe didn't land in my lap."

Quinn swallowed. "Yes, it was my shoe, but—"

Stuart interrupted. "No harm done, was there, honey?"

Sabina's stare did not seem sweet. Quinn changed the subject. "So, when's your wedding?"

Sabina flipped her hand, flashing her large diamond. "We haven't set a date. Stuart has to finish up some unpleasant legal business."

Quinn wondered if the unpleasant legal business was Stuart's divorce from his first wife or Miss May's death. "If the wedding is in Hickory Hills, I can recommend a good photographer and caterer."

Sabina gave a derisive laugh. "Why would I get married here?"

"Well, Miss May's farm is—"

Sabina cut Quinn off. "Stuart isn't interested in farming. He has his insurance business in St. Louis. We'll be living there."

"But I thought—"

Ace elbowed Quinn, and she realized Sabina might not know about Miss May's new will. Maybe Stuart didn't know about it either. Ace planned to file it as soon as they returned from their honeymoon.

"I hear you had an intruder out at your place the other day," Stuart said. "If Jackson's murderer isn't found, I might hire some security for the farm."

Sabina leaned forward as if suddenly interested. "Do they have any leads?"

"Zeus has been spotted everywhere," Ace said. "Last week he was in Hickory Hills. A few days later at the state fairgrounds in Springfield. Yesterday he was supposedly in Cairo."

Ace turned toward Stuart. "No need for security. I can look after the farm. I have some equipment stored in the barn. I hope I can still keep it there."

Stuart cleared his throat. "We need to talk about the farm." Stuart put a hand on Virgil's shoulder. "Sabina's brother is an appraiser. I asked him to estimate the value of the land."

Ace's brows shot up. "If you're thinking of selling, Stuart, I'll make you a fair offer."

Ace hoped eventually to acquire more tillable acreage. Buying now, after being newly married, would strain his budget, but Miss May's farm was near Ace's land, and he might not get another chance.

"I haven't made any decisions about selling," Stuart said.

Virgil handed Ace a business card with his name and contact information.

Ace examined the card. "What company do you work for?"

"I'm an independent contractor," Virgil said.

Ace pocketed the card and frowned. "Maybe we should talk business after the will is read."

Stuart nodded. "Of course, of course. Jackson was my aunt's attorney. Do you know who's taking over his practice?"

Ace tilted his head toward P.R., who was walking their way. "Jackson offered it to P.R. so you might ask him."

P.R. and Ashleigh walked up beside Quinn and Ace. "Ask me what?"

"About taking over Jackson's practice," Ace said.

Before P.R. could answer, a glass tinkled and Belle announced, "Food's ready."

After Reverend Stone said a blessing, Belle gave the instructions. "The Edlestons will go first, followed by the wedding party and their guests."

Taylor and Jason hurried over. "I'm an Edleston," Jason said. "I get to go first."

Taylor crossed her arms. Her lower lip began to tremble. Ace leaned over. "What's wrong, Lady Bug?"

"Jason said I'm not an Edleston, so I don't get to go first."

Ace glanced at Quinn for help. She put a comforting arm around Taylor. "Just because your name is still Taylor Matthews that doesn't mean you aren't part of this family."

Taylor wriggled free and stomped her boot. "That's not fair. I want to be Taylor Edleston."

Quinn raised her eyes back to Ace. He reached over and swiped Jason's cowboy hat. "Son, a gentleman always lets a lady go first."

Taylor skirted around Jason and threw him a smug look over her shoulder.

82

Jason stuck his hat back on. "Dad, you could adopt Taylor. Then we'd all have the same last name."

Ace didn't answer, but P.R. noticed the worried looks Ace and Quinn exchanged as they led the way to the buffet table.

"Does the flower girl remind you of anyone we know?" Ashleigh asked P.R.

"Well...she's stubborn like Quinn."

"I mean that burnished red hair. It's so striking." Ashleigh aimed her camera at Taylor and snapped several more pictures. She'd taken dozens of photos at the church. He hoped she wasn't getting wedding fever. He knew she'd been engaged and then the guy had broken it off.

P.R. and Ashleigh followed Stuart and his guests through the line. When they were seated, Ashleigh said, "I didn't know you were considering another job."

"I turned it down." P.R. took a big bite of his barbeque. "Although with food like this, Hickory Hills wouldn't be a hardship."

"Are you worried about being pink slipped?" Ashleigh asked.

He shrugged, not wanting to admit it.

"I can put in a good word for you with the partners," Ashleigh offered.

P.R. almost choked. He grabbed the mason jar and gulped down some water. "Don't do that." Help from Ashleigh might make him seem desperate.

As they continued to eat, Ashleigh filled him in on a political bribery case she was handling. In fact, most of their conversations this weekend had been about their clients.

His eyes wandered to Tomi, seated between Jason and Taylor at the head table. If Tomi was sitting next to him, they wouldn't be discussing work.

Craig clinked his glass and stood to make a toast. He checked the volume on the hand-held mic. "Testing." Satisfied, he turned toward Ace. "Growing up, I wasn't crazy about having a little brother."

Chuckles rippled around the room.

"In fact, I can honestly say we didn't like each other very much." He looked at Summer. "My wife was determined to bring my brother and me together." Craig laid his hand on Ace's shoulder. "Never underestimate the power of a good woman because here I am, best man at your wedding, and I'm proud you're my brother." He looked at Quinn. "I'm even happier to welcome his wife and her daughter into our family." Craig raised his champagne glass. "To Ace and his new family."

P.R. lifted his glass. "Hear, hear."

Craig handed Tomi the mic and she rose. Her cheeks were flushed, and her eyes flitted around the room as if searching for something to focus on.

He sensed her panic. He thrived on addressing judges and jurors. Yet each time he delivered an opening in court, for a brief moment panic shot through him and his heart revved up, just like it was doing now. What was that about? He wasn't speaking.

He found Tomi's eyes and smiled, silently urging her on. *You can do this.*

As if she heard him, she gave a slight nod and took a deep breath. "My name is Tomoe Kanai. To you, Tomi. I have great honor to be maid in wedding." She spoke slowly and even though she had a foreign accent, her words were clear.

"My friend is beautiful bride with beautiful heart."

Across the table, Sabina whispered to her brother, Virgil, "I can't understand what she's saying, can you?"

Stuart scowled. "Not when you're talking."

P.R. leaned forward, wanting to hear every word.

"In Japan we say, 'Bad marriage spell hundred year of bad harvest.' I wish good marriage for Laney and Ace and hundred year of good harvest." Tomi's hand flew to her mouth. "Oops, so sorry. I mean Ace and Quinn." Tomi raised her glass. "*Kanpai.* Cheers."

"*Kanpai.*" P.R. lifted his glass. His racing heart began to slow.

"She has something, doesn't she?" Ashleigh asked.

"What?" He turned to Ashleigh, not sure what she meant.

"Toma. She has a certain charm."

"Tomi," he corrected, surprised her name no longer felt foreign on his tongue, but familiar and delightful.

Ashleigh put her hand on his and smiled up at him. "Think how hard it would be to give a speech to strangers in a foreign language."

A man could easily get pulled in by Ashleigh, those heart-shaped lips and that buttery blonde hair. Even her hands were beautiful—long, slender fingers and nails polished in robin's-egg blue to match her tailored suit. But as her hand covered his, he didn't feel a thing. Not a spark or tingle.

Nothing. Maybe his sisters were right. Maybe he liked the chase better than catching the woman.

He hadn't always been so callous. In junior high he'd mooned over Mia, a short girl with strawberry blonde hair and braces. Finally he worked up the nerve to write her a note. After she answered, he began moseying by her locker and carrying her books to class.

At Christmas, he gave her his initial ring, and she wore it on a silver chain around her neck. They met at the movies, and he held her hand or slipped his arm around her shoulders. At the end of junior high, Mia taught him to dance for the Spring Fling.

The night of big event, she wore a pink chiffon strapless gown. As he led her around the gym floor, his hands sweated and he had to keep wiping them on his dress slacks.

A week later, Mia unexpectedly knocked on his front door. When he opened it, she burst into tears. Through sobs, she told him her family was moving to Florida.

He held her in his arms, and they vowed to stay in touch. Back then, he didn't have a cell phone. He emailed, sent a few letters and some silly cards, but it was too hard to love someone you couldn't see.

"It's just puppy love," his sisters said as he moped around the house. "You'll get over it."

Why did they think because he was fourteen, he couldn't feel real love?

A year later his dad died. Of course, that was worse than losing a girlfriend. He dropped out of the academy and enrolled in a public high school. At five feet three inches, he was a minnow in a sea of sharks.

His junior year he shot up seven inches. Girls who previously ignored him flocked around his locker, but he had given his heart away once and learned not to do it again.

That junior high experience hadn't changed the way he felt about women. He liked them and dated plenty. Yet, whenever a woman started to invade his thoughts, he found a reason to move on. He didn't want to risk getting hurt again. But as he watched Ace and Quinn cutting the wedding cake, P.R. couldn't help but think Ace was one lucky guy.

When the band started playing, Ashleigh squeezed his hand. "Let's go outside and listen to the music."

They walked through the French doors and onto a small patio. A stone path led to a lighted tent where a Western band was playing. Straw bales were arranged in a semicircle in front of the tent.

Ashleigh abruptly stopped. "You should have told me the reception was informal. I didn't know I'd have to sit on straw."

"Would you have worn jeans and cowboy boots?" P.R. asked.

She wrinkled her nose, but her answer was lost as the guests burst into loud cheers for Ace and Quinn as they began to dance. Several minutes later Taylor and Jason cut in. Taylor danced with Ace, and Jason with Quinn. Then Craig led Tomi into the circle with the others, and they danced, too.

P.R. watched, wishing he was the one with his arms around Tomi, and she was smiling up at him, not Craig.

When the song ended and another began, Craig waved to Summer, who joined them. Craig continued dancing with both women.

Craig definitely had his hands full. Ushers were part of the wedding party, reasoned P.R. "Excuse me," he said to Ashleigh. "I think my brother-in-law needs help."

P.R. walked down the path and into the spotlight. He tapped Craig on the shoulder. "Mind if I cut in?"

Craig stopped dancing and looked up at P.R. "Which woman do you want?"

CHAPTER SEVENTEEN

Tomi lowered her head as P.R. took her hand. She did not want him to see her smile of pleasure. She had not expected to be able to dance with him. He was with another woman.

Her heart skittered as he slid his arm around her waist and they began to dance. She must not think about his strong arms and how much she liked being held in them. "How your head?"

"Fine."

She raised her eyes to see if he was truthful. "No hurt?"

"Feel for yourself." P.R. lifted her hand off his shoulder and placed it on the side of his head.

His hair was softer than Japanese hair. The caramel locks felt as fine as silk. Fascinated, she ran her fingers through his hair and searched for the bump.

P.R. made a strange sound, almost like a moan. He grabbed her hand. "Stop."

She jerked back. "Did I hurt?"

He shook his head and pulled her into his arms. Their bodies swayed, moving together with the music and each other. An odd sensation uncurled in her stomach. Tomi yearned to put her head on P.R.'s shoulder and press her body against his the way Quinn was dancing with Ace.

As if he read her thoughts, P.R. tightened his hold and pulled her closer.

Her breath caught. He must be able to feel her heart throbbing. She could not let this happen. He was a playboy with many girlfriends. "Your girlfriend no mind you dance with me?"

He glanced toward the patio where Ashleigh stood talking to Sabina's brother. Virgil leaned in and whispered something in Ashleigh's ear, and they both laughed.

P.R. turned back to Tomi. "She doesn't seem to miss me." P.R. didn't sound jealous. Instead he asked a strange question. "Do you like cowboy boots?"

She raised her dress to her knee and stuck out her leg to show off her black leather boot. "I like."

P.R. let out a whoop and lifted her off the ground, twirling her around. She gripped his shoulders and held on. The wind hit her face and her hair fluttered behind her. Laughing, she threw back her head. She was free, like a song bird flying from its cage.

This is the way she imagined she would feel in America. No parents with overly protective rules. Here she could let go, be herself, and let her heart sing.

All too soon the song ended, and P.R. abruptly stopped. Her boots hit the ground, but he kept a steadying arm around her waist as she found her balance.

The wind picked up, gusting through the yard. The canvas on the tent started flapping, and the temperature dropped. Tomi crossed her arms and stepped away from P.R. Her eyes flitted around. Evil was near. Were the spirits searching for her, trying to take away her happiness?

She moved out of the light and looked for a place to hide so the spirits would pass her by.

"It's just the wind," P.R. said.

She shook her head. "No. Not wind." She did not try to explain the cold chill running through her. P.R. stood close enough that his warm breath caressed her cheek, but their worlds were miles apart.

The music started again. She wanted him to take her in his arms where she would be safe. She gazed up at him, hoping he would understand her need. When he did not take her hand, she asked, "Dance?"

He gestured to a nearby straw bale. "Maybe you should sit."

She did not want to sit. She wanted to be in his arms. He could protect her and drive away the evil which seemed to be creeping closer.

As he led her to the circle of hay bales, she placed her hand on his arm. That odd sensation uncurled in her stomach again.

He bowed respectfully. "Thank you for the dance." He reached for her hand, brought it to his lips and kissed it. His lips lingered on her fingers. He had to let go. He had to walk away while he still could.

Resolutely, he turned and strode toward Ashleigh. Halfway, he could no longer resist. He turned back to Tomi.

She was gone. He craned his neck, trying to see through the crowded dancers.

Ashleigh came up behind him and hooked her arm through his. "I was beginning to get lonely."

He turned to her. "Where are Virgil and the others?"

"Virgil saw someone he knew, and Stuart is dancing with Sabina."

Maybe that was a hint. "Do you want to dance?"

Ashleigh shook her head.

P.R. didn't understand why, but he felt relieved.

"I'm tired. I was thinking about going upstairs early." Her green eyes sparkled in a sexy come-hither look. For months, he had been hoping to score with Ashleigh. So why wasn't he high-tailing it up the stairs with her? Why were his eyes flitting over her shoulder searching for Tomi?

Ahh, there she was, dancing. His back stiffened. Tomi was dancing with Carter. What was Raven's husband doing here? He should be with Raven and their new babies.

Ashleigh stretched and yawned. "I'm exhausted."

The song had not ended, but Tomi pulled back from Carter. She seemed to be trying to get away. She broke free and squeezed through the other dancers, disappearing into the darkness.

P.R. balled his fist. He wanted to pummel Carter, but that could wait. Right now, he was worried about Tomi.

He stepped around Ashleigh.

She put her hand on his arm. "Hey, Cowboy, you're headed in the wrong direction."

He lifted her hand from his arm. "Your train leaves early tomorrow morning."

She tilted her head. Her green eyes looked puzzled.

Trying to make it clearer, he said, "Goodnight, Ashleigh."

Understanding sparked in her eyes. She didn't bother to answer. She waved, spun on her heels, and stalked through the French doors. Her nails were a deep purple.

P.R. had to find Tomi, make sure she was all right. He rushed toward the other side of the yard where she had disappeared. The other guests were crowded around the tent with the band. No one was on the unlit side of the Castle. He walked toward the side door that led into the kitchen. Maybe she'd fled inside.

He pulled open the kitchen door. Across the room, Belle was stacking glasses into the dishwasher. "Good timing, brother. I need you to carry out the trash bags."

"I'm looking for Tomi. Have you seen her?"

Belle swiped her hand over her forehead. "She hasn't been in here."

His sister sounded tired, and he'd learned arguing with his sisters never turned out well. He hefted the two large plastic trash bags and carried them out the door toward the alley.

Soft light spilled through the kitchen window, illuminating the stone path that led through the apple orchard and grape arbor. He followed the path to the alley and tossed the bags into the large dumpster.

As he turned back toward the Castle, the grape vines in the arbor seemed to move, but the wind had died. He crept to the arbor and peered over the top. Crouched close to the ground was Tomi.

Relief shot through him. "Are you all right?"

She sprang up and hurried around the arbor. "He's here. He's here."

P.R. reached for her and folded her into his arms, protectively. A tight knot of fear he hadn't realized was there slowly unraveled. "Who's here?"

She buried her head again his chest.

He stroked his fingers through her tangled hair and righted the daisies on her head. "Tell me who's here?"

Her voice was barely a whisper. "The bad man. The killer."

"Zeus?" P.R.'s head shot up. His eyes darted left and right. But all he saw was darkness.

CHAPTER EIGHTEEN

Bucky crouched behind the dumpster in the alley of the Castle. Music from the wedding reception drifted through the crisp night air. He'd driven out to Ace's to search the house again only to find a Belle's Bakery van parked in the lane. Several women were carting in dishes of food left over from the reception. He'd driven back to town to see if people were also loading up wedding gifts to take to the house.

So far, the guests seemed to be congregating near the tent where the band was playing. Bucky spotted Jason, smiling and teasing his sister, as he danced. Gone was that grim face he'd worn since the death of his dog.

Bucky had sprinkled ashes on the floor of Miss May's barn to see if the kid or anyone else had come snooping around. He was relieved when no footprints showed up. The death of a child was something you didn't get over. Captain didn't understand that. After Joey was gone, Captain expected life to go on as usual.

But Bucky couldn't just forget his brother. He became pious, going to church with his mother and praying daily for Jesus to bring Joey back. Mary and Martha believed in Jesus, and He'd brought their brother, Lazarus, back from the dead.

Bucky knew if he prayed hard enough, Jesus would bring Joey back, too. Bucky's fervent prayers enraged Captain. He ordered Bucky to stop.

But he couldn't stop. If he did, Bucky would be weighed down by the guilt that he'd started the fire.

One day, Captain heard Bucky in his bedroom, praying. Captain stomped into the room, yanked open the dresser drawers, and dumped out Joey's clothes. Next was the toy box.

Captain opened the second-floor window and pitched Joey's stuff to the wheelbarrow below. Bucky huddled in the corner, pleading with Captain to stop. But Captain had worked himself into a frenzy.

When nothing of Joey's was left in the room, Captain grabbed Bucky by the back of his shirt, pulled him down the stairs, and outside. Captain pushed the wheelbarrow heaped with Joey's things to the burn pile in the orchard.

After several trips, Captain held out a can of gasoline. "Pour it on the pile."

Bucky shook his head and crossed his arms. He couldn't burn Joey's things. It was all he had left of him.

Captain took off his belt, snapped it in the air. "Pour it on now."

Bucky flinched. He knew a beating was coming. But he closed his eyes and stood resolute.

The first blow from the leather belt struck his back so hard he toppled to the ground.

"Get up and start the fire."

Bucky rose, but he wouldn't pick up the red metal gas can.

Captain hit him again—and again. After half a dozen blows, Bucky no longer heard the slap of the leather belt or felt the thrashing. His mind drifted to a snowy December day. School had been called off, so he and Joey tromped over to Fifth Street hill. The steep brick pavement was too icy for cars to climb and was blocked off, making the hill a perfect spot for sledding.

He and Joey didn't have one of those fancy wooden sleds. They tied a rope to an old inner tube big enough for both of them. When they reached the top of the hill, Joey climbed on the front of the inner tube. Bucky pushed from behind. As the tube started sliding, Bucky jumped on.

Together, the boys went flying down the hill. The ride wasn't smooth. The rubber inner tube twirled and bumped on the icy brick pavement. But as the wind hit Bucky's face, he stretched out his arms, opened his mouth, and screamed.

He was still screaming even after Captain stopped whipping him and looped his belt back onto his crisply creased dress pants. When Captain stalked into the house, Bucky's screams changed to snivels and a gloat of triumph. The throbbing pain was worth it. He had been as brave as Flame Boy. He had stood up to Captain Evil and won.

Bucky hobbled over to the burn pile and pulled off one of Joey's flannel shirts. He wadded the red-plaid shirt into a ball and stuffed it under his T-shirt.

The back door creaked open. Bucky scurried away from the pile and turned toward the house. Captain walked toward him. In his arms he carried a brown cardboard box with 'DON'T TOUCH' printed on the side.

Bucky's stomach curled into a sickening knot. His comic book collection.

Captain strutted over to the burn pile and began tossing out the comics: Batman, Spiderman, Superman, and Pyroman.

Even more precious than his comics were the spiral notebooks hidden in the bottom of the box. Pages of paper filled with crude pencil drawings of his own comic book: Flame Boy, his sidekick, Joey, and their dog.

One by one Captain flipped the comic books onto the pile. "If you don't start the fire, I will."

Bucky couldn't breathe. Watching his prized comics go up in smoke was hard, but he couldn't lose Flame Boy.

Swiping his arm across his wet cheeks, he hunched over in defeat. He picked up the red metal can and pulled the cork out of the nozzle. The pungent smell of gasoline enveloped him. He stepped forward, tipping the can and splashing gasoline onto the pile.

Captain held out a box of farmer's matches. Bucky didn't want to touch the matches. He promised himself he would never strike a match again, not after what had happened last time.

Captain slid open the box and held up a single wooden matchstick. Bucky couldn't resist. He grabbed the match, struck it against the side of the box, and tossed it onto the pile.

Whoosh. Flames shot into the air. Beautiful red, orange, and yellow flames. One licked his forehead, singeing stray locks of his hair and eyebrows. He jumped back. The stench of burnt hair was nauseating. He bent over and vomited.

That night Bucky's body was too sore to sleep. He reached beneath his pillow and took out Joey's plaid shirt. He rubbed the soft red flannel over his blistered forehead. The shirt smelled of dirt, gasoline, and Joey. Caressing the shirt made him feel connected to his brother.

That day in the orchard watching Joey's things burn, Bucky lost more than Joey's possessions. Bucky lost a part of himself. Whatever good was left in him had vanished, just like Joey.

The wind in the alley picked up, rustling the leaves in the orchard. The music from the band stopped. Bucky scanned the guests. His eyes landed on the Japanese woman. She had seen him the day he'd fled from Ace's house. He moved away from the alley trying to get a better view.

She lifted her head and looked in his direction. He flattened himself against the band's trailer.

Had she seen him? The band began playing again, strumming like his heart. Jason didn't seem to be a problem, but now he had a new worry—that Japanese woman.

CHAPTER NINETEEN

For the first time since the wedding, Quinn was alone with Ace. She sat in the cab of his truck as he drove to Shawnee National Forest for their honeymoon. The radio pumped out love ballads, and with each passing mile, the heat between them sizzled.

The dash lights illuminated Ace's profile. The strong set of his jaw, the square of his wide shoulders, and the firm grip of his hands on the steering wheel made her heart sing. *Husband.* The word didn't frighten her the way it would have six months ago.

As a child, life had been a struggle. Winter mornings waking up with no heat and her mother passed out on the living room floor, drunk again. Quinn had learned to survive the hunger and cold. What never went away was the ache in her heart to be loved. She had yearned for someone to see her as special and love her no matter what.

Quinn wished she could go back and tell that little girl not to worry. Her life would be good, and when she grew up, she would find the love she needed.

"Are we close?" Quinn asked after they'd been on the road for an hour.

"You sound as impatient as our kids," Ace said.

'Our kids.' She loved hearing those words. She reached over and switched off the radio. Listening to love songs only increased her nervousness.

Ace turned off Route 13 and headed south on a curvy two-lane highway. On the dark, unfamiliar roads, he slowed to thirty-five miles an hour.

Inwardly she moaned. Now it would take forever. She had to think about something else besides being alone with Ace. She peered out the side window. The headlights illuminated tall pines and limestone cliffs.

"I didn't realize southern Illinois was so hilly compared to the flat land where we live."

"That's because you're a Hoosier," Ace teased. "But those flatlands with fields of corn and beans are beautiful."

"Spoken like a farmer. And since I'm a farmer's wife, are you going to put me to work in the fields?"

Ace chuckled. "I'd rather have you in the kitchen, barefoot and pregnant."

Quinn's cheeks flushed. She knew some women would take offense at the remark, but she liked the thought of being pregnant with Ace's child— eventually. Right now, Jason and Taylor needed time to adjust. She changed the subject. "You lived in Chicago for a while. What was it like?"

Ace frowned. "Do you really want to talk about my first marriage on our honeymoon?"

"Oh. I didn't think of it that way." Quinn had never met his ex. Stephanie had remarried and lived in England. "I wasn't asking about your marriage, but about Chicago."

"Chicago's okay to visit, but almost ten million people live there. That's a little too crowded for me."

Quinn picked up the Illinois map from the seat. "Where exactly does southern Illinois begin?"

Ace switched on the dome light so she could see the map. "According to people in Chicago, anything south of I-80 is considered southern Illinois."

She squinted out the window. "Not many houses along the road. A few million from Chicago could move down here."

"You can't live here," Ace said. "Shawnee National Forest is federal land. Although when Alcatraz closed, prisoners were moved to the federal penitentiary in Marion."

"Oh, where Zeus escaped from." Quinn checked the map again. "So how big is Shawnee National Forest?"

"I don't know. It stretches across the whole bottom of the state."

"What town is close to where we are staying?"

"Herod," Ace answered.

"Like King Herod in the Bible?"

"Yep. And the tip of Illinois is called Little Egypt."

Quinn pointed to the map. "I see Cairo and another town called Thebes. Do they have pyramids?"

"I guess some of the limestone cliffs might look like pyramids."

Concentrating on her surroundings helped Quinn with her jitters. Ace must have felt the same way because he told her about other towns like Equality and the region in Illinois named United States Saline, where slavery had been legal and slaves were used in the salt mines.

Finally Ace slowed the truck and pointed ahead. "Sasquatch."

Quinn eyes widened at the seven-foot statue along the side of the road. "Do you think we'll see Bigfoot?"

"I hope not," Ace said. "I don't want him carrying off my bride."

Quinn laughed. "Don't worry. I'm staying close to you."

"You'd better. There are lots of things I want to show you."

"Good." Quinn hoped what Ace had in mind had nothing to do with southern Illinois, salt mines, and Shawnee National Forest.

They turned off the main highway and drove up the lane to a rustic log cabin. Quinn hopped out of the truck and onto the porch. At the door, Ace punched in a security code. The light changed to green, and he pushed open the door.

Quinn started to walk inside. To her surprise, he swooped her up in his arms and carried her across the threshold. She laughed with joy. She hadn't expected him to be so romantic.

As soon as they stepped inside the cabin, Ace let her down.

"I wonder where the light—"

He put a finger against her lips. "I think we've done enough talking." He lowered his head and kissed her. His mouth was warm and soft. He ran his lips across her cheek and whispered in her ear. "I want you. All of you."

Heat surged through her. His hands slid down her shoulders to her blouse. He undid the top button. Then the next and the next. He slipped off her blouse and groaned. The sound sent shivers of pleasure through her.

Moonlight streamed through the window. Taking her hand, he followed the beam of light into the next room. He laid her onto the bed and piece by piece stripped off the rest of her clothes. Then he started on his own. But she had other plans. She stayed his hand and began undressing him. His shirt, his jeans, his briefs. She liked the briefs and what was beneath them.

He stretched out on the bed beside her. Her heart thrummed. Their bodies came together. Flames shot through her. His lips found hers, no longer soft and warm, but hot and sensual.

Every night for the rest of her life he would lie in bed beside her. How would she ever be able to sleep? Of course, not one inch of her body was thinking about sleep...

Yet sometime she must have slept because the next morning sunlight slipped through the mini-blinds, spilling onto the bed. Outside, song birds chirped their morning greeting. Her body felt relaxed. She kept her eyes closed as she remembered last night.

Her stomach growled. Was that bacon she smelled? She opened her eyes. Ace was lying beside her, his head propped on his elbow and his mouth turned up in that boyish grin she loved.

"Good morning, Mrs. Edleston. How did you sleep?"

She smiled. "Sleep? Is that what you call what we did last night?" She cupped his stubbly jaw, enjoying the rough feel. Her eyes moved to his bare chest, and she playfully weaved her fingers through his curly black hair. Then her eyes slid lower. A sheet covered him below the waist. She had no trouble remembering every muscular inch of him.

Ace pushed a lock of hair from her brow and brushed his lips across her forehead. "Are you hungry?"

"Very hungry."

"How about breakfast in bed?"

"M-m-m." Her body tingled. "Sounds good."

"The bacon is fried, and I can scramble some eggs."

"Oh." Her lips puckered. That wasn't exactly what she had in mind.

"First, come look at the view."

She liked the view in bed just fine, but her eyes widened as Ace tossed back the top sheet and rolled out. He strolled around the end, seemingly relaxed in his nakedness, something she had not yet learned to do. He reached down and clasped her hand, tugging her up.

He led her over to the window and rolled up the blinds. She squinted against the bright light. When her eyes dilated, her breath caught. She let out a long, "O-o-o-h."

Colorful red, yellow, and orange trees dotted tall limestone cliffs. God's design, she thought.

Ace's words echoed her thoughts. "Now I know why it's called Garden of the Gods."

"Do you think Adam and Eve felt this way when they saw all that God had created?"

Ace turned toward her, his eyes no longer focused on the view. "Magnificent," he echoed, as if noticing for the first time that she was standing next to him, naked.

Then he took her hand and led her back to the bed. "I think breakfast can wait."

CHAPTER TWENTY

Two hours later, Quinn bounded down the stairs of the cabin, wearing a sleeveless top, jeans, and comfortable sneakers. Her unruly curls were pulled back with a banana clip, and a backpack flopped against her shoulders.

Her jaunty steps slowed as the sun drifted behind black rain clouds. She glanced at Ace a few steps behind. "Not a great day for hiking. Maybe we should tour the salt mines. At least we'd be inside."

"Actually we wouldn't be inside." He squinted up at the dark clouds. "The salt mines here are mosquito-infested swamps. The salty water bubbles up out of the ground where holes have been bored."

"Oh." Quinn's idea of a salt mine was a coal shaft where men used picks and axes to break off chunks of salt from an underground vein. "If the water bubbles out of the ground, why did they need slaves? It doesn't sound like hard work."

"The hard part was cutting down the trees to keep the fires burning beneath the kettles of boiling water. They had to distill about a hundred gallons of water for one bushel of salt." Ace stepped closer and ran his finger down her nose. "The water smells like sulfur."

"Yuck. That rotten-egg odor is enough to change my mind. We might as well explore Garden of the Gods."

"Then we can take some photos of Camel Rock. It's the image on the back of the U.S. Mint's Illinois quarter in the wilderness series. Jason wants pictures to display with his coin collection."

"We may need an umbrella," Quinn said.

Ace strode to his truck and returned with a folded umbrella and a gun holstered to his leg.

Quinn's eyes widened. "Why do you need a gun?"

He handed her the umbrella. "Wasn't 'protect' in my vows?"

"Yes, but—" Quinn glanced at the peaceful forest surrounding the cabin. "Protect me from what? We haven't heard a car or seen a single person since we turned off the main highway last night."

"Critters. You know, snakes, bobcats, bears, and Bigfoot."

"You're not serious, are you?" Quinn didn't like snakes, although she knew she might encounter one in the woods, but she hadn't considered larger, four-legged animals. A finger of fear sniggled down her back.

Ace must have noticed because he slipped his arm around her shoulders. "The gun is just a precaution."

"If I see something, I'll probably scream loud enough to chase it away."

"Okay. You have your lungs. I have my gun."

She squatted to the ground and wiggled her arms out of the backpack. Inside were four bottles of water, brochures, bags of trail mix, a first-aid kit, and her camera. She tried rearranging, but the umbrella wouldn't fit.

She glanced up at Ace. "What should I take out?"

"I'll carry the camera."

Quinn handed the camera to him, and he hooked the case onto his belt. She slipped the umbrella into its place and then strapped on the backpack. "Good idea."

After more than an hour of hiking in Garden of the Gods, 'good idea' wasn't what she was thinking. The brochure described the trail as a quarter-mile flagstone path with panoramic views, including Camel Rock.

Quinn thought hiking would be a fun-filled adventure, trekking through the wilderness, enjoying the wild flowers.

The reality was much different. Sweat trickled down her back. Gnats swarmed around her eyes, and mosquitoes bit her bare arms. The uneven flagstones wound through dense clumps of trees and blotted out most of the light, making the trail seem like a dim tunnel.

She kept her head down and watched her feet so she wouldn't step on an uneven surface or a snake. The Observation Trail was one of the more popular in Shawnee National Forest, so she'd expected to see other hikers. So far they hadn't crossed paths with anyone. Maybe because it was Monday, or maybe the threat of rain had kept others away.

The uphill climb to the top of the bluffs was strenuous. She stopped sporadically to rest and to pick up some of the small pine cones scattered on the ground. Thinking about hanging them on their Christmas tree made her smile.

Ahead was a landing with two wooden benches. "Do you want to rest?" she asked Ace.

He kept walking. "If I stop, I might not get started again."

Quinn glanced wistfully at the benches. She didn't want to appear to be weak or be left behind. She stiffened her shoulders and continued the upward climb.

Five minutes later the trees cleared. Quinn followed Ace onto a bluff with a heap of boulders in the center. She stopped next to him, bent over, and laid down her pine cones. When she straightened, she was surrounded by nothing but sky. She stretched out her arms and slowly twirled. She felt like she was standing on top of the world.

The sun moved from behind the clouds, and its rays beamed behind Ace's head. With his muscular arms and wide stance he looked like a mighty god standing on Mt. Olympus. He began moving closer, a devilish glint in his eyes. Quinn backed away.

"Be careful," he warned. "Don't get too close to the ledge."

She turned and continued to the rim, inching her way across the rocks. When she reached the side, she peered over the edge. A forested ravine dropped at least a hundred feet. She scooted back until she stood safely next to Ace.

"Thirsty?" She didn't wait for an answer, but wiggled out of her backpack and grabbed two bottles of water. She handed one to Ace. The other she drank, letting the cool water trickle down her dry throat.

Across the canyon parallel to where they stood was another huge sandstone cliff. "Is that the camel?"

Ace turned toward the cliff. "It doesn't look much like a camel?"

She squinted at the opposite bluff. "Maybe the pointed rock is the camel's head and the rounded one behind is the hump."

Ace stared at the rocks. "That's a very flat head."

Quinn took out the brochure and read. "Millions of years ago this part of Illinois was a giant sea. A great upheaval moved the rocks on the bottom above sea level, forming sandstone plateaus."

"Does it tell about the glaciers?"

Quinn read on. "Over time, the exposed sandstone was shaped by wind and weather. No glaciers covered this area. They stopped north of Garden of the Gods."

"That doesn't explain why the head is flat," Ace said. "It could be from people climbing on it?"

"That's a pretty long leap between the hump and the head."

Ace finished his water. "Maybe that's why people die on these cliffs."

Quinn understood the temptation. The rush of leaping from rock to rock would appeal to death-defying thrill seekers. She wasn't one of them.

Ace handed Quinn the camera. "If that's Camel Rock, we'd better take some pictures."

Quinn snapped several photos, but was too far away. When she tried to get a good picture of the entire rock, the shape wasn't clear, and when she focused on the camel's head, she cut off the body.

As she continued taking pictures, Ace swatted at the mosquitoes buzzing around them. One landed on his forearm. He squashed it with his hand, but the mosquito left a large red welt.

"Did you bring any bug spray? These mosquitoes are giants."

Quinn bent over and checked her bag. She shook her head, wishing she had.

"Well, hand me a bag of trail mix."

Quinn tossed him the trail mix, then repacked the bag, putting the pine cones where the water had been. When she rose, she looked across the canyon. Two teenagers walked out onto the hump of the camel. The boy and girl, holding hands, were dwarfed by the size of Camel Rock.

Quinn raised her camera and searched for the people through her viewfinder. She couldn't find them. She lowered the camera. They were gone. She wanted a picture that would show Jason how huge Camel Rock was.

She handed Ace the camera. "Hold this and stay here. I'll hike over to the other bluff. Then you can take a picture of Camel Rock with me on its back."

Ace clutched the camera and crossed his arms over his chest. "Quinn, that's not a good idea."

"Why not? Jason will love it."

"Because I don't like you hiking alone. It's not safe."

She smiled and tried to erase his scowl. "You don't really think I'll run into Bigfoot, do you?"

"No, but you could run into other beasts."

Quinn slipped on the backpack, pulled her phone out of her jeans pocket, and checked the signal. "If I run into anything that looks dangerous, I'll call for help."

"You could slip and fall."

"Don't worry. I'm not planning on doing anything reckless." Off in the distance thunder rumbled, and the sun disappeared behind the clouds again. "I'd better hurry before the rain hits."

"Quinn—"

She gave him a quick kiss on the cheek, and before he could argue more, she ducked into the trees and disappeared.

CHAPTER TWENTY-ONE

Walking down the flagstone trail was much easier than going up, Quinn thought. Then rain started. She stopped at a fork in the trail. The dirt path led up, the flagstone path continued down. Camel Rock was above her, so she chose the dirt path with the steep incline and hiked up. The path narrowed to a secluded passage with overhanging branches and knee-high flora. Above her, raindrops plopped onto the leaves and dripped onto her head.

She continued walking through what felt like a rainforest. When the trees cleared, she stepped into an opening. Rain pelted her. She didn't get the umbrella out of her backpack. After the humidity, the rain felt refreshing. She tilted her head up and welcomed it. She just hoped the wet rocks wouldn't be too slippery for her to stand.

Cautiously, she worked her way to the center of the cliff and stood on what she thought was the camel's back. The entire area wasn't as big as she'd expected, and Ace wasn't looking in her direction. He was gazing farther out at the dark clouds. Just like a farmer, always checking the weather.

Crisscrossing her arms over her head, she shouted to Ace, "Over here. Turn around."

He didn't move. After several attempts, she gave up. The distance and the rain made it impossible for him to hear her.

She frowned. Maybe she wasn't even on Camel Rock. At the fork in the trail, the path had changed to dirt, which seemed odd since Camel Rock was a popular site. Maybe she'd taken the wrong one. But the flagstone path had gone down, which didn't seem logical.

She squeezed her eyes shut and silently willed Ace to turn and look in her direction. She opened her eyes. He was in the same spot. So much for mental telepathy. She'd just have to phone him.

She pulled her cell from her jeans and checked for a signal. A mosquito landed on her arm. She swatted at it with her phone.

Her backpack shifted, and her foot slipped. She teetered on the wet rocks. Her arms flailed as she struggled to stay upright. Her hands opened, grasping for something to hold onto.

Her phone slipped from her fingers and clattered against the boulders. It bounced off the rocks, spun in the air, struck another rock, then flew over the side of the cliff and disappeared.

Quinn gasped, and then nervously laughed. Instead of her phone, she could have slid on the rocks and plunged over the edge.

Then her gut clenched. What if Taylor tried to call her? Or Jason? Tomi's number was in the phone, along with all of her other contacts. She didn't have any of that information backed up.

Don't panic. It's okay. Even as she tried to convince herself, a knot formed in her stomach.

She hadn't actually seen her phone fall over the side. Maybe it was lodged in the rocks or caught in the underbrush. She unstrapped her backpack and took it off. She didn't want to lose her balance again. Crouching on her hands and knees, she crawled to the edge of the cliff. Cautiously, she inched toward where her phone had flipped into the air and disappeared.

Trees lined this section of rocks. Some shot up higher than the bluffs, making it impossible to tell where the ground ended and the sky began. She grabbed a limb and parted the branches, expecting sky. Instead more shrubs, along with tree limbs, were stacked in a pile. Why had the foliage been placed here? She carefully lifted branches off the pile as she searched for her phone.

One by one she removed the limbs until only the bare ground was left. *No phone.* Straightening, she sat back on her heels. Ahead was a narrow chasm between two huge rocks. The pile of limbs had hidden a stone passageway that resembled a twenty-foot tunnel. At the end was an opening barely wide enough for a person.

A beam of light shining through suggested a clearing beyond. She leaned forward, searching the downward slope for her phone. She didn't see it. But her cell could have slid through the opening and be lying on the other side.

She checked her watch. She'd been gone almost ten minutes. Ace would be worried. She should go back and tell him what happened, bring him here, and they could search together.

She glanced around to find something to mark her location. The surrounding rocks and trees all looked the same. If she left, she might not be able to find this spot.

Maybe if she waved to Ace again, this time he would see her. She wiggled back a few feet and rose. The rain came down harder, and Ace no longer stood on the bluff. Of course, he wouldn't stand out in the rain.

No use returning to Ace. He might be headed to her. But if she'd taken the wrong path, he might not find her. The knot in her stomach tightened. She needed her phone.

She'd leave the backpack. Ace would certainly see it. But if she slipped and was trapped, she'd be stuck without food or water.

She scooted to the middle of the cliff and retrieved her bag. She unzipped it and took out the pine cones. One by one, she dropped them in a line pointing to the edge where she'd found the stone passageway. She saved the last two, gripping them in her hand.

Satisfied she'd left a noticeable trail, she slung the backpack over her shoulders and headed toward the tunnel. As soon as she stepped between the stone slabs, the air cooled. A soft trickle of water flowed down the mossy green sides.

She placed a hand on the slimy side and descended the slope. As she walked, she kept her eyes on the muddy ground and searched for her phone. When she reached the end, she peeked through the narrow opening at a circular clearing, about the size of a camping spot. The area sported knee-high wild plants, mostly goldenrod. If her phone had slipped through, it would be hard to find. Still, she'd come this far. She had to try.

She dropped one of the pine cones in front of the opening and began to squeeze through. She couldn't fit, not with her backpack. She wiggled back, removed her pack, and held it behind her. She squeezed through and pulled her arm after her.

As she stood in the clearing, the rain stopped and the sun broke through the clouds. She was surrounded by giant limestone cliffs. Some of them had openings large enough for animals.

She took a deep breath and inched forward into the knee-high grass and yellow goldenrod. She pushed the weedy grass and goldenrod back and forth, searching for her phone. *Call me, Ace. Call me.* She repeated these words like a mantra.

Her phone rang. She jumped and then laughed aloud. Ace. He had heard her and called. Of course, he had. He had always been there when she needed him.

The musical ring of her phone sounded again, only behind her. She turned and searched the ground. There it was, lying in the grass a few inches from the opening. Relief washed over her.

She bent down and picked up the phone. A movement out of the corner of her eye surprised her. Her head jerked up. She started to turn.

Crack. Pain shot through the back of her skull. Her legs buckled. She reached out her arms to break the fall.

She thudded to the ground. The pine cone slipped from her hand.

CHAPTER TWENTY-TWO

Ace leaned against the trunk of a tree that he'd ducked under to get out of the rain. He squinted through the leaves at Camel Rock. Where was Quinn? Any minute he expected her to come prancing out looking great in those skinny jeans. Actually her long legs would look even better without them. He was ready to head back to the cabin and enjoy more honeymooning.

An urgency to hear Quinn's voice pulsed through him. *Call Quinn. Call Quinn.*

He pulled out his phone. Relieved he had a signal, he hit Quinn's number. Her phone rang three times and then stopped. His signal was gone. He gritted his teeth. He should never have let her leave. He should have flat out said *no*.

Well, maybe not in that way. He didn't want to butt heads with her on their honeymoon. Separating had been foolish. Quinn, however, wanted a picture on Camel Rock to make his son happy. *His* son. Ace needed to quit thinking of Jason in that way. From the beginning, Quinn had bonded with Jason, and he'd been eager to call her Mom.

Truth be told, Quinn was better at mothering than his ex. At least for this year, Stephanie was out of their lives except for Saturday mornings when she phoned Jason from London. That weekly contact seemed to be enough for both of them.

The urgency to find Quinn grew stronger. *Call Quinn. Call Quinn.* He shuffled between the trees, trying to find a signal. Nothing. He checked his watch. Quinn had been gone more than fifteen minutes. He didn't want to spend his honeymoon separated, even if it was for *their* son.

A closeup of Quinn posing on top of Camel Rock would make Jason just as happy. He slid his phone into his pocket and started walking.

Five minutes later, Ace stood in the drizzling rain on top of Camel Rock —alone. He frowned. Where was Quinn? Why wasn't she here?

Of course, she wouldn't be standing in the rain. She'd probably taken shelter under the trees. He cupped his hands around his mouth. "Quinn, I'm here. Where are you?"

Nothing moved in the trees or rocks near him. He called louder. "Quinn! Quinn!"

He felt foolish standing on a rock, calling his wife. He took out his phone. Three bars, a strong signal. He pressed Quinn's number and waited.

Her recorded voice answered, "This is Mrs. Ace Edleston. I'm probably busy with my new family. Leave a number and I'll get back to you."

In spite of his frustration, he grinned. After the beep, he playfully replied, "This is *Mr.* Ace Edleston. Where are you? Call me."

He tapped off and thrust the phone into his pocket against the bag of trail mix. The rain had stopped. He might as well sit and enjoy a snack while he waited.

He pulled out the nut-and-raisin mixture and tossed a handful into his mouth. The saltiness left a bad taste. A lump rose in his throat. He could barely swallow. Quinn had been gone more than half an hour. Even if she ducked off the trail during the rain, she should be here by now.

More minutes ticked by. The lump in his throat thickened. What if Quinn had taken a wrong turn?

He hadn't paid attention to the trail on his way to Camel Rock. He'd just dashed through the rain. Maybe he'd missed some clue along the way. He couldn't just sit and wait. He crumpled up the almost full bag of trail mix and rose.

Once on the path, he backtracked, examining the flagstones and tree trunks, checking for anything unusual. He came to a fork and stopped. The flagstone path was the one he had taken. It appeared to go down, but around the bend it turned right and started up again. The other trail was a dirt path that went up. Going up seemed logical. Maybe Quinn had chosen that one.

This time he plodded up the dirt trail. Within minutes, another bluff appeared. He walked to the center which was lower than Camel Rock. The sun had come out from under the clouds. He gazed around. If Quinn had followed this trail, where was she?

He cupped his hand to his mouth and called her. No one answered. He forced his feet to the edge of the cliff. Below, sandstones and trees lined a deep ravine. No skid marks on the rocks. No broken limbs on the trees.

He carefully backed away. His foot stepped on a pine cone lodged in the rocks. No tree branches stretched over this area. Yet a few feet away lay another pine cone. It seemed too coincidental for a second pine cone. Could these be ones Quinn had picked up?

He spotted a third. The cones seemed to be lined up. They couldn't have fallen out of her zipped backpack. She must have dropped them here for a reason.

Maybe she was leaving some kind of clue? If so, why? She had her phone. Reception was spotty, but she would eventually find a signal. Unless the battery on her phone went dead or unless...

The pounding in his head grew louder. He had to find Quinn. He took out his phone and called again. This time it went straight to voicemail.

He jammed the phone into his pocket and looked at the pine cones. They seemed to be in a straight line. Stepping carefully, he followed the line to the opposite side of the bluff. Limbs and shrubs were piled near the edge.

He inched closer to the debris. Instead of a ravine, a sloped passageway cut through the layers of sandstone. At the other end, sunlight poured through an opening and pooled onto the slanted stone floor. In the muddy stream of water lay a pine cone. He paused long enough to get his bearing and then stepped down into the passage.

He was surrounded by high walls and damp air. The hair on his arms rose. His skin prickled. Water trickled down the rock and dripped onto the short path. He continued along the slippery slope until he reached the end and the single pine cone. Ahead was the narrow opening. On the other side was a grassy meadow of mostly goldenrod. He sucked in a deep breath and tried to squeeze through the rocks. Halfway he became stuck.

He'd made it in; he had to make it out. He inched back, one way and then the other. Once freed, he surveyed the opening. It was wider at the bottom. He squatted down and wiggled through.

On the other side, he stood in the clearing, checking the ground, looking for a clue that Quinn had been there. To his left, a section of grass had been flattened and the goldenrod bent. His heart thudded. On the ground lay a pine cone—and Quinn's phone.

The flattened grass continued through the clearing. Had someone or something dragged Quinn? He picked up her phone and crept through the meadow, following the swath of bent grass.

The trail led to an overhanging bluff with a wide-mouth opening. The hair on Ace's neck rose.

He pulled out his gun and released the safety. Crouching down, he crept toward the cave.

CHAPTER TWENTY-THREE

Quinn's eyes were closed, her lids heavy. A nauseating smell of overripe cat litter filled her nostrils. Her eyes gradually opened.

She lay on her side, her cheek pressed against damp earth. She took short, shallow breaths, not wanting to fill her lungs with the musty stench of urine.

In front of her loose pebbles were scattered in the dirt. She fingered the small stones resembling grains of brown rice, except they were soft.

Dank rock walls surrounded her. She must be in a cave. She heard a *plop...plop...plop*. Water dripped somewhere behind her. Where was Ace? He would take care of it. But he wasn't here. She would call him.

Her phone. She'd lost her phone. She'd been searching for it in the meadow. How had she gotten here? She shivered. Maybe she wasn't alone. Maybe someone had brought her here.

Her eyes followed a dim light to a wide opening. Framed by rock walls, the blue sky and green grass beyond looked like a grade-school drawing she might have colored.

Something in the grass moved. A snake? She shuddered. She didn't want to think about what might be lurking outside in the weeds—or inside this cave.

She scanned the craggy walls above her. Clumps of short, thick masses hung down. Stalactites or stalagmites? Which cone-shaped icicle extended from the ceiling to the floor and which rose? *Like ants in the pants: the mites go up and the tights go down.* That's how she remembered the difference. But these stalactites weren't slender. They ended in rounded points, almost like brown noses.

Not stalactites. Bats!

Hanging upside down over her head was a colony of sleeping bats.

Her stomach roiled. Those pebbles she had fingered were bat poop.

Behind her, footsteps padded against the floor. She tilted her head toward the sound. The shadow of a man stretched up the wall. Stringy locks of white hair waved down his back. She stifled a scream.

Zeus!

She was trapped inside a bat cave with a serial killer.

Her heart tapped against her chest. Tomi had sensed Zeus at their wedding reception. He must have followed them. But why? What did he want?

Quinn had seen pictures of the albino in newspapers and on TV, but now, with his back to her, he was shorter than she'd expected, barely five feet six, yet stocky and broad-shouldered. He wore baggy jeans that sagged almost to his knees and a T-shirt stained with brown mud.

Maybe she could bargain with him. Give him what he wanted. But what did she have? He was holding her backpack, hacking at it with a knife. He growled like a grizzly and shredded her bag as if he had made a kill. When he finished, he flung it to the ground.

She wouldn't be able to reason with him. According to the news, he was a megalomaniac with grandiose delusions of power and judged his victims. Had he judged her for her past transgressions—for not being a mother to Taylor? That decision still haunted her.

She had to stay focused. She had to live for Taylor, for Ace, for Jason—and for herself.

Maybe she could rush him, jump onto his back, and overpower him. She was taller and wirier and would have the element of surprise. But the girth of his back and arms made him appear solid and strong. Plus he had a knife.

He'd used a knife to carve his victims, mark them with a red *Z*. Fear coursed through her. She needed a weapon. Her eyes darted around the cave. Nothing lay close. She might be able to claw him with her fingernails, but they weren't sharp talons. Maybe she could use her teeth. She couldn't fathom biting into his flesh.

Damp hair that had worked loose from her banana clip hung in her face. Her banana clip had metal claws. Maybe she could use it, clamp it onto Zeus' ear or nose. Then she could bolt from the cave.

But he had a knife and could hurl it at her.

What weapon did she have? Her eyes rolled up to the ceiling.

CHAPTER TWENTY-FOUR

Ace ducked into the dark cave and was surrounded by damp air. He flattened his back against the cool rock wall and waited for his eyes to adjust. He steadied his hand holding the semi-automatic, hoping he wouldn't have to use the gun.

Maybe he'd read the signs wrong. Maybe Quinn had just rushed through the grass and into the cave to get out of the rain. Maybe he'd find her inside, safe and dry.

A faint *drip, drip, drip* echoed from within the cave. Water. The dripping was followed by a sound he didn't recognize—*shink, shink, shink.* The hairs on the back of his neck rose.

His eyes dilated. He was standing near the front of a cavernous room that extended into blackness. The damp walls were carved with graffiti— initials like *SS loves LA* and words about somebody's mama. On the floor lay piles of loose rocks. And on the ceiling hung bats.

Ace sucked in his breath. The bats were asleep, but their hearing was as razor-sharp as their teeth. Their sonar, radar, or whatever they had, might detect his footsteps, or even his breathing.

Shink, shink, shink. That strange swishing noise hadn't disturbed them. Ace let out a slow breath. He didn't want to warn whoever or whatever was making that noise.

Light from the entrance of the cave radiated behind him. He would be a sitting duck, only not in a carnival shooting gallery, and the prize wouldn't be a fuzzy stuffed animal. It would be his life—or death.

He kept his back to the wall and inched forward. His boots sank and a pungent odor rose. He glanced down. Bile rose in his throat. The piles of gravelly pebbles were bat guano. He swallowed.

Next to his boot was the outline of a footprint, then another and another. Not Quinn's. She wore sneakers. These were boot prints, shorter and wider than his own. The tracks continued into the darkness. Ace crouched, careful not to make any sound as he followed them.

After more than a dozen steps, he stopped. His heart clenched. Ahead lay Quinn, stretched out on the floor, her back to him. She wasn't moving.

He tensed. He wanted to call out, run to her and make sure she was all right.

S*hink, shink, shink.*

Ace looked toward the sound. Across the cave was the outline of a man, his back to Quinn. Strings of white hair trailed over his wide shoulders.

Zeus.

Light glinted on something in his hand.

Shink, shink, shink.

A knife.

Zeus moved his arm back and forth. Was he sharpening the knife, readying it for a kill? Or cleaning it up afterwards?

Ace's gut twisted as if that knife had stabbed him. *Please, God, I can't be too late. Let Quinn be alive.*

His eyes darted to Quinn. Her arm seemed to have moved. Was he imagining it? Seeing what he hoped for? No, her right arm was inching up toward her head. Her fingers slid through her hair.

Ace focused on Zeus and aimed the gun at him. Without warning, Quinn leaped into a crouch and rose. She raised her arm and threw something at the ceiling. The bats screamed. Hundreds of them. The cacophony was horrendous. The bats squeaked and flapped their wings.

Ace was caught off guard. His weight shifted. He lost his balance. His finger jerked on the trigger and the gun fired. Bullets ping-ping-pinged through the cave. The bats screeched and swooped toward the light.

Zeus whirled around. Quinn took off, sprinting toward the entrance. Zeus aimed his knife at her.

"Quinn, get down," yelled Ace.

She didn't seem to hear him and continued running.

"Down!" he barked.

She began to zigzag from side to side.

Zeus threw the knife at her.

"Qui-inn-inn!"

Her legs stopped, and her body went slack. She toppled onto the floor. Ace rushed to her side and knelt on one knee. A knife wasn't sticking out of her back. Oh, God, no! Did one of his bullets hit her?

Behind them, Zeus lay on the ground, screaming and writhing as he held onto his leg. At least one of the bullets had hit Zeus.

Ace steadied his gun and kept it aimed it at Zeus. With his other hand, he prodded Quinn on the shoulder. "Where are you hurt? Did a bullet hit you?"

A movement caught his eye. Zeus was crawling on his belly toward them. His hand reached out and grabbed the knife.

Zeus hadn't been shot. Ace had foolishly fallen for the ruse. He aimed the gun, and just as he fired, Zeus leaped to his feet and charged. This time there was no mistake. The bullet struck Zeus in the side.

Zeus stumbled forward and threw the knife at Ace.

He dodged left, trying to avoid being hit. He wasn't fast enough. The handle of the knife smashed against his fingers. The gun slipped from his grip and thudded to the ground. He leaped forward to grab it.

Zeus was closer. He kicked the gun away and pounced onto Ace. Zeus was smaller, but the momentum of his body slammed against Ace and knocked him backward. His head thumped against the ground.

Zeus balled his fist and smashed it against the side of Ace's head.

A flash of white pain burst in Ace's eyes. He fought to stay conscious. He didn't know if Quinn was alive or dead, but he had to protect her.

He wrenched his knee beneath Zeus' injured side and levered his hands flat against Zeus' shirt. Ace heaved and pushed his knee into Zeus' wound.

Zeus roared, reared back, and grabbed his side. Ace rolled free and reached for the gun. His fingers touched the handle, but Zeus pounced on Ace, knocking the gun farther away.

Zeus grabbed for Ace's neck and wrapped his hands around it, squeezing tight enough to shut off the air.

Ace twisted and bucked, bucked and twisted, but Zeus pressed harder.

Ace couldn't breathe. He fought to free himself, but he was pinned too tightly. He needed air.

Zeus laughed manically.

Ace's body was weakening, going slack. His eyes closed. Blackness surrounded him. The laugh faded, sounding far, far away.

A shot rang out.

Zeus groaned. His hands fell away from Ace's neck.

Ace gasped. His chest heaved as his lungs filled with air. His eyes popped open. Zeus was falling forward. Ace shoved him aside, throwing Zeus' body against the ground.

Ace looked up at a mass of unruly curls. Quinn. Her face was caked with dirt and unimaginable filth.

But she was alive.

He had never seen anything more beautiful than his wife, standing over him, holding his gun.

CHAPTER TWENTY-FIVE

Monday afternoon, Tomi placed a plate of left-over cupcakes onto Ace's kitchen table. Jason and Taylor would be home from school soon and would want a snack. They'd ridden the bus in the morning, but P.R. had offered to bring them home.

Last night after the wedding reception, P.R. had taken Tomi back to the loft to wait for Quinn and Ace to return with the children. Taylor and Jason had begged to sleep at Ace's while Quinn and Ace were on their honeymoon.

Tomi felt more comfortable at the loft, but she had not wanted to disappoint the children. "Okey-dokey." Tomi liked using the new word Jason had taught her.

"I'm here until Tuesday," P.R. said. "Maybe I should sleep at Ace's, too."

Tomi and Quinn stared at him, their mouths agape.

"On the couch," he explained.

Ace thought P.R. staying close was a good idea. "Quinn, you haven't taken Tomi out to drive yet. Maybe P.R. should stay. He could bunk at your place."

Tomi was glad P.R. was next door. She felt safer.

The phone rang just as P.R.'s car pulled into the drive. She picked up the receiver. "*Moshi, moshi.*"

Quinn answered. "I called to tell you Zeus has been caught."

Tomi hoped she'd heard right. "Say again, please."

"Zeus has been caught. No need to worry."

Tomi collapsed against the wall. "*Yokatta!*"

"What?" Quinn asked.

"Good. Very good."

The sliding door opened. P.R. and the kids rushed into the kitchen, chatting. Gogo pattered after them. Tomi pointed to the cupcakes on the table and then put a finger to her lips to signal them to be quiet.

After she finished talking to Quinn and hung up, Tomi said, "Bad man caught."

Jason pumped his fist into the air, and Taylor clapped.

P.R. strode over and leaned on the wall next to Tomi. "Where did they find him?"

"In cave, near Quinn and Ace."

"At Shawnee National Forest?" P.R. asked.

"*Hai.*"

"But you saw him at the wedding reception."

"No see." She didn't know how to explain the evil that had whirled around her, not when his blue eyes were jumbling her thoughts. "Feel evil."

P.R. stroked his goatee. "O-kay."

He didn't sound as if he believed her, but he didn't laugh.

"Why did Zeus kill Jackson and break into Ace's house?"

She shrugged. "Quinn no tell me."

"Did she say how they caught him?"

Tomi glanced at Taylor and Jason sitting at the table eating cupcakes. She did not want them to hear. She cupped her hand and whispered to P.R., "Quinn shot him."

P.R. raised his eyebrows. "Quinn!"

The kids glanced over at them.

P.R. leaned closer and whispered in Tomi's ear, "Is Zeus dead?"

"No. In jail." She had to move away. He was standing too close, unnerving her, making her wonder what his warm lips would feel like pressed against her ear, her cheek, her lips.

She could not give in to her feelings. Her friends had warned her about Western men. She did not want to become just another comfort woman for an American playboy. "Quinn tell story when she come home tomorrow."

Tomi moved to the table. Taylor looked up, her lips smudged with chocolate icing. "Can we go for a bike ride?"

Tomi glanced back at P.R. She did not want their time together to end. "Maybe...later."

P.R. ruffled Jason's hair. "Does your dad have a bike I could ride?"

"In the shed next to mine."

P.R. looked toward Tomi. "I'd like to come."

———

P.R. rode the bike along the graveled road near Ace's farm. He pedaled faster, leaving Tomi, the kids, and the dogs behind. No skyscrapers. No traffic. No smog. Just fields of dried corn stalks almost ready to be picked.

He threw out his arms. A cool autumn breeze swept over him, stripping away the years. He felt boyishly carefree, the way he had after all his papers had been delivered.

On Mondays, he was usually at his desk, dressed in a suit and tie. Today he wore faded blue jeans and a plaid shirt. He'd asked off to be at the hospital when Raven gave birth. But the twins had arrived Saturday night. He could have returned to Chicago, and probably should have to consult with Ashleigh about the trial next week.

He told himself he'd stayed to spend more time with Raven and the babies, but he suspected the reason really was because of Tomi.

He glided to a stop and straddled his bike, waiting for the others. Tomi pulled up first. She looked fresh with her hair swept up in a ponytail. Her cutoff Levis showed off her legs and her stretchy white top revealed her curvy breasts.

She smiled at him, not just with her mouth and eyes, but with her whole face. Something inside him jumped, like a giddy school boy. She was definitely attractive, but what captivated him more was her simple joy.

When the kids caught up, Tomi took bottles of water from her basket and handed them to everyone. As they drank, the dogs scampered across the road. A rusted barbed-wire fence surrounded a concrete brick building with broken glass windows. A sign above the wooden gate read 'Springside Mine.' Posted below was the warning: *No Trespassing.*

Tomi pointed to the building. "What that?"

"An abandoned mine."

She twisted her lips the way she did when she didn't understand.

He tried again. "A place where they dig for coal."

She nodded. "Coal mine." She guided her bicycle toward the gate, and P.R. followed. "Quinn say mining have dark history."

"She was probably referring to the coal mine strike in Pana, a small town north of here. The owners brought in black laborers from Alabama to break the union. The miners didn't settle until they were offered a fair wage. That strike was in 1898, but it established the role of labor unions in America."

Jason pushed his bike up beside them and petted Bullet. "Last year our class visited the Chicago Science and Industry Museum. We got to see a real coal mine."

"That mine was moved to Chicago from right here in Franklin County," P.R. said. "Old Ben #17."

"Cool." Jason's eyes lit up. "Can we go in?"

P.R. shook his head and pointed to the *No Trespassing* sign.

Jason didn't give up. "Other people have been here."

Inside the gate, tire tracks crisscrossed through the finely crushed coal dust. "Belle said that a group of local businessmen are considering buying the mine and opening it for tours. The tracks are probably theirs."

"Why closed?" Tomi asked.

P.R. didn't know the specific reason. From Jackson, P.R. had learned Illinois produced high-sulfur coal that polluted the environment. The scrubbers to reduce emissions were costly, as was the safety equipment for the miners. But that explanation was too complicated. He finally chose one word. "Dangerous."

Tomi finished her water and pulled her phone from her pocket. "After 3/11, some Japanese mines reopened. Safe."

P.R. brows shot up. "Safe?"

"Nuclear power dangerous."

He had witnessed the damage coal mining caused to the workers and the environment. On TV he had seen the destruction of nuclear power. Both seemed dangerous.

"Look." She pointed to the horizon and her fingers brushed across his hand. A spark of electricity shot through him.

He turned. The sun was just beginning to set behind the cornfield, streaking the sky with pinks, purples, and fuchsias. He watched with her, transfixed by the vibrant Midwestern sunset.

"In Tokyo sun already up."

"What time is it in Japan?" P.R. asked.

Tomi looked at her watch. "Thirteen hours ahead. Eight a.m. Tuesday morning."

"I wish I was there," Taylor said. She picked up Gogo and hugged him. "Then it would be tomorrow and Mommy and Ace would be home."

Tomi put her arm around Taylor and her puppy.

Unlike Taylor, when they turned away from the setting sun and headed back toward the farm, P.R, wasn't ready for the day to end. "Anyone for a wiener roast?"

CHAPTER TWENTY-SIX

"Wiener roast good idea," Tomi said as she, Taylor, P.R., and Jason sat on hay bales roasting hot dogs over a small fire while Gogo, Bullet, and Nugget lay nearby.

Tomi had eaten hot dogs, but not roasted. The skin was brown and crunchy, the inside juicy. She finished her last bite and licked her lips. "Food makes me happy."

Across from her, P.R. stood and threw another log onto the fire. The flames leaped and the light flickered, making his hair glitter like spun gold. "Anyone for another hot dog?"

Taylor shook her head. "I'm ready for dessert."

P.R. turned to Tomi.

"Yes, please."

He forked an uncooked hot dog and circled the fire. He handed her the willow branch, and when she took it, their fingers touched. A spark seared through her.

P.R. must have felt it, too, because he stepped back, almost toppling into the flames. Tomi lowered her head and stuck the hot dog into the fire. As she roasted and ate it, she tried to quiet the pounding of her heart.

Next to her Taylor squirmed. "Now can I go to the house for s'mores?"

Tomi handed Taylor the willow stick. "No need more. We have some here."

Taylor giggled. "Not some more hot dogs. S'mores."

Jason jumped up. "I'll help you."

The two kids raced to the house, followed by the dogs.

Tomi looked across the fire at P.R. "Why they go inside to get some more hot dogs?"

P.R. walked around the fire and sat next to her, shoulder to shoulder. "S'mores are roasted marshmallows, graham crackers, and chocolate bars."

"*Oishi.* Sound good."

He turned to her. His breath was warm on her cheeks. "They are good and gooey."

He was too close. She tried to remember the American slang about desserts. His musky maleness, mixed with the smell of burning wood, muddled her thoughts. "I have sweet mouth."

P.R.'s voice was husky. "Yes, you have a very sweet mouth." He cleared his throat. "But I think you mean *sweet tooth*."

Her lips parted. "Oh."

He ran his finger across her lips in a soft caress. Shivers rippled through her.

"You're shaking." He stretched his arm behind her back, resting his hand on the hay. "Do you need a jacket?"

She shook her head. The night had turned chilly, but the fire and sitting beside P.R. warmed her. She liked sitting next to him. She liked the way he listened to what she said and the way he explained things. She liked almost everything about him.

She wanted to lean against his arm, let go, and give into these strange feelings churning inside her. But she had come to America to be an independent woman. She didn't want to switch from obeying her parents to obeying a man. Besides, after three months she must return to Japan, be an obedient daughter, and do what her parents expected of her.

The dogs barked, and she straightened as the kids ran back to the fire.

"Who wants s'mores?" Taylor asked.

When Tomi nodded, Taylor showed her how to roast a marshmallow, put it on the chocolate, and smash it between two graham crackers. After Tomi finished eating one, Taylor asked, "What do you think?"

"I want s'more." Everyone laughed.

As soon as the fire burned down, Jason said, "Let's tell ghost stories."

Taylor moved closer to him. "Tell the one about Williamsburg Hill."

Jason lowered his voice, "This boy and girl ran out of gas in the cemetery on Williamsburg Hill."

As he continued telling the story, the wind rustled the leaves. Shadows from the trees fell on the Quonset hut. A log in the fire popped. Tomi jumped up and looked around.

"It's only the burning wood," P.R. said

She shuddered. After Quinn had called, Tomi thought she would feel safe. The bad man was in jail. But she still felt uneasy, and the kids had school tomorrow. "Sleep time."

"Don't you want me to finish my story?" Jason asked.

P.R. threw his arm around Jason's shoulder. "I think you're scaring the girls."

Taylor stood and placed fisted hands at her waist. "I'm not scared."

"Maybe you aren't, but Tomi doesn't like ghost stories," P.R. said.

Jason looked at her. She didn't say anything, but started to gather up the food.

Jason reluctantly rose. "All right."

"Come on, Gogo," Taylor said.

"Remember dogs sleep in shed," Tomi said.

"Please." Taylor begged. "Gogo won't be any trouble."

"He get used to new home." Tomi looked toward P.R. for help.

He scooped up Gogo and called the other dogs. "I'll put them in the shed."

Taylor must have been too tired to argue. She let Tomi lead her and Jason to the house.

P.R. shouted after them, "I'll put out the fire and then come say good-bye."

Saying good-bye to P.R. was something Tomi did not want to think about. Tomorrow he would return to Chicago, and she didn't know if she would ever see him again.

When they reached the house, Jason shot up to his bedroom. Taylor leaned against Tomi and together they climbed the stairs. Taylor's new bedroom was next to Jason's. The walls had been painted a light purple. The double bed was covered with a princess spread of crowns and castles. Resting on the pillow was Lovey, Taylor's black-and-white stuffed cow.

A few other personal possessions had been moved from the loft. Palettes of paint and a can of brushes were on the dresser. Tomi hurried into the adjoining bathroom and ran water in the tub. After Taylor climbed in and began washing, Tomi scurried down the hall to Jason's room.

She rapped lightly on the closed door. "Jason, I come say good-night."

His voice boomed through the door. "I'm not a baby. I can go to bed by myself."

She turned the handle, but the door was locked. "Okey dokey." Quinn had told Tomi that Jason hadn't received much mothering, and she had taken pleasure in pulling up the covers and kissing his rosy cheek last night when she had tucked him into bed. But she understood and did not want to hover over him the way her parents did her. Reluctantly she turned away.

As she returned to Taylor's bedroom, Taylor padded out of the bathroom with a towel wrapped around her. "Will you sleep with me tonight?"

Last night, Taylor had begged Tomi to sleep with her since Gogo was in the machine shed. So she had crawled into the double bed, but Taylor had been restless, her arms and legs flopping most of the night. Tomi hadn't slept much. Her eyes stayed open, guarding against the lurking evil.

She did not want Taylor to be scared. "I come back after say good-bye to P.R."

Taylor put on her pajamas and climbed into bed, hugging Lovey. When Tomi turned on the nightlight, Taylor's eyes were already closed.

Tomi descended the stairs into the dark kitchen. Through the sliding glass doors, she saw P.R. standing outside on the deck. His back was to her, and a circle of yellow from the porch light outlined his tall, lean frame. He looked strong, not like a sumo wrestler, but like a sleek jaguar.

As if he sensed her presence, he turned and slid open the patio door. "Shut off the light and come outside."

She found the switch next to the door and turned it off. When she stepped onto the deck, P.R. moved toward her. The air was instantly charged with electricity—and him. Her body jolted.

"Fire's out," P.R. said. "Do you need anything before I go?"

She tilted her head to look up at him. She gasped. "Stars!" The sky was a black canvas filled with millions of twinkling silver dots. "I no see stars before. So beautiful."

"Never?" P.R.'s voice was filled with disbelief.

"In Tokyo lights burn all night, and here I no see night sky in country."

He weaved his fingers through hers and led her over to the steps.

They settled on the top one. He didn't let go of her hand as they leaned back and gazed up at the sky. "Close your eyes and make a wish," he said.

"Oh. Like Disney. When you wish on star." She closed her eyes and thought of Hiro and their childhood dream. The dream had come true. She was in America. She made her wish. *Let my spirit be free.*

She opened her eyes. P.R. was not gazing at the sky, but at her. Without the moon, the darkness drew them closer and enveloped them in a cocoon.

"Tell me about him," he said softly.

She did not ask 'who.' They connected on a level beyond words. "My brother should be here, not me."

She told him about the day Hiro had come home with news that his company was building a plant in America. Japanese workers would be sent to America for five years. The company offered to send Hiro.

Their father said he was number one son. He should help take care of the family and marry the girl they had selected for him. Their heated discussions continued for days. Even their mother wanted Hiro to stay in Japan. Finally, their parents wore him down.

"He said he would go next time and take wife." Tomi swallowed before she could go on. "A month later, tsunami hit." She paused again. "That five years ago. I come for Quinn's wedding...and for Hiro."

She looked up at the sky again. "Do you believe wishes come true?"

P.R. was silent for a long time. "Sometimes they come true, but you have to do your part, too, by putting them out in the universe and asking God for help."

"I want to hear about your god," she said.

"That would take all night."

She wouldn't mind listening to him all night. But when he didn't say anything, she said, "Your turn. Make wish."

P.R. closed his eyes. He felt foolish. He hadn't wished on a star since he was kid. He was used to working to get what he wanted, but a wish immediately popped into his head. *More days like today.*

Until recently, he'd been focused on his goals. Finish college, go to law school, earn a degree, pass the bar exam, and get a job. He'd done all of that. Last week, he'd checked out a condo on Michigan Avenue. Tomorrow he planned to put a deposit on it. But he was surprised by how much he liked being here, sitting with Tomi, enjoying the night sky. She fascinated him. The attraction was unexpected, and it changed what he thought was important in life.

She rose. "I go inside now."

He couldn't let her leave, not without holding her, touching her, kissing her. He scrambled to his feet and followed her to the door. "It was a good day," he said. Although that wasn't at all what he wanted to say.

"*Hai*. Good day."

He felt like an awkward school boy. He hesitated. He didn't know Japanese customs, but he knew what he wanted. Gently he touched her long hair, running his fingers through it. Her scent was intoxicating, like honeysuckle and fresh peaches. He slid his hands down her arms and settled them around her waist. He pulled her against him. She didn't push away.

He let out a breath, waited for her to get used to the feel of him. Was it his imagination or was her heart beating against his?

He leaned down. Her head tilted up, her mouth inviting him closer. He pressed his lips against hers in a gentle kiss. Her lips quivered, pulsing against his. Each pulse sent an explosion rocking through him. Rational thoughts disintegrated. He wanted more. He pressed harder, got lost in the feel of her.

Abruptly, Tomi pulled away from him.

He blinked, startled. He'd planned a quick tender kiss, but her mouth fit so perfectly with his. When he'd felt her soft lips, he wanted to explore them, but he must have offended her. Yet he didn't say he was sorry. He wasn't sorry. He wanted to do it again and again. He used every bit of restraint to keep from taking her into his arms and kissing her now.

Those lips were moving, saying something. "When you come back to Hickory Hills?"

His mind was still reeling. "What?"

"When you come back?"

Why was she asking when he would be back? He was here now. What was his plan? Oh yes, he had told Summer. "Thanksgiving."

"When Thanksgiving?"

He didn't care about the date. He cared about now. "In November sometime. About seven weeks."

Tomi moved farther away. *So, he does not care for me. If he did, he would return to see me.*

She had not expected it to hurt so much. She thought she had steeled herself against caring for him, but she didn't seem to be able to control her feelings when she was near him.

She should not have let him kiss her. But desire had flooded through her. She had been kissed before, but it had not been pleasant.

She'd thought maybe he felt the same jumble of emotions that coursed through her, but he was returning to Chicago, resuming his life there. So the kiss had meant little to him, something he probably did with most of the women he met. She'd ended the kiss and backed away for her own protection.

She wanted to be a free spirit. Now she understood that with freedom came choices. If she made the wrong choice, she would be hurt—and possibly she could hurt others.

His hand reached out and tucked a strand of hair behind her ears. She closed her eyes, reveling in the softness of his touch. He moved his hands to her shoulders and tried to pull her back to him.

She planted her feet and stiffened her body. She would not be won over by his easy smile, kind words, and a single kiss, no matter how wonderful that kiss felt. She willed herself to look at him, face reality. He was American. She was Japanese. It could never work.

"Thank you for today." She turned and slid open the patio door. "Have safe trip." She slipped inside and closed the door, leaving him on the other side. She did not turn on the light. She stood at the window as he walked down toward the lake where he had built the fire.

He went to the Quonset hut and returned with a bucket of water. He circled the hay bales, pouring on water and kicking the ashes several times to be sure no spark was left. When he finished, he looked back toward the house. She lifted her hand and waved, even though she knew he could not see her in the dark.

His shoulders hunched. He jammed his hands into his pockets as he strode toward the hickory grove and disappeared into the trees.

Tomi walked over to the stove. She needed a cup of tea to settle her nerves. Just as she put on the kettle, the dogs started barking. Tomi walked to the patio door and peered out. Seeing nothing but the night, she glanced up at the myriad of stars. She expected to be filled with awe, but without P.R. the magic was gone.

The dogs continued to bark. She looked toward the machine shed. A movement in the shadows startled her. Her heart leaped. P.R. had come back. She peered into the darkness and waited, but P.R. didn't appear.

Goosebumps rose on her arms. The dogs were just restless. Maybe Gogo missed sleeping with Taylor. The kettle on the stove whistled.

She returned to the stove and poured the water into her cup. She drank the tea. It did not settle her nerves.

CHAPTER TWENTY-SEVEN

After dark, Bucky parked his car at the Springside Mine. He popped the trunk and pulled out a five-gallon gas can. The stars blinked like lights in a slot machine and lit his way as he weaved through the cornfield toward Ace's house. The newlyweds were on their honeymoon, so the house would be empty. But there were too many places to search. He'd decided on a better idea.

At the end of the cornfield, he crouched down and inched into Ace's back yard. Dogs started barking. He stopped and looked toward the Quonset hut. The barking seemed to be from inside, but a man with his back to the cornfield was in the yard, walking near a circle of hay bales.

Bucky stepped back into the field. He pulled the stocking cap down on his head, not covering the long locks of white hair. He watched the man walk to the trees and disappear into the darkness. He waited to make sure he wasn't coming back.

Hunkering low to the ground, Bucky dashed out of the cornfield, the gas can swinging from his hand. He darted to the hay and latched onto one of the bales.

The dogs continued to bark. Ignoring them, he dragged the bale to the house. He stopped near the deck and tipped the can, splashing gasoline onto the hay and wooden boards. The scent of gasoline was intoxicating. His fingers itched to start the fire.

He pulled a box of farmer's matches from his windbreaker. Let the games begin. He liked to play Russian roulette with the matches. He would strike a match and let it burn as long as possible. He wouldn't put it out until the flame was ready to burn his fingers. Then he would blow. If the flame went out, he would light another match. But if the flame burned his fingers, he would drop it. *Whoosh.*

Game on. Bucky held up the first match and struck it against the side of the box. The match sparked. Sulfur filled his nostril. The smell was exhilarating. He held onto the match, the flame leaping and dancing in the dark. The beautiful colors inched toward his fingers.

The fire was getting closer and closer. He sucked in a deep breath and blew. The fire went out.

He stifled a triumphant laugh and pulled out another match. His record was ten matches. Maybe tonight he'd beat the record and strike a dozen. He held the second match next to the side of box, ready to strike it.

The dogs barked louder. He glanced up. Behind the glass patio door stood the Japanese woman, the one who had seen him fleeing from Ace's house. She was staring in his direction.

His hand froze. He dove to the ground, hoping the deck would hide him. Sweat beaded under his cap and trickled down his neck. Had she been watching when he lit the match? Had she seen his face?

Over the years, he'd started plenty of fires. Dilapidated houses, abandoned barns, empty churches... After the first fire, no one had been injured or killed. Now, though, he didn't have a choice. That pretty little lady was in the wrong place at the wrong time.

He waited under the deck for an hour. This time he didn't play Russian roulette. When he struck the match, he dropped it onto the hay. Flames shot up. He scurried to the cornfield. When he'd reached a safe distance, he turned and watched. The fire was magnificent and...deadly.

CHAPTER TWENTY-EIGHT

Bweee! Bweee! Tomi's eyes popped open. The nightlight illuminated the bedroom. Where was she? Not on her futon. Not in Taylor's bunk beds. She sat up. Taylor turned over and snuggled next to her. *Ah*, she was in Taylor's new room at Ace's house.

Bweee! Bweee! What was that shrill sound? *Bweee! Bweee!* Was it the alarm? Was it morning already?

She checked the clock. The hands pointed to 12:30. Why was the alarm ringing? She leaned over and pushed off the button.

Bweee! Bewee! The shrieking continued.

An acrid smell jolted her. Her eyes widened. Smoke.

Her heart thudded in her chest. She jumped out of bed and groped across the dimly lit room. She grabbed the knob. *Hot.* She jerked back. Smoke curled under the door and into the room. Fire!

Bweee! Bweee!

Her whole body began to shake. She sucked in a shallow breath. She couldn't panic. She had to get Taylor and Jason to safety.

She raced back to the bed and shook Taylor. "Wake up. Wake up," she said in Japanese.

Taylor sat up and yawned. "Is it morning already?"

"Hurry!" Tomi ran to the window and pushed back the curtains. She turned the lock and raised the window. A screen covered the glass, blocking their escape. She pressed her hands against the wire mesh and pushed. The screen fell, clattering onto the roof of the porch, less than a meter below.

Bweee! The fire alarm suddenly stopped, but the smell of smoke hung heavy in the air. She wrapped a fleece blanket around Taylor's shoulders and led her to the window. Tomi forced herself to speak slowly. "Climb out."

Taylor's sleepy eyes rounded. "I can't leave Lovey." She wiggled free and ran back to the bed, picking up the black-and-white stuffed cow.

Tomi looked at the dresser. The frog. Where was the frog Hiro had given her?

The bedroom door cracked. She grabbed Taylor, who held Lovey in her arms. She lifted her through the window and set her onto the roof. Then Tomi scrambled out, closing the window behind them.

She had to get Jason. "Stay here, Taylor."

Tomi balanced on the slanted porch roof. Above the house red and orange flames shot up, illuminating Jason's window. She slid her hand along the side of house as she crept across the shingled roof in socked feet. When she reached Jason's room, she pulled off the screen and pushed on the window. It wouldn't budge.

She pounded on the glass with her fists. "Jason! Jason!"

No answer.

She lowered her shoulder and lunged against the window. One, two, three times. The glass held. She lifted her foot, kicked her heel in short, swift, Karate-style jabs against the pane. The glass shattered.

She hoisted herself up and wiggled through the jagged glass. Shards ripped her skin. Blood trickled down her arm. Clenching her teeth, she ignored the pain. She had to find Jason.

The room was filled with smoke. She covered her mouth and fumbled through the dark, searching for Jason's bed. Her foot kicked the frame.

"Jason! Jason!" Smoked filled her lungs. She coughed, and her eyes watered as she patted the sheets feeling for him.

Her pupils adjusted to the darkness. The bed was empty. Her heart stopped. Where was Jason?

Smoke billowed under the door, fogging the room. She crouched down and crawled toward the door. A few feet away lay Jason. She lunged toward him and shook his arm. "Get up! Get up!"

He didn't move.

Coughing, she repeated it. Still Jason didn't move. What if she was too late? No, she couldn't be too late.

Her lungs burned. She had to get Jason out of the smoke. She grabbed his ankles and pulled him toward the window. Sweat poured down her face. When she reached the window, she punched out the remaining glass.

She coughed harder, barely able to breathe. Smoke stung her eyes. Wedging her hands under Jason's back, she rolled him into her arms and cradled his body against her.

Something hissed and popped. She glanced back. The door buckled and burst into flames. Fear engulfed her. Adrenalin kicked in. Using all her strength, she heaved Jason to the window. She straddled the frame and lowered him onto the roof.

Now all she had to do was crawl the rest of the way out.

Boom! The explosion rocked the house.

———

P.R. lay on Quinn's couch. He'd slipped off his shirt, but still wore jeans. He couldn't sleep. The couch sagged in the middle, and his bare feet stuck over the end, but the couch wasn't keeping him awake. Every time he closed his eyes, he saw Tomi.

He pulled his phone out of his jeans—12:35. Only five minutes since he'd last checked.

What had he been thinking when he told her he wouldn't be back until Thanksgiving? How could he wait seven weeks to see her? He couldn't even wait until 7 a.m.

He'd swing by this morning to make sure she didn't need anything before he drove to Chicago. Tomorrow he had to prepare for a high-profile murder trial. Tomi's sweet smile would go a long way in helping him make it through the week. Maybe if he worked late every night, he could take off Saturday. Then he could drive back to Hickory Hills to see Raven's new babies and spend time with Tomi.

His stomach clenched. He didn't even know if she liked him. When he had kissed her, her lips had been soft and oh, so sweet. But she ended it way too soon, and when he'd tried to kiss her again, she backed away.

His stomach knotted. She would be in the U.S. for only three months. He couldn't start something when she was leaving. Yet he couldn't imagine never seeing those almond-shaped eyes or hearing that delightful laugh again.

He swung his legs off the couch and slipped on his loafers. Maybe some milk would help him sleep. He shuffled into the kitchen and pulled a jug of milk out of the refrigerator. He found a glass in the cupboard.

He poured the milk, downed it, and walked over to the sink to rinse his glass. He peered out the window toward Ace's house. Light flickered through the clump of trees separating the two houses.

Must be lightning. The weatherman hadn't predicted a storm, but they were rarely right. Strange, P.R. hadn't heard thunder. The orange glow near the ground grew brighter. The light wasn't in the sky. The way it flickered, it almost looked like...

The glass slipped from his hand and shattered in the sink. Fire! He raced to the door and took the steps, two at a time. The air was heavy with smoke. He weaved through the hickory trees.

I have to get there in time! I have to! I have to!

He'd doused the campfire with water and checked it before he left. But he hadn't been thinking about the ashes. His mind had been on Tomi. What if some of the embers had been hot? What if his carelessness had caused a fire? What if something happened to Jason or Taylor or Tomi?

The dogs were barking. Was the Quonset hut on fire, too?

He raced out of the trees and into yard. The shed was fine, but flames licked up the back of the house. Oh, God! A red ball of fire shot into the air.

Boom! The back part of the house exploded, sending wood shooting from the house like deadly shrapnel.

———

Quinn bolted up in bed. Fear welled inside her. She couldn't breathe. Something was wrong. Terribly wrong.

Go home, go home, go home, throbbed in her head. Taylor, no Jason, Taylor and Jason. Their shrill screams vibrated in her ears.

"Ace! Ace!" He lay asleep beside her. She pounded on his back. "We have to go home!"

"What?" He rolled over, his voice gravelly. "We spent hours at the sheriff's office. Go back to sleep."

"We have to leave." She jumped out of bed and grabbed her cell phone from the dresser. She pressed Ace's home number and listened for it to ring. Nothing happened. No signal. She slipped on her clothes and threw the rest into the suitcase.

Ace sat up. "Quinn, what're you doing?"

She dropped his clothes onto the bed. "Get dressed. We have to go home."

He swung his legs out of bed and loped across the room. He wrapped his arms around her, coaxing her toward the bed. "We'll leave in the morning."

"No." She pushed him away. All the oxygen left the room. Her chest tightened. Her breathing became erratic. She took short breaths and then long gulps of air.

"Quinn, calm down. You're hyperventilating like that day in the garden shed. Take slow deep breaths."

She shook her head. This wasn't like the day in the garden shed. This was like the day in the Old Slave House when the mother voices had warned her.

She grabbed the suitcase and lugged it across the room. She opened the door. Once outside, she bent over, gasping for air. "Please, Ace, hurry."

Ninety minutes later Quinn sat in the front seat of the truck. The dash clock read 1:30. She peered out the window, searching for familiar landmarks. "Can't you drive any faster?"

"Quinn, I'm going seventy-five. Here's the turnoff. We'll be at the house in a few minutes."

Ahead the sky had turned to an eerie shade of orange. Her throat closed. She couldn't speak. Her entire body shook. Flames shot above the trees lighting up the night sky.

She gripped Ace's arm, but his mouth was open. He had already seen it.

A siren wailed behind them. Warning lights reflected in the rearview mirror. A fire truck. Ace clamped the steering wheel tighter. It couldn't be his house. Jason and Taylor were in the house. Tomi was with them. The coal mine or cornfield was on fire, not his house.

He floored the accelerator. The siren screeched louder. The ladder truck was speeding behind them. He kept his foot on the gas and slowed to the side of the road. The fire truck roared past and barreled into his lane.

Sweat beaded on his forehead. The kids. He had to get to the kids and Tomi.

He shot to the house and swerved into the lane. Halfway up, a barricade blocked the drive. He skidded to a stop, swung open the door, and leaped out.

Three fire trucks were parked on the lawn along the side of the house. He raced toward them. The back of the house was engulfed in flames. A dozen firefighters in yellow protective coats shot streams of water onto the blazing inferno.

Ace raced through the haze of smoke to the nearest fireman. "My kids. Where are the kids and Tomi?" Ace lifted his hand and shielded his eyes as he searched, hoping to see them huddled safely outside.

The fireman flung his arm out, blocking Ace's way. He pointed behind him. "Back there. Back there."

Ace wasn't going to be pushed away. He had to get to his kids.

Quinn rushed up to him. "Have you found them? Where are they?"

He didn't answer. His eyes darted toward the house. They couldn't be in the house. They couldn't.

The front of the house with the upstairs bedrooms was still standing. Maybe he wasn't too late. He turned and ran toward the porch.

"Stop!" another fireman yelled.

Ignoring him, Ace sprinted toward the front steps. The air shimmered with heat. His eyes stung. He lowered his head and pushed against the wall of hot air.

From behind, two firemen grabbed his arms and pulled him back. "You can't go in there."

He twisted loose. "I have to get inside."

"No. Get back! Get back!" More hands. Some gripped his shoulders, others grabbed his waist.

"Go to the Quonset hut." They continued to yell at him to go to the Quonset hut, but he didn't care about his safety. He wasn't going to seek shelter. He had to save his kids.

The roar of the fire filled his head. He could hear them yelling, but their words had no meaning. The fire blotted out everything. Like a fiery red serpent, the flames leaped and twisted in a macabre dance of destruction.

Rage flared inside him. He flailed, trying to fight off the hands pulling him back. But too many arms held onto him. They dragged him across the lawn, away from the house, away from his kids.

His legs buckled. He fell to his knees and dug his hands into the wet grass. He tried to claw his way back to the house, but they wouldn't let go of him.

Crack. The sound cut through the roar. The red receded. He lifted his head. The rafters gave way, and the roof caved in. Plumes of black smoke mushroomed above the peak of the roof.

"Nooooo!" He collapsed onto the ground. His fists pounded the earth. Jason, Taylor, Tomi—they were trapped inside. And he couldn't do anything. He couldn't save them.

Blazing heat ripped through his body and gutted him. He let out a primal cry. He was as powerless as Job. He lay prostrate on the ground and wailed as the ashes of his life rained down on him.

CHAPTER TWENTY-NINE

Quinn ran to Ace and lay next to him on the ground. Clouds of black smoke billowed from the burning house. The smell of charred wood hung in the air like a death shroud. She wrapped her arms around him, trying to hold them both together.

Her throat burned. Tears streamed down her face. Her entire body shook as she choked back sobs. Taylor couldn't be dead. Wouldn't Quinn feel it? How could her arms and legs move? How could she breathe if a piece of her were missing?

In the distance, a siren wailed. No need to hurry. The emergency for Taylor, for Jason, for Tomi, for all of them was gone—just like her world.

Tires crunched on the graveled lane. Quinn looked up. An ambulance swerved around the barricade. It sped past the house and lumbered into the back yard. Its headlights cut through the fog of smoke, illuminating the Quonset hut. Outside, next to the metal building, stood P.R. In his arms was Taylor.

"Taylor!" Quinn screamed with disbelief and joy.

Ace raised his head, his eyes red and vacant. "What?"

"It's Taylor! She's alive! She's alive!"

Quinn didn't wait for Ace. She scrambled up and ran toward Taylor. The air was thick and heavy. Her arms and legs moved like rusty pistons.

What was taking so long? She had to get to Taylor, touch her, hold her, make sure she was all right.

Where were Jason and Tomi? Did they get out? *Please, God, please let them be alive, too.*

She was halfway to the Quonset hut. The lights swirling on top of the ambulance blinded her. She stumbled. Plumes of ghostly smoke swirled through the air. She found her footing and continued running as she squinted against the light. She couldn't see Taylor and P.R. Where were they?

Panic seized her. Her throat closed. She couldn't breathe. Had she just imagined them, willed them to appear because she so desperately needed Taylor to be alive?

Quinn reached the Quonset hut. Light spilled through the open double doors onto the ground. She plunged inside.

She gasped. It hadn't been her imagination. In front of her stood P.R holding Taylor. She raced toward them.

Taylor launched herself from P.R.'s arms into Quinn's. "Mommy, Mommy."

Quinn clutched her daughter to her chest. She was able to breathe again. "Thank you. Thank you," she said to P.R. He quickly waved away her thanks and moved toward Tomi.

Ace rushed in and wrapped his arms around her and Taylor. He buried his head in Taylor's mass of tangled red curls and then pulled away. "Where are Jason and Tomi?"

Taylor pointed to Tomi, her arm covered with blood, her forehead swollen and bruised. Near her was a circle of paramedics kneeling on the ground.

"Jason?" Ace's voice filled with panic. "Where's Jason?"

Taylor's voice trembled. "He won't wake up. I gave him Lovey, but he still won't wake up."

One of the three paramedics rose and started to examine Tomi's head. On the ground lay Jason. He wasn't moving. A high flow oxygen mask covered his face. His skin was pink and mottled.

Ace rushed over and knelt down. "What's wrong? Jason? Jason?"

No response. Fear pulsed through Ace. He reached for his son.

A squat paramedic, who Ace knew as Junior, planted his hands on Ace's shoulders and pulled him back. He signaled with his head toward Tomi and P.R. "Stand over there. The chief will need to ask you some questions."

"I don't know anything. I just got here." Ace started to move back toward Jason.

Junior stepped in front of him. "The best thing for your son is for you to let us do our job."

Outside, another ambulance screeched to a stop. Two paramedics wheeled in a stretcher. Within minutes Jason was lifted onto it and whisked outside. Ace followed the stretcher, and hopped into the ambulance. No one protested.

He gripped Jason's hand and peered out the back, searching for Quinn and Taylor. He spotted Quinn holding Taylor as they were helped into the other ambulance. Tomi was with them.

P.R. climbed in the ambulance with Ace. "They said I needed to be checked out, too. Any change with Jason?"

Ace shook his head.

The door closed, and the ambulance screeched away. The wailing siren filled Ace's head. He looked down at Jason, so small and still. Ace's prayers had been answered. Jason was alive.

Now Ace confronted a new fear. When the paramedic shined a light into Jason's eyes, he hadn't blinked. Had Jason been hit on the head? Had he been deprived of oxygen?

What if Jason's brain had been damaged? What if Jason didn't wake up? Or what if Jason did wake up and he was a very different boy?

———

In the ambulance, P.R. sat next to Ace. He was holding Jason's hand, trying to reassure him. "I'm here, son. Right here. I won't leave you."

On the other side of the stretcher, a paramedic monitored Jason.

P.R. lowered his head. He felt sick. If only he could be sure he'd put the fire out. But he wasn't.

Ace's voice was strained. "I'll-I'll never be able to thank you for saving everyone."

P.R. kept his head down. He couldn't meet Ace's eyes. "Don't thank me. Thank Tomi."

"But you helped her."

"By the time I got there, the back of the house was in flames. Then something exploded."

"Exploded! Oh God, did something hit Jason on the head?" Ace asked. "Is that why he's not responding?"

Maybe telling Ace everything about the fire would help him and Jason. P.R. closed his eyes. He could see the fire from the loft, smell the smoke as he raced through the trees, and hear the sickening boom of the explosion.

He opened his eyes and cleared his head. "When I heard the explosion, I should have called 911, but all I could think about was getting everyone out of the house."

The fire was seared into him. Aloud, he recited the details, but in his mind he relived it. Not just what he had done, but what he had thought and felt.

He could taste the fear as he ran toward the burning house. The thick grass seemed to hold him back. His dad's words pounded in his head. "Screw-up. You didn't cut the grass short enough. You never do it right."

He pumped his arms, tried to run faster. This time if he screwed up, it wouldn't be just him. It would be lives—Jason, Taylor, and Tomi. He had to save them.

He raced toward the front of the house. He rounded the corner. He would have to kick in the front door. He wasn't afraid to rush into the burning house. He wasn't afraid to die. He was afraid his dad was right. He was afraid he had screwed up and was too late. That would be worse than death.

"P.R!"

It was Tomi's voice. Where was she?

"P.R! Up here!"

He craned his neck, expecting to see her at the upstairs window. Instead, she stood on the roof of the porch, waving her hands. Taylor was next to her, and Jason lay beside them.

Thank God. He wasn't too late. He didn't screw-up. They were alive.

Red and orange flames shot from the top of the house, cracking and popping. He had to get them to safety.

He hurried to the middle of the porch. "Taylor, jump. I'll catch you."

She hesitated.

He held out his arms. "Come on! You can do it!"

Tomi prodded her forward. Taylor shook as she moved to the edge. He stretched his arms. She threw Lovey down and he caught the stuffed cow.

"Now you," yelled P.R.

Taylor hesitated and then jumped into the air. He caught her and wrapped his arms around her.

She clung to him, shaking like a frightened fawn. "Something's wrong with Jason. He won't talk."

P.R. looked up at the roof. Jason lay on a blanket. He wasn't moving. He gave Lovey to Taylor and set her on the ground. "Tomi, lower Jason over the side. I'll catch him."

Tomi dragged the blanket with Jason lying on it to the edge of the roof. Then she pushed him over the side. P.R. awkwardly caught Jason in his arms. The boy was heavy and didn't move, but his body was warm.

P.R. pressed his fingers against Jason's neck and felt the thumping. He was alive and breathing.

Tomi threw down the blanket. P.R. knelt and laid Jason on it.

Only Tomi was left on the roof. He would have to coax her down. He stood, but before he could plant his feet, she leaped off the roof.

She was flying, like Wonder Woman soaring through the air. She smacked against his bare chest. He stumbled backward and wrapped his arms around her. She smelled of fire and smoke and felt like heaven. He never wanted to let go.

He would tell her that later. Right now he had to get them away from the house. "The machine shed," he yelled. It was metal and down by the lake, far enough away to be safe from falling debris.

He wrapped Jason in the blanket and hefted him into his arms. Tomi picked up Taylor. As he ran toward the lake, Tomi ran beside him.

They were running together. Her legs were shorter, but somehow she was staying with him, matching his distance. Their rhythm was one.

His feet raced through the grass. This time the words in his head were different. This time they were not his dad's words pounding him down telling him he couldn't do it. They were Tomi's words lifting him up telling him he could. "We make it. We make it."

"Yes, yes, yes," his heart answered. "Together we can do it."

Breathless, they raced to the machine shed and stopped. Behind the closed door the dogs frantically barked. He pulled out his cell phone and dial 911. Tomi unhooked the padlock and slid the door open. They ran into the shed. The dogs jumped and barked around them.

The fire department would be too late. The house would burn to the ground. The thick grass would scorch and die.

But the three of them were alive.

When he finished telling Ace the story, P.R. felt emotionally and physically drained. Ace had listened, but even after he'd heard the details, he still seemed to think P.R. was a hero. "They might not have made it off the roof if you hadn't shown up."

P.R. didn't agree. Tomi had rescued the kids from the house. She would have found a way to get them off the roof because somehow she'd found a way to rescue not just the kids, but him, too.

She believed in him. When she jumped from the roof, she hadn't called out for him to catch her. She flew to him and trusted that he would be there. And he'd caught her.

Ace said, "I'm grateful to both of you. You saved my kids—and my life."

Ace was right. It had taken both of them to rescue Taylor and Jason.

Then Ace asked the question P.R. had feared. "Do you know how the fire started?"

P.R. buried his face in his hands. He would have to own up to it. "Yes." His voice was barely a whisper. "It was my fault."

CHAPTER THIRTY

Tomi lay in the emergency room of the hospital, alone. The cubicle was cold and smelled antiseptic. A green curtain was pulled across the foot of the bed and blocked her view. Footsteps rushed up and down the hall, and somewhere a TV droned on.

Exhausted, she closed her eyes. The room turned hot. Flames shot up around her. She couldn't breathe. Gasping, she jerked up and gulped for air. She waited for the room to stop spinning and then collapsed against the pillow.

She had been trapped in the burning house, only this time Taylor's bedroom window wouldn't open. This time she couldn't get out.

But she had made it out. Earlier, Quinn had visited her. "Taylor's fine. They're keeping her overnight, just as a precaution, but-but Jason's still unconscious."

Jason's bedroom was at the top of the stairs. He had breathed in the most smoke. What if Tomi hadn't reached him in time?

What would happen to Quinn and Ace's marriage if Jason didn't recover? After Hiro's death, her own parents' marriage had cracked, until they found a new focus—Tomi and her life. Even in America, she couldn't break free from their expectations. She could feel their disappointment that she had not married.

Footsteps paused outside her room. Maybe it was P.R. She wanted to see him, make sure he was all right. He had saved them. He had charged across the lawn like a fearless Power Ranger and rescued them from the roof. She had tried to tell him how brave he was, but he looked away as if he felt guilty.

She wanted to reassure him. Where was he? Why hadn't he come to see her? Had he inhaled too much smoke? Her heart missed a beat. Maybe he'd gone back to Chicago.

A wave of loneliness washed over her. She was in a foreign country, and she'd lost her anchor. She wished she had the porcelain frog. Then she wouldn't feel so alone. Whenever she rubbed her fingers over the frog, she felt as if her brother were still with her.

Quinn and Ace had lost so much. She had only lost a few clothes and the frog. It seemed selfish to be upset over a tiny frog, even though it was all she had left of her brother—except her memories.

She unwrapped a memory, a happy time, the day she and Hiro had visited Tokyo Disneyland and had ridden Space Mountain. From the outside, the ride resembled a white, cone-shaped mountain. They joined the long line of people moving slowly. Once inside, they were surrounded by darkness. They inched up ramps that wound around the mountain, going up and up and up.

Half-way to the top, the ride no longer seemed fun. She couldn't see the roller coaster, but she could hear the clickety-clack of the wheels on the track and the screams of the passengers. She wanted to go back.

But she was trapped, packed inside with all the people. There was no way down.

Hiro squeezed her hand. "Don't be scared. I'm with you."

She held his hand, gripping it tightly until they reached the top. When they climbed into the coaster, Tomi's heart pumped. Then the ride took off, and they were flying down into a dark hole. She kept her eyes open, but she couldn't see where they were going. She didn't know when to lean right or left. She felt off balance.

The ride lasted three minutes. To her it seemed like thirty. She screamed all the way to the end of the tunnel. She didn't relax until the ride coasted to a stop.

She climbed out, laughing. She pulled on Hiro's arm, trying to coax him back in line. "Let's ride again."

"It won't be the same," he said. "This time we'll know where we're going."

"That's why it will be better."

But Hiro was right. Knowing what was ahead wasn't always better. She was glad she had not known that would be the last time she would go to Disneyland, or anywhere, with Hiro.

She also wished she did not know what lay ahead when she returned to Japan. Usually she could push it away, but today she couldn't.

Letting P.R. kiss her had been a mistake. She thought if she felt his kiss just once, she would be satisfied. But she wasn't. Before P.R.'s kiss, she hadn't known the mysteries of her body. That kiss had awakened them, and she couldn't go back.

Her father would be displeased. He always lectured her. She must be a good girl. She must guard her reputation. She must be pure, a virgin, when she married Yoshiro.

Yoshiro. The name sent prickly needles down her spine. The marriage had been arranged, just as her parents' and grandparents' marriages had been arranged. Most of her friends were fortunate. Their parents were not stuck in the old ways. They allowed their daughters to choose their husbands. But the old ways had worked for her father, so he thought they would work for her.

Her father and Yoshiro's father were best friends. They had grown up together, worked together, and now the two families would be united when Tomi became Yoshiro's wife.

Yoshiro was five years older than Tomi, and before the tsunami, he'd had a solid job. Her friend, Chie, always told her how lucky she was. Tomi did not feel lucky.

Yoshiro did not look at her the way Ace looked at Quinn. In fact, Yoshiro did not seem to even like her. He was not a tall man. He was a full inch shorter than she was. Standing next to him made her feel awkward.

He liked to joke about her height. "I have Amazon woman." She did not think her size pleased him. Nor did she think he was pleased when she expressed her own opinions rather than agreeing with him.

She had gone out with Yoshiro many times, but always in a group. He never tried to pull her aside and be with her privately. The night before she left for America, they had gone with friends to a movie. She couldn't even remember what they saw. Yoshiro sat next to her, chomping on his popcorn, while she nervously thought about what she must tell him.

When the movie ended, he rose, but she stayed seated and whispered, "We need to talk."

He sat and waved the others to go on without them.

She clasped her hands in her lap to keep them from shaking and kept her head down. "Tomorrow I go to America."

His voice was harsh. "So you disobey your father."

"No, he gave his permission." She took a long breath and forced out her words, "Because I agreed to set the wedding date when I return." Then she quickly added, "If you still want to marry me." She had hoped he would say he did not want to marry her. She had convinced herself it would be so. He did not seem to like her. Why would he want to marry her?

But Yoshiro put his arm around her shoulders as if claiming her as his prize. "I will honor my father's wishes."

He leaned closer. His breath smelled of tobacco. He thought smoking made him look more Western. He smoked Golden Bat, unfiltered cigarettes that left bits of dried tobacco between his large yellow teeth.

Suddenly he pulled her closer and pressed his lips against hers, kissing her. Even the salty popcorn could not disguise the taste of tobacco. She pursed her lips and quickly drew away. The kiss had been distasteful and made her mouth feel dirty.

She thought P.R.'s kiss would be much the same, except for the tobacco taste. But P.R.'s kiss had been tender. That kiss opened the door of the cage and made her heart sing. Now it would be even harder to close that door and return to Japan to marry Yoshiro. She must not let P.R. kiss her again. She must be a dutiful daughter.

Heavy footsteps walked down the hospital hallway. P.R. She sat up straighter and raked her fingers through her long hair.

The curtain opened. The doctor walked in. He stopped at the foot of the bed and read the tablet in his hand. "I have your test results."

Tomi blinked back tears of disappointment.

———

P.R. paused in the hallway outside Tomi's room and tucked the borrowed shirt into his jeans. His clothes reeked of smoke. His hair was filled with soot. He needed to shower. But even more pressing was the need to see Tomi, make sure she was all right.

His mind kept replaying her flying off the roof and into his arms. His chest had been bare and her nightgown thin. He could still feel her body, those feminine curves and the way she fit against him in all the right places.

He looked up and down the hospital corridor. No one was around to chase him away. He pushed back the curtain and slipped into the cubicle.

Tomi sat up in bed. Doc Morgan stood behind her. His stethoscope was pressed against her back. As she took deep breaths, her blue hospital gown slipped from her shoulder revealing the swell of her breasts.

He stared. Even in a hospital gown, she looked beautiful, but he was imagining how she would look without it.

"Breathe in and out again." Doc Morgan stopped and turned toward P.R. "What do you want?"

What he wanted was for Doc Morgan to remove his hands from his woman. *His woman.* What was he thinking? He wasn't thinking. He could only feel. He'd never felt this kind of jealousy spewing inside him.

Doc Morgan's tone was stern. "P.R., you need to leave so I can finish examining the patient before she's admitted."

"Admitted?" P.R. rushed forward. Fear gripped him. "What's wrong?"

Tomi looked up at him. "P.R., you okay?"

"I'm fine. What about you?"

"I fine, too." She smiled and he was able to breathe again.

Doc Morgan cleared his throat. "If you'll step out of the room, P.R., I can finish."

P.R. staggered back, bumping into a chair and almost knocking it over. "I'll-I'll go check on Taylor and Jason. Then I'll return."

———

In the adjoining room, Ace clutched Jason's hand as he sat in a chair next to the bed. The cold room buzzed with medical personnel. The emergency nurse went through a string of questions.

No, Jason wasn't allergic to any medication, at least that Ace knew of. No, he didn't know if Jason had breathed in anything toxic. No, Ace didn't know if Jason had hit his head. *No, no, no.*

Ace had a list of his own questions. Why was it taking so long? Why wasn't the helicopter here? Why was Jason still unconscious?

Ace didn't have those answers either.

He continued to grip his son's hand. They had removed Jason's clothes, and the blue hospital gown made him look so small. He was hooked up to an IV, an oxygen tube, and various other machines that blinked with numbers that people recorded on tablets and charts.

Ace glanced up at the large round clock over Jason's bed. It ticked off another minute. It was after three a.m. The longer Jason remained unconscious, the worse his condition would be.

Hickory Hills Community Hospital was more like a triage station that assessed the patients and then sent them on to another hospital. Jason was being helicoptered to Barnes in St. Louis.

Another minute ticked by. Ace looked back at Jason. Nothing had changed. Jason lay listlessly, his arms at his side.

Jason had to wake up. He had to. If he didn't...Ace wouldn't let his mind go there. Instead he thought about Jason's birth. When Stephanie told Ace she was pregnant, they weren't married. He wasn't sure he was ready to be a father, but he wasn't the type of guy to leave a woman holding the baby. His baby. So he married her. After all, it took two to tango.

The first time Ace held Jason, the world changed. Jason's tiny hand had clutched onto one of Ace's fingers, and as Ace drew him closer, Jason's heart beat against his. Ace had peered down at his son cradled in his arms. "Hey, little man."

Jason's bright eyes peered up at him, so trusting. Ace's chest swelled. He wanted to be a father—not an ordinary father—the kind Jason deserved.

Ace looked down at Jason now and mouthed those same words. "Hey, little man."

No response. Ace dropped his head. He had failed. He should have known something was wrong. Quinn had sensed Taylor and Jason were in danger. How could he have slept when Jason was gasping for air?

Ace glanced at the hospital clock again. Two more minutes gone. He looked back at Jason and willed his eyes to move. When Jason was first being assessed his eyes had twitched.

But later when Doc Morgan shined a light right into Jason's eyes, they hadn't flinched.

"What you saw was a reflexive movement," Doc explained. "Involuntary."

Ace stared up at the clock. Each minute ticked away another year of his life. Why was this happening now? After years of loneliness and frustration, he was on the verge of real happiness. When Stephanie divorced him, she had been awarded custody. Ace had been restricted to seeing Jason a few times a month and every other holiday. Ace wanted his son in his life every day. He wanted to be a full-time father.

In August, when Stephanie remarried, she had agreed that while she was living in London, Jason could stay with him. On Sunday, Ace had married Quinn. (Oh God, had the wedding been only three days ago?) For the first time in years, his life was good. If only Jason would wake up.

The world needed Jason, and Ace needed Jason, too. Ace wanted his son to experience life, have it all—grow up, graduate, get married, and have his own son.

It could still happen, if Jason would only wake up and give him that goofy grin.

The curtain rustled. Ace glanced at P.R. standing in the doorway. He motioned with his head for Ace to come into the hall.

Ace didn't want to leave. The nurse was preparing to intubate Jason. But maybe P.R. had news about Taylor. She seemed all right. Quinn was with her, but Ace was worried about Taylor, too.

Reluctantly, Ace let go of Jason's hand. "I'll be right back, son."

Ace walked to the doorway. Sounds from a TV down the hall mixed with the machines hooked up to Jason.

"Any change?" P.R. asked.

Ace kept his eyes on Jason. "No, and Doc Morgan said..." Ace cleared his throat. He couldn't finish. "What about Taylor?"

"They're keeping her over night, but she'll probably go home tomorrow."

"Good. Good." He didn't need anything else to worry about.

P.R. stroked his beard, the way he did when he talked about unpleasant legal stuff. "I'll stay with Jason if you want to make some calls."

Ace shook his head. "I don't want to leave. The helicopter should be here any minute."

"You need to phone Jason's mom, unless you've already called her."

Stephanie. That's what P.R. wanted to talk about. Ace knew he needed to call her. "I'll phone her later...when Jason wakes up."

Ace was glad P.R. didn't ask, what if Jason didn't wake up?

But P.R. had switched into lawyer mode. "Stephanie's in London. If she's going to come, it'll take a while."

Ace gritted his teeth and lowered his voice. "I do not want Stephanie here harping about how I couldn't take care of our son for a few weeks." Guilt weighed on him. He began to pace in front of the door.

"I'm your lawyer, Ace, and I'm advising you that Stephanie needs to know."

He glared at P.R. "Well, then, lawyer, you make the call."

P.R. paused and seemed to consider this. "I could do that. But are you sure you want me to? What if Jason were with Stephanie and her lawyer called you because Jason was in the hospital? How would you react?"

Ace stopped pacing. His shoulders slumped. "You're right. I should call her. You'll stay with Jason, won't you?"

P.R. nodded.

The TV sounds were louder. Someone must have changed the channel. Dogs were barking. It sounded like the movie he and Jason had watched about a dog's life.

Ace tried to move his feet. He stared at the clock again. He needed to call Stephanie, but he was afraid to leave. Maybe the helicopter would come while he was gone.

He looked back at Jason. His hand. Hadn't both arms been lying at his side? Now Jason's right hand was next to the railing.

Ace stopped breathing. He willed Jason's hand to move. Ace eyed the clock and then Jason. Clock...Jason...Clock...Jason. One minute passed. Then two. Jason's hand didn't move.

Ace looked at Jason's face. His eyelashes. They fluttered. Ace's heart hammered. Jason's eyes had twitched before. It was that reflexive movement that Doc Morgan had told him about. Not anything voluntary, just a natural involuntary twitch.

"Call me if anything changes," Ace said to P.R.

P.R. nodded and waved him away. "Make the call."

Ace willed his feet to move. They did, but they moved toward the bed. He was being drawn to Jason. He stopped near the side of the bed and patted the cowlick in Jason's hair. "I'll just be gone a minute, son. You know how your mother worries."

"Okay, Dad." The words were barely a whisper.

Ace leaned over the bed. "Jason! Jason!"

Jason's eyes opened.

Joy and relief washed over Ace.

"Dad...where's...Babe?"

Babe. Jason's puppy, the one that had died a few weeks ago. Ace didn't want to upset Jason, so he didn't answer the question. Instead Ace gathered Jason into his arms and pulled him tightly against his chest.

Machines started to beat.

But what Ace heard was the beating of Jason's heart against his, the way it had done the first time he had cradled Jason in his arms.

"Dad, where's Babe?" Jason asked again. "He was barking?"

The nurse tried to squeeze in next to him. "Sir, I need you to step away."

Reluctant to let go, Ace continued holding onto his son.

Jason coughed. "Dad, you're holding me too tight." Then Jason gave Ace that goofy grin. "You're slobbering all over me."

Ace choked back a sob. He stepped aside and let the nurse in.

But he already knew his son was back. This was his Jason, not a different boy, but the son he needed and loved.

CHAPTER THIRTY-ONE

Wednesday afternoon P.R. hurried along Michigan Avenue, skirting people as he rushed to the office. In the mornings on the way to work, he passed men and women swinging briefcases or balancing Starbucks' cups. Now the people he passed dangled shopping bags or talked on cell phones.

At least by this time of day the riffraff were gone. He didn't mind the musicians with their beat-up guitar cases propped open for a dollar or two. Music brightened the world. Even the men who hustled to shine shoes provided a service. But the freeloaders with their coffee cans and cardboard signs irritated him.

When he first started working downtown, he'd slip a dollar or two into an outstretched hand. He had a good paying job, so he could help out his fellow man. After all, who was he to judge?

"Sucker," the lawyer next to him smirked one day as P.R. dropped a dollar into a guy's bucket. The lawyer was a rising star in P.R.'s firm. "These guys just want money for booze or drugs."

P.R. shrugged. "That's on them, not me."

Now, though, P.R. had learned to do what most people did—walk by without ever meeting their eyes.

But today as he rushed toward his building, a voice from behind called out, "Hey, Mr. P.R. Where ya been?"

P.R. didn't turn around. He recognized the voice, a beggar who P.R.

used to regularly slip a few bucks. But he didn't have any bills smaller than a twenty. Besides, it irked him that the guy had somehow found out his name.

P.R.'s conscience nudged him. *At least turn around and wave.*

The guy called out again. "Hey, Mr. P.R. You just get back from Italy?"

Italy? Where did that come from? P.R. straightened his tie and pulled open the door. He strode to the elevator and punched the button for the tenth floor. He had more important things to deal with today.

As he walked into the law office of Spader, Kirk, and Lloyd, he hoped no one would waylay him for details about his extended weekend. He needed to get caught up on the Abrams' trial scheduled to begin Monday.

Alexander Abrams was accused of killing his twin brother for the family fortune. He had called 911 from his brother's estate and reported his brother dead. Alexander had also been shot.

His client said he'd been at his brother's when they'd heard an intruder. They separated to investigate. The downstairs was dark, and as Alexander rounded the corner in the living room, a bullet struck his shoulder. He fired back. He heard a thud and crept over to the lights. He flipped the switch and saw his brother lying on the carpet, in a pool of blood. It could have happened that way, and P.R.'s job was to make sure the jury believed it did.

As he hurried by the cubicles, no one looked up from their phones or computers. With all the recent cuts, everyone was extremely busy. Still it was odd not to see anyone's welcoming smile. His desk wasn't piled with papers either. Nothing but a yellow sticky note tucked into the corner of the desk pad. *See me. L*

Uh-oh. He hoped Mr. Lloyd wasn't replacing him on the Abrams' case. He and Ashleigh had spent months prepping for trial. The red light on his desk phone was blinking. He needed to listen to his messages. But first he'd talk to the head honcho.

As he walked out his office door, he came face to face with Ashleigh.

"I see you finally made it back."

P.R. hoped they could still have a professional relationship. "I can stay late and work with you on the Abrams' case."

She shook her head. "I have everything covered."

"Great. I need to see the boss. Then you can fill me in."

She gave him a quick wave of her hand with her fire-engine red nails and strutted away.

Ten minutes later, P.R. sagged in the chair in front of Mr. Lloyd's desk. *Fired.* The word punched him in the gut. Lloyd hadn't actually said *fired.* No one used that word anymore. *Pink-slipped, indefinite leave, down-sized* were today's buzz words. But the results were the same. He didn't have a job—or a pay check.

P.R. had worked for the firm for almost three years. He'd even dreamed about becoming partner. He waited for anger or hurt to well up inside him. Instead, he felt numb.

Mr. Lloyd peered at him over the half glasses propped on his prominent nose. "Of course, you'll be pleased with your severance package." Mr. Lloyd picked at an imaginary speck of lint on his suit sleeve as he waited for P.R. to respond.

What could P.R. say? Yes, he'd been through multiple associate reviews, but did he really want to work for a firm that thought he was easily dispensable? For the last twelve months, he'd been dreading this. But he'd convinced himself that if he worked hard, it would be the other guy, the slacker, not him. So P.R. had put in extra hours, not even billing the firm. He rarely took off, except for this weekend. And his success rate at trial trailed only that of Ashleigh's.

Mr. Lloyd cleared his throat. "Of course, your letter of recommendation will be stellar." Then Mr. Lloyd stood and stuck out his hand. "You're a fine lawyer, P.R. I wish it would have worked out differently."

P.R. rose and shook the man's hand. "So do I."

On his way back to his office, P.R. squared his shoulders and waited for his father's voice to scream at him. "Screw-up." But he didn't hear his father. Inside something had changed.

He'd just lost his job. His life plan had been shredded, but he wasn't as devastated as he'd expected. He had enough faith in himself to believe he'd find a job with another Chicago firm. He would update his resume, look up a few contacts, and make some phone calls. Finding another job wouldn't be easy. The search might take five or six months. At least he hadn't put money down on the condo.

When he walked into his office, a cardboard box sat on top his desk and next to it stood the stocky security guard. For the last year, the guard had escorted other pink-slipped workers out of the building. Each time P.R. imagined how terrible it would be and had been grateful some other poor bloke was carrying out a cardboard box. His face flushed with humiliation. Now he was that poor bloke.

Displayed on his desk were family pictures. He placed the pictures, face down, into the box and opened his drawer. Nothing much there. From the wall he took down the framed diploma from Northwestern and his certificate for passing the bar exam.

He closed the cardboard box with three years of his life bundled inside. "Guess that's it."

On the way out, he passed Ashleigh's office. She looked up from her desk and smiled as she gave him a dismissive wave of her hand. A troubling thought crossed his mind. Ashleigh had volunteered to put in a word for him. What if she had, only it hadn't been a good word? Maybe her nail polish should be called she-devil red.

P.R. rode the elevator down and stepped out of the building.

The beggar was still there. "Hey, P.R. Looks like you just got canned."

He cringed. Losing his job was humiliating. He didn't need a public announcement.

The man scurried up and stood directly in front of him. He gave P.R. a gap-toothed grin. "Well, now you can take that trip to Italy."

Italy. There it was again. For the first time, P.R. really looked at the guy with the stringy blond hair. Was this someone he knew?

During his freshman year, he'd transferred into the Chicago public schools and had been an outsider. In geography class the teacher had assigned the students to plan an itinerary for a two-week vacation in a foreign country. Since P.R. was fascinated by Greek and Roman mythology, he chose Italy. So did another kid named Peter. The kid's nickname was Peewee, although he actually stood a few inches taller than P.R. Peewee always wore a plain white T-shirt, except it was never white, and high-water pants.

After they were paired up, Peewee began hanging around P.R. They had little in common, but since P.R. didn't have any other friends, he was grateful to have someone to sit with in the cafeteria.

One day someone called Peewee P.W. For the rest of the year, they were the P's brothers.

Now P.R. studied the sunken cheeks and sallow face of the man in front of him. He wore a dingy T-shirt and high-water jeans. But this couldn't be

Peewee, could it? Then he noticed the guy's hands. His fingers curled into a fist, as he opened and closed them, the way Peewee used to do.

"Peewee?" The name just popped out.

The guy gave him that gap-toothed grin. "I wondered if you recognized me."

"No, no, I didn't," P.R. admitted. "Not until right now."

"I thought maybe that was why you used to give me money."

"What-what happened?" P.R. asked, trying to come to grips with this bedraggled beggar being the kid he'd known in school.

Peewee's hands opened and closed several times. He looked away and shrugged. Finally he said, "Choices, man, choices."

P.R. shuffled the cardboard box to one side and reached into his pocket. He pulled out a couple of twenties. "I won't be around here anymore." He pressed the bills into Peewee's hand. "Take care of yourself."

"Thanks, Mr. P.R."

"Hey, what's with that mister stuff? I'm just P.R. and you're P.W."

For a moment, their eyes met, and they connected as if they were once again sitting at the table in the high school cafeteria.

Peewee worked his mouth as if he were about to say something, but the phone in P.R.'s suit coat vibrated. He pulled it out. On the screen was a message from his brother-in-law Ben. *Need fire info. When in HH?*

Police business, P.R. thought. He looked up from his phone. Peewee had already moved on, shuffling down the sidewalk, opening and closing his fists.

Choices, the word echoed in P.R.'s head. He remembered his wish the night he and Tomi had watched the stars. *More days like this.*

He texted his answer to Ben. *ASAP.*

CHAPTER THIRTY-TWO

Friday afternoon, P.R. sat at the desk across from his brother-in-law, Sheriff Ben Campbell. P.R. finished reading his statement about the fire, signed his name, and pushed it back across the desk. Ben slipped the paper into a manila folder.

P.R. admired Ben. He wasn't one of those big-bellied, donut cops. Ben ran marathons, lifted weights, and kept himself fit.

Ben leaned back in his chair and locked his hands behind his head. "I guess we'll be seeing more of you, since you're taking over Jackson's law practice."

"It's temporary." P.R. had sent out a dozen resumes and made several personal phone calls. Until something came up in Chicago, he'd work at Jackson's law office.

"This weekend the boys have a big soccer tournament."

Soccer? P.R. had promised his nephews he'd come to one of their baseball games, but summer was over and he hadn't gone. Why not? He remembered looking up in the stands for his father and vowed to be there for his nephews.

"Have you seen the twins today?" Ben grinned. "Those girls are cute little pixies."

"Not yet," P.R. said. "When are they moving into that fancy new house Carter promised?"

"According to Raven, Carter needs to close a few more deals. We don't mind Raven and the twins staying at the Castle, but Belle can't help much with the babies."

"Mom isn't coming for two weeks, so who's helping Raven now?" P.R. asked.

A knock on the door interrupted them. Ben straightened in his chair and became all business again. "Come in."

A female police officer with a holster strapped to her hips stepped inside. "We're ready in Room Two."

Ben nodded. "I'd like to go over a few more details about the fire, P.R."

"I've told you everything I know."

But when Ben picked up the folder and rose, P.R. followed him out of the room and down the hall. His carelessness had endangered others. At least he could cooperate in the investigation.

Ben opened the door to the small interrogation room. P.R. walked in. At the table sat Quinn and Tomi. His breath caught. Tomi's hair was pulled back into some kind of fancy braid that hung over her shoulder. The style suited her delicate face and wide eyes. When those eyes met his, they lit up the room—and him.

On the drive from Chicago, P.R. had questioned his rash decision to temporarily move to Hickory Hills. Now, looking at Tomi, he couldn't deny the surge rushing through him. The room crackled with electricity. He felt something more than physical attraction.

He tried to make sense of it. What connected one person to another? He thought about those few seconds he had connected with Peewee. Tomi was from a foreign country. They spoke different languages. But he was drawn to her in a way he couldn't explain even to himself.

Ben cleared his throat. "Are you ready, P.R.?"

P.R. pulled his eyes away from Tomi and looked at Ben. "What?"

Ben closed the door and pointed with the folder toward the chair next to Tomi.

P.R. settled into the chair, and Ben sat across from them. "You've both given statements about the fire, but it might be helpful if we went over them together. Maybe it will jog your memories."

P.R. squirmed and rubbed his hands on the knees of his pants. He didn't want Tomi to find out the fire might have been his fault. Once she knew that, she would probably go back to thinking he was the devil.

Quinn glanced at her wristwatch. "Tomi, I have to pick up the kids from school. If you don't understand anything, ask P.R."

Tomi looked over at P.R. and smiled.

P.R. sank lower in his chair. He only wished he deserved that smile.

After Quinn left, Ben opened the folder and turned on the recorder. "I'm going to read each statement aloud. If you think of something, feel free to interrupt."

P.R. hoped Ben would go over his statement so fast Tomi wouldn't be able understand it. Ben, however, started reading Tomi's first.

P.R. listened intently. When Ben came to the question about possible causes of the fire, Tomi had answered *gas stove*.

"No," P.R. said. "That wasn't the cause."

Tomi folded her hands in her lap and lowered her head. "After you left, I boil water for tea. Maybe I no shut off stove."

He couldn't let Tomi think she was the cause. The kitchen was already engulfed in flames before the explosion. "It wasn't you," he quickly assured her. "I started the fire."

Her eyes widened.

His throat tightened, but he had to get it out, tell her what really happened. "I think some ashes might have been left from our wiener roast."

Tomi shook her head. "No fire in ashes. You put out."

"I thought I put them out. But—" A lump filled his throat. He couldn't tell her that he had been distracted by her and their kiss.

"You put out," Tomi said firmly. "I stood at window. You use water and kick ashes many times. No spark. Fire out."

She sounded so convincing. "Are you sure?"

"*Hai*. No fire." She turned to Ben. "P.R. hero. No start fire. Probably gas stove."

P.R. shook his head. "It couldn't have been the stove because—"

"Stop!" Ben raised his hands, palms outward. "I don't want either of you beating yourselves up. No one else we've talked to believes either of you caused the fire."

P.R. rubbed his chin. "Then what caused it?"

Ben turned off the recorder. "The fire marshals were here Wednesday and Thursday."

"Fire marshals?" repeated P.R.

"The fire chief noticed some things that looked suspicious. The final report isn't complete, so this is highly confidential. Quinn and Ace are the only ones outside the department who know that fire marshals found signs of arson."

"Arson?" P.R. repeated the word and then explained it to Tomi.

She put a hand over her mouth. "Oh, so bad."

"I hoped one of you might remember something suspicious about that day, a stranger asking for directions or an unfamiliar car driving by."

P.R. scratched his head. "We rode bikes to the old mine, but I didn't see any cars along the way. Do you remember anything unusual, Tomi?"

She shook her head.

"Well, if you think of something, no matter how small, give me a call."

After Ben finished reading, P.R.'s statement, Quinn hurried into the room. "Tomi, are you ready? The kids are waiting in the car."

P.R. wanted to talk to Tomi, but she rose, gave a little bow, and scurried out of the room.

After the door shut, P.R. sat there, thinking about what Ben had said. What if the fire marshals were right? What if someone had purposely set Ace's house on fire? But who would do that? And why?

CHAPTER THIRTY-THREE

Bucky parked his car in the alley and stared up at the light in the third-story window of the Castle. For the past few days, fire marshals and dogs had poked and sniffed through the rubble at Ace's house. When Bucky had set the fire, he hadn't been concerned about arson. He'd worn the white wig and beard and thought Zeus would be blamed.

But Zeus had been captured, and the Japanese woman standing at the door might have seen his face. She had gone to the sheriff's office for the past three days. Maybe she was working with a sketch artist. He didn't want to open the *Hickory Hills Journal* and see his face plastered all over the front page like the fire had been.

The *Journal* had printed a half-page picture of the fire and had listed the people in the house as Tomoe Kanai (Tomi), Jason Edleston, and Taylor Matthews. The man who had rescued them was Pleasant Rupert Montgomery, P.R.

Bucky hadn't known the kids were in the house. He was glad they hadn't been burned or died, but Tomi was a problem.

Today when he'd followed her from the police station, she had gone to the local B&B owned by the sheriff and his wife. Bucky could think of only one reason Tomi would be staying with the sheriff. Police protection.

As Bucky stared at the Castle, the light in the third-floor window went out. Time to make sure that Japanese woman wasn't able to identify him.

He slipped out of his car and crouched down. He followed the stepping stones through the orchard to the back door. These old houses were easy to break into, if a dead bolt hadn't been installed. He ran the credit card down the jam, heard a click, and turned the knob. The door creaked open.

Stepping inside, he pulled out his phone and shined the light around the kitchen. Across the room stretched a long counter. Next to the sink was a line of canisters and jars. He patted his pocket with the small bag of rat poison. He couldn't just mix the poison into the sugar the way he'd done at Miss May's. A major investigation would be conducted if a whole house full of guests keeled over.

He panned the cell light over the jars of loose tea labeled peach, raspberry, chamomile, and mint. On the end was a small green packet. He paused on the picture of a tea kettle and symbols going up and down. *Bingo.*

He crept across the room and took out his special seasoning. He opened the green packet and sprinkled the rat poison into the thin layer of loose tea. He shook the bag, mixing the tea and the poison. Tomorrow morning Miss Tomi's cup of tea would definitely predict her fortune—or misfortune.

As he began to close the packet, the cell phone in his gloved hand vibrated. He jerked. He wasn't used to the burner phone and fumbled several times before he retrieved his message. *Where can we meet? We need to talk. S*

The phone was supposed to be for emergencies. He didn't want to talk to *S,* but he might as well get it over. He typed in *Springside Mine, tomorrow, 10.* He pressed send and shined the cell back on the Japanese tea bag.

A noise startled him. He turned off the phone light and held his breath. Footsteps padded down the stairs.

He didn't want another bloody incident like in Jackson's office. He needed to finish and get away. Laying his cell phone on the counter, he hurriedly closed the packet of tea.

He tiptoed across the kitchen and pulled open the old wooden door. It creaked. He quickly closed it, turning the knob to make sure it was locked.

The moon had disappeared under a cloud. He squinted into the darkness, searching for the stones leading to the alley. He took several tentative steps and stumbled. He stopped and reached into his pocket for his phone.

His pocket was empty. He slapped his hand on his forehead. The cell phone was lying on the counter. He turned back to the Castle.

CHAPTER THIRTY-FOUR

Tomi turned off the light in the nursery. Both babies were asleep in their basinets at the foot of Raven's bed. At least for now.

Two days ago when Quinn and Tomi had visited Raven, the scene had been chaotic. The twins were squalling and Raven was sobbing. "Carter went back to work, and Mom isn't coming for two more weeks. What am I going to do?"

Tomi lifted one of the twins from Raven's arm and cooed softly in Japanese. The baby nestled against her and quit crying.

Raven blinked back tears. "That's amazing. Meggie is so fussy. She usually won't let anyone hold her, except me."

Tomi smiled down at the baby. A mothering instinct flooded through her. "I help."

Raven wiped her wet cheeks with her hands. "Really? Could you stay at the Castle with us?"

"*Hai.* If Quinn agrees."

Quinn hesitated, but Raven explained it would be for only two weeks, until Raven's mother came. Besides, Ace had moved into the loft. When Jason was released from the hospital, he would stay there, too. The loft, with its two bedrooms and one bath, would be crowded. But that wasn't the reason Tomi had volunteered. From the minute she picked up the baby, she had been overwhelmed with love.

She had never been around infants before, but she already knew what each twin liked and how they acted. Morgan was lively, always ready to go. Quiet Meggie liked to be held. Morgan slept as soon as her eyes shut. If Meggie's eyes were shut and her brow was wrinkled, it meant she wasn't sleeping.

Tomi tiptoed out of the nursery. Nightlights near the baseboards illuminated the hallway and stairs. She stopped in her room next to the nursery for a robe to cover her baby doll pajamas before she went downstairs to fix a cup of tea. She didn't expect to see anyone. The doors to the Castle were locked at nine p.m., and the kitchen was off limits to regular guests.

The wooden steps creaked as she carefully tiptoed down the three flights of stairs. On the main floor in the dining room, where the wedding reception had been held, she felt a cold draft. She shivered and drew the sash of her robe tighter. Ghosts and spirits could be lurking in the dark shadows.

She hurried into the smaller tea room. At the far end, swinging shutters, which reminded her of saloon doors in Western movies, led to the kitchen.

She pushed open the doors. Moon light from the tall window cast shadows across the wooden floor. As she stood in the dark, goose bumps rippled up her arms.

She hurried to the stove to fix a cup of hot tea. As the water boiled, she thought about P.R. She had tried to forget him, but today when he walked into the room at the sheriff's office, her heart betrayed her. She felt so much joy just seeing him, but they could never be together. She had promised to marry Yoshiro. Yet her heart would not listen.

The kettle whistled. She opened the package of barley tea, sprinkled some into her cup, and poured hot water over it. She set it on the table and waited for the tea to steep. Outside, the wind picked up. Something tapped against the window. She jumped. A tree branch scratched against the glass.

She laughed at herself. She picked up the tea, brought it to her lips. She blew on the hot liquid and set it back down to cool. She was still unsettled because Sheriff Ben had said the fire might have been set on purpose.

Memories of that night swirled in her head. After P.R. had left, the dogs had been barking. She'd walked to the patio door to look out. Until now, she hadn't remembered that odd feeling that someone had been lurking in the shadows. But she hadn't seen anyone. Just a feeling of evil. No use mentioning that.

She started to pick up her cup. Something squeaked. This time it wasn't a branch against the glass. Light from the opposite window shined on the door. The brass knob turned. Someone was on the other side of the door. Sheriff Ben was already home, and a guest would use the front door.

The door rattled as someone pushed against it. Sheriff Ben was upstairs. She would wake him. She jumped up, bumping her leg against the table. Her cup tipped over, and tea spilled onto the floor. She sucked in a breath.

The rattling stopped. Footsteps slapped against the brick stones leading to the alley.

Who could have been trying to get in? Sheriff Ben would know what to do. She didn't stop to mop up the spilled tea, but rushed through the swinging door.

The front door rattled.

Her hand flew to her mouth. The door squeaked open and closed. Footsteps sounded in the hallway.

Maybe a guest with a key had come in late. She waited. The light switch didn't turn on. The footsteps moved toward the dining room.

Next was the tea room, where she was standing. She had to hide. She dropped to her knees, crawled through the swinging door and into the kitchen. Her eyes searched for a place she wouldn't be seen. The corner next to the swinging door was dark. She flattened herself against the wall. When the person came into the kitchen, she could slip under the door and run upstairs.

She held her breath. The footsteps grew closer. Her heart jumped as the person walked into the tea room. She counted the steps: one, two, three, four. The saloon-style doors swung open.

Tomi rolled her eyes to the side. A large man stood in the middle of the swinging doors. Light from the window illuminated the outline of his body filling the frame, but his face was obscured.

The man took long strides into the kitchen.

What if this was the person who had started the fire? She had to run upstairs to protect the babies. She had to warn Belle and her family.

She pressed her back against the wall and slowly slid toward the door.

The man was near the table. She kept her eyes on his back and crouched down to slide under the swinging doors. The man's shoes squeaked. He began to glide across the floor.

He must have slipped on her spilled tea. He slid across the floor, his arms flailing. His feet shot up and he toppled backward. His body thudded against the table.

Tomi's hand flew to her mouth as she gasped.

CHAPTER THIRTY-FIVE

He grabbed the nearest chair and fell into it. A woman sprinted toward him. Arms, legs, hair flickered like disjoined pictures in a flip book. Then they all blended together. Tomi.

P.R. stretched out his arms. She rushed forward and tumbled onto his lap. He must be dreaming. He'd worked late at the law office and was bone tired. But now as he inhaled her intoxicating scent and ran his fingers through her long hair, he was rejuvenated. This was no dream. Tomi was sitting on his lap. Her robe slipped off her shoulders revealing baby-doll pajamas.

Why was she hiding in the kitchen? It didn't matter. All that mattered was Tomi, here in his arms, just where he wanted her to be.

"P.R. P.R." Her voice shook, and she looked like a frightened fawn.

He pulled her closer, reveled in the feel of that silky robe—and her. He planted tiny kisses around her ear and whispered her name. "Tomi."

His lips moved to her mouth. He kissed her gently and sighed as her lips pressed against his. Then she pulled away, plunging him back to reality. But he had felt the passion in the kiss. He wanted more, but something held her back. "What are you afraid of?"

"I hear noise." She pointed toward the kitchen door. "Someone try to break in."

"Oh." Had she purposely misunderstood? "That was me at the front door."

She shook her head. "No, kitchen door."

He spoke slower, making sure she understood. "No one was at the kitchen door. The lock on the front door is old. I had trouble with the key. I'm sorry I frightened you."

She slid off his lap and stood next to the back door. "Someone try to come in." She touched the knob. "This turn." She put her shoulder against the door. "Someone push." Her finger pointed to the lock. "Strong. No break."

P.R.'s brow furrowed. The sheriff lived here. That would deter most people from breaking in. Yet Tomi sounded convinced. Maybe he should check.

He rose and walked to the door. He turned the lock and opened the door. Tomi scurried behind him as he peered outside. Only a few stars twinkled, and the quarter moon moved under the clouds, sending shadows shifting in the dark. "Stay here while I check."

She grabbed his arm. "No. Not safe."

"I'll be fine. Lock up behind me." He didn't want someone sneaking in when he was gone. "I'll use my key and come in the front door."

She tugged on his arm, trying to keep him inside. "Stay."

She was definitely convinced someone had tried to break in. He pointed to his watch. "If I'm not back in five minutes, go upstairs and tell Ben."

He unfurled her fingers from his arm and stepped outside. He waited until the lock clicked and then crept down the brick stones toward the alley. He paused near the grape arbor where he'd found Tomi the night of the reception. Was she feeling bad karma again or had someone tried to break in?

He crept to the alley. A cat yowled, and he jumped. Now she'd made him jittery.

He looked up and down the alley. Nothing suspicious, except an overturned trash can. He returned to the house and circled it. He didn't see anyone. Relieved, he hurried to the front door and unlocked it.

He found Tomi in the kitchen, cowering in the corner, clutching a broom. He took the broom from her hands and set it aside. "No one was outside."

"Maybe we should wake Sheriff Ben."

"You can tell him in the morning." P.R. checked the back door, made sure it was locked, and then turned to face her. "What are you doing at Belle's?" He didn't add and 'in that thin robe and skimpy silk pajamas.'

"Help Raven with babies."

So Tomi was the one helping Raven until his mom came. That meant for the next two weeks, he would be able to see her every day. He moved closer and leaned forward ready to resume their kiss.

She scuttled away and flipped on a switch. Bright lights flooded the room. "So why you here?"

"I lost my job in Chicago." Saying it aloud made the gravity of it sink in. "I'm working in Jackson's office."

He slumped into a chair. He'd finally found a woman he wanted to spend time with and she didn't seem interested. Seeing her every day and not being able to touch her would be torture.

She tilted her head at him. "So sorry about job." Her face flushed. "Will you have cup of tea with me?"

He cleared his throat. "Tea would be nice."

She put the kettle on the stove, and while she waited for the water to boil, she wiped up the wet floor. She fixed his tea and then opened a packet of what looked like Japanese tea. She frowned and tossed it in the trash. Then she fixed another cup of tea like his.

When she put his tea on the table, he reached out and covered her hand with his. "Thank you."

She pulled her hand away and went back to the stove for her tea.

He'd grown up with three sisters, but women still baffled him. With Tomi, the cultural differences made it even more confusing. Maybe he needed to follow some ritual, such as dating first before kissing. Maybe women needed to be chaperoned. The possibilities of what he might be doing wrong were endless.

He'd give it one more shot, see what happened when he tried to kiss her. After she sat next to him, he put his finger under her chin, tilted her face up to his, and leaned forward.

She jerked back. She lowered her head and began blowing on her hot tea.

The message was clear. She didn't want him to kiss her. Maybe she didn't like his kisses. Maybe she didn't even like him. He searched her face, but couldn't find any answers.

He needed something stronger to fortify himself, but all he had was tea. He took a sip of tea. He'd have to swallow his pride and be direct. "Will you answer one question?"

She nodded.

"Why won't you let me kiss you?'

She peeked up at him and waved her hands. "No understand."

Her long black lashes fluttered and her face turned pink. She understood.

He cleared his throat. "I'd like to kiss you. Is there something I should do first? Maybe ask your permission?"

His honesty must have moved her because this time she did not pretend. "No need permission."

"So it's okay if I kiss you?"

She raised her cup and sipped her tea before she answered. "No."

His shoulders sagged. He hadn't expected her to be so blunt, but he needed the truth, no matter how painful. "Do-do you like me?"

Her eyes met his. She didn't hesitate. "I like. Good man."

He sat up. Relief swept through him. At least she liked him. "I like you, too," he said. "Usually in America when a man and woman like each other, they kiss. What do a man and woman do in Japan?"

She placed her cup in the saucer. "Maybe same."

"But I can't kiss you?"

She shook her head. "No kiss."

She said she liked him, and her eyes were looking at him in a way that made him believe her, so he must be doing something wrong. He tried again. "Why can't I kiss you?"

"No can marry me."

A laugh rumbled up in his throat. "Marry?"

Tomi's big brown eyes looked serious.

He choked back his laugh. He'd asked to kiss her. He hadn't proposed. He was a long way from marriage. He couldn't provide for a wife and family. Right now he didn't even have a steady job. All he owned was a car. "So if I promise not to marry you, I can kiss you?"

She pursed her lips and repeated, "No marry."

"Yes, I understand. No marry. But kissing. Is that okay?"

She angled her head and blinked her eyes at him. "Just kiss?"

He held his breath and nodded.

Her lips curved into a smile. "Maybe okay."

He could breathe again. He wasn't sure why she wanted him to promise he wouldn't marry her. Maybe *no marry* was a euphemism for not going to bed together. It didn't matter. He stood up and pulled her to him. He would have promised anything to hold her in his arms and feel her pressed against him.

He drew her closer and leaned down. Her sweet lips tilted up and met his. He groaned and forced himself to hold back, ease into it so she wouldn't pull away.

She didn't. Her lips pressed against his, giving back. He wanted more, so he gave more, opening himself up to her in a way he'd never allowed himself to do with other women.

Tomi melted into him. A passion she didn't know she had erupted. Heat rushed through her. P.R. had saved her from the fire and then again tonight. Being in his arms made her feel safe, yet her body quivered with a longing for something that could never be.

She had been honest with him, told him she could never marry him. But it didn't seem to matter. He was offering what she had come to America to experience—life without her parents watching over her, life where she could be free to make her own choices.

She should not get too involved. She was promised to Yoshiro. But she pushed away those nagging thoughts. She wanted to spend time with P.R., get to know him, and definitely kiss him, again and again. She could not walk away. She'd already crossed the line.

She made her choice. She chose him.

The door to her cage sprung open. She soared, flying higher and higher. Her soul was free.

CHAPTER THIRTY-SIX

Bucky lay on his belly, hidden in Ace's cornfield. The hood of his windbreaker and a black ball cap covered his head and obscured his face. Now that Zeus had been caught, he needed to be more careful. He didn't want to do anything that would link him to Jackson's murder or the fire.

Bucky propped his elbows up in the dirt and aimed his binoculars at the burnt remains of Ace's house. The smell of charred wood hung in the air. He took a deep breath and inhaled the heady scent.

The fire marshals were gone. Today, however, four other people were combing the area near the yard where a greyhound and two other dogs were staked. Bucky adjusted his binoculars and focused on Ace, his wife, Tomi, and P.R.

He was glad he wasn't one of those chumps stuck in an eight-to-five job. He had done that for ten years and brought home a decent paycheck. But he wanted more. His present job had a flexible work schedule which gave him time for extra-curriculars. So far, though, he hadn't been able to get near Tomi. After he'd broken into the B&B, additional police cars patrolled the area, and whenever she left the Castle, P.R. was always with her.

Vvvroom. The sound startled Bucky. He turned his binoculars to Ace sitting on a backhoe. He lowered the bucket and scooped up some of the charred debris. Then he swung the bucket over to the half-full grain truck.

Before Ace dumped the load into the truck, the others, donning masks and gloves, poked through the ruins.

A high-pitched squeal startled Bucky. He shifted the binoculars and watched as Tomi jumped up and down. She seemed excited and hugged everyone, but mostly P.R. She must have found something valuable.

Bucky zoomed in on her as she held out her hand. He focused, trying to get closer. The object in her palm was too small to see. All he could make out was the jade green color.

The wind shifted. The greyhound jumped up and started barking. Tomi went over to pet the dog, straining on the leash.

Bucky scuttled backward into the cornfield until he was far enough away. Then he stood, knocking against cornstalks and racing toward the mine.

The dog was barking. It sounded closer. The stalks behind him rustled. The dog must have broken loose.

The mine, surrounded by the barbed-wire fence, was just ahead. He looked over his shoulder. The dog raced out of the cornfield and flew toward him.

Bucky leaped over the fence, but he wasn't quick enough. The dog caught his pant leg. His sharp teeth dug into his leg. Part of his pants tore loose, and he tumbled over the fence. He rose and rushed toward the car, dragging his injured leg.

The greyhound flew over the fence. Bucky reached the car and opened the door. He slid in. The dog charged toward him. Bucky kicked the dog away, sending it flying, and slammed the door.

He didn't like to hurt dogs, but this dog needed a lesson.

CHAPTER THIRTY-SEVEN

Tomi began to settle in at the B&B. Deadbolts had been installed on all the doors, and a cell phone that didn't belong to any of the guests had been sent to a lab to be analyzed. Even additional patrols drove by the house.

With the extra precautions and P.R. at the Castle, Tomi no longer felt afraid. She loved taking care of the twins. She felt a fierce protectiveness that made her begin to understand her own parents. She delighted in watching Meggie and Morgan grow and discover the world.

Just like the babies, everything at the Castle was new to her, too, and she began to grow, only in a different way. After her brother's death, her happiness had been tamped down by guilt. Hiro should have gone with the family on the train to visit Uncle, not her. How could she be happy when Hiro had been swept away by the tsunami and his body never found?

Coming to America had been his dream. He would not want her to grieve for him while she was here. The day she had helped Ace and Quinn search through the rubble, she thought she had spotted the frog. But that was impossible. The frog had burned in the fire.

Still, she had bent down, reached into the ashes, and pulled out the object with the small spot of green. She ran her fingers over it, wiping away the layers of black soot. Her hands shook. It was not her imagination. She had found her precious frog.

As she held it in the palm of her hand, a sense of peace washed over her. Finding the frog was like a sign from Hiro. He was still watching over her, giving her his blessing. She started to heal in a way she couldn't have in Japan.

Tomi's routine revolved around never-ending diapers, laundry, and bottles, but Raven didn't expect Tomi to spend her entire day taking care of the twins. "You need time for yourself, too."

In the mornings, Tomi rose early and shared coffee with P.R. before he went to work. At night, the whole family gathered in the dining room, Ben at the head of the table and Belle at the other end. Their two boys sat on one side, and she and P.R. on the other. Raven chose to eat on the third floor to be close to the twins.

Sitting at the table and spending time with P.R.'s family made Tomi realize how much the tsunami had taken from her. She had lost more than Grandmother and Hiro. She had lost her entire village. Her parents now lived in temporary housing, surrounded by people she did not know.

With her brother missing and her familiar childhood home swept away, Tomi had floated like a piece of jetsam. Her roots were gone. She yearned for that sense of belonging.

After supper, she and P.R. would often sit on the porch swing or take a walk. She told him about the babies, and he told her about his clients, mostly coal miners with black lung.

The first weekend Carter came back to the Castle, he presented Raven a box of twelve, long-stemmed red roses. She was ecstatic, like a young school girl with her first beau.

Then he walked over to Tomi and pulled a single red rose from behind his back. "For another beautiful lady."

Tomi blushed and bowed. Carter looked dashing in his business suit and tie. He seemed like a thoughtful husband. She wondered why P.R. did not like him.

Then Raven went downstairs for vases. Carter took off his suit coat and stepped closer to Tomi. He wrapped his muscular arms around her. She thought he was going to give her a quick hug. Instead, he planted his large hand firmly in the middle of her back and pressed his body against hers.

His breath smelled like tobacco and reminded her of Yoshiro as he whispered in her ear, "I hear Asian women take very good care of their men."

She tried to wiggle free. His strong arms were like a steel trap. His mouth moved toward her lips.

She could not let him kiss her. Panicking, she pressed the stem of the rose against him. The thorns cut through his shirt and gouged his side.

He jerked back. "What the—"

She scurried across the room and picked up Meggie, who had started to fuss. Tomi did not say 'so sorry.'

She thought Carter must have 'yellow fever,' the nickname for the myth that all Eastern Asian women were sweet, innocent, and submissive. After the jab to his side, he would know she was not sweet and submissive. Tomi did not tell anyone. She was proud she'd been able to handle Carter herself.

But that night at supper, she was still shaken.

"So Tomi, what do you say?" P.R. asked.

She glanced up at him. She had been thinking about Carter's advances. "What?"

"Do you want to go to the movies," P.R. said.

She stared down at her spaghetti. "Maybe another night."

"Prairie Land Theater shows classic movies once a month. Tonight the movie is *Titanic*. I remembered you liked the song."

Tomi didn't lift her head. "I see movie—twice."

"Oh." The joy in his voice flattened. She raised her eyes. He no longer looked happy. She wanted to put the smile back on his face. "But I like to see again."

His smile stretched from ear to ear.

After supper she and P.R. walked the few blocks from the B&B to the theater. On the way, he told her about the movie house. "It was built in the 1940s and has most of the original furnishing. The movie screen is the largest one in downstate Illinois."

When they got closer, the lights from the marquee jutted out over the sidewalk and lit up the block. P.R. stepped up to the outside window and bought two tickets for less than twenty dollars. Tomi was surprised because in Japan a ticket was more expensive.

When they walked into the lobby, she smelled the buttery popcorn.

"You didn't eat much for supper. Would you like some popcorn?" P.R. asked.

"Yes, please."

He picked up two bags from the counter. "Popcorn and soda are included with the tickets."

"American theater so great."

P.R. chuckled. "City theaters cost a lot more."

Three rows of seats near the front had been removed. In their place were several comfortable-looking couches. Tomi thought they would be fun to sit on, but they were already taken, so they sat near the back.

When the lights went out, P.R. put his arm around her, and she leaned her head on his shoulder. She had always fantasized about Leonardo DiCaprio. When his face appeared on the movie screen, he was as handsome as she remembered, and his blue eyes were captivating. But when P.R. turned his blue eyes on her, they were real and made her heart catch.

The haunting sound of "My Heart Will Go On" filled the theatre. The first time Tomi saw *Titanic*, she'd thought the movie was romantic. Now she didn't want to be like Rose. She didn't want to find love only to lose it.

Was this love she felt for P.R.? She tried to analyze her feelings, but whenever he was near, she became confused. Something was happening between them, and she didn't understand it. Not ever seeing him again would be like not breathing. When she returned to Japan, would the song be true? Would her heart still go on?

The next day when she and Raven were folding baby clothes, Raven said, "I think he likes you."

Tomi stalled and tried to come up with a way to explain Carter's behavior. "Who?"

"My brother."

"Oh." Relieved, Tomi smiled.

"Be careful. I don't want you to get hurt. My brother's a rake."

"A rake?" She looked up the word on her new cell phone, but did not understand.

That night when she and P.R. sat on the porch swing, she told him what Raven had said. "Please explain *rake*."

P.R. frowned. "Don't listen to my sister. If anyone's a rake, it's Carter."

Tomi didn't like to talk about Carter, so she changed the subject. "I have favor."

P.R. stopped swinging and turned toward her, giving her his full attention. "Just ask."

She liked the way he listened to her, as if everything she said was important. But she wasn't sure how he would respond. "I need to practice driving car."

P.R. stroked his goatee. "Do you have a license?"

"I apply for International license and have it."

Quinn had offered to take Tomi driving, but Quinn was overwhelmed by her new family and building another house. Before, Tomi would have given up. Now she felt a strong determination.

"I'll think about it," P.R. said.

Tomi slumped against the porch swing and tried not to show her disappointment.

The next night after supper, P.R. dangled a set of keys in front of her. "Ready to go for a drive?"

She jumped up from the table and threw her arms around his neck.

Dakota and Dallas chanted, "P.R. has a girlfriend. P.R. has a girlfriend."

Was it true? Did P.R. think of her as his girlfriend? He merely grinned and took her hand as he pulled her outside to the car parked in the alley.

"Raven offered to let us use hers." P.R. opened the passenger door on the Dodge Charger. "Carter bought her a new van so it would be easier to take the twins."

P.R. slid behind the wheel. "I'll drive out of town and then we can switch places."

On the way Tomi watched the street signs and concentrated on the directions. Once they were in the country, P.R. pulled the car to the side of the road. Tomi reached for the door handle.

He placed his hand on her arm. "Don't get out or turn around. I think we're being followed."

Tomi's eyes widened as she stared up at the rearview mirror. A full-sized sedan swung out from behind the Charger and sped down the graveled road, a cloud of chalky dust pluming behind.

"I didn't see the license plate number, did you?" P.R. asked.

Tomi shook her head.

P.R. squinted. "Not much down this road. The loft, Ace's, the mine, and Miss May's. Let's wait until the car comes back."

They waited twenty minutes. The car never returned.

Tomi squirmed in her seat. "Maybe I no drive."

P.R. was insistent. "Yes, I want you to practice."

Patiently, he went over the instructions. Then he let her drive up and down the country road several times before they returned to town.

Driving was only one of her new experiences. Each day Tomi awoke ready to embrace her life. The next weekend she didn't have to worry about Carter. He phoned Raven and said he wouldn't be back until the day her mother came.

Tomi was glad. Raven, however, was depressed. Not only was Carter gone, but her milk had dried up and she could no longer breast feed. So her sisters planned a spa night to pamper her. They used the guest room with the Jacuzzi. Summer gave Raven a manicure, Belle gave her a pedicure, and Tomi gave her a massage. Then they all took turns doing the same for each other.

Tomi had never had a sister. She envied the shared bond among the three women, but they didn't make her feel like an outsider. They even teased her about liking their brother.

"Hey, you could be our sister-in-law," Raven said.

Sisters-in-law. The word flitted through her head. What would it be like to have these three women as sisters? Even though she was in a foreign country, how easy it seemed to fit into this family. She liked the idea of belonging here.

But she quickly pushed the thought away.

CHAPTER THIRTY-EIGHT

The night before Tomi was to move back to the loft, P.R. took her driving again. "It's almost dark. Go straight ahead under the arched metal sign that spells out Mitchell Park."

"Park is pretty," Tomi said as she drove through the entrance flanked by brick pillars.

P.R. agreed. "Captain Mitchell donated the forty acres to the city. On the right is a Civil War cannon. Turn left at the Chautauqua pavilion."

Tomi tried to repeat the name.

"The Chautauqua was for a program in the 1920s that brought culture and education to rural areas."

They drove by the bowl-shaped swimming pool closed for the season. "It's an above ground pool with the dressing rooms below. Only three were built like it in the U.S." P.R. continued to tell Tomi about the park as they drove by the baseball fields and tennis courts.

They neared the playground with the arched footbridge and small island. "Can we stop?" Tomi asked.

"You're the driver."

She parked the Charger in the empty graveled lot in front of a giant, two-sided slide. She jumped out and sprinted across the playground. Leaves fluttered around her bare ankles, and her loose hair swished across the back of her dress.

P.R. slid out of the car. He had on the khakis and plaid shirt he'd worn to the office. He felt foolish running after her, so he leisurely strolled over to the footbridge.

He stopped next to her. A light breeze rippled across the surface of the lagoon, and the colored lights on the fountain reflected on the water.

"Like bridge in Japanese garden."

He put his arms around her shoulders. "Do you miss Japan?"

She sighed. "Sometimes, but so peaceful here."

P.R. gazed at the maples and oaks, their leaves shimmering in oranges, russets, and golds. Beyond the trees, a fiery pumpkin sun slipped toward the horizon, leaving streaks of purples, pinks, and fuchsias.

He had never experienced fall in southern Illinois. In Chicago with its tall skyscrapers and fast-paced life, the seasons sped by like the cars on the Dan Ryan Expressway. He didn't want his days with Tomi to race by, one after another. He wanted them to slow down so he could experience life with her. Then when she left, he would have no regrets.

Tomi leaned against him. "Do you miss Chicago?"

"I love Chicago. It's my home."

"But you move here?"

"It's temporary."

He had his life all mapped out. Practicing law in Hickory Hills was only a detour. He'd spent his school years struggling financially, but now he'd paid off his loan and even begun to save so that when he retired, he would have a nice little nest egg. As soon as another Chicago firm offered him a lucrative job, he'd move back to the city.

Tomi, however, didn't seem bored with this little burg. She was captivated by its simple beauty, like the stars and the sun setting over the park.

She made him pause and look at life differently. He had begun to appreciate this town and its relaxed pace. Here he could be part of his nieces' and nephews' lives and maybe even start his own family. Well, he'd need a wife for that.

Tomi's words echoed in his head. *No marry.*

Without Tomi standing next to him would he feel the same way about this place? Or himself?

"I'd like to show you Chicago."

She gazed up at him. "Would we see baseball game?"

"Maybe." Right then he decided to check on some Cubs tickets.

Being with Tomi made him want to be more. When she looked up at him, like she was doing now, his chest swelled. He wanted to be worthy of the admiration in those sparkling brown eyes.

He wasn't sure how she had so easily become a part of his life. She was as necessary as his morning cup of coffee. If he didn't see her before he left for work, his day started off-kilter. He wasn't the only one. She had won over his whole family.

As soon as Dakota and Dallas were home from school, his nephews scampered after her like playful puppies. His sisters were a tightly knit trio, but they had embraced her, too.

He hadn't been surprised by Summer. She would take in any stray and had flocks of girlfriends. Raven, however, was wary of other women, probably because of Carter's roving eye. Yet P.R. often heard Raven and Tomi giggling just like they were sisters. Maybe it was because of the loving way Tomi took care of the twins, mothering them as if they were her own.

Even Belle, who was busy running the B&B, cooked special dishes for Tomi. Tonight Belle had surprised Tomi with a red velvet cake. "In honor of our guest who's leaving tomorrow."

Leaving.

P.R was not looking forward to Tomi moving back to the loft. It was only a few miles away, but she had brought joy and laughter into all their lives, and he would miss her. Too much. What would happen in December when she really left and was an ocean away?

Tomi's voice cut through his pensive mood. "Let's swing." She took his hand, threading her fingers through his, and walked across the playground.

On the way, she paused at the wooden gazebo and pointed down at the concrete stamped with TMHK Foundation. "What does it mean?"

"Those are initials," P.R. explained. "The gazebo was built in honor of a woman who loved life, but didn't live to see her daughters grow up."

Tomi nodded and walked over to the swings. She let go of his hand and sat on the middle one. Then she patted the swing next to her.

The thick chains and U-shaped rubber seats were strong enough to hold him. He had pushed his niece and nephews here, but he couldn't remember the last time he'd swung.

As he hesitated, Tomi began pumping her feet. Her dress billowed around her shapely legs and her long hair flowed behind. Shivers rippled through him.

He plopped onto the swing next to her, jarring him back to reality. He was just spending time with Tomi. That was all. Nothing good would come of fantasizing about anything more.

He pushed his reliable brown brogues against the ground and began pumping his feet. Soon he was flying beside her. The wind hit his face. With each pump, the years sloughed off, until once again he was a carefree boy with nothing better to do than swing away the day.

Tomi turned toward him. Her lips curved into a teasing smile. "Jump."

Before he could protest, she was flying through the air. Like an Olympic gymnast she sailed farther and farther, defying gravity. When she landed, both feet stuck.

Whirling around, she gave him a triumphant bow. Then she crossed her arms and laid down a challenge. "Jump past."

He was tempted to let go and sail through the air. Then he remembered his fall from the ladder. He certainly didn't want to crack his head again. He quit pumping. The swing slowed. The boy inside him slipped away.

Those carefree days of slides and swings were gone. His childhood had ended at fifteen when his dad died. While other boys in the neighborhood shot hoops or played baseball, he cut grass and delivered papers so he could save for college.

Nothing much had changed after he passed the bar. He still worked long hours and saved money for the future. When he did go out, he ended up at some frivolous party.

Tomi waved her hands. "Jump."

Behind her was the wooden gazebo dedicated to the young woman whose life had ended too soon. He wasn't even thirty, and somehow his life had derailed. When the law firm downsized, it didn't matter how many hours he'd given to them. He'd been axed. Now he would have to dip into his retirement.

Retirement. What about now? Was he ready to give up living before his life even started? He loved Chicago. Yet it had taken only a day and a half to pack up and leave. It surprised him how little he thought about his old life or the city.

As he sat on the swing, he felt as if he were at some kind of crossroad. Go forward or stay stuck in the past.

His hands tightened on the chains. His feet began pumping, harder this time. Then his fingers were slipping away from the chains. He let go. He was soaring through the air. He didn't look down. He was flying forward, reaching out, ready to embrace whatever lay ahead.

———

Thirty minutes later, P.R. still had a boyish grin on his face when he and Tomi walked through the back door of the Castle. Tomi started to hand him Raven's car keys.

"Just hang them here." He pointed to the hooks next to the kitchen door. "Raven said the car is yours whenever you want to drive it."

Tomi's brown eyes lit up. "Really? So generous." Before she hung the keys on a hook, she held them in her hand, letting them linger, much the way he'd done the day he'd driven and experienced a taste of freedom. "I really like your sisters."

"They like you, too, and tomorrow you can meet my mom."

Over the years, he'd brought a few women home, but his mom finally said, "Wait until that special girl comes along."

Tomi was certainly special, but their relationship would be short-lived. Still, he wanted them to meet. "If your suitcase is packed, I can carry it down for you tonight." The Castle didn't have an elevator, so lugging a suitcase down three flights of stairs would be difficult.

"Thank you. I almost ready."

He followed her up the winding staircase. While she went into her room to finish packing, he knocked on Raven's door. When he entered, Raven had her back to him, diapering one of the twins. She flipped her long black hair off her shoulders and turned. Her bright smile faded. "I thought you were Carter. He said he might come home early."

P.R. bit back a sarcastic comment about Carter. It would only hurt Raven. The three-week old twins were changing daily, but Carter hadn't been home much. He crossed to Raven. "Well, my nieces are as beautiful as their mother."

Raven blushed and finished diapering Meggie. Then she handed the baby to him. The first time he had held one of the twins, he was nervous, but Tomi had patiently showed him how to support the baby's head and cradle her in his arms. Now he looked forward to spending time with them.

The adjoining door opened. Tomi propped her suitcase against the wall. "All packed."

Meggie turned her head toward Tomi. Yes, he thought, even the babies recognized her voice and wanted her attention.

Tomi didn't disappoint. She walked over and planted a tender kiss on Meggie's forehead.

P.R. passed the baby to Tomi. "I'll put your suitcase downstairs next to the kitchen door and then come up to say good-night."

He picked up her suitcase and started down to the kitchen. He hoped Tomi wouldn't be too busy to spend a few minutes alone with him. He thought about holding her in his arms and kissing her, especially since tomorrow night she would be at Quinn's.

As he climbed back up the stairs and approached the last landing, Tomi walked out of Raven's room. He took the rest of the steps two at a time and pulled Tomi over in front of her closed bedroom door.

She put a finger to her lips. "Sh-sh. Babies."

That was okay. Talking wasn't what he had in mind. He wrapped his hands around her and inhaled the peachy scent of her hair as he pressed his body against hers.

Their eyes met. Her turned-up mouth seemed to be waiting. He bent down and moved his lips gently over hers. Then something exploded, and all his pent-up passion spilled out. He tightened his hold, and his lips pressed harder. Everything around him faded. He melted into her and was lost in the taste.

He continued to kiss her, finding it harder and harder to pull away. Tonight they were standing right outside her bedroom door. He thought about pushing it open and leading her to the bed. He thought about the way she would feel stretched out beside him.

He thought...the warmth of her lips and her body suddenly stopped. He blinked, and as she came into view, her eyes looked sad.

She reached back and pulled open the door. "Sayonara." She shuffled inside and closed the door behind her.

He stared at the wooden door separating them. She had never used the formal Japanese word to say good-bye. What did that mean? Had he gone too far? Had she sensed that tonight he had not wanted to stop?

As much as he would like to open the door and fulfill his fantasy, it was a line he had put down, and he was determined not to cross it.

CHAPTER THIRTY-NINE

Tomi lay in bed surrounded by darkness. Usually moonlight shone in through the dormer above the bed, but tonight rain pelted the windowpane.

The dreary weather matched her mood. Tomorrow she would leave the Castle, which meant she would leave P.R., the twins, Raven, Belle, and her family.

During the past two weeks while Tomi stayed at the Castle, Ace and his brother, Craig, had worked on the loft. They had converted the lower part of the barn that had been used as a garage into a bedroom for Jason, another bathroom, and a family room. According to Quinn, who called or stopped by every day, only the studs and drywall were up, but that was enough for Jason to sleep there.

Tomi had missed Quinn and wanted to talk to her about so many things, especially P.R. Maybe she could help Tomi understand her feelings. She didn't know why she couldn't control the flood of emotions that swept over her whenever she was near him.

In Japan, dating happened at a much slower pace. Here, time was her enemy. She had agreed to let him kiss her. Now she wanted to give him more. But she couldn't.

She didn't have romantic feelings for Yoshiro, but he was an honorable man. She must be an honorable woman, not a soiled bride. Several of Tomi's girlfriends were married. Most had married for love; some for convenience. Now she understood what could be between a man and a woman, and she wanted more than a marriage of convenience.

But her parents knew what was best for her, so she would marry Yoshiro.

She had come to America to experience freedom. Now she understood freedom did not make her free. She was free to see P.R., but she couldn't keep her emotions in check, at least not the way she had planned.

Tonight P.R.'s kisses had been different. At first they had been tender. Then they had changed. His lips had filled with heat. They took away her breath and made her body strain against him, wanting more.

Something quivered deep in her belly, a small tremor before an earthquake. Her feelings scared her. She wrenched herself away.

What would have happened if P.R. had reached around, opened the bedroom door, and pulled her inside? Would she have been strong enough to deny the need pulsing through her?

Leaving the Castle was for the best. She would be away from P.R. and temptation. Tomorrow P.R.'s mother would come. She would want her son to find a pretty American girl.

Tomi closed her eyes and finally gave in to sleep.

Bweee! Bweee! She bolted up. Fire!

The twins. She flew across the bedroom and pulled open the adjoining door. The babies weren't lying in their bassinets. She whirled around. Raven's bed was empty. Tomi had to find them, get them to safety.

Smoke clouded the air. Her eyes burned. She closed her eyes and when she opened them, she was in her room. The babies were lying on her bed, kicking and crying.

She rushed to the window and shoved it open. How could she jump down three stories with two babies? P.R. Where was P.R? He would help her.

Her frog. She had put it in the pocket of her robe. She turned from the window. Where was her robe? No time. A wall of thick smoke separated her from the babies. She lowered her head and plowed through it.

She couldn't breathe. She needed air. Her lungs burned. She gulped in hot acrid smoke. She coughed and jolted up in bed, wide awake.

The room was dark. She was drenched with sweat. She breathed in. No smoke. No babies crying. No fire. How long before she could close her eyes and not relive the nightmare of the fire?

Her pulse raced. She reached for her robe at the end of the bed. She'd go downstairs and fix some tea. She slid her feet into the slippers and padded across the room. She pulled open the door. The hallway was dark. She stepped out of the room and thudded against someone.

A man's hand clamped over her mouth, stifling her scream. He pushed her against the wall. Her eyes dilated.

Carter. He wasn't supposed to return until tomorrow. Was this part of her nightmare? His breath smelled of whisky and tobacco.

"Sh-sh! You don't want to wake the babies." His lips moved up her neck.

Her skin crawled. This was no dream. She tried to wiggle free. "Please, please."

"I knew you wanted me."

"No! Stop!" She placed her hands on his chest and shoved. He didn't budge.

She pushed harder.

He pressed his lips against her. The tobacco taste gagged her. She couldn't open her mouth. She couldn't cry out. Raven would be devastated, maybe blame Tomi. She had to get away. Hiro had always helped her, always protected her from bullies at school.

She reached into her pocket. Her fingers grasped the frog. A new strength surged through her.

Carter's lips pressed harder. She bit back a scream and swallowed her bile. Her hand tightened on the frog. She lifted it out of her pocket and swung it against the side of his head, hitting him near the temple.

He jerked back and uttered an oath. She twisted free and ran toward the stairs. She didn't know where she was going, only away from Carter.

She raced down the steps, her long hair flying behind. When she reached the bottom, she glanced over her shoulder. She didn't see him, only heard his steps.

Her mind whirled, searching for some place to hide. The kitchen. She ran through the dining room, into the tea room, and pushed open the swinging doors. Light streamed in from the window, pooling onto her suitcase next to the door. Above, hung the row of keys.

She wasn't trapped. She could leave, go to the loft. She dropped the frog into her pocket and lifted off a set of keys, felt them in her hand. Yes, these were Raven's car keys.

She grabbed the handle of the suitcase.

The wooden steps creaked. He was coming down the stairs.

Fumbling, she unlocked the dead bolt and pulled the door open. She rushed into the darkness, dragging her suitcase behind her.

Rain drizzled onto her face and soaked her robe. She darted into the shadows of the orchard. Raven's car was parked in the alley in front of another car. Probably Carter's rental.

A light appeared in the kitchen window. Any second Carter would come after her. She opened the door on Raven's car and threw the suitcase into the back seat. Her hand shook as she poked the key into the ignition and turned the switch.

The car roared to life. Her headlights flooded the alley. She turned on the windshield wipers, but didn't buckle up or check the mirrors or do anything else P.R. had taught her. She stomped on the accelerator. The tires spun in the gravel. She sped down the alley, rocks spitting behind her.

At the corner, she cranked the steering wheel and careened onto the street. Her eyes glanced at the clock on the dash. Midnight. The road was wet and deserted. She kept her foot pressed to the floor and drove toward the loft.

She checked the rear view mirror.

Nothing.

She let out a nervous breath. She drove on. Her eyes flitted to the mirror again. Car lights shined behind her. She gasped. Carter. Her body shook. She had been foolish to flee. At least at the Castle other people were around. The country road was deserted, and she was miles from the loft. No one could help her. She was alone.

She pressed down on the accelerator, harder. The Charger fishtailed and sped ahead. She looked in the mirror again. The other car swerved into the opposite lane and drove up beside her. It didn't pass. The car continued speeding next to her, inching her to the side.

She gripped the steering wheel tighter. She was driving too fast. The road was wet. She could lose control or hit the ditch and flip over. She let up on the gas and eased her foot on the brake. The other car shot ahead, splashing water onto her windshield.

When it cleared, her headlights shined on a large oak near what once had been a lane. Sometimes P.R. had used it to turn around. Maybe she could park the car and hide in the overgrown grass and weeds.

She switched off the headlights and coasted toward the tree. If she missed the lane, the car would sink into the muddy ground.

Blinking, she waited for her eyes to adjust to the darkness. Shadows crept across the windshield. She turned, hoping she hit the lane. The tires spun forward. She inched ahead and shut off the engine.

She swiveled around in her seat and stared out the back window. An owl hooted. She jumped. She hadn't checked the locks. She clicked them, made sure no one could yank open the doors.

Headlights shined on the road, moving closer. She held her breath. They continued on. Was it Carter? She watched the clock. Five minutes passed. She turned on the engine and backed onto the road.

She kept the lights off and drove for what seemed miles. Ahead was Quinn's lane. She turned onto it, hoping the extra key was still hidden in the turtle at the bottom of the steps.

Within minutes, she parked the car, found the key, and rushed up the stairs. Unlocking the door, she slipped inside and relocked it. She pressed her back against the door and slid to the floor. Her body shook. She wrapped her arms around her knees. Tears streamed down her cheeks.

She was safe.

CHAPTER FORTY

On Sunday evening, Bucky slipped into the small A-frame chapel with stained glass windows and sat in the vacant back row. The sanctuary was alive with gospel music being pounded out on the upright piano near the altar. A few people were scattered around the pews. Most, however, sat behind the first two rows of boys, whose ages spanned from five to fifty-five.

The chapel south of Springfield was part of The Farmstead, a residential home for boys. The private facility was established by Aunt Sophie for children whose parents could no longer take care of them—or in some cases no longer wanted to take care of them. The Farmstead, set on twenty acres, raised its own chickens and cattle and, when possible, the residents did daily chores, like gathering eggs and milking cows.

Aunt Sophie had been a loving, no-nonsense woman who never had children of her own. During her life, she took in dozens of boys. Twenty-four-hour care was expensive, but most families felt the cost was worth it.

Before Aunt Sophie died, she set up a trust so The Farmstead could continue her mission. Aunt Sophie believed every child was precious to God. On the chapel wall behind the altar were Jesus' words, "Suffer little children, and forbid them not, to come unto me."

When the hallelujah song ended, a choir of a dozen boys in full-length blue robes stood and began singing "Amazing Grace."

In a wheelchair at the end of the first row sat one of the older residents. A monk's ring of white hair circled his bald crown. The man in the wheelchair lifted his arms and started conducting the choir. His large hands were crooked and scarred, but swayed in perfect time.

Bucky was mesmerized by those disfigured hands. He watched them, letting the music wash over him and lift his spirit.

The minister, in his long black robe, stepped behind the lectern. The sermon was on forgiveness. Bucky needed forgiveness.

Today was Joey's birthday. Memories swirled in his head of that birthday long ago, and he couldn't forgive Captain—or himself. Last night he almost wrecked his car trying to run Tomi off the road. For two weeks, he hadn't been able to get near her. By now she would have already told the authorities whatever she had seen. Killing her would only add to his sins.

The plan to hurry along Miss May's death had seemed simple. Then Jackson had complicated matters. Bucky didn't want to keep killing. Maybe sitting here in church, he would be able to hear that quiet voice that used to be in his heart before Jesus let him down and Joey hadn't come back.

The piano in the chapel started playing to signal the end of the service. The minister raised his hands. "Go in peace."

Bucky stood and waited for the residents to come down the center aisle. He reached into the front pocket of the windbreaker, fingering the police car he'd taken from Jason's bedroom. When the middle-aged man in the wheelchair neared the last pew, Bucky squeezed into line. He inched over until he stood beside the wheelchair. Then he gently laid the black-and-white police cruiser onto the man's lap and whispered, "Happy birthday, brother."

The man's hands, wrinkled with purple scars and skin grafts, snatched the toy. He lifted his head, and his child-like eyes lit up. "You came. I knew you'd come, Bucky."

CHAPTER FORTY-ONE

P.R. was disappointed that Tomi had left without saying good-bye. When she hadn't come down for coffee with him before he went to work, he thought maybe one of the twins had kept her up or she'd overslept. So he'd phoned her. She didn't answer her phone or return his message. After three days, he called Quinn, but she said Tomi was just busy.

So he waited for her to come to the Castle to see the twins—and him. But after a week, P.R. knew something was wrong. Maybe he'd gone too far that last night when he'd kissed her with such passion.

He tried to put her out of his mind by plunging into work. Each morning, he woke, went for a three-mile run, grabbed one of Belle's muffins, and was at his desk by six a.m. At the office he could focus and sometimes forget Tomi, for at least an hour or two. He'd moved on from other women. Why couldn't he forget her?

He certainly had enough challenging legal work. He spent hours going over the files for the lawsuit against Illinois Coal for unsafe mining practices. The statistics on black lung puzzled him. In recent years, more government legislation had been passed to prevent black lung, yet the cases had steadily increased. Some of the documented reasons were longer working hours, pressure to produce additional coal, and advanced machines that generated more dust. None of that was new.

But Jackson had filed a suit against Illinois Coal for three of his clients who had previously been denied black lung benefits. Two had died, so he had filed on behalf of their families. Vera Anderson, a waitress at the Blue Moon, had lost her husband to black lung, and Carrie Hall, P.R.'s office manager/paralegal, had lost her dad.

Carrie was another person Jackson had helped. She'd been enrolled in college for two months when her dad had been diagnosed with black lung. He planned to quit at the end of the month, but a beam fell on him and crushed his spine. Carrie's mother was a recluse who had never learned to drive. So Carrie dropped out of school to take care of her parents. Now she was a paralegal and had a photographic memory. She could rattle off dates and court cases better than most of the people he'd worked with in Chicago. P.R. was glad she had agreed to continue to work, even if it was only temporary.

The third client, Dale Miller, was still alive. Talking to Miller might help P.R. find what he needed. He checked the calendar in the appointment book on his desk.

Jackson had used the black, dog-eared notebook for his schedule. P.R. used a digital planner, yet he didn't have the heart to discard what Jackson had called his bible. P.R. used it to reference Jackson's previous appointments in the months before he died. P.R. made a note in his digital planner for Carrie to schedule an appointment with Miller for next week.

P.R. opened one of Miller's files and combed through the contents. Coal companies lost very few legal battles, so Jackson must have found something that made him think he could win a lawsuit against Illinois Coal. But what?

P.R. laced his fingers behind his head and leaned back in his chair. The last time he stopped in this office to see Jackson, his mentor had been sitting at this very desk, doodling.

When Jackson had spoken about the lawsuit, his eyes glimmered. "This time we have a shot at winning."

P.R. had given a low whistle. "How?"

Jackson stopped doodling and leaned toward P.R. "It's better not to write everything down. Other lawyers are working on this case. Some of them supposedly on the miners' side are on the take."

P.R. wondered if Jackson had become paranoid. Jackson must have sensed P.R.'s skepticism.

"Remember that TV exposé that proved a number of the prestigious doctors at Johns Hopkins had been getting money from the coal companies for years?" Jackson tapped his finger on the side of his head. "I got it stored right up here."

P.R. was curious. "What is it?"

"Only me and God know. But I think I've found the so-called 'smoking gun.'"

"So why did you mention it if you aren't going to share it with me?" P.R. asked.

"I'm willing to let you in on it, after you haul your legal mind down to Hickory Hills and take over my practice."

But P.R. hadn't agreed to take over the practice, so whatever Jackson referred to as the 'smoking gun' had been snuffed out with him. And P.R. had until the week after Thanksgiving to find it.

The phone on P.R.'s desk rang. He picked it up. "You have a call from Ace Edleston on line one," Carrie said.

"I'll take it." P.R. eagerly punched line one. "Good to hear from you, Ace."

"I have a legal matter I want to discuss. Do you have time to see me today?"

"Sure, why don't we meet for coffee at the Blue Moon in about thirty minutes?"

"I can come to your office," Ace said.

"No. I need a break."

After Ace agreed and hung up, P.R. closed the Miller file. He had a few things to discuss with Ace, too. Maybe if they chatted over coffee, he would tell P.R. why Tomi hadn't returned his calls.

CHAPTER FORTY-TWO

Across the street from the law office, Bucky ducked out of the drizzling rain and sat at a window booth at the Blue Moon. The blackboard propped next to the door listed today's special as meatloaf, mashed potatoes and gravy, and corn. Bucky didn't plan to eat.

On a rainy day the downtown diner was the perfect spot to eavesdrop on the local coffee drinkers. Maybe he'd hear some news about the murder or the fire.

A stout waitress handed him a menu. "Coffee?"

Bucky nodded to the gray-haired woman with Vera on her name tag as she poured steaming coffee into his cup. She didn't crack a smile. Bucky knew the type—a big woman who lived a small life. Vera moved on to the next table and the next, filling coffee cups without a word or a friendly smile.

The bell over the restaurant door jingled. A young woman, holding onto an open umbrella with one hand and a chubby boy about eight with the other, hurried inside. The blond, curly-haired boy dropped the woman's hand and clumsily ran across the room to Vera, hugging her thick waist. His wet hair dampened her crisp apron.

The child said something that sounded like, "Nana, Nana."

The boy's speech impediment and pigeoned toes reminded Bucky of Joey at that age, not so much because of his disabilities, but because of his wide smile. As soon as the boy had walked into the Blue Moon, he'd brought sunshine with him. Even Vera smiled.

The boy released Vera and hurried to the red-leather stools in front of the counter. He plopped down and whirled around, giggling. The woman, probably his mother, scurried after him. She grabbed his shoulders, stopping him from spinning, and shook her finger at him.

The scene reminded Bucky of the times his family had gone out to eat. Captain wanted Joey to act normal, but his brother had never been normal. When Joey was born, Captain and his wife, Blanche, had been stationed overseas. Since the pregnancy was her first, Blanche wanted to fly back to the States.

Captain said women had babies all the time. Some even squatted in the field and went back to work the same day. He didn't see any reason for Blanche to run home to Mama. Her place was beside her husband.

Blanche's labor had been difficult, more than twenty hours. When Joey was born, the umbilical cord was wrapped around his neck. The doctor revived the baby.

"It's a blessing," his parents said before they knew Joey's brain had been deprived of oxygen for too long.

"It's a blessing," Captain said eleven years later when he lied to the world and announced Joey had died from burns in the fire.

For forty years Bucky had blamed himself for Joey's death. He didn't learn of his parents' secret until two years ago when Captain died.

At the reading of the will, only Bucky and his sister sat in the lawyer's office. His mother was ill with cancer and could not attend. Bucky asked the lawyer why a trust had been set up for Joey since his brother had died when he was eleven.

"Died?" The lawyer frowned. "I saw Joey last week."

The lawyer took Bucky to The Farmstead. Bucky hugged his brother, and for the first time in forty years, a joy that he thought was gone sprang up in him.

Vera interrupted Bucky's thoughts. "Are you ready to order?"

No one had been seated near enough to his booth for him to pick up any gossip. "Just coffee."

Vera took the menu and huffed away. The few coins in her half-moon apron jingled with each step. She was probably going to expect a tip for her sour-mouthed service. Maybe when Vera went home, she lined up her tips on the kitchen table, counting the nickels, dimes, and quarters. Maybe she was saving for a better place for her grandson than a tar-papered shack next to a rumbling railroad track.

That's what Bucky wanted for Joey, a place for them to live together and finish their lives in comfort, to make up for all the years Captain had robbed from them.

When Bucky had learned Joey was alive, he confronted his mother. He couldn't believe she had agreed to such a heinous plan. His mother, who was in the last stages of breast cancer, had pleaded with Bucky to understand.

After Joey was moved to The Farmstead, she'd cried for weeks and had even gone to see him. She begged Captain to bring Joey home. Captain refused, but promised her what she wanted—another child.

Bucky remembered his parents' fights had ended when his mother gave birth to a healthy baby girl. Bucky was ten when his sister was born. To him she was just a pest.

Captain, however, doted on his new daughter. She was never the object on his wrath. Bucky became his new whipping boy.

The bell over the front door of the diner jingled. Bucky glanced up from his coffee. In walked Ace with that lawyer who had been hanging around Tomi.

Vera led the men to the booth behind Bucky and then stopped at his table. "More coffee?"

Bucky put his hand over his cup. "Give me the special."

CHAPTER FORTY-THREE

Ace sat across from P.R. at the Blue Moon, stirring his coffee and waiting for P.R. to brag about the Chicago Cubs. For the second year in a row, the Cubs were in the playoffs for the National League Championship.

Ace was a Cardinal fan and felt sorry for his friend. The Cubs were cursed. Last year they'd clinched the division and hadn't won a single playoff game. The Cubs hadn't even won the World Series since 1908.

P.R., however, didn't look like a happy Cubs fan. His shoulders slumped, and the twinkle in his eyes was gone. He'd even shaved off his mustache and goatee. "So did they have a sale on razor blades?"

P.R. ran his hand over his smooth jaw. "Can't a man shave without everyone making it a federal offense?"

Ace raised his eyebrows.

P.R. confessed, "I did it for Tomi. But I haven't even seen her. Do you know what's going on?"

When Ace had called about a legal matter, he'd hoped P.R. wouldn't ask about Tomi. Ace took a sip of coffee and avoided P.R.'s probing eyes. "Like what?"

"Like why she's too busy to see me."

Ace put down his cup. "Maybe you should ask her."

"I've tried. She won't answer my calls or return my messages. You must have noticed something."

"I've been in the fields." At least that was true, and today Ace would have picked the cornfield next to his house if it hadn't rained. He didn't want to lie to P.R., but he'd promised Quinn he wouldn't tell anyone, particularly P.R., about what had happened the last night Tomi stayed at the Castle.

P.R. plowed ahead. "My mother's been here a week, and Tomi said she wanted to meet her."

"You know, P.R., what women say isn't always what they mean."

Ace wasn't about to divulge that Carter had been a little too friendly with Tomi. Quinn urged Tomi to tell Raven, but Tomi didn't want to cause trouble. Besides, Carter could just deny it.

Quinn had convinced Tomi that Ben should know about Carter, so it wouldn't happen to another guest. Tomi agreed, but she wouldn't talk to Ben, so Ace had done it.

Ben had not taken it well. Without saying why, he had given Carter an ultimatum to find another place to live before the end of the month. Raven and the twins were welcome to stay, but Raven had made it clear if her husband had to leave, she would leave, too.

"Has Carter found a place yet?" Ace asked.

P.R. shrugged. "He's been looking all week, but the less I talk to that guy the better."

"Finding a place to rent isn't easy. After the fire, Quinn and I searched for a house. That's when we decided to remodel the loft and live there until we can rebuild."

"How are the house plans coming?" P.R. asked.

"So far I haven't found a carpenter. Everyone I've called is tied up until spring."

"I might be able to help. A former client is a great carpenter, but he has a record, so not many people are willing to give him a chance."

Ace hesitated. "I'd better talk to Quinn about that."

"I could stop by tonight and talk to Quinn myself, maybe even help with the remodeling."

Ace waved away the suggestion. He didn't want P.R. falling off another ladder, but P.R. pressed on, obviously determined to see Tomi. Ace might as well tell P.R. part of the truth. "Quinn's worried about your relationship with Tomi."

P.R. leaned back and seemed genuinely surprised. "Why?"

"She doesn't want her friend hurt."

"Why would Quinn think I'd hurt Tomi?"

"Your love'em-and-leave'em reputation isn't exactly a secret," Ace said.

"I just want Tomi to enjoy her time here. Besides, she's the one who's leaving."

P.R. had a point, plus Ace had gone through his own agony before Quinn and he had worked out their problems. He pulled his cell phone from his pocket. "I'll call Quinn and ask her and Tomi to meet us for lunch."

P.R.'s eyes brightened. "Don't mention me."

Ace punched in the number and talked to Quinn. "They'll be here in about half an hour," Ace said after he hung up. "What time do you need to get back to the office?"

P.R. shrugged. "It's not like Chicago."

"So you ready to move to Hickory Hills permanently?"

"I'm liking it better than I expected. If I decide to move here, would you sell me some land near Summer's house?"

Ace was surprised that P.R. didn't seem to miss his big-city bachelor life. "I could probably let go of a five-acre tract."

"I'll keep that in mind."

Vera stopped at their booth. "More coffee?"

Ace nodded. "And menus. Two others will be joining us for lunch."

Vera refilled the coffees and returned with menus. P.R. pushed his aside. "I want to talk to you about a note Jackson scribbled on his calendar the week before he died. I think it says 'Call Ace.' Did you meet with Jackson back in September?"

"No, but if it was around the time Miss May died, Jackson might have wanted to discuss Miss May's new will."

"Stuart filed the will two weeks ago."

Ace leaned across the table and lowered his voice. "Miss May changed her will in July. She named me executor."

"Does Stuart know?" P.R. asked.

"I doubt it. Miss May didn't want him to know. The will Stuart filed is probably the old one, but Miss May made it clear the previous will is null and void. You should have a copy of the new one at the office."

"I don't remember seeing it. But I'll check." P.R. pulled out his phone and made a notation. "What's in the new will?"

Ace looked around. The lunch crowd hadn't come in yet so most of the tables were empty, but the booths in front and behind them were filled. "This is for your ears only. Miss May left a million dollars to the town to build a new library."

P.R. eyes widened. "That's great for the town."

"She earmarked the yearly profits from two hundred acres for upkeep, and she gave me the option to buy the hundred acres I've been farming."

"So what's left for Stuart?"

"He inherits the rest of her land and the home place, if he lives there for five years."

P.R. let out a low whistle. "Stuart's not going to like that. When did you file the will?"

"I planned to file it after we got back from our honeymoon, but the house burned."

"So your copy was destroyed?"

"I thought so. Then yesterday we dug up the basement safe, and I found the will." Ace reached into his jacket pocket and pulled out Miss May's will. He handed it to P.R.

P.R. scanned it. "Any idea why Miss May wanted Stuart to live on the farm for five years?"

"My guess is it had something to do with Stuart's fiancé, Sabina. Miss May thought the woman was a gold digger and would talk Stuart into selling the farm and spending the money."

"Did Stuart ever show any interest in the farm?"

"Not that I know of, but he used to come visit Miss May regularly. After Sabina, those visits dwindled."

P.R. handed the will back to Ace. "This looks like it would stand up in court, but Stuart's bound to contest it."

"Would he have a chance?"

"He might. He could argue that Miss May wasn't of sound mind or that you coerced her." Then P.R. asked, "When did you file it for probate?"

"I haven't filed it yet."

"In Illinois you have thirty days after someone dies to file the will."

"Thirty days!" Ace glanced at the calendar on his watch. "That means I have to file it today."

The bell over the door jingled. Ace turned just as Quinn and Tomi walked in. The man who been sitting in the booth behind them rushed out, bumping into Tomi. He knocked the umbrella from her hand and didn't bother to stop.

Quinn retrieved the umbrella and led Tomi over to their booth. "Ace, you didn't say we would be having company." Quinn's tone let everyone know Ace might have some explaining to do later.

Tomi saw P.R. and gasped. "P.R., is that you?"

He sheepishly grinned. "I didn't think you'd forget me so soon."

Tomi flushed. "You look so...different."

Quinn sat next to Ace, leaving Tomi to slide in beside P.R.

P.R. handed her a menu. "Is different good or bad?"

Tomi studied P.R.'s clean-shaven face. "I like," she said and smiled.

His stomach did a little flip flop, and his world righted again.

CHAPTER FORTY-FOUR

Tomi peered out the passenger side window of P.R.'s car, searching for the Chicago skyline. "When we get there?"

P.R. chuckled. "You asked the same question fifteen minutes ago."

Tomi bit back her usual 'so sorry.' She did not want anything to spoil this weekend with P.R. He was taking her to an American baseball game. Not just any baseball game. He had tickets to the last playoff game. If the Cubs won tonight, they would be in the World Series.

When he'd asked her to go to the baseball game with him, she was so happy she had thrown her arms around him. At first he had hugged her back, but then he politely released her and stepped away. That's when she knew things were not quite the same, and it hurt more than she expected.

She glanced over at him. Without his mustache and goatee, he looked younger, almost boyish. Yet his jaw was firm and solid, the way he was. Something in her chest twinged. Longing? Need? She clasped her hands together in her lap so she would not reach over and run her fingers down his smooth cheek.

For a brief moment, P.R. turned and smiled at her. Then his eyes focused on the road. "I have a question."

"Okey dokey." She hoped P.R. had not found out about Carter.

"If I do something you don't like, will you tell me?"

She relaxed. "No problem."

P.R.'s eyebrows knitted together. "It was a problem, Tomi. You didn't return my calls for a week."

Seven days. Those seven days had been a problem for her, too. She had missed him and the babies, but with Carter at the Castle, she was too scared to go back. She had called Raven for updates on the twins and had asked about P.R.

Then one day Carter answered Raven's cell phone. "We miss you."

The phone slipped from her hand, and she quit calling.

Tomi had little experience with men. Carter made her wary, even of P.R. When she was near P.R., he made her come alive in ways she didn't understand. He made her want what she couldn't have. Those feelings frightened her.

So she had ignored his calls, convinced not seeing him would make her forget. But each passing day, she missed him more. At night she lay awake on the top bunk until Taylor was asleep below. Then she would press her cell phone to her ear and listen to P.R.'s messages just to hear his voice.

P.R. cleared his throat. His usual confident tone sounded strained. "I want you to know I respect you."

She did not like being so respected. Since they had met at the diner, P.R. would drop by the loft after work, but he didn't hold her hand, and when he left, he didn't kiss her. Since he had shaved, she wondered what his kisses would feel like without his whiskers.

"There it is." P.R. pointed ahead.

Tomi looked out the window at the sprawling city and tall buildings. Chicago was a major city. She had expected it to be larger, more like Tokyo. But when they arrived at Wrigley Field, she expected the stadium to be smaller.

In fact, as they watched the baseball game, she peppered him with questions. Why was the ball a different size? Where was the fan club? The chanting?

By the seventh inning she was frustrated. After one particularly bad call from the umpire behind the plate, she couldn't take it anymore. She stood up and yelled at the umpire in Japanese. Then she fisted her hands on her hips and glared at P.R. "Why you no yell at him?"

P.R. seemed surprised. "You want me to yell?"

"He wrong. More fans should yell. Show displeasure."

P.R. agreed. The pitch was definitely a strike, but he didn't want to upset her so he'd curbed his usual colorful comments. She, however, had shouted loudly enough for both of them.

"In Japan, everyone yell at umpire. Like battle. Teams are warriors and umpire is enemy."

She asked him strange questions like why didn't they blow a whistle for a foul ball or when would the drums play and where were the balloons. A Japanese baseball game must really be interesting.

He'd thought bringing her to the game was a good idea, but she looked so doggone cute in her rolled up jeans, Cubs shirt, and baseball cap. He was already in agony. The Cubs were ahead and had led the entire game, but he kept waiting for fate to snatch the victory away. And Tomi jumping up and screaming was driving him crazy.

By the ninth inning, the Cubs still led five to zero but his nerves were frazzled. He and Tomi stood with the sea of fans and remained standing to support their team. The Cubs were three outs away from going to the World Series. The first out was easy. Four pitches and the batter struck out.

The second player stretched the count to three and two. Then it happened. The pitch was low. The umpire signaled ball four, and the player walked.

P.R.'s stomach knotted. He lowered his head. The curse was back. The Cubs would blow it. The Dodgers would score five runs, tie it up, and send the game into extra innings. Then the Dodgers would win and go to the World Series.

Tomi touched his arm. Electricity charged through him. "They win. You see."

All around the stadium, fans held up signs. "It will happen," and, "We believe."

After a lifetime of watching and hoping, P.R. found it hard to believe it would happen.

Then Tomi slipped her hand into his. He latched onto it like a sky diver clutching a ripcord. Hand in hand they stood as the third batter strutted to the plate.

On the first pitch, the batter connected. The ball rolled to the left field. The shortstop caught the grounder and threw it to second. The second baseman caught the ball and threw it to first. A routine four-three-two. A double play.

The announcer shouted, "Cubs win! Cubs win!" The stadium went wild. Fireworks exploded. The Big W was raised over Wrigley Field.

P.R. couldn't believe it. He let out a victory yell, picked up Tomi, and spun her around. Then he was kissing her, and she was kissing him back.

Once his lips touched hers, his restraint was gone. He was lost. He couldn't remember when a simple kiss had meant so much.

The fans jostled him. His lips slipped away. He kept his arm securely wrapped around her waist. He was in no hurry to let go of her. His team was a winner. He looked down at Tomi and smiled. Her brown eyes smiled up at him. He was a winner, too.

Two hours later, he was still smiling when he led Tomi up the back steps of his childhood home. As he opened the door, he put his finger over his lips. "Sh-sh. It's after midnight. The lights are on, but Mom's probably asleep."

When they walked into the kitchen, he stopped short. His mother sat at the table, dressed in a long flannel nightgown and pink fuzzy slippers.

He felt like a teenager who'd been caught sneaking in after curfew. "Mom, what are you doing up?"

"I watched the game, of course."

"I'm sorry you had to watch it alone."

"Oh, Al came over."

Mom had mentioned Al, Officer Levy's dad, more than a few times. P.R. wondered if they were more than friends.

Before he had time to consider that, his mother rushed over and threw her arms around him. Then she turned and hugged Tomi. "And I wanted to meet my son's mystery woman."

Tomi blinked up at him. "Mystery woman?"

Instead of explaining, he introduced them. "Mom, this is Tomi. Tomi, this is my mom, Irene."

Tomi pressed her palms together and bowed respectively. "*Hajimemashite.*"

Irene bowed and repeated the formal Japanese greeting.

Tomi's eyes sparkled at the unexpected gesture of welcome.

"I've been practicing." Irene led them to the table. "Sit down. I want to hear every detail of the game."

As P.R. gave his mom almost a play-by-play account, Tomi glanced around the warm kitchen with white metal cabinets and worn linoleum. She imagined P.R. as a boy sitting at this square wooden table with his sisters. Summer, Belle, and Raven had told Tomi stories about P.R. How much fun the four of them must have had sharing family meals in this kitchen with this spry woman.

P.R. didn't look like his mother, although they had similar blue eyes and fine blonde hair. She was shorter than Tomi, more like Raven, and talked with her hands the way Raven did. Other features, like her nose and mouth resembled Summer or Belle.

When Tomi yawned, Irene rose. "Better get you to bed." She led them up the narrow stairs to the converted attic. "This was the girls' room. The grandkids sleep here now."

Three twin beds were lined up under the slanted ceiling. Each bed was covered with a gingham-checked spread of a different color: yellow, blue, or green. Gingham curtains hung at the dormer windows. Irene pointed to a small trunk. "Extra blankets and towels are in the cedar chest."

Tomi nodded as Irene said good-night and left. Now Tomi was alone with P.R. The excitement of the night changed to tension. After the Cubs won the game, P.R. had kissed her, but everyone was hugging and kissing, sharing a happy moment together. If he kissed her now, it would be personal.

He didn't step closer. "Do you need anything before I leave?"

You, she thought. I need you to take me in your arms and kiss me the way you used to. I need you to want me again. She couldn't say those words aloud, so she shook her head.

"Okay. I'll see you in the morning." He turned and walked toward the door.

She wanted to run after him. Pride kept her feet rooted to the floor. Her heart ached. Each slap of P.R.'s shoes against the creaking floor was a crushing blow. When he reached the door, he turned. "So where do you want me to take you tomorrow?"

She was caught off guard. "Tomorrow?" She was thinking about today.

He took one step toward her. "You said you wanted to see Chicago."

Her mind couldn't focus. She repeated, "See Chicago."

He took another step toward her. "What do you want to see?"

Her heart raced. She couldn't think, couldn't remember what was in Chicago.

He stopped in front of her.

She couldn't breathe.

He reached out and touched her hair, letting his fingers run through it. His hands moved to her shoulders. "Do you want to go to Navy Pier and ride the new Centennial Wheel?"

"Yes." Her answer had nothing to do with the question.

His warm breath grazed her cheek. She closed her eyes and waited. At first he merely skimmed his mouth across hers. Her parched lips soaked in his gentle touch and yearned for more. Then he pressed his mouth against hers. This kiss had nothing to do with baseball. This kiss was for her, and so was the next and the next.

He couldn't stop kissing her. He had tried to stay away. He had walked to the door with every intention of leaving. But he couldn't. Just as he couldn't continue to lie to himself.

He wanted this woman in his life, now—and always.

Always?

The word frightened him. It wasn't possible. She was from Japan and would return in December. He had known her less than two months. He didn't have a steady job or a tidy nest egg or any of the things in his life plan. Yet when he was holding her and kissing her, she made him feel as if anything were possible.

Even always.

CHAPTER FORTY-FIVE

P.R. stretched his arm across the back of the enclosed gondola as he and Tomi rode to the top of the Centennial Wheel at Navy Pier. He missed the old Ferris wheel, but on this crisp October Sunday when the harsh wind blew in from Lake Michigan, the new ride was more practical.

They could enjoy a spectacular 360-degree view of the lake on one side and Chicago on the other. But his eyes were fixed on Tomi's smiling face. He leaned closer. "What did my mother whisper in your ear before we left this morning?"

Tomi turned to him with a Cheshire cat grin. "Girls' secret."

He laughed. "Just like my sisters. I can never pry anything out of them."

The ride descended and they stepped out of the gondola. "Where to next?" He had already taken her to Grant Park, where she posed in front of Buckingham Fountain. They'd gone to Millennium Park where she'd snapped pictures of them reflected in Cloud Gate, a silver sculpture nicknamed The Bean for its shape.

Tomi looked up at the skyline and pointed to the tallest building. "We go there."

P.R. frowned. "The Sears Tower? Well, the Willis Tower now."

"Is that building with glass ledge?"

P.R. nodded. He hadn't been there since The Ledge was added. His dad had been working on the elevators at Willis Tower the day he had a massive stroke and died.

P.R. tried to talk Tomi out of going. "It's not the tallest building in the U.S. anymore. It's like the sixteenth in the world. I'm sure Tokyo Tower is more impressive."

"Tokyo Tower no have glass ledge."

P.R. tried again. "The Centennial Wheel has a gondola with a glass bottom. We could ride in that car."

The sparkle in Tomi's eyes disappeared.

He had promised to show her Chicago, and Willis Tower was considered one of the major attractions. He didn't want to go, but somehow Tomi's happiness had become more important than his own.

He looped his arm through hers. "We can walk."

Her eyes lit up, and he thought going was worth it until he stepped into the elevator at Willis Tower. He moved to the rear and pressed his back against the sleek silver side. The car filled; the doors shut.

He pulled on the collar of his leather jacket. No air seemed to move. He was being crushed. His dad had talked about this elevator, a top of the line Schindler. As the car rose, the pressure changed. On the display in front of him the numbers flew by, ten floors at a time. A large television screen above the doors showed images of famous places around the world. The elevator rose higher than the Sphinx of Giza, the Roman Coliseum, the Statue of Liberty, the Gateway Arch, the Eiffel Tower, the Empire State Building, and then they passed the 99th floor. They stopped on 103.

P.R. exhaled. The ride had taken a little more than a minute, but sweat streamed down his back. He waited for the doors to open. They remained closed.

A man in front, wearing a Cubs cap, asked, "Do we have to push something?"

The teenage girl next to him tapped on the door as if that would open it.

A third person called out, "Hey, we're in here." Her hollow laugh increased P.R.'s tension.

Tomi tugged on his arm. "What wrong?"

P.R. couldn't talk, couldn't breathe. He had to get out of here. His dad used to brag how he kept the city moving up and down. He boasted that no elevator he'd worked on ever malfunctioned. But his dad didn't work on elevators anymore.

As a boy, P.R. resented the long hours his dad spent away from home. Now P.R. understood his father a little more, especially after he'd been terminated. A reliable income was important, especially for a man with a family.

The elevator doors slid open. The people in front of him rushed out. P.R. couldn't move his feet.

Tomi touched his hand. "Everyone gone."

He swallowed.

"You okay?"

When he didn't answer, she took his hand and led him out of the elevator onto the skydeck. He felt the ground beneath him and could breathe again. They circled the tower and read facts about Chicago and the construction of the building. Then Tomi coaxed him onto the glass ledge that extended four feet from the building.

He didn't look down, but out through the glass at the overcast sky. "On a clear day you can see four states: Illinois, Indiana, Michigan, and Wisconsin."

Tomi put her hand on her stomach. "Feel like plum pit."

He nodded and they stepped back inside. When they were ready to leave, they entered the elevator. This time he took her hand, gripping it tightly. As they descended his stomach dropped, but Tomi squeezed his hand and everything felt right again.

Next, they stopped at Water Tower Plaza and ate Chicago-style pizza. Tomi purchased souvenirs, a glitzy Cubs hat for her friend Chie and smaller tokens for others.

P.R. eyed all her bags. "We better leave before you have to buy another suitcase."

Tomi nodded. "Take presents to coworkers. Sometimes people don't say they go on holiday. Then they no have to bring back souvenirs."

"I'm glad I never had to buy for the law firm. They have more than one hundred lawyers." As they walked out of Water Tower Plaza, dark clouds appeared. "Any place else?"

"I want to see office."

P.R. was sorry he'd mentioned his law firm, but he took her arm. "Hurry. It could rain."

They walked half a block and stopped in front of the tall building. He pointed up. "My office was on the tenth floor, the third window from the corner."

As he looked up, a strange sensation rippled through him. He hadn't been downtown since being let go. He felt like the two-faced Janus, looking back at his old life and ahead at his new life. He was surprised how little he missed the law firm and how much he enjoyed life in Hickory Hills.

"P.R.!"

He didn't need to turn around. He recognized Peewee's voice. Why did the vagabond have to show up now? He certainly didn't want to talk to him with Tomi. He put his hand on her elbow to steer her away.

"P.R.!"

Tomi slowed. "Someone call you."

P.R. pretended not to hear and nudged her forward. "Let's hurry before we get caught in the rain."

Peewee called out again. "Hey! Hey wait!"

Tomi stopped. Peewee scuttled in front, blocking their path. "I thought that was my old friend."

Peewee looked much the same. Dingy white shirt, high-water pants, and gap-toothed grin. "Get your old job back?" he asked.

"No." The word came out harsher than P.R. intended.

Peewee didn't seem to notice. "Tough times, man. Tough times."

"Yeah, they are." The wind picked up, bringing with it a cold bite. Tough times for Peewee meant no jacket to protect his thin arms and no cap to cover his stringy blond hair.

Peewee fixed his eyes on Tomi. "Who's your pretty woman?"

P.R. felt a manly pride at the words 'your woman.' Reluctantly he introduced her. "Tomi, this is an old friend from high school, Peewee."

P.R. was shocked when Tomi bowed in the same polite way she had for his mother.

Peewee slapped P.R.'s back. "Thought maybe you'd end up with an Italian babe, but looks like you did better."

P.R. reached into his pocket and pulled a bill from his money clip. Not sure if he held a twenty or a fifty, he slipped it into the palm of his hand. He didn't want Tomi to notice the money. He extended his hand to Peewee as if to shake good-bye. "Take care of yourself."

Peewee shook P.R.'s hand and snatched the money.

Thunder rumbled, and the clouds darkened. "We better go." P.R. tried to guide Tomi away.

Her smile faded. She didn't budge. "Maybe friend need ride?"

P.R. stopped. "What?"

"Going to rain. Friend no have coat."

What did she want him to do? Take off his jacket. He wasn't giving Peewee his expensive leather coat.

Tomi eyes slid from P.R. to Peewee. "Help friend."

He had helped his friend, but Tomi didn't know he had given Peewee money. A rain drop landed on P.R.'s nose. He looked skyward just as it began to sprinkle. Then the dark clouds ripped open. The three of them dashed toward the building. Soaked, they huddled under the wide overhang sheltered from the rain.

As quickly as it had begun, the rain stopped, and the sun began to shine. Peewee moved away from the building. "Just like the monsoons in Afghanistan."

P.R.'s mouth dropped open. "You were in Afghanistan?"

"Enlisted in the Army right after high school. You know, see the world and all that. Thought maybe I'd make it to Italy. Almost did, but two weeks before my R&R, a truck in front of the convoy hit a land mine. I got shrapnel. Some of my buddies weren't so lucky."

For three years P.R. had walked by his friend almost every day, but until a few weeks ago, he hadn't known who he was. But even when he'd learned the beggar was Peewee, he hadn't taken the time to find out what had happened to him.

Peewee shouldn't be living on the streets. He was a veteran. The country should take better care of veterans. Not just the country, P.R. should do his part, too.

"Do you need a ride?" P.R. asked.

"Naw. It's a good day. Lots of Cubs fans."

P.R. reached into his jacket and took out his wallet. He found one of his old business cards and handed it to Peewee. "The cell phone number is the same. Give me a call next week."

P.R. looked over at Tomi. She smiled up at him with pride. He didn't want that smile to disappear. He checked his other pockets and took off the coat. "Here, you might need this."

Peewee latched onto the leather coat as if he had been thrown a lifeline. "Thanks, man. I owe you."

"No, man. I owe you."

CHAPTER FORTY-SIX

The next Monday, Quinn called down the hall, "Hurry up, Taylor. Breakfast is ready. You don't want to miss the school bus."

She returned to the kitchen and filled the bowls with oatmeal. Tomi carried them to the table.

Jason opened the front door, letting in the cool October wind. He took off his Cubs hat and hurried to the table. Shivering, he blew on his hands. "It was Taylor's turn to feed the dogs, not mine."

Quinn began making Jason's lunch. "Taylor can take care of them tonight." The dogs had been moved from the Quonset hut to the garden shed behind the loft. The distance wasn't far, but the October air was too chilly for Jason to be outside in just a Cubs T-shirt and jeans. "I found your jacket in the Quonset hut. It's on the hook by the door. You can wear it to school today."

Jason scowled. "I don't want to wear that old thing."

Quinn's eyebrows rose. Jason used to love that jean jacket. She thought he'd be happy it hadn't burned with his other clothes. She finished making his sandwich and set his lunch box on the table. Jason hadn't touched his oatmeal. "Why aren't you eating?"

"I don't like oatmeal," Jason mumbled.

"Oh." Quinn didn't know that. Or if she did, she hadn't remembered. Mondays were hectic, but today was worse. Last night had been the fifth game of the World Series. The game was played in Cleveland and started in Illinois after eight, which was bedtime for the kids.

Jason had begged to stay up. "Please, please. It might be the Cubs last game."

Taylor pleaded, too. Quinn let Ace make the decision. But Ace wasn't here to help her get the kids off to school.

At least the Cubs had beaten the Indians, but the game was only their second victory. One more loss and Cleveland would win the World Series. Then Cub fans, like P.R. and Jason, would say what they'd said for the last 108 years. "Wait 'til next year."

Quinn handed Jason a bowl of brown sugar. "Sweeten your oatmeal with this."

"It's not sour. It's mushy."

"We're out of Cheerios. I'll go to the store tonight."

Jason opened his lunch box and peeked inside. "What kind of sandwich did you make?"

"Grape jelly."

"I don't like jelly sandwiches without peanut butter."

"You know we can't have peanut butter. Taylor is allergic to it."

Jason wasn't a picky eater, and he'd never asked for peanut butter before. Something must be bothering him, but right now she didn't have time to figure it out. Ace had left for the field and would have a truckload of corn waiting for her to haul to the elevator.

"I go to store," Tomi offered.

"Thanks." Quinn didn't know how she would manage when Tomi returned to Japan. Marriage and joining the two households were harder than she expected. "Could you check on Taylor?"

Tomi rose and shuffled down the hall to Taylor's bedroom.

"Taylor's not going to school today," Jason said.

Quinn's mouth dropped open. "Why not?"

"She doesn't want to be in the Halloween parade."

Halloween? She glanced at the wall calendar above the stove. October 31. How could she have forgotten?

Tomi hurried into the kitchen. "Taylor no feel well."

Quinn didn't have time for one of Taylor's tantrums. She marched down the hall and into the bedroom. Taylor lay in bed, the covers pulled over her head.

Quinn took a deep breath and gathered her patience as she sat on the edge of the bunk bed. "What's wrong, Lady Bug?"

Taylor peeked from beneath the covers, her red curls springing around her head. "My tummy hurts."

Quinn put her hand on Taylor's forehead. "No fever. I'm sorry I forgot about Halloween and didn't make you a costume."

Taylor stuck out her bottom lip. "I hate Halloween."

Quinn patted Taylor's wild hair. "I'll buy you something to wear and bring it to school." Surely she could find a costume at the local store.

"I don't want to be in that stupid Halloween parade."

"You'll be wearing a mask. No one will know it's you. "

Taylor sat up. "Please, Mommy. I just want to be me." Her whole body shook, and her eyes filled with fear. This wasn't the pleading of a child too tired to go to school. Taylor was scared.

Quinn's stomach heaved. Oh, no! Taylor had acted this way Fourth of July when she'd refused to wear the Miss Liberty costume Quinn had made.

Pictures of Taylor dressed in pageant gowns and ballet costumes swirled through Quinn's mind. Taylor had been traumatized when her stepfather had dressed her in his deceased daughter's clothes. It would take Taylor a long time to overcome that.

Quinn tried to keep her voice steady. "I'll write a note to your teacher and pick you up early. That way you won't have to be in the Halloween parade."

Taylor threw her arms around Quinn's neck and covered her face with kisses. Quinn reveled in her daughter's slobbery kisses. They made up for all the hectic mornings.

Quinn walked back into the kitchen. Jason still hadn't eaten. Maybe Halloween was his problem, too. "I'm sorry I didn't think about today being a holiday."

"Taylor made me throw away the note the school sent home last week."

So Taylor had been worrying for days and Quinn hadn't noticed. Her old doubts about being a good mother resurfaced. She shouldn't be too busy to pay attention to her daughter. Quinn knew how it felt to be neglected. As a child, her mother had paid little attention to her, but plenty of attention to each new man.

Quinn wanted to make sure Taylor and Jason knew she loved them. She needed to figure out what was going on with Jason. "Do you want me to buy you a costume and bring it to school?"

Jason pointed to the Cubs shirt. "A bunch of us guys are going as baseball players."

"I'll get you a mask."

"Naw. Baseball players don't wear masks, except for the catcher."

"Good point."

Taylor pranced into the kitchen and started taunting Jason. "Ha-ha-ha. I don't have to wear a costume, and I get to leave school early."

Quinn handed Taylor her lunch money. "Hurry up and eat."

Taylor sat and quickly finished her oatmeal.

Quinn wrote Taylor a note and gave Jason his jacket. "Wear this to school until I can buy you a new one."

"That's not fair. Why do I have to wear that dumb jacket? Taylor doesn't have to wear a costume, plus she gets out of school early."

"I like jacket," Tomi said, obviously trying to help.

Jason threw on the jacket and stomped out of the house. Taylor skipped after him. When they were gone, Quinn sank into the chair.

Tomi pointed to the table. "Jason forgot lunch."

Quinn groaned. Jason hadn't eaten breakfast. He couldn't skip lunch. She'd just have to squeeze in some time to stop by the school after she delivered the corn to the elevator.

———

Quinn and Tomi stood outside the front door of Hickory Hills elementary school, a three-story red brick building built in the 1920s. Quinn held Jason's lunchbox in one hand and pushed the intercom with the other. She wondered what Tomi would think of American schools.

In Japan, students, not custodians, took care of the school buildings. They swept the halls, dumped the garbage, and even cleaned the bathrooms. Since Japan had a low crime rate, the buildings were left open.

"American schools have to be locked for safety," Quinn explained.

As if to reinforce her words, a siren wailed in the distance. Quinn automatically reached for her coat button. 'Hold your button for an ambulance' was a childish superstition, yet Quinn's fingers wouldn't release their tight grip on her button.

A woman's voice on the intercom asked, "May I help you?"

"Quinn Edleston and my friend. We're here to—"

The door clicked. "Mrs. Edleston, I've been trying to reach you. Jason—"

Quinn didn't wait for her to finish. She pulled open the door. Something was wrong with Jason. She could hear it in the woman's shaky voice.

Quinn hurried to the principal's office and Tomi followed. An attractive blonde named Dorothy sat behind the desk.

"Jason, where is he? What's wrong?" Quinn asked.

"He's in the nurse's office. The ambulance should be here—"

"The ambulance is for Jason?"

The woman nodded.

Quinn grabbed Tomi's hand. Together they shot out the door and down the hall to the nurse's office. Jason lay curled up on the cot, holding his stomach. His eyes were blood-shot and sweat rolled down his pale cheeks.

Jason's lunchbox slipped from Quinn's hand as she knelt beside the cot. "Jason, what happened?"

When he didn't answer, Quinn looked up at the nurse. "What-what's wrong with him?"

"The teacher said after recess he started stumbling and slurring his words. She thought he was clowning around until he vomited. When she questioned him, he said he didn't eat anything today, except part of a brownie."

The door opened and two paramedics wheeled in a stretcher. Quinn recognized one man as Junior, who had been on duty the night of the fire.

Quinn stood next to the cot, feeling helpless as the men prepared to transport Jason. When they lifted his small body onto the stretcher, he grabbed Quinn's arm. His words were slurred, but Quinn thought he said, "I don't want to die."

"You aren't going to die," Quinn automatically said.

He let go of her arm and doubled over as he screamed with pain. Quinn's heart pounded. She no longer felt as sure as she had sounded.

Jason's eyes searched for her. "Don't...leave."

She touched his arm. "I'm right here."

Quinn reached into her coat pocket and handed the keys to Tomi. "I'll ride with Jason in the ambulance. Go to Taylor's classroom and pick her up. Meet us at the hospital."

Five minutes later the ambulance arrived at the hospital. The paramedics whisked Jason into the emergency room. Quinn stopped at the desk to give insurance information and phone Ace. When he answered, the lump in her throat made it almost impossible to speak. "Jason...hospital...come."

Ace asked a string of questions. She answered, "Hurry."

As she entered the emergency room, Doc Morgan turned toward her. "We've pumped Jason's stomach. Is he allergic to anything?"

"Not that I know of." Jason's body jerked uncontrollably.

"What did he eat today?"

Quinn felt guilty. "I fixed oatmeal, but I don't think he ate any, and he left his lunch at home. That's why I went to school." Then she remembered what the nurse had said. "Maybe he ate a brownie."

Jason's body was still convulsing when Tomi led Taylor into the room. Taylor gripped Jason's jean jacket and hurried over to Quinn.

Taylor shouldn't be in here, Quinn thought. "I'll take Jason's jacket. You and Tomi wait outside for Ace."

Taylor held onto the jacket. "Don't give Jason his jacket. It'll make him sad."

Quinn bent down to Taylor. "Why would his jacket make him sad?"

"Because he wrapped Babe in his jacket when he carried him home from Miss May's."

"Babe?" Tomi asked.

"Jason's puppy. He blames himself because Babe died." Maybe that's why Jason thought he was going to die.

Quinn pried the jacket from Taylor's fingers. "I won't give the jacket to Jason."

Quinn waited until Tomi and Taylor left before she reached into the pockets on the jacket. The first was empty. In the second one, she felt something and pulled it out. Her hand shook as she held up a small plastic baggie. Inside was a half-eaten brownie, hard enough to have been there for several weeks.

Babe had eaten a brownie before he died. Had Jason eaten part of this brownie? Was he going to die, too?

CHAPTER FORTY-SEVEN

On Wednesday night, P.R. and Tomi, along with Quinn, Ace, and Taylor, were seated around Jason's hospital bed watching the final game of the World Series. Last night the Cubs had tied the series, and tonight they played for the championship.

The Cubs had an early lead, five to one, but P.R. was too nervous to enjoy the game. By the bottom of the eighth, the Cubs still led six to three. Then the curse happened. The goat returned. The Indians hit a three-run homer and tied the game, six to six.

P.R. rose. "I can't sit. I need to walk."

"You no watch?" Tomi asked.

On TV, the dark clouds above the Indians' stadium matched his mood. His team was going to lose—again. Watching was too painful. "Come get me when the game is over."

P.R. paced the hallway, past the nurse's station to the exit and back. The outcome of the game wasn't life or death. Being at the hospital reminded him of that.

For hours after Jason had been admitted to the ER, the family prayed he would live. Their prayers were answered. Jason was alive and cheering for the Cubs.

From Jason's vomiting, abdominal cramping, and blood in the urine,

Doc Morgan suspected Jason had ingested poison, possibly the same poison that had killed Babe.

"It's a miracle," Doc said. "A few more hours and Jason might have had some major damage."

The Cubs needed a miracle, too.

When Tomi rushed into the hall, P.R. was in agony. "Did they lose?"

Tomi shook her head.

He couldn't believe it. "They won?"

She shook her head. "Bottom of ninth they tied."

He slapped his hand against his forehead.

"And rain delay."

He groaned. "If the game continues much longer, I'll need a hospital bed."

Tomi must have understood his misery. "Go to Castle," she suggested.

"Good idea." Hospital visiting hours ended at eight. The staff had bent the rules to let all of them in Jason's room past ten.

Five minutes later, P.R. and Tomi walked into the family room of the B&B where Belle, Ben, and their two boys huddled around the TV, eating popcorn. "Is the rain delay over?" P.R. asked.

"Not yet." Worry clouded Belle's eyes. "How's Jason doing?"

"He'll probably be able to go home tomorrow."

"What a relief!"

Ben set down his bowl of popcorn. "Want a drink, P.R.?"

P.R. shook his head. He didn't think his stomach could keep anything down.

Ben rose. "Join me in the kitchen." The words sounded like an order, so P.R. followed him.

In the kitchen Ben grabbed a bottle of water from the refrigerator. "What do you know about how Jason got sick?"

"Only what I've heard. Why?"

Ben took a swig and sat at the table. "Ace said Doc Morgan suspects poison. If it's poison, I'll need to question Jason about where the poison might have come from."

P.R.'s throat went dry. He removed a bottle of water from the refrigerator and sat across from Ben. "Jason said he ate part of a brownie that Miss May gave him."

Ben nodded. "That's the rumor I heard. Did Tomi tell you anything else?"

"She said Quinn sent Jason to check on Miss May, who hadn't been in church. Stuart was supposed to come that day for his birthday, so Miss May made his favorite brownies, but he called and cancelled."

"So what happened to the brownies?" Ben asked.

"Tomi said that Miss May gave Jason two brownies in a plastic bag and told him not to eat them until after supper."

"My boys would have devoured both of them."

"Exactly. While Jason was biking home, he reached into the pocket of his jacket for the brownies. Babe ran in front of Jason's bike and he crashed."

"So what happened to the brownies?"

"According to Jason, Babe gulped one of them down, and Jason stuffed the other into the bag and put it in his pocket. Babe acted weird and wouldn't follow him home, so Jason wrapped him up in his jacket and carried him. That night Babe died."

Ben rubbed his hand over his face as if taking it in. "So this happened back in September, the day before Stuart found Miss May?"

P.R.'s eyes widened. "Ben, you don't think—"

"It's a possibility," Ben said. "First, the dog dies. Second, Miss May dies. Third, Jason almost dies. The dog and Jason both ate brownies. Suppose Miss May ate one, too?"

"But why would the brownies be poisonous unless—unless someone wanted to kill Miss May. But who would want to do that?"

"Ace mentioned Miss May had drawn up a new will that named him executor instead of Stuart. Rumor is when Ace filed it, Stuart foamed at the mouth like a rabid dog."

"Do you think Stuart might have tampered with the brownies?"

"I'd need proof before I make any accusations about murder."

The kitchen doors swung open. Tomi's hands flew to her mouth. "Murder?"

Ben rose and put a reassuring hand on Tomi's shoulder. "Nothing for you to worry about." He glanced over Tomi's head and mouthed to P.R. "Don't repeat any of this."

P.R. nodded.

Tomi's voice trembled. "Game begin."

Ben hurried back to the family room, but P.R. remained seated. Tomi walked over and extended her hand. "Come. Enjoy game."

Enjoy? He couldn't enjoy the game, but if the Cubs won, he wanted to see it. He took Tomi's hand. "You'll be our good luck charm."

The rain delay lasted seventeen minutes. When the Cubs stepped up to the plate in the top of the tenth inning, the batters seemed ready to hit the ball. The Indians walked two crucial players, and the Cubs scored two runs. When the Indians came up to bat in the bottom of the tenth, the Cubs led eight to six.

Tomi squeezed P.R.'s hand. "See, Cubs win."

P.R. crossed his fingers. Then the Indians scored again, making it eight to seven. P.R. began to fidget, but the Cubs held onto the lead. They had their miracle.

"Holy cow!" Tomi was right. He picked her up and swung her around. "They did it! The Cubs won the World Series!"

CHAPTER FORTY-EIGHT

Two days later, Tomi and P.R. drove to Chicago. Along with a million other people, they stood along Michigan Avenue, cheering the Cubs as they rode by in red double-decker buses. After the victory parade, P.R. and Tomi crowded into Grant Park for the rally.

The November day was sunny with fifty-degree weather. They wrapped their arms around each other's waists and swayed as they joined together and sang "Go Cubs Go."

"I wish Dad could have seen the Cubs win the World Series," P.R. said to Tomi.

"I wish brother could have come to America."

"You came." P.R. leaned over and kissed the top of her head. He pushed away thoughts that in a month she would be leaving. Today was for celebrating.

The next few weeks flew by. P.R. took Tomi bowling and roller skating. He taught her to play UNO and monopoly. She fixed him Japanese food, such as rice balls, and took him to a Kabuki production of *Macbeth*. The actors were male and spoke Japanese. P.R. had read the play in high school and understood enough of it.

At work, the days seemed to run together. Word had spread that he was temporarily in Jackson's office. People who had put off legal matters began scheduling appointments.

The week before Thanksgiving, P.R. came into the office early as usual. Whenever he had spare time, he perused the files devoted to the coal miners' lawsuit. He wasn't the only lawyer working on the case, but Jackson had been lead attorney, so P.R. was thrust into that position. That hadn't set well with Miller's lawyer, Randy Jeralds.

Jeralds was flamboyant with flowing white hair, and a handle-bar mustache. From the beginning he and P.R. butted heads, probably because Jeralds didn't like some whippersnapper being in charge when he had over thirty years of experience.

At nine Carrie knocked and peeked her head around the door. Today her hair was streaked with green. "Dale Miller is here."

"Send him in."

P.R. rose as Mr. Miller shuffled in pulling a portable oxygen tank. The records showed his age at fifty-four, but he appeared twenty years older. He wore faded bib overalls and a flannel shirt that made him look Jack Sprat thin.

Miller dropped into the chair in front of P.R.'s desk. "Don't get out much these days."

P.R. didn't ask Miller how he was doing. Miller had cancelled the previous appointment and didn't look well today. P.R realized he should have gone to Miller's house.

P.R. reviewed the basic facts. "So how long did you work for Illinois Coal?"

"Started the day I turned eighteen. Worked in the mines for thirty years." He stated it like a badge of honor.

At first, when P.R. had helped Jackson on the black lung cases, P.R. hadn't understood why men chose to be coal miners. They had to know the job would probably shorten their lives. After P.R. talked to the miners and took their depositions, he realized choice had little to do with the decision.

The miners wanted what most men wanted—enough money to support their families. They wanted to put food on the table and clothes on their children's backs. Other jobs in southern Illinois were scarce. Even mine jobs often depended on who you knew or what family member already worked in the mines.

P.R. found it hard to imagine working underground, sometimes in twelve-hour shifts, and then ending up fighting for every breath the way Miller did now.

Miller fisted his hand. "Even wearing those masks I could taste the coal dust. When I had to leave, I took part of the mine with me." He pounded his fist on his chest "It's right here."

P.R. had viewed the chest x-rays. Miller was right. His lungs were riddled from black coal dust.

Each word Miller uttered was labored. "I'm not worried about myself. It's the missus and my daughter." He doubled over and coughed so hard P.R. thought he might crack his ribs. After several minutes, Miller hacked up a thick glob of yellow phlegm and spit it into a tissue. He examined the phlegm, pushing it around with his index finger.

"See that." He pointed to a speck of black. "It's killing me. But them lawyers for the coal company say I don't have black lung."

Miller looked up and focused his rheumy eyes on P.R. "Have you met my daughter, Dahlia? Pretty girl. Smart, too. She used to work in the mine office. Now she works down at Johnston's Grocery."

P.R. had not met Dahlia, but he remembered her flowery signature on several requisitions for mine supplies.

"I'd sure like to be able to take care of her financially before I pass."

After Miller left, P.R. poured himself another cup of coffee. He spent the next hour digging through Miller's files. When he finished the last one, he closed it in frustration. His hand hit the coffee cup, tipping it. He grabbed the handle, righting the cup before coffee spilled onto any legal documents. Jackson's black appointment book fell off the desk onto the floor. The notebook lay open to August 15.

P.R. leaned over and scooped it up. Jackson had drawn one of his doodles, something that looked like a surgeon wearing a mask. Had Jackson been ill? Maybe he had a doctor's appointment that day.

Jackson had been doodling in his appointment book the last time P.R. stopped in the office. He flipped the pages until he found that date, August 22. On the page under his name was a picture of a pistol with a plume of smoke curling from the end. Had Jackson found out he had a terminal illness?

That didn't make sense. Jackson had been excited. He talked about the lawsuit and thought they had a chance to win. He'd even said something about a 'smoking gun.'

P.R. placed the appointment book on his desk. He didn't feel that same excitement. Time was running out. The trial was scheduled for the week after Thanksgiving, and he still hadn't found anything that would help him win.

He stared at the doodle of the surgeon. Michelle said Jackson's doodles always meant something. Maybe Jackson had left P.R. a clue.

He leaned back in his chair and turned to the page with the gun, August 22. He flipped the pages back and forth between August 15 and August 22. Surgeon. Gun. Surgeon. Gun. Surgeon...

He jerked up and paused on the picture of the surgeon. Maybe it wasn't a surgical mask. Miller had mentioned wearing a mask.

P.R. had read something about respiratory masks. He jumped up and hurried to the boxes stacked along the wall. He thumbed through the files until he found the one labeled safety equipment. He pulled out a list of equipment that Illinois Coal had requisitioned from the Workers' Safety Equipment Company (WSEC). He paused on the order for respiratory masks, signed by the president of Illinois Coal, Leland Little, and the office manager, Dahlia Miller. That must be the pretty daughter Miller had mentioned.

After P.R. read over the files, he leaned back in his chair and whistled. Maybe Mr. Miller would get his wish. Maybe he would be able to leave something substantial to his wife and daughter.

Maybe P.R. had just found the smoking gun.

CHAPTER FORTY-NINE

P.R. was happy Tomi would be celebrating her first Thanksgiving with his family at the Castle. His mom had come down from Chicago and brought Al Levy. Actually Al had brought her, since Mom usually rode the train when she visited. Carter was also home for a rare visit.

Ben deep-fried two turkeys injected with special herbs. Belle prepared the family's other favorites—dressing, noodles, mashed potatoes, and gravy. Summer brought the green bean casserole. Raven whipped up pumpkin and pecan pies, and Quinn baked cloverleaf rolls.

"And what did you bring?" P.R. asked Tomi as he greeted her at the door.

She pointed to her stomach. "My appetite."

He chuckled. "No leftovers this year."

He threw his arm around her and led her into the dining room. Tomi's eyes rounded at all the dishes of food.

At noon, twelve adults and six children gathered at the farmhouse table. Ben seated himself at the head. Ace took the other end. The family joined hands as Ben thanked God for their blessings, particularly the miracle that Jason was with them today. He also gave thanks for the new additions to the family, Quinn and Taylor, and their special guests, Tomi and Al.

As the bowls of food were passed around, P.R. glanced over at Ben and Belle. They had uprooted their family from Chicago so their boys could be nearer to their cousins. Ben had become a small-town sheriff, and Belle had turned the Castle into a B&B. The move to Hickory Hills had worked for them.

Ace was all smiles today, too. "Our first Thanksgiving together," he said to Quinn.

"I remember when Thanksgiving was just another day." Quinn gazed around the table. "Now I have an entire family."

As a boy, P.R. had enjoyed the hectic holidays. He hadn't realized how much he missed them and how much he wanted to have more holidays like this with Tomi. Ben and Ace had overcome obstacles to make their marriages work. Maybe he and Tomi could overcome their differences.

"Ready for the trial next week?" Ace asked.

P.R. smiled. "I might be buying that land we discussed."

"Glad to hear it," Ace said. "I'm sure we can work something out."

P.R. wanted to have a serious conversation with Tomi, but he was afraid he might scare her away. He didn't know how much longer he could pretend they were just friends. He loved her and wanted her by his side.

Maybe next weekend they could go away together, just the two of them. Then he could show her how much she meant to him.

He glanced over at Tomi and frowned. She had barely touched her plate of food. "You're not eating."

"Too much."

She had never complained about too much food before.

Cries from the baby monitor next to Raven rose above the chatter at the table. First one twin and then the other wailed. Raven put down her fork. "I'd better check on them."

Carter rose. "Honey, you stay and finish your dinner. I'll go."

Raven gave him an appreciative smile and then pointedly looked at Ben. P.R. wasn't sure what had happened between Ben and Carter, but obviously something had because the tension between the two men was thicker than the Thanksgiving gravy.

After Carter left, Tomi's appetite improved. She finished everything on her plate and asked for a second helping of noodles which she quickly slurped down.

"You must really like Belle's noodles," P.R. said.

"*Hai.* I slurp to show cook appreciate very much."

"Pass the noodles," Jason said. Soon all the kids were slurping noodles.

"Please don't tell them about belching," Quinn said.

"I want to know," Taylor said.

"After finish good meal, if you like, you belch." Tomi let out a big belch, and everyone laughed.

Jason, not to be outdone, produced a bigger belch. Then the other kids began to belch.

Finally Belle said, "Anyone belching must be too full for pie."

The noises quickly stopped.

Tomi sampled bites of the pumpkin and pecan pies, and then devoured slices of each. "My first Thanksgiving." She patted her belly. "Ate too much."

"You can always come back next year." As soon as the words slipped out of his mouth, P.R. knew he'd made a mistake. The smile on Tomi's face disappeared.

He shouldn't have said anything about next year, not here, surrounded by his family. He wanted to talk to her in private. He needed to tell her how he felt, convince her that together they could figure out a way to make it work.

Taylor, seated on the other side of Quinn, said, "We'll see Tomi next year. We're going to Japan."

P.R.'s eyebrows rose. "You are?" No one had mentioned that to him.

"Yep. We're going to Tomi's wedding."

"Wedding?" All the food in his stomach heaved. He turned to Tomi. "What's Taylor talking about?"

Tomi dropped her fork and avoided his eyes.

Taylor didn't seem to notice the awkward silence. "I think Tomi should stay here and marry P.R., but she said she would marry another man."

"Anyone want more pie?" Belle asked.

Heat flooded through P.R. He couldn't breathe. He scooted back his chair and rose. "Tomi, I'd like to talk to you in the kitchen." He threw down his napkin and marched into the kitchen.

He took deep breaths, trying to slow his pulse. The words 'Tomi's wedding' pounded in his head. One minute he'd been planning their future and the next he discovered she already had plans for her future—plans that didn't include him.

The doors behind him swung open and Tomi walked into the kitchen. He didn't turn around. "Is it true?"

She didn't answer.

He repeated the question, slower and louder. "Is it true? Are you marrying someone else?"

"Yes," Tomi whispered.

The word stabbed his heart. He'd hoped what Taylor said was just a child's misunderstanding. But he was the one who had misunderstood.

Tomi put her hand on his shoulder. "Why mad?"

He whirled around. Pain and anger flared up in him. "You didn't tell me you were engaged."

She stepped back, away from his accusing eyes. Her shoulders stiffened. She drew herself up. "I told you. No marry."

"Yes, but...that's what you meant? The whole time you were what, having some kind of fling?"

"No understand fling."

It didn't matter if she understood 'fling.' He understood. From the beginning, their relationship had been a sham. A one-sided affair. She'd never been serious. Oh, she'd been clever, acting so innocent. Even now she looked up at him, wide-eyed and perplexed.

For the first time in his life, he'd given his heart to a woman, only to find out she didn't want it. She'd never wanted it. She already loved someone else.

"So sorry."

Her stock phrase. The words only fueled his hurt. "Who is he?"

She did not want to say his name, did not want to bring him here in the kitchen between P.R. and her.

P.R.'s face grew red, his eyes hard. "Tell me," he demanded.

"Yoshiro," she spat out the name with the same distaste she had for the man, but P.R. was not listening to the sound or he would have heard her heart breaking.

"And you love him?"

She did not love Yoshiro. How could P.R. think that? She loved him, but she couldn't tell P.R. she loved him. That would hurt him more. He might think they could be together. But they couldn't. When she returned to Japan, she and Yoshiro would register the date of their marriage.

She couldn't lie. She would never love Yoshiro. In time she might become fond of him. But she had no heart to give him. She had already given it to P.R. He was the man she loved. He was the man she wanted to marry. But it was impossible.

She cast her eyes down and remained silent.

P.R. opened the back door. Cold air rushed into the warm kitchen. He was walking away.

She stepped toward him. "Don't leave."

He turned. His eyes were filled with hurt. She wanted to wrap her arms around him, kiss him, and make him happy. Her voice trembled. "Nothing changed. I still here."

"Maybe nothing has changed for you. But everything has changed for me."

He slammed the door. He didn't say good-bye, but she knew it was over.

She had been counting the days, dreading only three short weeks before she left. Now those three weeks seemed unbearable.

It was her fault. She should not have spent so much time with him. Maybe then she would not have fallen in love. But love wasn't a choice. She couldn't stop it flowing from her heart anymore than she could stop the tears flowing down her cheeks.

Tomi stood in the kitchen, alone and shivering. The slam of the door reverberated through her, echoing the door of her cage as it once again slammed shut.

CHAPTER FIFTY

Bucky pulled into the driveway of the white bungalow in Springfield, Illinois. The 'For Sale' sign was staked in the yard near a wheelchair ramp that led to the front door. He turned to Joey in the passenger seat. "What do you think about living here?"

"I live at The Farmstead." Joey proceeded to recite his address.

"If we play our cards right, we might be able to live here." Bucky didn't get the joyous response he wanted, so he added, "Maybe we can have a dog."

Joey's eyes sparkled. "I like dogs."

Bucky patted his brother's shoulder. "Me, too."

He reached into the pocket of his coat and pulled out the listing sheet that Sherry Sparks, the real estate agent had emailed him. The three-bedroom, two-bath house was handicap accessible. The two-car garage wasn't attached. He'd have to enclose the walkway so Joey wouldn't get cold or wet when he was wheeled to and from the car. The property was a few miles from The Farmstead, in case Joey wanted to visit.

The staff warned Bucky that Joey didn't adjust to change well, but Bucky knew Joey would be better off when they were living together. Until recently The Farmstead had been a charitable home. Then the facility had been bought by a corporation with directors who expected a profit. Costs skyrocketed.

Within a year of Captain's death, his mother died, and Bucky became executor of the trust. His mother's medical costs had eaten up the money Captain had left, so Bucky had begun to dip deeper into the trust for Joey's care.

The interest rates on the money in the trust couldn't keep up with the increases. A friend who worked for the State of Illinois had given Bucky a tip for an easy way to make big money.

The state planned to change Route 51 from a two-lane highway to a four-lane. A parcel of land that the state would eventually need was for sale. The acreage was in Vandalia, north of Hickory Hills, and wasn't prime Illinois farmland, so Bucky snatched it up for a reasonable price. When the state wanted to buy the land, Bucky would hold out for a sizable profit that would allow Joey and him to live comfortably for the rest of their lives.

But Illinois was in debt. The Democrats and Republicans were locked in a power struggle, and so far no annual budget had been passed for 2016. The highway project was put on hold. It might be years before the state optioned to purchase the land that Bucky had bought with money from the trust.

Bucky had put his house in St. Louis up for sale. It listed for almost a million dollars. After a year on the market and the house hadn't sold, he had borrowed money to pay for Joey's expenses. Two months ago the money had run out, and within thirty days his loan was due.

Desperate, Bucky had come up with another way to pay for Joey's care. Miss May's estate. But that had been a bust after Ace filed her new will.

Then, Bucky's luck had returned. He received an offer on his house. Not as much as he wanted, but a good chunk of money.

Unzipping the inside pocket of his coat, he ran his fingers over the cashier's check, reassuring himself it was still there. So on this Thanksgiving Day, he had plenty of blessings. Joey was alive, and they were together.

"Movies," said Joey. His eyes twitched the way they did when he got upset.

"I said we'd look at the house first, and then go to the movies." Bucky did not tell Joey it was a Batman movie. As boys, Bucky pretended to be Batman, and Joey was his faithful sidekick, Robin.

Miss Sparks was late. She hadn't wanted to interrupt her Thanksgiving dinner, but agreed to a showing in the afternoon. He reached for his cell just as a yellow Volkswagen pulled into the drive behind him.

An attractive blonde in her twenties climbed out. Instead of stopping at his car, she waved and hurried to the house. As she walked up the ramp, her spiked heels were so high she had to hold onto the railing to keep her balance. She would be a pushover.

Bucky retrieved the wheelchair from the trunk. He helped Joey into it and pushed him up the ramp. The Realtor seemed to be having trouble with the lockbox. He leaned over to help just as she punched in the correct four-digit code. Bucky stored away the information. It might be useful later.

Sherry opened the door, and Bucky pushed Joey inside. The floor plan seemed perfect. The bedroom off the living room could be his office. The other two bedrooms, one for him and one for Joey, shared an adjoining bathroom, which was good in case Bucky needed to help Joey in the middle of the night.

After they'd gone through the house twice, Sherry stopped in the kitchen and leaned against the counter. "Well, what do you like?"

Bucky listed a number of problems—not enough outlets, limited counter space, and plush carpeting that made it hard to maneuver a wheelchair.

Sherry put on her selling smile. "You won't find a house in this neighborhood for a more reasonable price."

"With some remodeling, I could probably make it work." Bucky shot her a low-ball offer.

Sherry's smile vanished. "I doubt if the sellers will come down that much."

"The deal will be cash, and I want to close within thirty days."

Her eyes brightened. "Cash is good, but consider upping the amount."

"I'll take my chances. Write up the deal."

Sherry pulled up the forms on her phone. "We can use an electronic signature."

He scanned the standard contract, signed it, and handed her a check for the earnest money.

They shook. "I'll let you know within forty-eight hours."

Bucky had a feeling Sherry would soon be handing him the keys to his new home.

Joey, eager to go, waved as the car putted out of the drive. "Now movies."

Bucky didn't want to go to a multiplex conglomerate with eight generic theaters. Prairie Land Theater was a long drive, but it was similar to the movie house they had gone to as boys. He'd discovered it the night he'd followed Tomi and watched *Titantic.*

As Bucky wheeled Joey into the theater, the smell of buttery popcorn filled the lobby. Movie posters lined the walls. Along one side was a glass candy counter and on the other a soda fountain. Bucky picked up two bags of popcorn and handed them to Joey, who held them on his lap. Bucky juggled the cups of soda and pushed the wheelchair down the aisle. In the middle section, rows of seats had been removed for couches. Bucky helped Joey onto a couch. Now his brother could enjoy the show seated like everyone else.

Too bad today would probably be their last trip here. After Sabina found out the stipulations in Miss May's new will, she told Bucky she had no intention of living in Hickory Hills.

He suspected she might already be cheating. He'd spotted her in St. Louis with some guy named Carter. Sabina said they were old friends who had bumped into each other and had gone to the pub to catch up. When Bucky asked how they knew each other, Sabina answered, "College." Carter said, "Work."

Bucky would go to the mine next week, pick up the gear he'd hidden, and clear out of Hickory Hills.

The theater lights dimmed. The theme song from Batman began, and the dynamic duo flashed on the big screen. Joey started bouncing up and down. He giggled as Robin exploded with his favorite saying, "Holy spontaneous combustion!"

The cell phone in Bucky's pocket vibrated. He pulled it out. A message from the Realtor. Just as he thought. The sellers were eager to accept a cash offer.

He read the message and frowned. The offer had been rejected. The price was so low, they hadn't countered.

Holy spontaneous combustion! They wouldn't be able to sell a house that was nothing but ashes.

CHAPTER FIFTY-ONE

P.R.'s desk was scattered with documents for the lawsuit to begin in two days. He glanced at the clock across the room. It was after twelve, but food was not what he wanted. He wanted Tomi.

For the past five days, he'd thrown himself into work trying to forget her. But he didn't know how to stop his longing. He didn't just miss her. He missed his life with her. She had shown him a different world, one where people did not close their eyes to a homeless man like Peewee.

P.R. wanted to be part of her world again. But Tomi had made her choice. She loved someone else.

Jealousy rose up in him like a bitter viper. At least an ocean separated him from that man. In less than two weeks, that ocean would also separate him from Tomi. Then what would he do?

Now he held on to the slim hope he might see her. That had happened Sunday at church. He'd been praying about Tomi, and when he opened his eyes, she was sitting in the pew two rows in front of him.

He had a hard time concentrating on Reverend Stone's sermon, "God's Plan for our Lives." What kind of plan did God have for P.R.'s life? He'd studied hard, graduated from law school, had a successful job, and then bam. Fired.

Working in Hickory Hills was supposed to be a short-term solution. Yet, with Tomi and most of his family here, he'd begun to see a different path, maybe a better one. Was that God's plan? If so, what kind of curve ball was God throwing him now?

After the church service, Tomi walked down the aisle toward him. Their eyes met. Just for a second he thought her eyes were filled with longing. And something else. Regret. Had she regretted their time together? Even knowing the outcome, he didn't regret their relationship. She had changed him.

After their trip to the baseball game, he'd contacted Pacific Garden Mission in Chicago, a shelter for homeless men. The Mission had accepted Peewee. Now it was up to him.

A knock sounded on his office door, and Carrie walked in. Today she had a purple streak in her hair. "I'm back from lunch. You need to take a break."

Carrie was right. He put on his overcoat and crossed the street to the Blue Moon. He'd been eating at the diner, hoping to see Tomi. He'd hinted to Ace and Quinn. Neither had given him hope.

Tuesday's special was the horseshoe, a hamburger and fries smothered in cheese. As he slid into a booth near the window, Vera hurried over. "The usual?"

He nodded. The horseshoe was one of his favorites.

She poured him a cup of coffee. "Looks like I'll be hanging up my apron."

He stared at her. "Why's that?"

"After the trial, I'll have enough money to retire."

"Nothing's guaranteed, Vera."

Vera stomped away, and when she returned with his order, she wasn't smiling.

He began to eat, but even his favorite meal didn't taste good today.

"Got a minute to discuss a legal problem?"

P.R. looked up as Stuart May slid into the seat across from him. Stuart was impeccably dressed in a tailored, pin-striped suit, but the expensive clothes couldn't hide his haggard look.

The locals liked to buy P.R. a cup of coffee, and in return they expected an hour of free legal advice. He didn't mind helping out a working man with a wife and kids, but Stuart could well afford P.R.'s fee.

He was about to suggest to phone the office when Stuart said, "I got a call from the sheriff."

That piqued P.R.'s interest. He picked up a French fry and nibbled on it as he listened.

"He wants my permission to exhume my aunt's body. Seems as if her death might not have been from natural causes." Stuart turned up the cup on the table and signaled to Vera. "What happens if I don't give my permission?"

"Why? You have something to hide?"

"I heard there may have been poison in the brownies my aunt baked. In September some field mice were getting into the barn. The cats had run off, so my aunt told me to buy poison at Scholtz's Hardware. Yesterday Jim Scholtz asked me how that rat poison I bought had worked."

P.R. hadn't expected Stuart to be so forthcoming. "And how did it work?"

Beads of sweat popped out on Stuart's forehead. "If you're asking, if I used it on my aunt, of course not. Why would I?"

Vera stopped at the table and poured Stuart's coffee. When she left, he leaned forward. "Did Jackson ever talk to you about my aunt's will?"

"Not that I remember." P.R. didn't add that Ace had talked to him about the will.

"I don't get it. Why would my aunt make Ace executor?"

"Did you two have a falling out?"

"Not really. My aunt didn't much care for Sabina, and the feeling was mutual. But I've always done my duty by my aunt. I called every week and visited at least once a month."

Duty. The word hung in the air. Maybe Miss May knew Stuart acted out of duty rather than any real love for her.

"The sheriff also asked if I'd lost my phone. Any idea what that's about?"

P.R. shrugged. He knew a burner phone had been found in the kitchen the night Tomi thought someone had tried to break in. Maybe the sheriff had linked the phone to Stuart.

"What do you think I should do?" Stuart asked.

P.R. took out his business card and handed it to him. "If you want legal advice, call my office."

"I have an attorney in St. Louis. He's tied up right now. I just thought I'd run some questions by you." Stuart glanced at P.R.'s business card—white with simple black lettering. "Classy card."

Tomi and he had worked on the layout. He'd been anxious to show them to her, but they hadn't arrived until the day after Thanksgiving.

CHAPTER FIFTY-TWO

Tomi sat in the rocking chair near the wood stove, knitting a sweater for Meggie. Heat shimmered from its black, pot belly, but could not warm her. Knit, purl, knit, purl. The rhythmic *click, click, click* of the knitting needles usually soothed her.

Tomorrow was the last day of November. P.R.'s trial.

"Tomi, phone." Quinn walked into the great room and held out her cell.

Tomi shook her head. "Busy."

"It's not P.R. It's Raven."

Tomi dropped the knitting into her lap and reached for the phone. "How are you? How babies?"

"They're kicking and trying to roll over. They miss you," Raven said. "I miss you, too. Please come see us."

Tomi hesitated. She had not been to the B&B since Thanksgiving. She did not want to chance meeting Carter or P.R.

As if Raven understood, she said, "P.R.'s busy at the office and Carter's gone."

Tomi thought Carter had left on a business trip. But an hour later at the B&B, Raven told her Carter had left permanently.

Raven had found messages on Carter's phone from another woman. He said the woman was a client and the messages were business.

Raven plopped onto the bed. "The only kind of business those messages could have been was monkey business."

"Monkey business?" Tomi asked.

"Never mind. I told Carter to leave." Now Raven seemed to regret her decision. "I thought he would come back, but he hasn't returned my calls. I don't even know where he is."

Tomi walked over to Raven and hugged her. She did not like Carter, but she did not want Raven to feel as lost as she did without P.R.

Raven must have noticed Tomi's sad face. She sniffed back her tears. "I'm glad we're still friends, even if you don't like my brother."

"I like. He good man."

"He's different with you. Caring and sweet. I haven't seen that side of him since he was a boy."

Tomi didn't admit to Raven how much she cared for P.R. He must never find out the truth.

"Maybe it's better that you don't love him," Raven said. "Love hurts too much."

Tomi felt that stab of love. She had not just fallen in love with P.R., she had fallen in love with his whole family.

As if on cue Meggie woke and began to whimper. Tomi hurried over to the bassinet and picked her up. She began singing in Japanese.

The baby's whole face lit up. Tomi's heart danced. She hugged Meggie to her chest, never wanting to let her go.

When she left Hickory Hills, she would leave behind everything that made her heart sing. Without the music, her heart would be too heavy to dance.

CHAPTER FIFTY-THREE

P.R. walked into the St. Clair County Courthouse and unbuttoned his gray suit. Jackson could have filed the lawsuit anywhere in the state, but he had opted for the Metro-East area. With its rich coal history he would have a good pool for jury selection, but he hoped it wouldn't come to that. P.R. had defended other clients and had been invested in the verdict, but today he would be fighting for fair monetary compensation for coal miners and their families.

By eight a.m., his three clients and their attorneys had convened around the long table in the conference room. Carrie, his paralegal and also a client, sat next to him. Vera and Dale Miller, flanked by their attorneys, sat across from them. Carrie's lawyer, Karen Boverman, was at the end of the table in her motorized wheelchair.

Miller's lawyer, Randy Jeralds, impatiently twisted one end of his handle-bar mustache. "This better be good, Montgomery. Calling a meeting two hours before we're due in court."

P.R. clenched his jaw. He wasn't about to be baited by Jeralds.

Vera's attorney had the same dour expression as Vera and seemed to share Jeralds' annoyance. "Anything you needed to tell us could have been handled by a phone call."

Heeded by Jackson's warning of corruption, P.R. had purposely kept major details to himself. "I apologize for the inconvenience, but I think you will find the meeting necessary and beneficial."

With a wave of his hand, Jeralds dismissed P.R.'s words. "You're as windy as Jackson."

From the end of the table Karen Boverman spoke up. "We're already here. Let P.R. explain."

P.R. smiled at Karen. He had collaborated with her on a workman's comp case and understood why she was a well-respected lawyer. She didn't allow her lifetime battle with MS to diminish her practice. Karen fought for her clients' rights the same way she fought for her own.

P.R. motioned for Carrie to pass out the thick manila folders. "Turn to the ruling from OSHA banning respiratory masks manufactured by Workers' Safety Equipment Company."

Jeralds opened his folder and scowled. "This is old news. OSHA banned those masks in the 70s."

Before P.R. could respond, Dale Miller began to cough. Today Miller appeared even more gaunt. He coughed so hard his frail body shook. Carrie rose and left the room. She returned with a bottle of water and handed it to Miller. He gave her a weak smile of thanks as he took the bottle and drank.

P.R. instructed the lawyers to look at the next document. "This is a requisition from Illinois Coal dated 2010 ordering two dozen respiratory masks from WSEC."

Karen was the first to spot what P.R. had discovered. "The model number and style number are the same as the ones OSHA banned."

P.R. nodded. "Exactly. Illinois Coal has continued to buy and distribute ineffective masks that were banned by the government."

Jeralds objected, "That should fall on WSEC. They should have stopped manufacturing those masks."

"The masks can be used for other businesses," P.R. said.

Jeralds wasn't placated. "Even if the coal company ordered those masks, how do we know our clients used them?"

P.R. flipped through his folder. "On the last page is the supply distribution sheet for those respiratory masks. Beside the long list of names, only three had signatures and dates verifying they received that make and model of WSEC's mask. Those that signed for the masks are our clients."

Miller bolted up. "You mean them masks weren't doing me no good?"

Jeralds put a hand on Miller's shoulder and settled him back into his seat. "Even if the coal company bought and distributed masks that were banned, it's going to be hard to prove culpability."

"I don't agree," Karen said. "It's the coal company's responsibility to provide safe equipment. If they didn't know the masks were banned, they were negligent."

Jeralds rolled his eyes as if it should be clear to everyone how ridiculous that was. "We all know what's going to happen today. The coal company's lawyers will ask for a continuance and the judge will grant it."

P.R. shook his head. "Not after we show them all the facts." He handed the lawyers another document. After they read it, even the sour-faced Vera and her lawyer were smiling.

An hour later, P.R. and his three clients sat at the same table in the conference room. This time his clients and their lawyers were lined up on his side of the table. Across from them were the two defendants—Leland Little, the owner of Illinois Coal, and the president of the board of directors. Next to them were their four lawyers, dressed in black suits, each with a different colored tie.

At first the defense lawyers blustered the way Jeralds had about being called to a meeting before court. P.R. waited until they finished grumbling before he presented the information. The Black Suits were not concerned about OSHA's decades-old ban, but they began to squirm when they discovered Illinois Coal had continued to order those masks.

Sitting directly across from P.R. was the lead lawyer for Illinois Coal. Red Tie had made a career out of finding loopholes for the coal companies. In his most infamous black lung case, the lawyer had a chest X-ray thrown out of court because no date appeared on the X-ray.

The miner died before he was able to have another one. The death certificate listed the cause of death as black lung. The man's widow received a pension of $800 a month.

Red Tie glared across the table, not at P.R. but at Jeralds, whose red face matched the man's tie. "The president of the company and the board of directors didn't order those masks. That decision was made by the office personnel."

"Your clients reviewed these reports." P.R. pulled out the end-of-the-year financial statement with the income and expenses. Under equipment expenses was the cost of two dozen masks from WSEC.

"You can't expect our clients to know the make and model numbers of all the mine equipment," another lawyer said.

The owner of Illinois Coal, a squat pretentious man, was unable to remain silent. "We have always put the welfare of our miners first."

P.R. focused on the man. "I'm glad to know that. Then you'll compensate these miners for buying respiratory masks that were banned."

The man's eyes began to blink nervously. "I'm sure the masks we provided met government standards."

"A copy of those standards is in your folder. Before 2014 the government regulations limited the respirable coal dust to two milligrams per three cubic meters of air. Now the government standards have been lowered to one and a half milligrams. According to OSHA's tests, the masks Illinois Coal provided allowed three milligrams. That's twice the legal limit."

P.R. addressed the man's lawyer. "Is your client ready to swear under oath he had no knowledge that the respiratory masks Illinois Coal supplied were the same ones that were banned by OSHA?"

Red Tie and Little conferred in whispers. When they finished, the lawyer answered, "My client assures me he had no knowledge his mine was supplying ineffective masks." The lawyer closed the file and began to rise. "If this is all you have…"

"It's not." P.R. drilled the lawyer with his eyes until the man sat. "Please remind your client that perjury is a crime."

Little's face puffed out like a blowfish. "I would not have authorized purchase of those masks if I'd known they were banned."

"But you did know." P.R. took out an additional document and handed one to each lawyer. On the front was OSHA's ruling banning the masks.

Miller's lawyer only glanced at it. "We've already seen this document."

"Please turn the paper over."

On the back was a requisition request. Written at the bottom was a note in Dahlia Miller's flowery handwriting. "Is this the correct make and model you want to order?"

Below the note was written one word. *Yes.* Beside it was the initials *LL. Leland Little.*

CHAPTER FIFTY-FOUR

The next day P.R. drove to Chicago to celebrate. When he pulled open the heavy wooden door of Paddy's Pub, a boisterous cheer greeted him. As he strode to the bar, other lawyers slapped him on the back and shook his hand.

A few months ago, he would have boasted about the huge settlement Illinois Coal had agreed to pay, but Jackson had done the work. P.R. had merely been the closer.

Jeralds had urged P.R. to negotiate for a higher amount. Countering again could have made Illinois Coal go to trial. Juries were unpredictable. Even if they did win, the verdict might be appealed. The case would be tied up in court for years. Dale Miller didn't have years; he had months. So P.R. had accepted a confidentiality agreement that would give each of his clients, roughly three million dollars after settlement fees.

Sitting at the bar, P.R. tried to keep up with the foaming glasses of beer shoved his way. The pub was too noisy, so he didn't hear his phone ring, only felt the vibrations. He pulled it out of his pocket and checked the number. His old law firm.

He slid off the stool and strolled to a secluded hallway leading to the restrooms. When he answered, Mr. Lloyd congratulated him several times. "We'd like to have you back at the firm."

Stunned, P.R. leaned against the wall as Mr. Lloyd offered him a substantially higher salary.

P.R. was flattered. "That's very generous." The proposition soothed some of the humiliation of being fired. Then he pictured packing up the office in Hickory Hills and telling his family and clients good-bye. Practicing law in Hickory Hills had renewed his passion. He had helped honest, hard-working people.

"I appreciate the offer, sir, but I plan to stay in Hickory Hills." Until that moment, P.R. hadn't realized he wanted to take over Jackson's practice. Permanently.

P.R. disconnected the call and pocketed the phone. A woman with long blonde hair obscuring her face hurried toward the restroom. She bumped into him, "Excuse me."

P.R. thought he recognized the voice. "Ashleigh?"

The woman looked up. "P.R.!" She flung her arms around his neck and sobbed.

He hadn't expected such an outburst from Ashleigh. He held her, waiting for her to quit crying, before he asked, "What's wrong?"

She opened her purse and pulled out a tissue. "I just received some bad news."

He didn't want to pry, but she was obviously distraught. "Can I help?"

"It's my fiancé." She stuck out her left hand and flashed a large diamond ring.

"Congratulations. Do I know the lucky guy?"

"Truman Regal. I think you've met him."

P.R. had met the guy and didn't like him much. "When's the wedding?"

Ashleigh started to tear up again. "Truman just found out he has some serious health problems. We might have to postpone the wedding."

For years, the guy had an on-and-off relationship with Ashleigh. P.R. wondered if it was a ploy to avoid commitment. "I hope it works out for you."

Ashleigh tried to smile. "I heard you settled against Illinois Coal. Congratulations."

"And I heard you won the Abrams case."

Mentioning work seemed to take Ashleigh's mind off her personal problems. She filled him in on how Abrams had taken the stand, against her advice. His testimony had swayed at least one person because the jury was deadlocked.

Ashleigh gave him a smug smile, obviously pleased with the outcome. P.R. doubted if he would have felt the same. His settlement with Illinois Coal, however, made him proud of his profession.

"Mr. Lloyd called. He offered me my old job." P.R. didn't mention the salary.

Ashley's red-rimmed eyes widened. "That's wonderful. When will you be back?"

"I'm staying in Hickory Hills."

"Seriously?" She obviously didn't think that was a good career move. "Truthfully, I'm worried I might be next."

P.R. reached into his pocket and pulled out his new business card. "I could always use an assistant."

She palmed the card. "I don't think I'd ever be that desperate."

They hugged good-bye, and P.R. strode back to the bar. As he settled onto a stool, a cute brunette sidled up and flounced onto his lap. She whispered in his ear that she was ready and willing to help him celebrate.

P.R. picked up his glass of beer and drank. Why not? He'd come to Chicago to celebrate. But the beer tasted as flat as the evening. Even spending the night with a beautiful woman had lost its appeal. He couldn't pretend the way he used to do. He wasn't that person anymore.

Tomi had shown him who he could be, and even though she had chosen someone else that didn't mean he couldn't still strive to be a better person. He glanced at his watch and wondered how soon he could slip away.

He nudged the brunette off his lap and checked Google Maps for the distance to Pacific Garden Mission.

Thirty minutes later an Uber driver pulled up to the mission and let P.R. out. Above the door of the red-brick building hung a giant cross illuminated with two simple words: JESUS SAVES. P.R. believed that. He hoped Peewee did, too.

P.R. found Peewee in the kitchen, wiping off tables. He wore an apron, his white T-shirt, and high-water pants. When his old friend saw him, his face lit up with a wide smile. It warmed P.R. more than the cheers at Paddy's.

P.R. stuck out his hand for Peewee to shake. Peewee whipped off his apron and threw his arms around P.R.

When he pulled away, his eyes gleamed with hope. "I went home for Thanksgiving," Peewee said. "And my family invited me back for Christmas."

Before P.R. left the mission, he stopped at the office and wrote out a check. He handed it to the black woman at the desk. "Here's a donation for the mission and a little extra Christmas bonus for Peewee."

"Bless you, brother."

And he did feel blessed. Without Tomi, he wasn't looking forward to Christmas, but at least he could use some of the money from the settlement fees to brighten the holiday for others.

CHAPTER FIFTY-FIVE

On Friday Bucky parked the Buick behind the concrete building at Springside Mine. This trip would be quick, just in-and-out to gather his gear. He removed a flashlight from the glove compartment and looked around before he climbed out of the car. Even if someone did notice the Buick, it wouldn't lead to him. He'd rented it under the name Bruce Wayne. He didn't think Batman would mind.

He scurried across the black coal dust glittering in the evening sun. His fingers tingled. Hidden inside was the red gas can. He had big plans for tonight. He would return to Springfield and torch the white bungalow where he and Joey would not be living.

He stepped inside the mine. Cold damp air assaulted him. Hairs rose on the back of his neck. He thought about being trapped, of slowly running out of oxygen. His hands shook. Ghostly scenes of dead miners swirled around him. He switched on the flashlight and craned his neck up. The timbers in the mine were old. Unstable.

He shook off the thought. He'd been in and out of the mine half a dozen times in the last three months. The beams had creaked and groaned, but nothing had happened.

He walked forward, searching for where he had hidden his things. The yellow beam danced along the wall and landed on the rock he'd used to cover the hole. He lifted off the rock and pulled out the sleeping bag, stuffed with snacks and his disguise. He'd come back for the gas can.

He threw the bulky bag over his shoulder and retraced his steps. Just as he exited the mine, a car door slammed and a man climbed out.

The man turned toward the mine. Bucky shined the flashlight into his eyes, blinding him.

The man raised his arm to shield his eyes. "Sabina, is that you?"

Bucky recognized him as the man at the pub with Sabina.

"Sabina, turn off that light. It's me, Carter."

Bucky slipped his hand into the pocket of his windbreaker and curled his fingers around the gun. The sleeping bag on his shoulder shifted. The wig and beard tumbled onto the ground and lay at his feet. Bucky hoped the guy wouldn't notice. No such luck.

"Hey, I didn't know we were role playing. Are you going to be Santa?"

Bucky rushed forward.

Carter's eyes widened as he realized the wig wasn't for Santa and Sabina wasn't holding the flashlight. He opened his mouth, "Zeus."

Bucky raised the butt of the gun and cracked it against Carter's skull. His legs gave. He folded onto the ground like a cheap accordion.

Bucky should have shot him, but he didn't know who might be close enough to hear the gunfire.

As he looked around, a car careened through the mine gate. The flashy red Mustang screeched to a stop and parked next to his Buick.

Sabina. Her slinky black dress and spiked heels definitely weren't mine gear.

Seeing Carter lying on the ground, she rushed over and knelt beside him. She glared up at him. "What did you do?"

"Not much...yet."

She stood up. "I'll take care of him."

He pointed to the wig and beard on the ground. "He saw the disguise. I can't let him ruin everything."

"No!" She screamed in her high-pitched voice. She continued to harangue him. Each word bore into his skull like an electric drill grinding on and on. He gritted his teeth, trying to shut out her never-ending drone. She got right into his face. "This has to stop. Now!"

Rage swelled inside him. "It was supposed to end tonight. But your boyfriend," he emphasized the word *boyfriend*, "got in the way. What was he doing here?"

Sabina fidgeted nervously. "We were just having a business meeting. Nothing for you to worry about."

Bucky raised his eyebrows. "Business?"

Sabina twisted the huge diamond ring around on her finger. "Well, if I have to live in Hickory Hills for five years the wedding's off."

That would be just like Sabina. Fickle. "Well, you invited Carter here. You need to help me clean up this mess. Find his keys and drive his car back to town. I don't want anyone knowing he was at the mine."

Her red lips puckered. "What about my car?"

"Give me half an hour. I'll pick you up at the diner."

She bent down and rummaged through Carter's pockets until she found his keys. Rising, she placed one hand on her hip and dangled the keys under his nose. "This is the last time I'm doing anything for you."

"What about the money you owe me? What about Joey?"

"You're crazy if you think I'm taking care of Joey."

Crazy. The word was like a firing pin. It released his explosive anger. He lifted his gun and pointed it at Sabina.

The smirk on her face disappeared. Her eyes widened in fear. She stepped back, wobbling on her spiked heels.

He cackled and crooked his finger on the trigger as he pretended to shoot. "Bang. Bang. The witch is dead."

She jumped. "You are crazy." Fisting the keys, she turned and stumbled toward Carter's SUV.

He raised the gun and squeezed the trigger. A bullet pinged on the ground next to her feet. She kicked off her heels, sending them flying into the air. She didn't stop to pick them up, but darted toward the car, her long black hair trailing after her.

Within minutes, the black SUV shot through the mine gate. The tires spit out cinders, leaving a cloud of dust behind.

Bucky's hand shook so badly he was afraid he might drop the gun. He'd scared her. Really scared her. Even more, he'd scared himself.

If Sabina hadn't fled, God help him, he might have pulled the trigger.

CHAPTER FIFTY-SIX

Friday evening, while Quinn and Ace went to the movies, Tomi, Jason, and Taylor rode their bikes along the country road toward the mine. Bullet and Gogo trotted behind. The December day was warm, jacket weather.

Suddenly Bullet shot across the field of disked corn stalks. The greyhound's nose pointed forward, his long body stretched out like a speeding bullet.

"Look at Bullet run." Jason's voice was filled with pride. "No wonder he was a champion racer." Tomi could tell Jason no longer thought of the dog as Miss May's, but his own.

After a few minutes, Bullet circled back to Gogo and, like a patient grandparent, nudged the puppy with his nose, gently prodding her along.

In four days Tomi would return to Japan. She had hoped being outside would lift her spirits and chase away thoughts of P.R. But he was always with her.

Unexpected tears sprang to her eyes. She pedaled faster, spurting ahead as Bullet loped by her side. By the time she reached the mine, sweat rolled down her neck. She stripped off her jacket and dropped it into the basket on the front of her bike.

Bullet, begging for attention, rubbed against her leg. She leaned down and petted the dog's short gray coat. When she stood, she shaded her eyes with her hand. Ahead, the sinking sun streaked the sky in purples and reds, the color of blood. She stood on the desolate country road, her hands by her sides. Her whole body shaking. She had never felt so alone.

Finally Jason pulled up next to her and Taylor was seconds behind. Tomi wiped the back of her hands across her wet cheeks and put on a happy face. The wind picked up and the gate on the mine creaked open.

"Look." Jason pointed to the unlocked gate. "We could go inside."

Taylor frowned. "The sign says *No trespassing.*"

Tomi pulled her phone from the pocket of her jacket lying in the basket and checked the time: four-thirty. "Dark soon. Go back."

She was relieved when Jason didn't argue, but turned his bike around and yelled to the dogs lying in the field. "Here, Bullet. Come on, Gogo."

The three of them lined up across the road and headed back to the loft as the dogs lagged behind.

"I wish you could stay for our Christmas program," Taylor said. "We're singing *Mary Did You Know.*"

A wave of sadness washed over Tomi. "I wish, too."

"We can sing it for you now." Taylor began singing and Jason joined in, their voices blending naturally.

Tomi pedaled slower, falling behind as she listened. Christianity was confusing, but she could relate to Mary, a young woman who was about to become a mother.

The dogs began to bark. Tomi thought it was because of Jason's and Taylor's loud singing.

"Race you back," Jason said after they finished their song. He shot off. Taylor sped after him.

The barking grew louder. Tomi glanced over her shoulder. A black SUV charged through the mine gate. It swerved onto the graveled road, careening from side to side, headed toward her.

Ahead, Jason and Taylor were in the middle of the road. Tomi screamed, "Look out!"

Their heads turned. Jason's bike wobbled. He lost his balance and fell against Taylor, knocking them into the grassy ditch along the side of the road.

Tomi jumped off her bike, letting it fall to the ground. She sprinted forward and dived onto them, protecting them with her body. She looked over her shoulder. The SUV struck the back of her bike, flipping it into the air. Her jacket sailed skyward. The sleeves stretched out like wings as it flew across the road.

The bicycle thudded, bouncing against the ground. The front wheel broke loose, swirling several feet into the air before hitting the gravel pavement and rolling down the road. The rest of the bike collapsed on its side, the rear tire still spinning.

Tomi didn't get a good look at the driver. Long black hair blocked the woman's face. Jason jumped up and shook his fist at the fleeing vehicle.

Taylor stood, her pants ripped at the knee. "My good jeans."

Jason walked over and put a comforting arm around his sister. Then he retrieved the bike's wheel for Tomi. "I don't think you can ride it."

She stared at the crumpled frame, her body still shaking. "I call someone to pick us up."

She carried the bike to the opposite side of the road and laid it in the grass. Then she tromped into the field where her jacket had landed. She reached into the pocket. Her phone wasn't there. She tried the other pocket. Empty.

As she slipped on her jacket, she turned to Jason and Taylor, who had followed her. "Phone fell out. Help look."

The three of them spread across the field, searching through the corn stubbles. The sun was almost gone now. They might not find the phone before dark. "Jason, Taylor, go back to loft and call...," she started to say 'P.R.' But he wasn't part of her life anymore. She didn't want Quinn and Ace to leave the movie. "Call Sheriff Ben. He help."

"Okay." Jason hopped onto his bike. "Come on, Taylor."

"I'll stay with Tomi."

"No, go with Jason." Tomi didn't like being alone on the dark country road, but Taylor and Jason would be safer back at the loft.

Jason must have sensed Tomi's uneasiness. "I'll leave Bullet with you."

Grateful, Tomi latched onto Bullet's collar, holding the dog beside her.

Taylor climbed onto her bike. "Come on, Gogo."

"Lock door," Tomi called as they pedaled their bikes down the road. Once they were out of sight, she began kicking the cut-up corn stalks, searching for her phone. She kept her eyes down. Something silver glinted in the soil. Releasing Bullet, she raced toward what looked like her phone. And there it was, lying face down in the dirt. She stooped and picked it up.

Jason and Taylor wouldn't be at the loft yet. Quinn and P.R. were on speed dial, so Tomi scrolled through her contacts searching for Ben.

Bullet began to bark.

She looked up. The greyhound shot across the field, obviously chasing something. Maybe a field mouse. She couldn't let the dog out of her sight. He'd run away before, and it had taken hours to find him.

She dropped the phone into her pocket, this time zipping it up, and sprinted after Bullet. She chased the dog across the field. He jumped over the barbed-wire fence surrounding the mine and disappeared behind the concrete building.

Her heart lurched. By the time she reached the mine, it would be dark.

CHAPTER FIFTY-SEVEN

Gripping Carter by the ankles, Buddy dragged him into the mine. His flashlight was hooked to his belt, illuminating the way. He regretted that he hadn't shot Carter. The man seemed to weigh a ton of coal.

Bucky wiped the sweat from his brow and heaved. He dragged him farther into the mine. Once he reached the shaft, he'd just shove him over the side. The body might not be found for years.

The gas can was ahead. He'd pick it up on the way out. The shaft should be just a little farther. He moved slowly, careful not to make a wrong turn. Once he'd done that and wandered around, lost. He needed to finish quickly and drive into town to pick up Sabina. He didn't want her blabbing.

He spotted the mine shaft and stopped. He heard something. Was that a dog barking?

———

Tomi raced through the mine gate and headed toward the concrete building where Bullet had disappeared. "Bullet! Here, Bullet!"

A voice in her head warned, *Go back! Go back!*

Waiting for Sheriff Ben would be the smart thing to do, but she had to find Bullet. She neared the building and slowed to a jog. The windows were broken shards of glass. The door hung askew on its hinges. A perfect haunt for ghosts. Goosebumps rose on her arms.

She rounded the corner and stopped short. Two cars were parked there —one cherry red and the other beige. She tiptoed to the red sports car and peeked inside. A designer purse with MK on the gold clasp lay on the seat.

She walked behind the beige car with 'Buick' on the rear and peered through the driver's window. A paper with a picture of a house lay on the dash.

She took out her phone to call Sheriff Ben. She didn't have time to search through her contacts. P.R. was on speed dial. In a moment of weakness, she pressed his number.

Bullet started barking again. He was near the mine entrance. She had to reach him before he went inside. She cut off the call and raced toward the mine.

The dog sprinted into the tunnel. At the entrance, she skidded to a stop. "Bullet! Bullet!"

She waited, hoping the dog would come prancing out. He didn't. She took a deep breath and squinted into the darkness. Her heart pounded. She needed to tell someone where she was. She'd call P.R again. She took out her phone. No signal.

The dog barked louder. Maybe he was in trouble. Her hands shook as she turned on her phone and aimed the light into the mine.

A narrow tunnel lay ahead. The ceiling was low, supported by wooden timbers across the top and sides. She stepped into the mine and was immediately swallowed by darkness.

———

The phone rang just as P.R. shut his office door. He had worked twelve long hours. The call would probably be someone wanting a divorce. Half of his new clients seemed to be stuck in bad marriages. He'd let the answering machine pick up.

The phone rang again. The sound cut through his weariness. Not his office phone, his cell. He must have left it on the desk.

He hurried across the room and picked it up. "Hello."

Silence.

"Hello. Hello."

He checked the screen. *Tomi.* His heart thudded. He hadn't talked to her since Thanksgiving. He held his breath and redialed.

The call went straight to voice mail. His shoulders sagged. He didn't leave a message. He wanted to talk to her in person. He dropped his phone into his pocket and rushed out the door.

He jogged to the car, his earlier weariness gone. As he opened the door, his phone rang again. He fumbled in his pocket and answered on the third ring, expecting Tomi's lyrical voice.

"Hey, P.R."

Jason. He slumped against the car and tried to hide the disappointment in his voice. "Hey, pal. What's up?"

"Uh, I called to tell you something."

"Got a legal problem already?" he teased.

"No. It's—it's about Tomi."

He straightened. "Tomi. What's wrong?"

"Her bike was wrecked."

He gripped the phone tighter. "Was she hurt?"

"She's okay, but her bike isn't."

P.R. frowned. "Did she ask you to call me?"

"No. She told me to call Ben so he could help with her bike."

"Oh." Disappointment set in. "Where is she?"

"Out by the mine."

"Springside Mine. Is Quinn or Ace with her?"

"They're at the movies. She's alone, except for Bullet."

Before P.R. could ask any more questions, Jason said, "Well, I just thought you'd want to know. Bye."

Frustrated, P.R. stared at his phone. Tomi shouldn't be out by the mine, alone. Is that why she had called? It didn't matter why. He'd do anything to spend time with her.

He dropped his phone back into his pocket and climbed into his car. Maybe this was his chance. If he could reach the mine before Ben, he could talk to her, tell her how he felt before it was too late.

CHAPTER FIFTY-EIGHT

Bucky listened. The barking continued. He didn't want to hurt another dog. He still felt bad about Jason's dog.

Footsteps. He peered through the blackness toward the entrance. Had Sabina come back?

"Bullet!" The name echoed through the tunnel.

He recognized the voice. That Japanese woman. What was she doing here? Had she seen him drag Carter into the mine? Maybe she'd sicked a dog on him. Well, he'd take care of both of them.

He switched off his flashlight. The barking grew closer.

Carter groaned.

Bucky ignored him. He needed to lure Tomi toward him. He crouched down and crept forward. His leg bumped a wooden beam. Overhead the timbers creaked. He silently swore.

She must have heard the noise. Ahead, light shined onto the wall. "Bullet."

Something growled and then lunged at him, nipping at his legs. It must be the dog. He kicked. His boot connected with the dog's ribs. Sharp teeth ripped through his pant leg. He bit back a scream and booted the dog away.

The animal flew across the tunnel. It thudded against the opposite side and whimpered.

Bucky took out his gun. He flattened his back to the wall and waited.

———

Tomi stopped and listened. Bullet was whimpering. Maybe he was hurt. She held up her phone and shined the light from side to side. As she inched forward, the air grew cooler. She drew her jacket tighter. Her voice quivered, "Bullet?"

No answer. She steadied her free hand on the cold wall. Above, something creaked. Coal dust sprinkled onto her face and into hair. She brushed it from her cheeks and pulled the elastic band from her ponytail, shaking out her hair. Her phone light dimmed. The battery was low. She should go back.

Bullet whimpered again. She couldn't give into her fears. Bullet needed her. She plunged ahead, groping with her hands. She felt something on her shoulder. More coal dust. She reached up.

An arm snaked around her neck. She screamed. A large hand covered her mouth, cutting off her air. She clawed at the hand, twisting to get free.

A deep male voice whispered in her ear, "Don't move unless you want me to use this gun." She felt hard metal pressed against her ribs. "Turn off the light."

She slid the phone down her leg and turned off the light. Fear curled in her stomach. Who was this man? Why did he want to hurt her? She struggled to breathe. Her lungs burned. She fought not to faint.

The man switched on the flashlight hooked to his belt. A yellow circle spread across the floor and landed on Bullet. His eyes were closed. His tongue lolled out of his mouth.

She struggled harder. The man tightened his hold. "See what you made me do."

What had he done? Was Bullet dead? She rolled her eyes to the corners trying to see who was holding her. He was taller than she was, and the arm around her neck was muscular.

His hand over her mouth loosened, but the gun poking into her side made her afraid to scream. She inhaled. Cold air rushed into her mouth and soothed her throat.

She had a partial view of the man's face. She had seen him before, but where? Like a negative being developed, pictures of Quinn's wedding reception slowly appeared. Near the French doors three people clustered together. One of them was Stuart. Next to him was a tall woman with black hair. Tomi's eyes widened. The driver of the SUV. Standing beside that woman was the man behind Tomi.

She didn't know his name, but she was convinced he was about to kill her. She looked at Bullet. His eyes opened. He growled.

The man lowered his hand to her neck. "Tell your dog to shut up, or I'll shut him up."

"Sh-h-h, Bullet. Sh-h-h."

Bullet whimpered and tried to stand. His legs buckled.

She wanted to help him. "He hurt."

"Shut up and move." He pushed her forward. She dug in her heels. They struggled in a strange back-and-forth gait as they slowly moved deeper into the mine. Time slowed. Her legs felt as if she were moving through sludge. What seemed like hours was probably no more than fifteen minutes.

They must be going in a circle. Twice they'd shuffled past the same red can. Was the man trying to confuse her or was he lost? So far, he had only threatened her, but she knew he would eventually kill her. She had to find a way out.

Her phone was still in her hand. But she didn't have a signal. If she could turn it on, maybe enough charge was left for her to shine the light into the man's eyes. But which direction would she run? She slid the phone underneath her jacket and pressed it against her body to mute the sound. She pushed the 'on' button. Vibrations tingled against her side, but the man didn't seem to notice. She slipped the phone from beneath her jacket, making sure to keep it close so he wouldn't see the glow around the screen.

In the distance a car door slammed.

The man heard it, too. "Be quiet." He clamped his hand over her mouth. She bit down, sinking her teeth into his fleshy fingers. He jerked his hand away, but his arm stayed wrapped around her neck.

She raised her phone. For an instant the beam of light illuminated the tunnel in front of her. Another man holding a lit match stumbled toward them. Had he come to save her or hurt her? She had to get away.

She turned her wrist and aimed the light at the man behind her. He raised his hand to protect his eyes. She twisted free and faced him.

His gun was pointed directly at her.

The man behind her yelled, "No-o-o-o!"

She spun toward him. His face was twisted into an angry rage. He threw down the match and charged forward.

Her eyes widened. Carter.

He lunged, hitting her and pushing her aside. She slammed against the wall and slid to the floor. Her phone flew from her hand. Its light went out.

Ping! A bullet whizzed over her head, splintering the beam above her. The wall rumbled. Coal sifted onto her.

Carter rammed the man in his chest. Another gunshot exploded. Carter clutched his stomach and toppled onto the man. They both crashed against the beam on the other side.

Crack.

The walls shook as rocks began to fall from the ceiling.

Ping. Ping. Ping. Bullets ricocheted around the tunnel.

"Tomi!"

"P.R.?" Was she imagining it, wishing he would come? She had phoned him, but how would he know she was at the mine?

"Tomi!"

Now was her chance. She tried to stand. Her legs held. She ran toward the voice. Ahead Bullet wobbled to his feet. She slowed, grabbed his collar, and pulled him with her.

Rocks began to fall all around her. Dust filled her throat. She coughed and covered her mouth. She maneuvered around the rocks toward the entrance. A light shined ahead.

Her heart surged. P.R.! He was here, running to her. Relief and happiness flooded through her. She rushed toward him.

The tunnel rumbled. A rock struck her head. She didn't want to endanger him. "Go back! Go back!"

He wasn't going back. Tomi was in danger. P.R. lengthened his stride, weaving to avoid the falling rocks. One hit his shoulder. He winced, but charged ahead. He had to reach her. With each step, his feet pounded out her name. *Tomi. Tomi. Tomi.*

He found his rhythm. He was running the way he had run the night of the fire. Her words echoed in his head. "We make it. We make it."

She was just beyond his reach. Bullet limped behind her. P.R. stretched out his arm. Their fingers touched. He clasped her hand.

Boom!

He was lifted off the ground and propelled backward. He tightened his hold on her hand, but he couldn't feel her. All he could feel was air.

CHAPTER FIFTY-NINE

"P.R.! P.R.!"

He lay face down on the ground. Someone was calling his name, shaking his shoulder. He didn't want to wake up. Tomi was running toward him, her face streaked with black. He reached for her. Nothing was there.

He lifted his head. His eyes flitted around, searching for her.

A flashlight shined in his face. "Are you okay?"

He recognized Ben's voice. "Where am I?"

"Springside Mine."

P.R. jerked up. Tomi had been in the mine. He had been holding her hand. He jumped to his feet. A sharp pain shot through his head. He staggered. "Tomi, where is she?"

Ben stood and put a steadying hand on P.R.'s shoulder. "I searched the building and the cars. All I found were these." He held up a pair of high heels.

From the size, P.R. knew they weren't Tomi's. "She was in the mine."

Ben shined his flashlight toward the mine about twenty feet ahead. A huge pile of rocks blocked the entrance.

A roar exploded deep inside P.R. He grabbed Ben's flashlight and raced toward the mine. He ignored his throbbing head. He waved the light from side to side, searching near the entrance. "She has to be here." His voice was desperate. "Tomi! Tomi!"

Ben ran up beside him. "Where is she?"

"I don't know. I'll look on this side of the entrance. You check the other side."

The two men separated and combed the area around the mine. Five minutes later, they met in front of the blocked entrance. "She's not here." Ben gazed at the pile of rocks. "She must be trapped inside."

P.R. wouldn't...couldn't accept it. He rushed to the rocks and scrambled to the top. Dropping to his knees, he placed the flashlight next to him and began to dig, clawing at the rocks like a crazed animal.

Ben climbed up beside him and picked up the flashlight. "P.R., it's too late."

"No. She's alive. I know she's alive." He continued to tear at the rocks, tossing them behind him.

"If she's in there, you could send more rocks tumbling down on her."

Ben was right, but P.R. couldn't wait. She might run out of oxygen. As Ben radioed for responders, he continued to dig. He only needed a hole large enough to crawl through.

Ben picked up the flashlight. "I'll move the squad car and shine the headlights at the mine."

P.R. merely nodded.

Ben rushed away with the light. P.R. continued to burrow. His hands moved like pistons. One rock. Another rock. He had to find Tomi. He had to reach her in time. Doubts slogged through him. What if he didn't find her? What if she was crushed beneath the rocks?

He moaned. A hand touched his back. He shrugged it off. "Leave me alone, Ben."

"I help."

"Tomi?" He rose and whirled around. He couldn't see her in the dark, but sensed her presence and grabbed for her. His foot slipped. He teetered, tightening his arms around her.

Together, they slid down the rocks and tumbled onto the ground, rolling away from the mine. When they stopped, she lay beneath him. He was dizzy with the sensation.

Propping himself up, he touched her hair and ran his fingers through the tangled strands. She stared up at him. He wasn't dreaming. She was alive.

A swell of protective love washed over him. Unchecked tears streamed down his cheeks. "I thought—I thought I'd lost you."

She swiped her hand across his wet cheek and pointed toward the slag pile. "Land there. Maybe faint."

But now she was awake, and her heart sang. P.R. had come for her. He had risked his life.

"Are you okay?" P.R. asked.

She heard the concern in his voice, but couldn't answer. Her body ached, but not as much as her soul. Nothing had changed. She must return to Japan and marry another man. But life was fleeting. Maybe she didn't have next month or next week. Maybe all she had was now. Today. She was alive. P.R. was alive. And they were together.

She reached up and wrapped her arms around his neck. She drew him down to her. His lips touched hers and then pressed harder.

His kiss unleashed something in her. She couldn't think. All she could do was feel the rightness of it.

She pressed her lips against his, thinking the words she must never say. *I love you. I will always love you.*

His kisses were magic. They transported her to Navy Pier. She was spinning round and round on the Centennial wheel.

She wanted to stay in the moment. Too soon, he pulled away. "Tomi."

She waited, dreading, yet hoping, he might say the words she must not hear.

"Tomi, what-what were you doing in the mine?"

"The mine?" Her head stopped spinning. She was jolted back to reality. A picture flashed in her head. Carter stumbling toward her, pushing her away. She heaved against P.R.'s chest. "Carter and other man in mine."

"Carter?" P.R. asked.

She rolled away from him and scrambled up. She ran toward the entrance now lit by the headlights of the squad car.

Ben stopped her and wrapped his arms around her. "Are you okay?"

She wrenched free and pointed to the mine. "Get Carter out." Then she remembered and added, "Bullet."

She scrambled to the top of the rocks. She didn't see the hole P.R. had dug. The rocks shifted under her feet. She slid backwards, bracing herself to hit the hard ground.

Instead she fell into P.R.'s arms. She struggled against him, but he held onto her and whispered, "You belong here. Always."

CHAPTER SIXTY

The paramedics arrived and transported Tomi and P.R. to Hickory Hills Community Hospital, where Doc Morgan checked them over. They had sustained minor scrapes and bruises and were admitted overnight for observation.

"You're lucky you weren't killed," Doc Morgan said to Tomi as a nurse helped her into a wheelchair.

"Carter not lucky. He in mine."

"Carter?" Doc peered over the rim of his black-framed glasses. "What was Carter doing at the mine?"

Tomi didn't know, but Ben also had questions the following day when he came to the loft to interview her and P.R. The four of them, Quinn, P.R. Ben, and Tomi, sat at the table in the great room. Ace was at the mine searching for the men.

"If it's possible, Ace will find them," Quinn said. "After all, he found Bullet."

"How's the dog doing?" Ben asked as he placed a portable recorder in the center on the table.

"He's at the vet's with a broken leg," Quinn said. "I promised Jason I'd take him there after school."

Ben nodded. "I'm ready." He pressed *record*. "This is Sheriff Ben

Campbell. Today is December 3. I am interviewing two witnesses about the incident at Springside Mine in Hickory Hills. Please state your full names."

"Pleasant Rupert Montgomery." He nudged Tomi.

"Tomoe Kanai."

Ben pulled a manila folder from the briefcase. "We're trying to identify who might be trapped in the mine." He removed several papers from the folder. "We checked the registration for the two cars parked at the mine. The red Mustang has a Missouri license registered to Sabina Barnes."

P.R.'s eyebrow rose. "Stuart's fiancé?"

Ben nodded. "We questioned her this morning."

P.R.'s throat tightened. "Is Stuart trapped in the mine?"

"That's what I hope Tomi can tell us." Ben slipped a picture of Stuart May from the folder and placed it in front of Tomi. "Is this the man who attacked you in the mine?"

Tomi studied the picture. "No. He not in mine."

P.R. breathed a sigh of relief.

"That matches Sabina's story. She said Stuart left Hickory Hills to check on some property in St. Louis. We're still trying to reach him."

Ben removed two other pictures and placed them on the table. One was a copy of an Illinois driver's license, the other a photograph of a man and woman standing in an apple orchard.

Tomi pointed to the woman. "I think she drove SUV from mine."

"That's Sabina," P.R. said.

"Do you remember anything else about the SUV?" Ben asked.

"Color black."

"Carter drives a black SUV," P.R. said. "But why would Sabina be driving Carter's vehicle?"

"We found Carter's SUV parked in front of the Blue Moon." Ben slid the driver's license closer to Tomi. "Do you recognize this man?"

Tomi studied the picture on the license. "Mine dark." Her eyes shifted from the license to the photograph and back. "Sorry. Both men look same."

Ben gave Tomi a reassuring smile. "We think they might be the same man."

P.R. frowned. "So who is he?"

Ben turned to P.R. "A driver's license was discovered in the glove compartment of the rented Buick parked at the mine. The name on the license is Bruce Wayne." Ben chuckled. "I'm pretty sure Batman hasn't decided to help me clean up crime in Hickory Hills."

P.R. picked up the picture of the man and Sabina. "I think I've seen this man." He handed it to Quinn. "Wasn't he at your wedding?"

Quinn looked at the photo. "Yes. I remember asking Ace to introduce me, but I don't remember his name."

"His name is Virgil Barnes. Sabina's brother," Ben said. "According to Sabina he might be the other man in the mine."

"So why were Sabina and her brother at the mine?" Quinn asked.

Ben slipped the photos back into the file. "Sabina said she asked Carter to meet her at the mine. She was evasive about why, but it wouldn't be hard to guess."

"Poor Raven. How's she doing?" Quinn asked.

Ben cleared his throat. "We haven't told her about Carter. No use worrying her until we have a positive ID."

Tomi lifted her chin. "Carter in mine. I see him."

Ben reached into his briefcase. "We found some interesting items in the trunk of the rental." He pulled out a clear evidence bag. Sealed inside were a white wig and beard. "Do these look familiar?"

Tomi gasped. "Zeus!"

"When Zeus was captured, he denied murdering Jackson and ever being in Hickory Hills. Whoever is trapped in the mine might have been masquerading as Zeus."

Quinn frowned. "Tomi saw Zeus running from our house. But you think it might have been this Virgil Barnes? Why would he break into our house?"

"Sabina said Bucky, that's what her family calls Virgil, needs money to pay for their brother's care. Joey lives at The Farmstead in Springfield. I called Springfield this morning. Their records show that Joey Barnes's account is more than $100,000 in the red."

"We don't have that kind of money in the house," Quinn said. "And we never found anything missing."

"Sabina admitted she owes her brother a large sum of money. She planned to repay it after she married Stuart May."

P.R.'s eyes lit up. "Now I'm beginning to understand. Stuart thought he would inherit Miss May's land and money. Maybe he mentioned it to

Sabina and she told her brother. This Bucky might have gotten tired of waiting and hurried Miss May's death with poison."

"But why would he break into Jackson's office and kill him?" Quinn asked.

P.R. stroked his chin. "Ace confided that Jackson had drawn up a new will for Miss May. When I checked Miss May's file, I couldn't find it. Maybe Virgil broke into the office and stole the new will. Jackson might have tried to stop him."

Quinn's eyes widened. "That makes sense. Ace had a copy of Miss May's new will at his house. Virgil could have been looking for it. We thought it had been destroyed in the fire, but discovered it in the fire-proof safe in Ace's basement."

Ben nodded. "I certainly have a better picture now. Tomi or P.R., can you think of anything else about the man or the mine that might help us?"

"I never saw anyone but Tomi in the mine," P.R. said.

"I see two men and..." Tomi stopped. She remembered walking in a circle. "Also I see red can, one like Ace use to put gasoline in mower."

Quinn gasped. "A gas can! Maybe that man set fire to our house."

P.R. let out a sigh. "If that's true, it's a big relief. I still have this feeling I might not have put all the ashes out."

Tomi nodded. "I wonder if I left stove on."

"The gas can could explain the explosion in the mine." Ben turned off the recorder and stood to leave. "If the man in the mine is Sabina's brother, finding him alive would certainly clear up a lot of unanswered questions."

Quinn's phone rang. "Hello." As she listened, her hand shook. When she ended the call, she said, "That was Ace. They found Carter and other man identified as Virgil Barnes. They-they didn't make it."

CHAPTER SIXTY-ONE

The next morning Quinn and Tomi drove to the B&B to comfort Raven. Tomi felt sorry for her friend. Thirty-one was too young to be a widow.

Tomi didn't liked Carter, but she did not tell Raven. Tomi hugged Raven and told her a different truth. "Carter push me away from man with gun. He save me."

Tomi hoped Raven could hold onto those words in the bad days ahead, when other facts about Carter would come out.

On the way back to the loft, Tomi stared out the windshield as they passed the courthouse, the Blue Moon, Prairie Land Theater, and Mitchell Park. So many places reminded her of P.R. She folded her hands in her lap. "So hard."

Quinn agreed. "Death is never easy."

"Not death." Tomi understood about the harshness of death. Now she understood another harshness. "Life."

"Oh, Tomi, I'm sorry your visit has been filled with tragedy."

Tomi shook her head. "Make me stronger. Experience happiness, sorrow, love, and death. When I plan trip, I think only about coming. I never think about leaving."

"You'll always have a home here," Quinn said.

"Home." Tomi's voice filled with longing. *Home* was what she had found in Hickory Hills. A place where she had become the woman she wanted to be, not the woman others expected her to be. And now she had to leave.

"You can come back anytime," Quinn said.

Tomi's back stiffened. "Never come back."

Quinn was surprised. "Why not?"

Tomi remained silent.

Quinn swallowed. "It's P.R., isn't it?"

They had discussed P.R. many times, but Quinn didn't think Tomi had been honest about her feelings. "I've seen the way you look at him. You love him."

Tomi squared her shoulders. "I cannot."

"He looks the same way at you, Tomi." Quinn's heart ached. Tomi had found something rare—a love that transcended race, language, and country. How could she walk away from that kind of love? "I know you have to go back to Japan. But I don't understand why you have to marry Yoshiro."

Tomi sighed. "For family."

"But you don't love him."

"Father give word to Yoshiro's family. Cannot disgrace him or Yoshiro."

"But surely your father will understand. He would want you to be happy. Tell him about P.R."

Tomi shook her head. "He not be happy. He be angry. Yoshiro's father was best friend. Everyone happy if I marry Yoshiro."

"But will you be happy, Tomi?"

"Family come first."

Quinn started to reason with Tomi. But was what Quinn thinking reasonable? For P.R. and Tomi to be together, one of them would have to leave his or her country. P.R. didn't speak Japanese. He wouldn't be able to practice law in Japan.

Tomi seemed happy here, but her trip had been only ninety days. Would she be happy if she left her family, friends, and country permanently?

Quinn stared out the windshield. Life was not laid out straight like the road ahead. She sighed and agreed with Tomi. "So hard."

––––––

On her last night in Hickory Hills, P.R. had asked Tomi to go out to dinner with him, but she declined. "I want to spend last night with Quinn and family. You understand."

No, he didn't understand. Not when it came to Tomi. She had turned his world upside down and now she was leaving.

"You come. I cook. Make special dishes."

So now he sat at the table in the loft with Quinn, Ace, Taylor, and Jason, counting the minutes until he could be alone with Tomi. He tried to concentrate on using chopsticks, but the way she looked muddled his mind.

She wore a traditional silk kimono with her hair swept off her neck and held up with two lacquered hair sticks. He wondered if she was making a statement. I am Japanese; you are American.

P.R. focused on using his chopsticks. He picked up one small grain of sticky rice. If eating with chopsticks was some kind of challenge, he was determined to show her he could do it. He stabbed at his food and picked up a bigger bite. He wanted to prove their differences didn't matter.

Since the mine accident, he'd had little time alone with her. Family, church friends, and Jason's and Taylor's classmates had come to say good-bye. They brought food, cards, and so many souvenirs that Tomi had shipped a box back to Japan.

"Do you like?" Tomi asked.

Thinking about her made the sticky rice hard to swallow. He gulped and nodded. He liked everything about her and wanted to be alone with her, hold her in his arms. He felt whole when he was with her.

He more than liked her, but he had never said those three simple words. Down to the marrow of his bones, he loved her.

After the meal Quinn rose. "Ace and I will clean up. Tomi, you and P.R. play with the kids."

Jason said, "Let's play Sorry. I want to beat Tomi. She always wins."

"So sorry." Tomi giggled, obviously not sorry.

As the four of them played the board game, P.R. kept checking his watch, but Tomi seemed to be having fun. She delighted in drawing the 'sorry' card. She won the first game, Jason the second.

"That's enough." P.R. gathered up the pieces and put them in the box.

"One more game," begged Taylor. "I haven't won."

P.R.'s patience was frayed. He wanted to be alone with Tomi when he gave her his gift, but he reached into his pocket and pulled out a small box wrapped in red-and-white paper with a blue bow. "Here."

Tomi's eyes lit up. "So beautiful." She removed the bow and then carefully unwrapped the box. When she saw what was inside, her smile lit up the room.

He removed the gold Seiko watch and showed her the dual dials for two time zones.

"I already set it." P.R. pointed to the top hands. "This is U.S. time. Below is Japanese."

"Cool," said Jason staring at the dark-faced watch.

"What time is it in Japan?" Taylor asked.

Tomi stopped smiling. "Already tomorrow."

"Time for bed," Quinn called.

"If we were in Japan, we wouldn't have to go to bed," Jason said.

"But you're not," Quinn said. "And tomorrow we need to leave early for the airport."

As Quinn hustled the kids off to bed, P.R. slipped the watch onto Tomi's wrist. The band was too big. "I'll take out some links." He started to remove the watch.

"Do later." She waved his hand away, and the sleeves of her kimono fluttered. Maybe he'd made a mistake. Maybe he should have bought her something more personal like diamond earrings or a pearl necklace. But he'd wanted her to look at the watch and know what time it was in Hickory Hills and hopefully think of him.

He reached over and took her hand. "Let's go outside,"

She hugged herself and pretended to shiver. "Too cold."

He marched to the front door and retrieved her coat. He held it out, waiting until she tucked the sleeves of her kimono inside. Then he took her hand and led her out the front door to the small landing at the top of the stairs.

The moon was full. A myriad of stars twinkled across the night sky. Tomi gazed up, her eyes as bright as the stars. His heart quickened. In the silence, he thought he could hear her heart beating, the rhythm matching his own.

He inhaled her scent, wanting to fill himself with her. But not this formal woman in a kimono and topknot. He reached over and removed her hair sticks, laying them on the wooden railing. One by one he found the hair pins and slid them out. Then he ran his hands through her thick silky hair, letting it cascade around her shoulders. In the moonlight, her hair shimmered like an ephemeral mist.

He soaked in the sight of her. This was his Tomi. He would remember her quiet beauty for the rest of his life. He cupped her face in his hands and planted tiny kisses on her temples, her nose, her cheeks. With each kiss he wanted to leave a part of him with her.

Tomi blinked up at him. "Tomorrow…"

"Sh-sh." He tucked a lock of hair behind her ears and kissed her lips, silencing them. "We have tonight."

He slipped his hands beneath her coat. The silk of her kimono felt as smooth as he imagined her skin would feel. His restraint broke. Crushing her body against his, he silently cursed the layers of clothing separating them. He captured her mouth with his. Gentle at first, then harder as he poured out the feelings he hadn't been able to say.

He wanted all of her. He fought to remember his strength. He didn't want to frighten her. But she didn't seem frightened. Her lips and body answered with their own needs. They locked together as one.

He finally came up for air. He was buoyed by the way she clung to him. Maybe she loved him, too. Maybe love could conquer all their obstacles. Maybe they could be together.

"Tomi." The sound of her name cut through the night and seemed to break the gossamer web surrounding them. He hurried on. "I need to talk to you. I want to tell you—"

She placed her fingers on his lips. "No need for words."

"Yes, I need to tell you—"

"No!" The word was loud and harsh. "Do not say words that can have no meaning."

His brows drew together. "They have meaning."

"To you." She flipped her hair over her shoulders. "No meaning to me."

Her words puzzled him. "How can you say that if you haven't heard them?"

"I speak first." She paused until she had his attention. "You good man. My wish for you is happy life."

"I'm happy…when I'm with you. I—"

She raised her hand, stopped him again. "Today no last. Tomorrow come. I marry Yoshiro and be his wife."

"But I love you." It was not the way he wanted to tell her. He'd blurted it out like a petulant school boy.

She was silent. The words hung in the air.

He held his breath, waiting for her answer.

Her reply stung. "So sorry."

Before he could gather his wits, she turned away, opened the door, and walked into the loft, slamming the door between them.

CHAPTER SIXTY-TWO

Early the next morning, Tomi climbed into Summer's van. At O'Hare she would board a plane and leave America. Tomi thought she was prepared to say good-bye, but when the door on the van slid shut, all the air whooshed out. She felt trapped.

"Ready?" Ace called from the driver's seat. Quinn sat next to him in the passenger seat. Taylor and Jason sleepily huddled on the back bench. And Tomi sat in the middle seat, across from P.R.

Nooo! her heart screamed. She would never be ready to leave the people she loved. Yet stoically she clicked her seat belt, and the van pulled away.

Her eyes blurred with tears as they passed the fields and farmhouses. Everything was moving too fast. She wanted it to slow down, to soak everything in around her. One last time.

She turned toward P.R., who was dressed in a starched white shirt and creased slacks as if he were prepared for court. His mouth was set in a grim line. Except for a few curt words, he had not spoken to her this morning.

Saying good-bye would be hard. But she had been thinking about her pain—not P.R.'s pain. His sisters and Quinn had warned her he was a playboy. So Tomi thought she was just another in a long list of women he would soon forget. Until last night.

The moonlight shining in his crystal blue eyes revealed everything. He was not saying pretty words just to flatter her. When she stared into his eyes, she saw the truth. He loved her.

Too late she realized what she had done. She had encouraged him, given him hope that they could be together. She had to quash his hope.

So last night, she silenced his words, made sure he knew his love could not change her responsibility. Then she had turned away and closed the door, not just on him, but on herself.

Today she wore the same black suit, white blouse, and high heels she had worn three months ago. But she was not the same woman. Here she had not been expected to conform to her parents' wishes. She had experienced freedom and explored who she could be.

She had found more than she ever believed possible. In each harrowing challenge, she had reached deep and discovered her inner core. She was strong and capable. In her quest to find herself, she had also found a man who loved and accepted her. It was the kind of life-changing love that singers wrote songs about and actors played out on the big screen.

But with each turn of the tires, she moved away from that love—and P.R. The trip to Chicago would take four hours. The flight to Japan would take thirteen more. Then a different life would begin. Countless hours, one after another, stretched ahead. Without P.R. Without his love.

She folded her hands in her lap and sighed. *Shogonai.* She must accept it.

Too soon they arrived at O'Hare. Ace parked the van in the passenger zone in front of the airport, and everyone piled out.

Quinn threw her arms around Tomi, clung to her, shaking. "This isn't good-bye. I'll see you in Japan."

Ace hugged her next. Even he teared up. Taylor and Jason wrapped their arms around Tomi's waist, begging her to stay. When Quinn pried them loose, Tomi turned to P.R. She didn't know how she would be able to say good-bye.

She took a deep breath and searched for her new-found inner strength. She must be strong, not just for herself, but for him.

He picked up her suitcase, much the way he'd done the first time they met. "I'll carry it."

She squared her shoulders. "No need."

"For me there is." P.R. stepped over to Ace, who had retrieved a luggage cart and was piling on the other two suitcases. "I'll go with Tomi, and then visit Mom. I can take the train back home."

He had never used the word *home* for Hickory Hills before and wondered if it would feel like home when he returned without Tomi.

As the van pulled away, he stood next to her, waving good-bye to Jason and Taylor, their faces pressed against the back window. Then P.R. wheeled the luggage cart into the main terminal.

Tomi had her printed boarding pass, so they stood in line to check her bags. He willed the line to slow down. Each step forward was a step closer to losing her. He marveled at how calm she appeared. A few tears had leaked out of her eyes, but she did not seem tied up in knots as he was. Last night he hadn't been able to sleep. He couldn't convince himself she would walk away from him and his love.

The weary-eyed woman at the ticket counter waved 'next,' and Tomi stepped forward. As she showed the agent her passport, P.R lifted the two bulky suitcases onto the scales. The largest weighed forty-nine pounds, two ounces.

P.R. tried to joke. "You have a few ounces left. Maybe you should buy another souvenir."

Tomi took his words seriously. "No time."

He walked with her toward the departure gate. On the walls were posters of the World Series Cubs and Navy Pier. In the corridor, they passed people chatting, babies crying, and dogs barking. The intercom blared out gate changes and plane delays. Yet he was silent. He had not even touched her, afraid if he did, the skein of nerves knotted in his stomach might unravel.

But he couldn't hold back any longer. In desperation, he reached for her hand. She didn't pull away. He gripped it tighter, silently pouring out his love. She didn't say a word, but as always gave him what he needed. This time, he needed her strength.

They reached the security check-point. He continued to clutch her hand as he turned and faced her. "So when will you come back to America?" he asked, wondering how long before he would see her again.

She didn't meet his eyes. "One trip."

Panic seized him. He squeezed her hand. "What-what do you mean?"

"Many places to see. Never come back to America."

He couldn't think, couldn't breathe. "But you'll phone or text?"

She dropped his hand and shook her head.

The finality hit him. Until this moment he had somehow convinced himself today was not the end. Tomi would come back to him. Divorce wasn't as common in Japan as the U.S., but it could happen. Or maybe like Raven, Tomi would be widowed. She might have a child or two when they met again. But they would meet again.

Of course, he would not marry. He would establish his law career and become financially stable. All he had to do was wait. Eventually, they would be together.

Now his foolish dreams shattered. He could go on if he had hope. But she had jerked that hope away. She was never coming back. He would never see her, never talk to her, never touch her again.

Desperate to hold onto to her, he pulled her into his arms. He wanted to take in all of her. The scent of her hair, the curve of her body, the beating of her heart against his.

Too soon, she stepped away. She reached into her suit pocket and pulled out a small green frog, the one she'd uncovered in the ashes of Ace's house. "For you." Her hand shook as she placed it into his palm. "Sayonara."

A lump formed in his throat. He stared at the frog. When he looked up to thank her, she had slipped into the crowded line. He stood there, holding onto the frog and watching her. He willed her to turn around. If she turned around and looked at him, it wasn't hopeless. She would come back to him.

She unbuttoned her suit jacket.

Turn around. Look at me. I'm here. I need to see your face one more time.

She slipped off her jacket and folded it onto the conveyer belt.

Turn around. I'm here. I need to see your face one more time.

She walked through the metal detector.

Turn around. I need to see your face.

She put on her jacket and buttoned it up.

Turn around. Turn around. Turn around.

She walked down the corridor, head up, shoulders squared.

She did not turn around.

CHAPTER SIXTY-THREE

Tomi hefted her two large suitcases onto the luggage cart. Her body ached. The flight from Chicago to Tokyo had been long and cramped. She pushed the unwieldy cart into the main terminal at Narita International Airport. She heard throngs of people chattering in Japanese. She passed shops filled with Japanese souvenirs: Hello Kitty toys, pot-bellied sumo wrestlers, and ninja warriors. She smelled the aroma of steaming rice and spicy curry.

Nothing had changed. Yet she didn't feel the welcoming embrace of returning to her homeland. Some slight shift had occurred deep within her, like tectonic plates hidden beneath the Earth's surface.

"Tomoe! Tomoe!"

She no longer thought of herself as Tomoe. In her heart she would hold onto who she had been in America. Tomi.

She turned and spotted Chie in the swarm of people dressed in black suits. Her friend wore a Lolita-style white blouse, a ruffled pink mini-skirt, and knee-high socks. Chie was short and pudgy with a moon face that always seemed to be smiling.

The girls had grown up in Ishinomaki, a fishing village more than three hundred kilometers from Tokyo. After graduation Tomi had attended the university while Chie stayed to work in her family's fish market. When the tsunami hit on 3/11, Chie had lost everything. Her house, her family, even the market had been swept away, but Chie refused to leave.

Tomi had moved to Tokyo and secured a teaching position, where she met Quinn. In March, when Quinn had returned to the U.S., Chie came to Tokyo and roomed with Tomi. The move had outwardly changed Chie, but inside she remained the same, good-natured girl.

Now, as the two hugged, Tomi hoped she could draw on Chie's bubbly spirit. Tomi had none left.

Tonight she and Chie would stay at their apartment in Tokyo. Tomorrow they would make the three-hour train trip to Ishinomaki to see her parents and Yoshiro.

Back at the apartment, Tomi gave Chie the glitzy Cubs hat. Chie immediately put it on and pranced around their one-bedroom apartment, the size of six tatami mats.

Exhausted, Tomi changed into lounging pants and folded herself cross-legged onto the floor. Chie plopped next to her and filled their glasses with sweet plum wine. The two clinked glasses and toasted. "*Kanpai.*"

Tomi relaxed and chatted, the Japanese words coming naturally to her.

"Tell me about American men," Chie said.

"Laney is called Quinn now. Her husband is a good man."

Chie's smile widened. "You find good man?"

Tomi wanted to confide in Chie, but Tomi suspected her friend would not approve.

When she did not answer, Chie teased, "Boyfriend might make Yoshi jealous."

Tomi never called Yoshiro by his nickname. Tomi shifted the conversation. "You had a new boyfriend."

Chie waved her hand. "He went bye-bye."

Many Japanese women were not in a hurry to marry. Chie, however, wanted to become a wife and mother. "I just need to find a man like Yoshi," Chie said.

Chie handed Tomi a fashion magazine. On the cover were two pictures of a Japanese bride. On one side the bride modeled an American wedding gown and on the other a kimono. "Will you wear kimono and American dress?"

Some Japanese women chose to wear a traditional kimono for the wedding ceremony and an American bridal gown for the reception. Tomi pushed the magazine aside. She was too tired to pretend to be happy about the wedding.

"Last week I saw Yoshi," Chie said. "He's still sad."

In July, two months before Tomi left for the States, Yoshiro's father had unexpectedly died from a heart attack. Tomi's and Yoshiro's fathers had been best friends since boyhood. Tomi's father took the death of his friend very hard.

A sliver of hope pricked Tomi. "Maybe Yoshiro will want to postpone marriage?"

Chie shook her head. "Yoshi thinks the wedding and a baby will help his family get over the grief."

"Baby!" Tomi tipped over her glass, spilling wine on the magazine.

Chie jumped up to get a cloth. When she returned, she wiped up the wine. "Yoshiro is fine man. You're lucky."

Tomi poured herself more wine. Tomorrow she would see Yoshiro. He would expect her to set a wedding date. She did not feel lucky.

The next day Tomi's head ached as she rode the afternoon train to Ishinomaki. She had expected Chie to come with her.

"It's different now. No one's there for me," Chie said.

Tomi agreed. Their hometown was different. When she stepped off the train, she was never prepared. The earthquake and tsunami had leveled 50,000 buildings and killed more than 3,000 people. The rubble had been cleaned up, but the city center was gone and had not been rebuilt.

Tomi braced herself for the usual wave of grief. It didn't come. In America she had been able to accept the loss of her grandmother and brother. Her old life was gone, swept away like parts of the city and its people. What remained was her future.

With her suitcase trailing behind, Tomi trudged up the hill from the train station to the temporary housing where her parents lived. She walked between two rows of corrugated tin apartments. The eighty units, built by the government after the disaster, needed repair. Foundations sagged, screens were ripped. Doors hung open on empty units.

Tomi had urged her parents to leave, too. Their answer was always the same. "Where would we go?" They were displaced people. Their community of friends was gone.

Tomi arrived at her parents' and slid the door open. The familiar childhood phrase tripped off her tongue. "Tadaima. I'm home."

Her heart sank. This two-room apartment, each room smaller than a

Western hotel room bore no resemblance to the home where she had grown up.

Even though the apartment was not familiar, her mother, sitting at the table, drinking green tea, and waiting for her to walk through the door, was. Her mother was small, barely five feet, with graying hair pulled into a bun. As usual she wore a Japanese-style apron, with long sleeves gathered at the wrists. At home, her mother wore the full apron, not just when she cooked, but also to protect her clothes.

As soon as her mother saw Tomi, she jumped up to greet her. Her mother rushing toward her with outstretched arms warmed Tomi's heart.

Her father, stooped and thin, shuffled into the room. Tomi was shocked at how much older he looked. He had always been a robust man. Now he appeared to have been flattened like the seawall around their city. Later she must take her mother aside and ask if he was well.

When her father greeted her, his leathery face, usually stern and judgmental, broke into a wide smile. As the three of them wrapped their arms around each other, Tomi was surprised by how happy they were to see her. Unexpected emotions bubbled up. Her parents loved her, and she loved and had missed them, too.

They had always tried to support her and give her what they thought was best. They had paid for her piano lessons and cram school. They had sent her to university, and when she became a teacher, her father's chest had puffed out like a peacock. They had even begrudgingly consented to her trip to America.

The last five years, cramped in temporary housing, had been hard. Marrying Yoshiro and living nearby would make them happy. She was their only remaining child and was glad she could repay them for all they had done.

Soon her parents would rebuild. She and Yoshiro would live a short distance away, and Yoshiro's mother would also live with them. Tomi's grandparents had been an important part of her life. Her children would have their grandparents near, too. Yes, life was as it should be.

Tomi spoke to her parents in Japanese. "When will you rebuild?"

Instead of answering, Tomi's mother removed her apron and gestured with her hands toward the door. "We talk later. Many people waiting to see you."

Her parents led her to the large community building where they had planned a party in her honor. Tomi entered and looked around at the long tables filled with people all smiling at her. She knew a few by name, but most were strangers. When her father walked over to a table of men, Tomi leaned closer to her mother. "Has he been ill?"

Her mother shook her head. "He cannot accept that our home and his best friend are gone."

Her mother nudged her to a table filled with many of her favorite Japanese foods. "Eat, eat. You're too thin."

Her mother handed Tomi a plate, but Tomi was too nervous about seeing Yoshiro to eat. She glanced at her watch. Six p.m. Her eyes strayed to the time in the U.S. Five a.m. The day would just be starting for P.R. He would wake up, go for his run, and come back to eat breakfast. Alone. The way she felt even in the midst of these people.

Like her father, she understood what it meant to lose someone. She understood the loss of her brother and grandmother. Now she understood another loss. She sighed. She must move on. She would get over it. But not soon. No, not soon.

She looked around the large room, searching for Yoshiro. She was not anxious to see him, but she had expected him to be here to greet her. "Where are Yoshiro and his mother?"

Her mother's hand flew to her mouth in surprise. "Didn't Yoshiro tell you?"

Tomi sensed something bad. "Tell me what?" She had not heard from Yoshiro since she left.

"After her husband died, Yoshiro's mother moved to Nagano to live with her eldest son and his family."

Tomi frowned. "So where is Yoshiro?"

Her mother ladled spicy curry over her rice. "He found a good company to work for in Nagano."

"He moved to Nagano?" The room swayed. Tomi tried to steady herself. Nagano was more than three hundred kilometers away. After 3/11, jobs were scarce. Yoshiro had been a businessman, but took a position at a nursery trimming trees and shrubs. She was happy that he'd secured a better job, but shouldn't he have discussed the move with her?

Her mother continued to pile food onto Tomi's plate as if eating would solve her problems. "You'll like living there."

She gripped her mother's arm. "Will you and Father move to Nagano?"

Her mother looked away, but not before Tomi detected the sadness in her eyes. "Your father said we stay here."

Maybe Tomi could convince Yoshiro to move near her parents. "When will you rebuild?"

Her mother shrugged and handed Tomi the plate filled with food. "Bad rumors. Maybe years."

Tomi almost upended her plate. "You can't live this way for years."

"No one's left from our old neighborhood."

Tomi couldn't believe her parents planned to continue to live in their cramped apartment. They deserved better.

Her mother gestured around the community room. "We try to make new community." Her mother began filling her plate. "Yoshiro works long hours. He can't come until New Year's. Then we will discuss the wedding."

Now she must not only marry Yoshiro, but also move away from her family.

The room swirled. Tears stung her eyes, blurring her sight. She felt as if she had been slammed by another tsunami and swept out to sea. And she couldn't find anything to hold onto.

CHAPTER SIXTY-FOUR

On Christmas Eve, P.R. along with the rest of the family, gathered around Summer's piano to sing Christmas carols.

How much different the holidays would have been if Tomi were here. They would have decorated a Christmas tree, gone caroling with the church, and sneaked kisses under the mistletoe.

He had to stop obsessing about Tomi. But he didn't know how. He felt the way he did when he'd lost a case. Worse really.

During the day he focused on his clients, legal briefs, and judges' rulings. But walling himself off from his feelings for Tomi came at a hefty price. The nights were agony. If he slept, he dreamed of her, and when he woke, she was his first thought.

He kept going over what he could or should have done differently. He'd presented his case and told her he loved her. Her decision was to marry someone else. He'd have to accept the verdict. But how?

At least the settlement for the coal miners had come through. His clients would have a Merry Christmas, and with his fees, he bought five acres of land from Ace.

Now at the piano Summer struck up *Deck the Halls*. He couldn't belt out even one cheery *fa la la*. He slipped into the kitchen where Raven had taken refuge.

"Do the twins need me?" she asked.

"Relax. Belle is watching them."

Outwardly Raven looked stunning, svelte and thin, in a silver-sequined strapless dress. Long black hair fanned out, covering her bare shoulders. But her dark eyes showed confusion and sadness. She didn't know how to face life as a widow.

She emptied the champagne bottle and lifted her glass. "To a very unmerry Christmas."

"You've got that right." He crossed the room and planted a brotherly kiss on her cheek. "We should be celebrating Christmas at Mom's like we always do."

Raven took another drink and raised her glass again. "To our sister Summer, who's always fixing our lives, whether we like it or not."

Summer's fix-their-lives idea this year was to host Christmas in Hickory Hills. "It'll be easier for Mom to come to my house instead of us dragging the presents and food up there."

Her plan made sense, but the family had always celebrated Christmas in Chicago. It was tradition. To P.R.'s surprise, Mom was delighted. He was the lone grumbler. Just another part of his life slipping away. He made sure Summer knew he didn't like it.

She wasn't sympathetic. "Your unhappiness has nothing to do with where we celebrate Christmas. It's about Tomi. So get over it."

In a moment of weakness, he put out his hands, palms up, and pleaded. "How? Just tell me how? I'm here and she's there."

Summer didn't have any answers, but she had taken him into his arms and hugged him, letting him know she cared.

His plan to make it through the holidays included indulging in some yuletide cheer. But when he'd gone to Chicago to celebrate, it hadn't worked then, and it wasn't working now. Drinking a keg of beer, a flask of whiskey, or a bottle of champagne wouldn't change reality—or fill the gnawing hole Tomi had left.

Raven wasn't having any trouble downing the liquor. She picked up the champagne bottle and tried to find one more swallow. When she didn't, she chucked it into the trash. "Will you go buy another bottle?"

He wouldn't help his sister down that self-destructive path. "Raven, you've had enough."

Her bottom lip jutted. "I thought you would understand."

"I do, but drinking won't bring Carter back."

Raven opened the refrigerator and pulled out a bottle of beer. "I don't even like beer. Tomorrow I'll have a big fat honking headache." She pointed the bottle at him. "And it will be your fault."

As she struggled to unscrew the lid, Summer's daughter, Kat, and Taylor raced into the kitchen. They wore matching red velvet dresses, and their black patent leather shoes clattered against the tile floor.

Taylor grabbed P.R.'s hand. "Time to open presents."

Kat skipped over to Raven. "Let's go."

Above the girls' heads, P.R. mouthed to Raven, "Don't disappoint them."

Shrugging, Raven set the beer on the counter and let Kat lead her into the living room. He and Taylor followed.

The large Christmas tree, twinkling with lights, cast a warm glow around the room. Stacked beneath the pine tree was a huge pile of presents, and lined up in front was a row of squirming children. This year, even his nieces' and nephews' smiling faces didn't bring P.R. his usual joy.

For the past few weeks, his sisters had been whispering about him. They were probably plotting to cheer him up. His family loved him, so he would pretend to like his gifts. But nothing they gave him could lift his spirits.

Eager to open their presents, Taylor and Kat plopped down next to the other kids. Summer's husband, Craig, unhooked the furry Santa hat from the tree and tossed it to P.R. He didn't react quickly enough. The stocking hat flopped on the floor.

P.R. usually enjoyed playing Santa, but he picked up the hat and threw it back to Craig. "Your house. You play Santa."

Craig gave him an understanding nod and shoved the hat onto his head.

The traditional order of opening presents was youngest to oldest. Craig sifted through the stack until he found a present for one of the twins. "To our sweet Morgan."

Taylor hopped up and carried the gift to Raven, who held the twins on her lap.

"I'll open it for her." Taylor ripped off the red-and-white striped paper and lifted out a frilly pink dress. A chorus of *ahs* followed.

Craig found another present. "And to sweet Megan."

P.R. strode across the room and scooped up Meggie. Now that he'd decided to stay in Hickory Hills, he would help Raven with the twins as much as he could. He bounced Meggie on his knee and opened her present, a matching pink dress.

When it was P.R.'s turn, Craig shook his head. "Nothing for you."

P.R. was by-passed two more times. On the third round, he felt slighted. "Hey, what about me?"

Jason, sitting cross-legged on the floor, grinned back at him. "All you're getting this year is a lump of coal."

P.R. ruffled Jason's hair. "Thanks a lot, pal."

Whatever his family was up to, P.R. hoped the gift wasn't Summer's idea. Once she had given Craig and Ace a fishing trip to Canada. At the time, they hadn't been speaking. But the trip repaired a relationship that had been damaged by their parents in childhood.

In July, the family had chipped in to buy an American Girl doll for Taylor's birthday. He glanced at Taylor, cradling the blue-eyed, freckled-face Kit. Taylor was an important part of their family, and he hoped Quinn would be able to adopt her.

After all the boxes were opened, Taylor jumped up and unhooked a white envelope from the tree. She skipped over to P.R. and suddenly became tongue-tied. She swayed back and forth, her face getting redder.

Jason marched over and snatched the envelope. He handed it to P.R. "This is from all of us."

P.R. ripped the envelope open and frowned. No card. Instead he held an airline voucher. Did his family think a vacation would cheer him up? Even fleeing from wintery Illinois to an island paradise wasn't going to make him happy. "Are you sending me away?"

A nervous titter rippled through the room. "Well, you haven't been the easiest person to live with," Belle said.

He looked from Belle to Summer. "So where have you decided I should go?" Knowing Summer she would already have planned his destination and itinerary.

Summer shrugged. "The name of the airlines might give you a hint. If not, there's a schedule in the envelope."

Aloud, P.R. read the letters on the voucher. "JAL." Still clueless, he pulled out the schedule. Circled were several flights from Chicago to Japan.

"Japan!" He blurted out the word with more venom than he'd intended. He gripped the voucher. He had tried to hide his pain, but his family had seen it. They knew losing Tomi had cut into his soul. He was touched that they cared enough to try to fix it. He didn't want to break down. Not here. Not now.

He took a deep breath. He'd never considered going to Japan. It wasn't logical. His passport was up to date, but what would the trip accomplish? Tomi had chosen another man. No matter how much he yearned to see her, he couldn't just fly over there and wreck her life. She was happy.

He forced a smile. "Thanks." But he felt as if Santa had just given him that lump of coal.

CHAPTER SIXTY-FIVE

Quinn stared across the room at P.R. as he tried to sound grateful for his Christmas present. He wasn't convincing. She stood. "I think I'll get more fruitcake. What about you, P.R.?"

"Good idea." P.R. rose and followed her into kitchen. When the door banged behind them, he shook the envelope at her. "Were you part of this?"

Quinn squared her shoulders. "Sort of. I told Summer I didn't think it was a good idea."

"You've got that right." P.R. slapped the voucher onto the table. "I can't just fly to Japan and interfere in Tomi's life. She made her decision. She chose to go back to Japan."

"Her stay was up."

P.R. began to pace. "Yeah, but she chose to marry some other guy."

"Not because she loves him."

P.R. stopped in mid stride. "What—what do you mean?"

"Tomi's parents and Yoshiro's parents made that decision when Tomi and Yoshiro were children."

"This is the 21st century. Japan doesn't do that anymore."

"Some families do. You know how hard tradition is to change. You didn't even want to have Christmas here."

P.R. waved his hand as if dismissing the argument. "So she's marrying him out of duty."

"Not exactly. I don't quite understand. It's honor and respect, too. When I was in Japan, I saw how much elders were revered. Tomi will not go against her parents' wishes."

"So when is the wedding?"

Quinn hesitated, not sure how much she should tell P.R.

"You can give me the date, can't you?" P.R.'s face turned ashen. His breath hitched. "Is-is she already married?"

Quinn shook her head. "No, she's not married."

P.R.'s legs folded and he collapsed onto the nearest chair.

Quinn hadn't been convinced P.R. loved Tomi. Really loved her. But tonight she saw the truth. Tomi wasn't just one of his girls. She was The One. He would not forget her. He couldn't. The same way Quinn couldn't forget Ace after she'd fallen in love with him at sixteen.

Quinn pulled a chair out and sat across from P.R. "I haven't been honest with you."

P.R. lifted his head.

"I thought when Tomi returned to Japan she would accept her marriage to Yoshiro. Instead, when she calls, she asks about you."

"What have you told her?"

"Just about your work and moving to Hickory Hills. I didn't tell her how unhappy you are."

P.R. nodded as if in agreement. "But she's happy, right?"

"Truthfully, she doesn't sound happy."

P.R. let out a groan. "That's what I've been holding onto. I just need to know Tomi is happy."

"I think she's hurting as much as you."

"What has she said?"

"Nothing, but she hasn't even seen Yoshiro."

"Why? She's been back over two weeks."

"I don't know. Whenever I ask about him or the wedding, she changes the subject."

P.R. took out his phone. "Give me her number. I'll call her and find out what's going on."

Quinn reached across the table and laid her hand on his arm. "If she hasn't told me, she's not going to tell you."

He dropped the phone onto the table. "So what should I do?" He picked up the voucher and fingered it. "How can I use this? I don't know where Tomi is."

"Summer asked if I would help you if you went to Japan."

P.R.'s eyes sparked. "So are you going to help?"

"I promised Ace I wouldn't tell you unless I was convinced you needed to go."

She reached into her pocket and pulled out her own airline voucher.

CHAPTER SIXTY-SIX

On New Year's Eve, Tomi, along with millions of others, went to the Meiji Shrine in Tokyo for the first visit of the year. Before entering, Tomi stopped at the communal water tank to perform the ritual cleansing. She held the wooden dipper under the running water and purified her hands before she brought the cleansing water to her lips. Now she was ready to enter the Shinto shrine dedicated to Emperor Meiji and his wife, Empress Shoken.

Towering pines and cedars flanked the giant cypress gate. The *torii*, the largest in Japan, stood twelve meters high. Even though she had come here many times, she was always filled with awe.

As she inched along the sacred path and through the massive gate, she tightened the belt on her long coat and turned up the fur collar. The mass of people sheltered her from the sharp wind, but inside she felt a bone-chilling aloneness. Most of her life, she had celebrated New Year's with her family at the temple in Ishinomaki. But the tsunami had ended that tradition.

On New Year's Day she still returned to her hometown, but for the past five years, she and Quinn had come to the Meiji Shrine on New Year's Eve. Each year their prayers were the same. Quinn prayed for her daughter. Tomi prayed for her family and for a chance to go to America and experience love.

Her wishes had come true, yet she wasn't happy. Her parents were even less fortunate. A few days after Tomi returned from America, three city officials had come to talk to her parents. They showed them blueprints for a memorial for the people lost in the tsunami. The construction would begin next spring and be finished in 2021. Her parents were thankful that their son and others would be remembered.

Then a short, white-haired man puffed out his chest and announced the location. Part of the 3/11 memorial would be built on her family's ancestral land. The new sea wall would keep the land from flooding again. The man pontificated about what an honor it was to have their land chosen.

Of course, her parents would be amply compensated. Now they could rebuild anywhere. Anywhere except on the land that had been in their family for centuries. The news crushed her parents. Her father's dream of home disappeared. Her mother sat at the table, her eyes vacant as she drank pot after pot of green tea.

Tomi talked to them about moving with her after she married Yoshiro. But they couldn't fathom it. They were afloat, untethered, as if the tsunami had swept in again. This time it had taken away their future.

The temporary housing was too cramped for Tomi to stay for more than a few days, so she had returned to Tokyo to live with Chie. She had quit her teaching job to go to America so her long days were filled with a heavy sadness. Finally she confessed to Chie, "In America I fell in love."

Chie glared. "You love another man more than Yoshiro?"

"I do not love Yoshiro." Tomi's blunt words angered Chie. They argued. A rift separated the two childhood friends. After Christmas, though, something changed. Chie no longer seemed angry and was always smiling. The two grew close again.

Tonight, Chie had not come to the shrine. "I will meet you at midnight by the sacred camphor tree."

"Where are you going?" Tomi asked.

Chie merely smiled.

Now, as Tomi stood in line at the shrine, she checked her watch. 11:30. For nearly an hour, she had shuffled along the crowded path, usually a ten-minute walk. Ahead was a second cypress gate, and beyond, the main offering hall. She reached into her coat pocket and reverently ran her fingers over the small silk pouch she'd purchased last New Year's Eve. The amulet had been lucky. Her wish had come true. She had gone to America and found love.

Since returning to Japan, she had tried to quell her feelings for P.R. The pull was too strong. Tonight she would rid herself of him. She had slipped a small scrap of paper inside the silk pouch. Written on it was P.R.'s full name. She would dispose of the amulet and her love for P.R. Then she would be an obedient daughter and live the life her parents had chosen for her.

The wave of people pushed her forward through the second *torii* toward the main offering hall. The shrine, rebuilt after World War II, was constructed of cypress, its peaked copper roof green with age. The shrine wasn't as ostentatious as the Golden Pavilion in Kyoto, once covered in gold leaf, nor as breath-taking as the Great Buddha of Kamakura, a giant bronze statue that weighed 121 tons. But to her, the Meiji Shrine surrounded by 100,000 trees was a sacred sanctuary and a place of renewal.

As she waited, snow began to fall. Large, fluffy flakes danced around her like playful spirits. She thought of her grandmother and her brother, and no longer felt alone.

When it was her turn, she climbed the steps, bowed, and tossed her yen into the offering box. To get the attention of the gods, she bowed and clapped twice. The ritual was familiar, but instead of her usual requests, other familiar words filled her head. *Our father, who art in heaven.* P.R. had called it the Lord's Prayer.

Silently she repeated the words, and a warmth entered her body. Calmness spread through her. When she finished, she bowed again. Almost as if in a trance, she bought a small wooden plaque and moved to a table in front of the sacred camphor where rows of prayer requests hung on a wall encircling the trunk. She drew two symbols on her plaque and hung it on the wall. She stepped back and read, *Happy marriage.* An image entered her head. She was dressed in a white wedding gown. Next to her stood P.R.

No! No! She must wipe away those thoughts. She would buy another amulet and focus on her new life. She moved through the crowd to a small canvas booth with colorful charms. She was drawn to the silk pouches, similar to the green one in her pocket.

The vendor greeted her and wished her a Happy New Year. Tomi automatically repeated Happy New Year to the grandmotherly woman, but even as Tomi said it, she wondered how her new year could be happy. She pointed to a small red pouch and paid. As she dropped it into her pocket, she turned away and gazed at the throng of people waiting to make their offerings.

It was after midnight. Where was Chie? She checked her phone. No calls or texts.

Off to the side people tossed their old amulets into a burning fire. She moved toward the flames. The snow fell harder, and her legs lumbered along like heavy cypress logs. She must do this. She must purge herself of the past—and P.R.

Near the fire the air shimmered. Heat from the flames warmed her cheeks. She hesitated, not wanting to let go of the special charm. She squinted through the flames, searching for Chie.

The crowd was a sea of black hair, except for a tall, blond-haired man rising above the rest. The hair looked so much like P.R.'s that pain sliced through her. The smoke must be blurring her vision. Not just his hair, but the shape of his head and shoulders looked like P.R.'s. She must be mad. P.R. couldn't be in Japan at the Meiji Shrine.

She blinked. But he was still there. For days she had been consumed by him. Her mind must have snapped. She must drive away these thoughts before she crossed into crazy land.

She reached into her pocket and pulled out the amulet. The man spotted her. His eyes locked on hers.

"P.R.!" The name slipped out of her mouth as the amulet slipped out of her hand. She looked down at the fire. The flames licked at the red silk. Red! She had thrown away the wrong charm.

Her eyes darted back to the crowd. The man was still there. She fisted her hands and rubbed her eyes. The man who looked like P.R. was parting the crowd and weaving toward her.

Joy shot through her. Her stiff legs became agile. She tried to move toward him. The crowd was too thick. It pushed her back. She bobbed up and down. There he was. No, there. And now there.

She bounced like a pogo stick. Up...down...up...down. The crowd shifted. She stumbled backward. She fought for footing on solid ground and righted herself. She squinted toward the wave of people. Where was he? She couldn't see him. Where was her P.R.?

She closed her eyes and willed him back. She searched the crowd and couldn't find him. It was a hallucination. P.R. wasn't in Japan. Her mind was playing tricks on her.

She was in crazy land.

CHAPTER SIXTY-SEVEN

Tomi was gone.

P.R. searched through the sea of people, craning his neck. Where was she? He'd just seen her. He knew it was Tomi. Even in this mass of people he'd been able to find her.

His eyes had been drawn to the bonfire and a woman in a long black coat. Her head was down, but he'd known it was Tomi. She was different. Sad in a way he'd never seen before. Her shoulders hunched, her body listless.

"Tomi."

He didn't know her name had slipped from his lips until Quinn asked, "Where?"

P.R. pointed to the fire. "Over there."

He didn't wait for Quinn or Chie. He threaded through the crowd, one foot here, another there. Then he came up against a solid wall of bodies. He could see Tomi, yet he couldn't reach her. Their eyes connected. Adrenalin shot through him.

He tried to move forward. He was hemmed in. He inched back, became blocked again. He looked up, and she had vanished. His entire body sagged.

Coming to Japan was impulsive, impractical, all the things he wasn't. He always planned everything. But once the idea had taken hold, he couldn't let go. He didn't even have a plan, didn't know how he would be able to convince her to give up everything—her family, her friends, and her country—to marry him. But he had to try.

He stopped at the foot of the steps leading up to shrine and waited for Quinn and Chie. "I saw Tomi," P.R. said. "But now I don't know where she is."

"Sacred camphor tree," Chie said in English.

P.R. looked around. "Where's that?"

Chie pointed to the shrine. "Make request first."

P.R. started to protest. He had waited too long, but he wasn't sure what Tomi's reaction would be. Some divine intervention would help.

Following Chie and Quinn, he climbed the steps. He repeated the ritual, until they placed their hands together and closed their eyes. Then he prayed to his God, the one who had helped him through the death of his father, the one who had helped him through law school, the one he needed to help him persuade Tomi to marry him.

Quinn elbowed him. He opened his eyes and climbed down the steps. "Now what?"

Quinn pointed to the wooden plaques. "Buy one of these and write your New Year's wish on it."

He frowned. "I thought we just prayed for our wish."

"When you write it down, the Shinto priests will pray for it, too."

More divine intervention couldn't hurt. He bought the plaque and walked to a table where he wrote down his wish.

Quinn pointed to the side of the shrine. "Now you leave it at the camphor tree where Tomi is waiting."

"Finally." He had replayed this moment over and over in his head. It wouldn't be like a romantic movie where she threw herself into his outstretched arms.

Quinn had warned him, "In Japan showing affection in public is frowned on." Then she added, "Tomi once told me she dreamed of being able to walk down the street holding hands with the man she loved."

He wanted to be that man.

He approached the wall of wishes around the sacred camphor. Tomi stood, waiting. He wanted to run to her, but all he could do was inch forward. When he was less than ten feet away, her eyes found his.

He held his breath, waited for those beautiful dark eyes to light up. Instead her eyes closed and she shook her head.

Disappointment stabbed him. Had the trip been a colossal mistake? He stopped in front of her. "Tomi?"

She opened her eyes and blinked. "Go away. You aren't real."

He reached out and slid his thumb over her smooth cheek. Electricity sparked through him. "Tomi. It's me. I'm here."

She gasped. "P.R.! Is it really you? I'm not in crazy land?"

He chuckled. "If you are, we're there together." He felt dazed and a little crazy, too. His tongue twisted on the words that he'd practiced for days. "*Akemashite omedetou gozaimasu.*"

Joy spread across her face. "Happy New Year." But her eyes stayed sad. "Why you come?"

Her question thudded against his heart. Not exactly the greeting he had hoped for.

She crossed her arms and waited.

His mind was jumbled, his mouth numb. He reached into his pocket and pulled out his plaque. He opened her hand and placed it on her palm.

Her eyes widened as she read what he had written. *To marry Tomi.*

CHAPTER SIXTY-EIGHT

The bus swayed, rocking Tomi back and forth, lulling her as she dreamed she was at the Meiji Shrine dressed in a silk kimono.

A priest asked, "Will you, Tomoe Kanai, take this man to be husband?" Why was the question in English?

She peered through a netted veil. The man standing next to her was P.R. She was no longer at the Meiji Shrine. She was in a long white wedding gown, standing at the altar in Hickory Hills. Reverend Stone was waiting for an answer.

The bus swerved. Tomi awoke. She squeezed her eyes shut, trying to recapture the dream. According to legend, the first dream of the New Year was supposed to come true. But she hadn't finished the dream. She needed to know how it ended.

A warm breath caressed her cheek. She peeked out of the corner of her eye. "P.R.!" She clamped a hand over her mouth. It wasn't a dream. P.R. was on the bus next to her. Across the aisle, Quinn and Chie also slept.

Tomi closed her eyes again. She wanted to finish her dream, say 'I do,' and marry P.R. If only that were possible.

P.R. was traveling to Ishinomaki to meet her parents and ask her father for permission to marry her. Yoshiro would also be there today to discuss the wedding.

P.R. would no longer be a secret. Her parents and Yoshiro would know that she had fallen in love in America. Instead of the knot in her stomach tightening, it loosened. She was relieved. She no longer had to pretend.

Denying her true feeling had weighed on her soul. New Year's was for leaving the past behind and embracing the future. She did not want to embrace a future with Yoshiro, but if she must, she would do it honestly.

The brakes squealed as the bus pulled into the station. For the last five years she had regularly made this trip from Tokyo to Ishinomaki. Each time she returned, the city seemed less and less like home. Always before she would think the next time would be better, the next time her parents would have a permanent house. Now she knew that dream was impossible. Just as her dream to marry P.R. was impossible.

When the four of them left the bus, it was 6 a.m. and still dark outside.

P.R.'s hair had tufted from sleeping, his eyes groggy. "Which way?"

Tomi pointed to the lockers in the bus station. "For suitcases. Then we go to Hiyoriyama Park."

P.R. frowned. "At night?"

"To see first sunrise. New Year's tradition."

"Bring luck," Chie added.

Quinn looked from Tomi to P.R. "We could all use some luck."

They followed the line of people trekking up the hill high above the city. As they neared the top, P.R. reached over and took Tomi's hand, the way he had many times. But they were in Japan. She could not let him hold her hand in public. She tried to slip her hand away, but he laced his fingers through hers and held onto it. She gave in. This was what she wanted. Him and the freedom to be herself.

At the park, she led P.R. past the *torii* gate to a boulder away from the crowd. They sat together, waiting for the sun to rise. Too soon the first ray of light split open the dark expanse of sky, tinting it in shades of pink. The crowd sighed in a chorus of *ahs*.

Then a yellow orb burst forth, glinting down on the white-capped waves of the water and the fishing boats moored at the harbor. As the sun rose, it illuminated the city of inlets and tall buildings, protected by a new seawall.

"Now I know why Japan is called land of the rising sun," P.R. said.

She turned to him, her eyes filled with love.

He squeezed her hand. "I've missed you. Missed the peace I feel when we're together."

Yes, peace. That's the way she felt, too, even though she knew it could not last.

P.R. scanned the city below. "Where was your home?"

Tomi pointed to a small square of land. "There. South of the park."

P.R. studied the barren land for a long time. "Before I talk to your father, I want to talk to you." He cleared his throat. "Tomi, I need to be sure this is what you want, too."

In the dream her answer had not come. Now it did. "Yes."

P.R.'s smile was as bright as the sunrise.

Then she added, "If father give permission."

His smile slipped away. "I'll ask your father later. Now I'm asking you." He looked toward the harbor. "If you marry me, will you be able to leave this?"

She peered up at him. "Ishinomaki?"

"Your home."

Home. The word was only a distant memory, a feeling of safety and love that she had once known. Now it stirred inside her again. Not because of where she was, but because of who she was with.

She reached over, put her hand on his chest. "You are my home."

313

CHAPTER SIXTY-NINE

"We get luggage later," Tomi said to P.R. as they left the park. "Now meet parents."

As the four of them walked down the hill, he inhaled the salty ocean air. His stomach clenched. He rubbed his hand over his stubbly chin. Beneath his coat, his clothes were rumpled from sleeping on the plane and bus. His disheveled appearance certainly wouldn't make a good first impression on her parents.

He looked toward the harbor where the gulls circled and cawed as they searched for their morning catch. They swooped in and out like the nagging doubts flitting through his mind. When he argued a case in front of a jury, he had to convince twelve people. Now he had to convince only one. But his future hinged on that one man's verdict.

He reached into his pocket and wrapped his hand around the tiny porcelain frog. He hoped it would bring him the luck he needed.

Halfway down the hill, the temporary housing where Tomi's parents lived came into view. The two long rows of prefab modulars with corrugated tin roofs were similar to what FEMA used to house disaster victims. But her parents had lived there for almost six years. A new understanding swept over him.

They had lost their home, their ancestral land, and more importantly, their son. They had nothing left—except their daughter. Now he had come to ask them to give her up, too.

They stopped outside the end unit. On each side of the door stood a pot with a small pine tree and several bamboo shoots. Similar New Year's decorations lined the fronts of other doorways.

"Always in pairs. For male and female." Tomi looked up at him and blushed. "Like us."

"Like us," he repeated, hoping there would be an *us*.

Tomi slid open the door. They stepped inside and were greeted by a rush of warm air and the fragrant smell of steamed rice. As they slipped off their shoes, coats and gloves, P.R. scanned the hotel-sized room with a kitchenette at the far end. Stacked along the walls, from floor to ceiling, were cardboard boxes and plastic totes, not jumbled, but orderly and neat. Tomi had told him her parents lived in temporary housing, but he had never imagined it being similar to a cramped storage unit. Anger at the indignity roiled inside him.

Tomi's cheery voice filled the small room and calmed him. "*Tadaima.* I'm home."

A woman, with graying hair tied into a knot, turned from the stove and shuffled toward them. Although shorter and older, she resembled Tomi and moved with the same quiet elegance. "*Okaeri nasai,*" she said.

"It means welcome back," Quinn explained to P.R.

At the sound of Quinn's voice, the woman spun around and let out a surprised cry. She rushed toward Quinn. The two hugged, and tears streamed down Quinn's face. "She calls me Second Daughter."

The woman tilted her head toward P.R. and raised her hand to indicate his height.

Quinn nodded and nudged P.R. with her elbow. He put his hands together, palm to palm, and bowed as he recited the traditional Japanese greeting Quinn had taught him. "*Hajimemashite.*"

The woman bowed and returned the greeting. P.R. faced Tomi's father, a thin man with thick gray hair. P.R. bowed, and repeated in Japanese 'how do you do.' Tomi's father pulled himself up to his full height of five feet, five inches and greeted P.R.

Both parents bobbed their heads and smiled up at him. Then Tomi's mother winked at Quinn and said something in Japanese.

Quinn frantically waved her hands. "No, no. Not my husband. Friend."

The woman frowned. She arched one brow and eyed him suspiciously. P.R. shifted from foot to foot. He had not expected Tomi's parents to think he was Quinn's husband.

Tomi's parents began questioning her. Their voices rose. He didn't understand the words, but he felt the shift. As if someone had thrown open the window, the warm words of welcome blew away. Replacing them was a gust of Arctic air.

Tomi finally said. "Eat now. Talk later."

Her mother scurried to the kitchen and began filling bowls from a big pot on the stove. Tomi waved for them to sit on the floor.

The six of them sat, lotus style, sipping warm bowls of miso soup for breakfast. P.R. listened to the conversation in Japanese. Not being able to speak directly to Tomi's parents or understand what they were saying was more uncomfortable than he'd expected.

Chie said something about Yoshiro that made Tomi grimace, but her parents looked relieved.

P.R. couldn't wait any longer. He turned to Tomi. "Ask your father if we can talk in private."

Tomi put down her bowl. "Now? Are you sure?"

P.R. nodded.

Tomi spoke to her father. He rose and gestured for P.R. to follow. Quinn, who had offered to translate, got up, too. The three of them walked into the adjoining room also piled with neatly stacked boxes and totes. A futon was rolled up and pushed toward the wall. Two turned-over wooden crates served as tables for personal belongings.

P.R. folded his legs and sat on the floor facing Tomi's father. Quinn knelt to the side. Before they began, Tomi's mother entered carrying a tray with a bottle of sake and cups. After she poured the sake, she bowed and left.

"First you must drink," Quinn said. "Then talk."

P.R. needed a sharp mind, but he politely took a small sip and silently practiced the Japanese words Quinn had taught him. He addressed Tomi's father in Japanese. "Mr. Kanai, I would like permission to marry your daughter."

Tomi's father put down his sake. His eyes measured P.R. Then he began to speak. Quinn waited until the old man finished before she translated. "Another man also comes here today to ask for Tomi's hand in marriage.

316

His father was my best friend. I gave my word that I would give his son permission to marry my daughter."

So her parents had arranged Tomi's marriage. P.R. cleared his throat and continued in English. "That was many years ago, before 3/11. The world and Japan are different now."

At the mention of 3/11, the man's eyes darted to a framed photograph propped on a wooden crate. In the picture were two small children wearing bathing suits. The boy, holding up a string of fish, faced the camera and smiled. The girl, a few inches shorter, gazed up at the boy with admiration. P.R. couldn't see the girl's face, but he knew it was Tomi and her brother.

P.R. rose and picked up the photo. "I'm sorry for your loss. Tomi told me about Hiro. He was a good son, and Tomi is a good daughter. Even though she is not a young girl, she will honor your wishes."

As Quinn translated, P.R. studied the photograph, and then handed it to Tomi's father. His gnarled fingers shook as he reached for the picture.

P.R. said, "At one time, daughters were dependent on their fathers. They needed their fathers to make decisions for them. Tomi is educated. A teacher. She is also very spirited. If she marries someone she does not love, her spirit will die." He pointed to the girl in the picture. "She will no longer be the girl you see. Then you will have lost both of your children."

P.R. sat and gazed across at Tomi's father. After Quinn translated, the man met his eyes and for the first time P.R. thought they connected. Two men who loved and understood the same woman.

The next question was the one P.R. had dreaded. "He wants to know if you marry his daughter, will you live in Japan?" Quinn said.

P.R. knew Tomi's father would not like the answer. "I'm a lawyer. I do not know Japanese laws or the language. Tomi said her brother's dream was to come to America, but you were against it. Now it is Tomi's dream to live in America. Don't take away her dream, too."

As Quinn repeated the words, P.R. pulled out his phone and scrolled through the photographs. He found pictures of the land he had purchased from Ace.

P.R. handed his phone to Tomi's father. "We would live here. On my land."

The man's eyes widened as he looked at the grassy field leading to the lake. Then Tomi's mother entered the room and rapidly spoke to her husband.

Quinn explained, "Yoshiro called. He will be here soon. She told her husband to finish quickly."

Finish? He had just begun. A spark of interest had lit up in the man's dark eyes when P.R. had shown him the land. What could he say in five minutes to prove he loved Tomi and wanted what was best for her?

This was his last chance. The summation. He scanned the room filled with boxes. He saw nothing of value. *Nothing!* He turned back to Tomi's father who was still clutching the phone and looking at the land.

P.R. reached into his pocket and took out the porcelain frog. When he showed it to Tomi's father, the old man's eyes began to water. P.R. held the frog in his hand as he talked fervently about his plans for the future. His future, Tomi's, and her family's. He spoke from the heart. When he finished, the room was silent. Finally, Tomi's father returned the phone.

Quinn said. "He will hear Yoshiro. Then he will make his decision."

P.R. rose and bowed. At least Tomi's father hadn't immediately rejected P.R.'s proposal.

When he walked into the adjoining room, Tomi jumped up. "What did Father say?"

Before P.R. could answer, someone knocked on the door. Tomi's mother shuffled to the door and slid it open. A short Japanese man wearing a Siberian fur cap entered. The hat covered most of the man's face, except for his gun-metal black eyes. P.R. had never seen the man before, but he knew it was Yoshiro. His eyes circled the room to Chie, Tomi, and finally to him.

The two men studied each other. P.R. had imagined his rival would resemble a samurai warrior or possibly a sumo wrestler. The man, who removed his hat, coat, and gloves, looked ordinary, lean, not muscular, with straight black hair and a flat nose. The two men met in the center of the room like opponents in a boxing ring. They bowed politely and introduced themselves.

As P.R. turned away, Yoshiro's upper lip curled into a sneer. So their feelings were mutual. P.R. had taken an instant dislike to Yoshiro, not only because the man was his rival, but because Yoshiro's eyes had zeroed in on Chie first. That told P.R. everything. This man, who had come to claim Tomi for his wife, did not love her. He was not worthy to be her husband.

Tomi's mother took Yoshiro by the arm, steering him toward the kitchen and the table laden with Japanese delicacies. She motioned to P.R., too.

He could not sit across from Yoshiro politely eating. The walls and boxes collapsed in on him. He felt trapped. "I need some air." He grabbed his coat and stalked outside.

The corridor between the two rows of modulars sheltered him from the harsh January day. As he paced from one end to the other, his emotions vacillated between hope and despair. He thought he had connected with Tomi's father through the picture, the frog, and the land. His spirits soared.

Then P.R. remembered the firm set of the man's jaw and remembered he had given his word. Then his hopes plummeted. Ten minutes later, when he was at the far end, he turned toward the apartment and Yoshiro walked out.

Such a short time. Was that good or bad?

Yoshiro's back was to P.R. The man paused and pumped his gloved fist into the air *"Banzai! Banzai!"* he shouted. His steps were jaunty as he swaggered away, down the road toward town.

P.R. did not need anyone to translate. He understood the victory cry. Yoshiro had won. The words *banzai, banzai* pounded in his head, beating him down. He thought he was a strong man. He thought he had prepared himself for defeat. But nothing could prepare him for the ache coursing through his body.

He stumbled toward the door and stopped in front of the small pines. Male and female. A pair. The natural order of things. But for him there would be no natural order. No Tomi. No *us.* He could not go back inside. He could not look into Tomi's beautiful soul and know he would never share a life with her.

Tears threatened. He clenched his hands into fists. He wanted to fight. But who would he fight? He jammed his hands into his pockets and willed back the tears. He lowered his head and blindly walked away from everything he ever wanted.

CHAPTER SEVENTY

Tomi rushed out of the apartment to find P.R. She tightened the coat around her and peered down the row of modulars. Where was he? Yoshiro had been gone more than fifteen minutes, and P.R. hadn't returned.

She hurried to the end of the housing and circled around. When she reached her parents' corner unit again, she turned toward the city. Maybe P.R. had walked to the bus station to get their luggage. But he was not on the road to the harbor. He must have gone in the opposite direction, up the hill.

She found him at the park, sitting on the boulder where a few hours earlier they had watched the sunrise. His head was down, his hands clasped together as if in prayer.

Quietly she settled herself next to him. He lifted his head and gazed at her. She had so much to say that emotion overwhelmed her. The words stuck in her throat. Tears streamed down her cheeks.

She waited for him to wrap his arms around her, press his body next to hers so she could feel the rhythm of their hearts beating as one. But he sat there, unmoving, looking lost.

She swiped her hands across her cheeks. "Why you no tell me about land?"

He shrugged. "It doesn't matter now, but I wanted it to be a wedding present."

"Why you offer my parents land?"

"To help them. I didn't understand about the tsunami until I came here. I saw where your parents live and how little they have left. I couldn't ask them to give you up, too. And I knew you would not be happy if you left them here."

She threw her arms around him. "You great man."

The feel of her undid him. He folded her into him and reveled in her scent. He ran his hands through her long hair and down her curvy body. He wanted to remember every inch of her. She thought he was a great man, thought he was strong. He was strong—when he was with her.

He should release her. She belonged to another. Yet he couldn't convince his hands to move. Maybe a dose of reality would help. "When-when are you marrying Yoshiro?"

She pulled back. "Yoshiro," she spat out his name. "He not good man for me."

So she knew he did not love her. If possible his heart ached more—this time for her.

"When Father told Yoshiro memorial park to be built on our land, Yoshiro no ask Father to move to Nagano. Then Father understood Yoshiro did not know my heart. Father said you know my heart."

"But he still wants you to marry Yoshiro?"

"Hard for Father to change. He gave word. Must save face."

P.R. understood about a man's word. He couldn't fault her father for that. The pain of having her so close and yet knowing she was unattainable tore through him.

"Father say Japan change. I am new generation. Smart woman. He see I changed, too. I do not have to live in old ways. He gave Yoshiro permission to ask me to marry him. But Father gave me permission to make own choice. When Yoshiro asked me to marry, I say *no*."

Had he heard right? Yoshiro had proposed and Tomi had said *no*.

"Yoshiro put on false face. Stomp foot. But he glanced at Chie and smiled."

P.R.'s mouth went dry. He let the words sink in. Tomi was free. She could choose her own husband. Now if she said *yes,* he would know it was her choice, he would know she truly loved him.

He slid off the rock and knelt in front of her. He reached into his pocket and pulled out the frog. He opened his hand and held it out to her.

Tomi blinked at the porcelain frog. "You want to give back?"

He turned the frog over. Hooked around its front foot was a diamond ring. "Tomi, will you do me the honor of becoming my wife?"

Her heart jumped as she picked up the frog and slipped the band of diamonds onto her finger. A perfect fit, like they were. "I want to be wife."

P.R. rose and pulled her into his arms. "*My* wife." His words sounded possessive.

She tilted her head. "Even if you husband, I not always obey."

He threw back his head and laughed. "I wouldn't want you any other way."

She didn't care if she was in Japan. She didn't care who saw her. This was the man she loved. The man she wanted to marry. "Yes. Yes." She pressed her lips against his, letting her body melt into his. Heat radiated through her.

Then reality jolted her. "How possible? I Japanese citizen. You American. We cannot just register date and go to temple to marry."

He cupped her face in his hands. "Tomi, I'm a lawyer. I'll figure it out. Trust me."

Trust. Yes, she did trust him. Of course, he would find out what needed to be done.

"Will your parents come to America to live?" he asked.

"Before today they give up. Then Father see land. He like very much. He say, if I choose America, he try life in new place."

P.R. reached into his pocket for his phone. He found the pictures and showed her the land. "This is where I want us to live."

She stared at the screen of green and the blue water beyond. But she saw more than a grassy field and a lake. She saw her future—a boy and a girl romping through the grass. A man and woman, holding hands, smiling and watching over them protectively. Behind them shuffled a stooped man and a woman, holding a parasol to shade them from the Midwestern sun.

She returned his phone. "I like."

"I like, too." But he was not staring at his phone. He was looking toward the harbor and beyond. They had crossed oceans to find each other. This morning they had watched the first sunrise of the New Year. He knew their marriage wouldn't happen tomorrow. It might take several weeks, possibly months, but she loved him. She had chosen him. There would be an *us*.

He laced his fingers through hers. She did not try to pull away. She walked beside him, step by step, as they made their way down the hill toward their new life—together.

THE END

———

Don't miss out on your next favorite book!

Join the Satin Romance mailing list
www.satinromance.com/mail.html

THANK YOU FOR READING

———

Did you enjoy this book?

We invite you to leave a review at your favorite book site, such as Goodreads, Amazon, Barnes & Noble, etc.

DID YOU KNOW THAT LEAVING A REVIEW...

- Helps other readers find books they may enjoy.
- Gives you a chance to let your voice be heard.
- Gives authors recognition for their hard work.
- Doesn't have to be long. A sentence or two about why you liked the book will do.

ACKNOWLEDGMENTS

Thanks to all my readers who enjoyed *Friends Forever* and have been waiting for the second book in the Hickory Hills series. Thank you for the notes, texts, calls, and comments that encouraged me to keep writing.

Thanks to the Iowa Writing Festival and their instructors. Hope Edelman's classes changed my life. Sara Saffian steered me in the right direction. Mary Kay Shanley taught me to write the hard stuff. Ami Silber so generously shared her knowledge of the craft.

Thanks to Akira Kurihara and Dave and Patty Duez for reading this book before it was ready for print.

Thanks to my critique group—Marilyn Gardiner, Sue Hemp, Debbie Miseles, Angela Myers, Elaine Orr, and J.D. Webb. All are wonderful writers and friends.

Thanks to my writing partner, LJ Hippler, for his friendship and continued support.

And most of all thanks to God for giving me the muse and blessing me with a wonderful family who allows me to be who I am—my husband, Larry; my children, Missy and Nelson, plus Christina; and my grandchildren, Hali, Payton, and Madison. Every day you give me so much joy and enough material to write a library of books.

ABOUT THE AUTHOR

Sue Stewart Ade lives in her hometown of Pana, Illinois with her husband, Larry. They have two children, Missy and Nelson, and three grandchildren. Sue has taught creative writing in high school and college. Her short stories have been published in anthologies and have won awards at Indiana University, Midwest Writers, and Central Indiana Writers. *Friends Forever* was a finalist in the Pacific Northwest Literary Contest. In 2017 "Pumpkin Blossoms" was published in the anthology *Food and Romance Go Together, Vol. 1*.

Sue wrote her first novel in fifth grade to share with her girlfriends at slumber parties. She enjoys sharing her writing with friends and family.

sueade.net

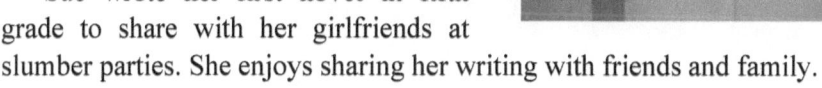 facebook.com/SueStewartAde

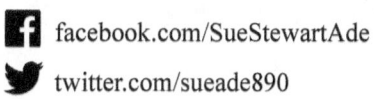 twitter.com/sueade890

www.ingramcontent.com/pod-product-compliance
Lightning Source LLC
Chambersburg PA
CBHW032241010726
47494CB00002B/575